Dirty Angels MC, Blue Avengers MC & Blood Fury MC are registered trademarks of Jeanne St James, Double-J Romance, Inc.

Keep an eye on her website at http://www. jeannestjames.com/or sign up for her newsletter to learn about her upcoming releases: http://www. jeannestjames.com/newslettersignup

Author Links: Jeanne's Blog * Instagram * Facebook * Goodreads Author Page * Newsletter * Jeanne's Review & Book Crew * Twitter * BookBub

BLOOD & BONES: REV

Blood Fury MC, Book 8

JEANNE ST. JAMES

Jeanne
ST. JAMES

———

Photographer/Cover Artist: Golden Czermak at FuriousFotog

Cover Model: Dylan Horsch

Editor: Proofreading by the Page

Beta readers: Andi Babcock, Sharon Abrams & Alexandra Swab, Author Whitley Cox

Blood Fury MC Logo: Jennifer Edwards

Character List

BFMC Members:

Trip Davis – *President* – Son of Buck Davis, half-brother to
Sig, mother is Tammy, Runs Buck You Recovery

Sig Stevens – *Vice President* – Son of Buck Davis, mother is
Silvia, three years younger than Trip, helps run Buck You
Recovery

Judge (Judd Scott) – *Sgt at Arms* - Father (Ox) was an Original, owns Justice Bail Bonds

Deacon Edwards – *Treasurer* – Judge's cousin, Skip Tracer/Bounty Hunter at Justice Bail Bonds

Cage (Chris Dietrich) – *Road Captain* – Dutch's youngest
son, mechanic at Dutch's Garage

Ozzy (Thomas Oswald) – *Secretary* – *Original* – manages
club-owned The Grove Inn.

Rook (Randy Dietrich) – Dutch's oldest son, mechanic at
Dutch's Garage

Dutch (David Dietrich) – *Original* – Owns Dutch's Garage,
sons: Cage & Rook

Dodge – Manager at Crazy Pete's Bar, did time with Rook
in jail

Whip – Mechanic at Dutch's Garage (formerly known as the prospect Sparky)
Rev (Mickey Rivers) – Mechanic at Dutch's Garage (formerly known as the prospect Mouse)
Shade (Julian Bennett) – Works at Tioga Pet Crematorium (formerly known as the prospect Shady)
Easy – Works at Tioga Pet Crematorium
Tater Tot – *Prospect* – Works at Crazy Pete's
Possum – *Prospect* – Works at Crazy Pete's
Castle - *Prospect*
Scar - *Prospect*
Bones – *Prospect*

Ol' Ladies:

Stella – *Trip's ol' lady* - Crazy Pete's daughter, owns Crazy Pete's Bar
Autumn (Red) – *Sig's ol' lady* – Accountant for the club's businesses
Cassidy (Cassie) – *Judge's ol' lady* – Manages Tioga Pet Crematorium
Reese – *Deacon's ol' lady* – Civil law attorney
Jemma – *Cage's ol' lady* – Hospice Nurse, Judge's younger sister
Chelle (Rachelle) – *Shade's ol' lady* – Elementary school librarian
Jet Bryson – *Rook's ol' lady* – Works at Justice Bail Bonds, Adam Bryson's sister

Former Originals:

Buck Davis – *President* – Deceased, Trip & Sig's father
Ox – *Sgt at Arms* – Deceased, Judge & Jemma's father
Crazy Pete – *Treasurer* – Deceased, Stella's father

Others:

Tessa – Trip's younger sister, Cage and Jemma's house mouse

Reilly – Reese's sister, works at Dutch's Garage

Henry (Ry) – Judge's son

Daisy – Cassie's daughter

Syn Stevens – Sig's half-sister

Saylor – Rev's sister, Judge and Cassie's house mouse

Dyna – Cage's daughter

Josie (Josephine) – Chelle's younger daughter

Maddie (Madison) – Chelle's older daughter

Jude – 12 yro rescued by Shade, Shade & Chelle's adopted son

Silvia Stevens – Sig's mother, Razor's former ol' lady

Tammy Davis – Trip's mother, Buck's former ol' lady

Bebe Dietrich – Cage & Rook's mother, Dutch's former ol' lady

Clyde Davis – Buck's father, Trip & Sig's grandfather, deceased

Lizzy/Billie/Angel/Amber/Crystal/Brandy – Sweet butts

Max Bryson – *Chief of Police* – Manning Grove PD, Bryson brother

Marc Bryson – *Corporal* – Manning Grove PD, Bryson brother

Matt Bryson – *Officer* – Manning Grove PD, Bryson brother

Adam Bryson – *Officer* – Manning Grove PD, Bryson's cousin, Teddy's husband

Leah Bryson – *Officer* – Manning Grove PD, Marc's wife

Tommy Dunn – *Officer* – Manning Grove PD

Teddy Sullivan – Owner Manes on Main, Adam Bryson's husband

Amanda Bryson – Max's wife, owner Boneyard Bakery

Carly Bryson – Matt's wife, OB/GYN doctor

Levi Bryson – Adopted son of Matt & Carly Bryson (birth mother: Autumn)

Prologue

FOR I HAVE SINNED

HE HATED IT.

Hated her.

Hated them.

All of them. Every last one.

He hated kneeling.

He hated praying.

He hated the endless drone of their voices.

He even hated the ten wooden chairs that formed a circle around him.

In those chairs sat his mother and nine other women from their church. When the women had entered the room, they refused to look at him and his mother demanded he keep his eyes lowered to the open book in his hand.

Why?

Because Michael was a sinner.

His spine, from his tailbone to the top of his neck, felt ready to splinter.

The skin on his bare knees was about to split open from kneeling on the stack of wooden rulers.

His muscles cramped from keeping perfectly still so the bible balanced on his head wouldn't tumble to the floor.

His arms trembled from holding the "good book" open in his hands.

He wasn't allowed to move except to turn the wafer-thin pages.

His mouth moved as he followed along with the passage but not one word escaped. His eyes didn't need to focus on the tiny print on the well-worn pages because he had been forced to read the bible so many times he knew the passage by heart.

Not that this particular scripture meant anything to him. It didn't.

Because he was a sinner.

He was born one.

He would die one.

And in between, he planned on living a life full of sin.

Keeping his head tipped down to hide it, one corner of his upper lip pulled up into a sneer.

He would remain in the center of that circle surrounded by these women and their monotone voices until the elder, the one who looked like a walking corpse, decided he had atoned for his latest transgression.

In the meantime, if he dropped the bible, he'd get ten lashes. If he stood without permission, he'd get twenty. If he told them all to fuck off, he had no idea how many lashes he'd be *blessed* with, but a bar of soap would be forced into his mouth, and he'd be locked in his room without supper. To think about his inexcusable actions, he would have to sit in a wooden chair with his hands in his lap, his feet flat on the floor while he continued to pray and ask for forgiveness until his father came home.

His father would be the one to decide whether the prayer circle was enough punishment for his latest offense. If it wasn't, he'd dole out whatever punishment he deemed worthy and wouldn't stop until the man was satisfied

Michael had learned his lesson. And, of course, Michael vowed to never do it again.

The thought of dealing with his father made him lock his joints and make sure his head didn't wobble even the slightest bit.

He no longer believed in God. Because if there was one? He or she wouldn't allow his parents to hurt him or Sarah the way they did.

In the churches his friends attended, they were told God was full of love and forgiveness. That Jesus died for their sins.

In his parents' church, they were taught to fear God. That he was always watching. He would judge them and how they lived their lives before he decided if they were worthy to take that final walk through those pearly gates.

Michael knew if anyone was denied entrance to Heaven, it should be his parents. Not him. Not Sarah.

If his parents were welcomed into God's embrace, then he wanted nothing to do with it.

Nothing at all.

But if he continued on his current path, he was told he wouldn't be welcomed, anyway. That he would be locked out.

Because he was a sinner.

Last night he had committed what his mother told him was an egregious sin.

Today's prayer circle had been formed because she caught him this morning in his sister Sarah's bed.

This was a sin his father would never allow to go unpunished. The prayer circle would be a start, but it certainly wouldn't be the end.

The gasps of his mother and then her screams had woken both him and Sarah from a deep sleep. He only saw a blur as she rushed over to the bed and grabbed handfuls of his hair, using it to yank him out of the bed and onto the floor.

Her face had been a mottled red, a mask of fury, when she tried to continue dragging him across the floor. He'd been too heavy and she hadn't been strong enough. He'd also resisted by pressing his weight and his fingernails into the worn wood planks to prevent her from hauling him out of the room.

He'd only gotten a quick glance at his sister to see her sitting up in her bed, once again crying. Her shocked, pale face had become almost translucent. Her mouth gaped open and the words she screamed to stop their mother went ignored.

He had climbed into Sarah's bed last night when he'd heard her crying through their shared wall. His only motive was to comfort her because no one else would. Eventually, she cried herself out and fell asleep. Unfortunately, so did he.

His first mistake was trying to comfort his sister. To chase away her pain and tears.

His second was holding her in her own bed.

The third was him falling asleep once she stopped crying and her steady breathing also lulled him into sleep.

The fourth was never waking up so he could return to his own bed before morning, like he normally did.

The fifth was him remaining asleep until his mother walked in to wake his sister.

His sixth was getting caught.

His mother automatically thought the worst. It hurt that his own mother didn't trust him. She believed him guilty when his motives were completely innocent.

She refused to hear his excuses because she saw evidence she would not dismiss.

She noticed something a teen boy hadn't been able to control.

Something he could never control.

His erection wasn't from holding his five-year-old sister. It was because he was fourteen and didn't know how to control it. It happened often when he least expected it. It also happened at the oddest times.

It happened enough to be embarrassing.

It happened in school. At the bus stop. While playing baseball. In the middle of the night. In the middle of the day.

Even during a long, boring sermon in church.

He wished it didn't happen, but it did.

And his mother wouldn't hear that it meant nothing.

All he'd wanted to do was comfort his sister from whatever their father had done to her last night. For whatever sin their father perceived his daughter had committed. Whatever reason he came up with to punish her. A made-up excuse to lock the door of her room with him inside.

The more he fought his mother to keep her from dragging him from Sarah's room, the angrier and crazier she got. Spittle flew from her mouth and clung to her lips. Her hands curled into claws. Her words got harsher, louder and more hurtful.

All she was doing was upsetting Sarah. Michael didn't want to upset his sister any more than she already was. So, he reluctantly climbed to his feet and allowed his mother to yank him from her room. He never once looked back.

He was forced into a tub of searing hot water and the brush she gave him to scrub his sins clean didn't have soft bristles. They weren't even firm. They were like a Brillo pad against his skin.

She stood over the tub and supervised him as he scrubbed every inch of his body until it was red and raw. She made him scrub his penis until the tender skin bled and the bristles left visible scratches behind.

"You scrub that filth off your skin. You scrub those sins

5

free of your soul. You wash away those ugly, ugly, forbidden thoughts."

When the water was pink and cold, when his mother's anger had turned to exhaustion, she forced him to stand in the tub and turn in a circle to make sure he got every spot. Once she pulled the drain plug, she left him standing there shivering with his hands over his raw, burning privates.

He hadn't cried. Not once.

Instead, he had taken himself elsewhere to a far-away place. Anywhere other than that bathroom. Because he couldn't cry.

His father told him over and over real men don't cry.

If he cried, it only made things worse.

But he wanted to cry. Not because of the burn of his skin but because his parents only saw what they wanted to see, they never listened to the truth.

They saw him as a wayward child who needed more discipline.

The same as Sarah.

Their goal was to teach her how to be a good and obedient wife for her future husband. How to be a good mother to her unborn children.

For Michael, it wasn't the prayer circle, it wasn't the scrub of the brush, it wasn't his mother's harsh words that he feared. It was what his father would do when he came home later.

Last night, their father had made Sarah cry.

Tonight, it would be Michael's turn. Only, he would have to hide every single tear.

Chapter One

Rev stood under the Toyota Avalon absently watching the dark motor oil piss from the engine into the oil drain dolly.

He could change oil in his sleep. He probably had a few times after partying late some nights and coming into work like a hung-over zombie. He only had to make sure he looked alert enough while he worked so Dutch wouldn't crack him upside the head with a wrench. His melon had been close to being dented a few times.

In truth, he appreciated the gruff old fart. He only never told him because Dutch probably wouldn't give a fuck and, instead, yell at him to get back to work.

But it was Dutch who had given him a job of sweeping floors and doing bullshit work a few years ago when he finished his last stint in Dauphin County Prison and had nowhere else to land.

He'd been sitting in a diner in Harrisburg, eating his first good breakfast since he'd been released and scanning the want ads in the day-old paper some other patron had left behind.

He hardly had any skills but the ad for Dutch's Garage said the owner was looking for an apprentice to train. Rev had read between the lines and figured the owner basically wanted an able body to work for shit pay.

It just so happened Rev was able and willing to work. Also willing to dig his feet in somewhere for a spell—at least until his sister got out of juvie—to put some scratch in his pocket and stay out of the joint.

He borrowed the diner's phone, called the number in the ad and was told to get his ass up to Bumfuck, Pennsylvania pronto, so that was what he did. Since he didn't have wheels, it took longer than expected to hitchhike his way from Harrisburg up to Manning Grove and, after doing a couple of questionable things along the way to snag a ride, he finally made it.

And managed to arrive alive and in one piece, *thank fuck.* But with empty pockets, no place to stay, no wheels, and, of course, no morals, which helped him do what he needed to do to get some of the basics he needed, like food in his belly and clothes on his back.

The salt-and-pepper-bearded Original had taught him to turn a wrench just like he'd taught everyone else in that garage. Dutch liked to train them young and keep them.

For years, the man had dealt with mechanics coming and going like a revolving door, but between his two sons, plus Rev and Whip, he now had a steady crew. Well, steady now that Rook wasn't landing in jail every few months. *Hell,* now that none of them were landing behind bars anymore. Though, that had more to do with Trip, the BFMC president, than Dutch.

Rev had done a little bit of time here and there. Nothing like Rook. Mostly for minor shit and certainly not for grand theft or aggravated assault on pigs like Dutch's oldest son.

However, there was one person Rev would've liked to have murdered. Instead, he tended to push that impulse out of his mind instead of dwelling on it. The hatred for the man wasn't worth Rev doing a lifetime bid in prison. Or even a permanent vacation on death row.

No, the man wasn't even worth a fucking second of thought.

Rev spat into the floor drain under the lift and watched the foamy, slimy wad slip through one of the metal drain holes.

With the weather nice as fuck today, all the bay doors were wide open. That allowed Rev to see Rook return from a test drive. As soon as the other man parked the repaired cage in the lot and climbed out, Cujo launched himself from the bottom drawer of Rook's rolling toolbox and beelined it outside to his daddy like the man had been gone for days instead of barely fifteen minutes.

Rook leaned over, scooped up the nasty little fucker and headed inside. He stopped only feet from Rev. "You got nothin' better to do than stare at dirty oil? Plenty of other shit to do while that drains."

Rev flipped him the bird.

Rook smirked. "Asshole."

"Dickhead."

Rook plopped the Chihuahua onto the floor. "Sic his ass, Cujo!"

The three-pound dog ran circles around his owner with his tail up, barking up at him. Rook pointed to Rev. "Not me, asshole, him!"

Rev laughed. "A stupid motherfucker just like you."

"Just jealous he don't like you."

"I prefer pussy."

"We got plenty of them runnin' around out back."

"The kind that don't bury their own shit," Rev clarified.

Suddenly a blonde was there, her hands on her hips, which drew his eyes to them. They were now slightly fuller than a year ago when she first elbowed her way into the club and also took over the garage's office like a drill sergeant.

Every time she bitched about the extra couple of pounds she'd put on and how she planned to go on a diet, Rev would run down to Dino's Diner, buy her a loaded buffalo burger and an order of their famous loaded fries and bring them back for her.

Of course, she couldn't resist.

He didn't feel bad one fucking bit because, even though the blonde looked smoking hot before, those curves just added to her sizzle.

It also added to his fantasies.

Whip's fantasies.

Dutch's derelict dreams.

Probably Rook's, too, before he got collared by Jet, as well as Cage's before Jemma.

Having wet dreams about Reilly wasn't the same as the real thing, though. Kind of like how Pepsi wasn't close to being the real Coke.

Rev blinked at their shop secretary, wondering why she was getting in the middle of his and Rook's ball busting.

"Go away, woman," Rev ordered, turning his back to her. Sometimes if he ignored her, she went away.

"Don't be a dick."

Sometimes she didn't.

Reilly fit right in at the garage. She could give shit as good as she could take it.

She did not cry. She did not whine. The good was she had a dirty mouth and a dirty mind, but the bad was she could bitch—loud as fuck, too—like a typical woman.

Rev grabbed his crotch, shaking it. "Why don't you suck mine?"

Reilly cocked an eyebrow and pursed her lips as she stared at where his hand had landed. "Nah. If I wanted to pick my teeth, I'd use a toothpick."

Rook howled loudly, causing Cujo to break into another round of yapping. He shook his head and went back to his bay with a grin, his ferocious black-and-tan rat on his heels.

"Why you buggin' me? Can't you see I got work to do?"

"Work? You're just standing there holding onto your tiny dick."

"How you know how tiny it is?"

"Please. It's not like any of you give a shit about privacy when you're sticking your pin pricks into a sweet butt or hang-around out at the farm. I think I've seen all of your packages. Or lack of them."

Whip lifted his head from the engine compartment of the cage he was working on in the next bay. "Who's got the biggest?"

Reilly put a finger to her lips and turned her eyes to the ceiling like she was thinking hard. After a second or two, she grinned and said, "Dutch. He puts the rest of you to shame."

Loud complaints went up from him, Cage, Whip and Rook, while Dutch, who was rebuilding a carb at one of the work benches, hooted out loud and pumped a wrinkled fist into the air.

"How 'bout you go grab a ruler, we all line up and you get on your knees to measure them?" Rev suggested. If she did it naked, it would be even better.

"How about no?"

"Then how about you turn around and march that luscious ass back where you belong in the office."

"So you can stare at it?"

Rev shrugged. "Of course. I know you work it so we watch it. Don't even bother to fuckin' deny it."

She wiggled her eyebrows and her hips. "Do I?"

"Ever wonder how many loads have been shot into a fist with you, that ass, and your mouth in mind?"

She blew him a noisy kiss. "I'm glad I can be of service."

He snorted at her teasing. "Go, Reilly."

"I didn't come out here to bust your microballs."

He waited.

"I came out here to give you a message."

He frowned, pulled a rag from his coverall's pocket and wiped off his grimy hands. "What message?"

She held out her hand. Within her fingers was one of those pink pages off the notepad she used for phone messages.

He stared at it. Anyone who knew him called or texted his cell phone. Who the fuck would be calling the garage to get ahold of him?

This couldn't be good.

Her fuckable lips took a downward turn. "Well, I'm assuming this message is for you."

He snagged the slip of paper from her fingers and glanced at it.

"Isn't your last name Rivers?" she asked, sidling up to him and bumping his hip with hers.

"Yeah."

"Who is Michael Schmidt?"

"That's who they asked for?"

"Yes." He could feel her nosy gaze on him as she said, "I thought your real name was Mickey Rivers."

"Yeah."

She pointed to the name on the paper he held. "Then who is Michael?"

He stared at her handwriting and the blood drained from his face. "Go away, nosy."

She stepped back and said sharply, "You're welcome, Rev."

He glanced up to see her chewing on her bottom lip. "Thanks," he said distractedly. Not only from the message but from what she was doing.

He crumpled up the pink paper in his fingers, stared at the wrinkled ball and scratched the back of his neck.

He took a couple of deep breaths and glanced up again.

Reilly still stood there with her green eyes locked on him. "You okay?"

"Why the fuck wouldn't I be?" he asked, doing his best to hide any reaction he was having or about to have. Actually, he wasn't even sure how he felt. His thoughts had been thrown into a blender and the button for the highest speed pushed.

"You look like you've seen a ghost."

He had.

"Do you know who that is?"

He sure did. "Didn't I fuckin' tell you to go the fuck away?" he snapped. "Leave me the fuck alone, Reilly."

She was not the kind of woman who would break down from simply being told to fuck off. Hell no. She had almost been killed by her former asshole boyfriend because she didn't *know* how to back down, even if it was in her best interest and for her safety to do so. Like Rev, if you told Reilly not to do something, she did it anyway to prove she could.

That attitude was why she had been beaten to within an inch of her life.

Why she bore a scar along her temple.

Why she was hospitalized by that motherfucker douchebag. The man, in the end, she torched while he was still breathing.

She ended up getting the final revenge.

She ended up pushing that button on the incinerator because she could.

She ended up killing that abusive motherfucker because she wanted to.

Even so, no valid argument existed that the bastard didn't deserve every second of that suffering.

Rev wouldn't be surprised if she hadn't walked away

after that, brushing her hands together while wearing a big shit-eating grin.

Though, none of them, not one, who witnessed what happened would ever be able to forget it. Even her sister had puked right afterward and quickly left town to try to deal with it and everything else that had gone on that day.

Reilly acted like it never happened. Like it had been just another day in Manning Grove. She never talked about it and no one brought it up around her, either.

But today, for some reason, when he told her to get fucking lost, something crossed her face he wasn't sure he actually saw. A possible illusion. Maybe in his shock of reading the name on the paper he now fisted, he had only imagined that flash of hurt.

It was there, then it was gone.

"You're a dick," came from Whip, who was now standing there watching the two of them, his jaw tight and his hands on his hips.

No matter what a pain in the ass Reilly was, they all were protective of her. Not because she was Reese's baby sister, but because she was now a part of their club. She was deeply entrenched in the Fury sisterhood, even though she wasn't an ol' lady.

She had wanted it and made it happen. It didn't matter what anyone, including Reese, thought about it.

That was also the reason she was always someone's backpack on the club runs. No one but regulars or ol' ladies were usually included. Reilly didn't fit either of those two titles. Nobody was fucking her, even though most of them wanted to.

At least once.

Maybe twice.

"Was there a fuckin' point where you thought I wasn't?" he barked at Whip. He closed his eyes and ground out a, "Fuck."

He took a deep breath, then a second. When he opened his eyes, he expected Reilly to have gone back to her office. Expected her to get far away from him since he was acting like a miserable prick.

But he was having a hard time concentrating on anything but that name and phone number in the center of the wad of paper.

He was surprised she still stood there. But then, nobody was more stubborn than Reilly.

Okay, maybe her older sister Reese. He didn't know how Deacon put up with her, even as hot as she was. But the man was happy. Reese must be hella hot in bed for the man to deal with that battle axe.

But it wasn't Reese standing before him. Instead, it was Reilly, whose hand automatically went up to pull her blonde hair forward to cover the scar on her temple. She did it all the time without thinking. No matter how often she was told that the scar didn't take away from her looks, she still self-consciously tried to cover it.

He reached up to snag her wrist and pull her hand away. Once he released it, she dropped it to her side. She blinked her big fucking green eyes up at him in surprise when he tucked the strand of hair she'd been pulling at behind her ear, instead, totally exposing the still slightly pink line along her right temple from her forehead to the top of her cheekbone.

"Sorry," he whispered. He was sorry for being such a dick when she didn't deserve it.

It was more than that. He was also sorry that her asshole boyfriend had bashed her head open with some kind of fucking knickknack leaving that scar while trying to kill her.

Reilly blinked once, twice, then whispered, "What?"

Normally, he would smile at her shock at him apologizing but he just couldn't drum one up. Not right now.

No, right now his head hurt, and he needed to go

outside to clear it. And to get away from all of the curious eyes turned their way. Not only from how he acted but by what was currently happening between him and Reilly.

Reilly was an untouchable. Totally off-limits. To him. To anyone and everyone with a dick in the club. He had no fucking clue why, since she was an adult and certainly not a virgin. Even so, she'd been put on the no-fly list for all the Fury members.

He guessed if he didn't wear a Fury cut, he could get away with sliding between her thighs. But he did, so he couldn't.

It was just one of the rules the guys followed to keep in good standing in the MC. As much as he hated rules, this was one he did his best not to break.

However, Reilly was distracting him from what he really needed to do. It wasn't finishing the oil change. It was to go outside where he had some privacy and call the name and number back. To find out why the fuck this person felt the need to hunt him down and turn his life upside down in the process.

To bring everything he'd buried deep back to the surface.

To stir up memories he and his sister Saylor had done their best to forget.

Maybe he should just toss the wadded-up note into the trash and go back to living his life. Simply ignore it and tell Reilly to never take a message from that person again. But if he told her that, she would want to know why. The woman had a way of digging you didn't realize was actually digging until it was too late.

She was a goddamn pro at it.

She should've been a lawyer just like her sister. In fact, Reese would probably love that for her, instead of her sitting in the office of a garage in Manning Grove surrounded by horny bikers who wanted to do dirty things to her baby sister.

He sighed and realized she was *still* standing there watching him, a concerned look on her face.

He needed to get the fuck away from her. He strode over to his toolbox, snagged his cell phone and didn't stop moving until he was out the back door, in the warm mid-April weather and staring sightlessly out over the boneyard.

He took a breath.

And another.

He went over to the picnic table they sat at during lunch or to burn a fatty and settled on the wood bench facing the storage yard, keeping his back to the building. He dug into his open coveralls and into the front pocket of his jeans, pulled out his metal pipe and an old prescription bottle full of bud. He had tossed the pink paper ball onto the table and occasionally took a peek at it while he packed the premium bud tightly into the bowl.

He dug into his other front pocket and pulled out a Bic, put the brass pipe to his lips, tipped the flame to the bowl and inhaled the smoke until no room was left in his lungs. He held it deep, until his lungs screamed for oxygen, then blew out the smoke on a frustrated breath.

He took another long hit, then another, and sat there until the sharp edges had slightly dulled.

He snagged the wad of paper and used his fingers to flatten it out against the worn wood of the tabletop. Not enough fucking pot existed in the world for the call he was about to make.

He shouldn't make it.

He should just use his lighter and burn the paper to ash to rid himself of the temptation.

But he was curious.

He couldn't imagine why anyone from his past life would

bother to reach out to him unless it was either something major or bad news. Or both.

More than anything, he wanted to know how that person even tracked him down. How the fuck did he find him? Why would he think Rev would care enough to hear any news?

In truth, today's technology didn't make it difficult for anyone to be found, even when they weren't using their legal name. One had to work very hard to go totally off the grid and never be found again.

He honestly never thought anyone would bother to look for him.

He was wrong.

He set his phone next to the now wrinkled paper and decided he needed another hit of pot first. When he was done with that, he picked up his phone and plugged in the number written in Reilly's neat print on the paper.

He stared at the Send button for a couple of heartbeats, then, before he changed his mind, he tapped the green icon. He put the phone to his ear and dread filled his chest as the ringing filled his ear.

Maybe he wouldn't pick up.

Maybe he wouldn't pick up.

Maybe—

"Hello?"

Rev's jaw shifted when he heard a voice he hadn't heard in a long time. Older but still familiar.

"Hello?" Another pause. "Anyone there?"

Rev should hang up.

"Michael?" The voice sounded kind of hopeful.

Fuck. "Yeah."

"Oh, blessed be! God is good! I've been trying to find you for the past three weeks."

"You found me."

"What a relief. You made it quite difficult, you know."

On purpose.

You never did anything. You never stepped in. You turned a blind eye. You are no better than them.

"But I prayed and prayed for God to guide me. And He came through. He found our lost lamb."

The searing heat of anger began to flicker like a flame in Rev's chest. "Ain't lost."

A long hesitation came from the other end of the phone, then, "Yes, you've lost your way, nephew. But it's easy to find it again. For you and Sarah. God is always willing to help."

Sarah.

He hadn't heard that name in a long time. The same amount of time since he'd heard the name Michael.

"Sarah died," Rev said flatly.

A deep gasp filled his ear. "Oh no, Brother Michael. May the good Lord be with Sister Sarah. God's embracing His child in His loving arms."

That made Rev want to puke.

The "good lord" hadn't been with her when she was a child, so why the hell would he be with her now? Why didn't their god embrace her in his loving arms back then?

Why didn't the "all-seeing" and "all-knowing" divine being do something to stop them?

He refrained from asking those questions because he didn't want the conversation to last any longer than necessary. He wanted to know why the fuck his uncle had searched for him.

And managed to find him.

"That news is quite devastating. I will add Sister Sarah to my prayers, of course. I'm not sure whether to tell that sad news to your mother or father yet. They have enough of a heavy burden to deal with right now."

Rev hoped that heavy burden crushed them. But even with whatever they were dealing with, wouldn't being told their daughter was dead be important?

Of fucking course not.

"That why you hunted me down?"

"Yes, I felt you needed to know and figured you'd want to come home."

"Why the fuck would I wanna come home?"

Home. That was no longer home and hadn't been for over ten years.

Home was where family was and the Fury was now his family. Everyone inside the garage behind him was family. Not the man on the phone.

"I... I..." his mother's brother stuttered. Most likely from Rev's choice of words. "Please don't use such foul language."

Fuck that. "You reached out to me first, Matthew. You don't fuckin' like it, hang the fuck up and never call the garage again."

"It's upsetting to hear that Satan still has a firm grip on your soul, Brother Michael. I will also continue to pray for you every night."

Satan had a firm grip on his soul. *Jesus fuck.* "Yep. He sure as fuck does."

"You can repent and rid yourself—"

"Why the fuck did you find me?" Rev yelled into the phone, not having the patience to hear his evangelical bullshit. Shit that was shoved non-stop into his ears since birth and until the day he escaped those restrictive chains.

"Your mother needs you right now."

He dropped the hand holding his phone, stared with disbelief at the screen for a second, took a deep breath, then put it back to his ear. "She told you to fuckin' call me?"

"No... She doesn't know. I... She's suffering, Michael. You need to make things right with her."

My fuckin' name ain't Michael!

"That's why you fuckin' called me? To make things right with my mother?"

"That's not the main reason. It's your father. A few weeks ago, she happened to mention she hoped you and Sarah would make peace with him before he passed."

"He's dead?" That was one thing he could shout "hallelujah" to.

"Not yet. He's almost at the end of his life journey and is getting ready to begin his glorious afterlife in the arms of God."

Rev rolled his eyes and sighed. "So, the fucker ain't kicked the bucket yet."

A sharp noise came through the phone. "You still have time to make things right between the two of you. You still have time to make things right with God. You can denounce the devil in your soul, Brother Michael."

Rev ignored the devil and God shit. Instead, he concentrated on the bullshit of making things "right" between him and his father. "How's he gonna make things right with me? He gonna apologize? He gonna let me do the things he did to me, and to Sarah, to him?"

More silence. Silence that was telling as fuck.

"Apologize for trying to raise you and your sister the way the good Lord intended?"

Christ. His stomach was churning right now. Absofuckin-lutely churning to the point of sharp pain. "What's wrong with him?"

"He's being tested by pancreatic cancer."

Rev doubted pancreatic cancer was some sort of test from God. Even so, it couldn't have happened to a nicer guy. "You try a prayer circle? You all believe that'll cure what ails ya."

Matthew inhaled sharply. "I can see Satan's tight hold on you is making you unwilling to take the healing steps I hoped for. You have a blessed day, nephew. I'm sorry about Sister Sarah. May she rest in peace and in the glory of God."

"You're not fuckin' sorry!" Rev screamed into the phone even though his uncle had already hung up. "You're not fuckin' sorry," he whispered, tossing his phone onto the picnic table. He dropped his head in his arms, felt a foreign sting in his eyes, and his breath stuttered. "You ain't fuckin' sorry at all."

Fuck them.

Fuck. Them. All.

He started when a warm body pressed against him and fingers plucked gently at the spiky hair at the top of his head. He cleared the thick from his throat and blinked a few times to rid himself of the sting, then reluctantly lifted his head.

Reilly stood with a hip pressed to his arm and her big green eyes turned down toward him. "You okay?"

This wasn't her being her normal nosy self. Genuine concern tinged her voice. That made the ball of tension in his chest grow until he thought it would burst through his skin.

"Yeah."

"Liar."

He didn't put any energy behind his soft, "Go away, woman."

Like he figured, she ignored him and, using his shoulder for balance, climbed between the attached wood bench and picnic table to sit next to him, wrapped an arm around his back and pressed her cheek into his bicep. "Bad news?"

The answer to that question wasn't simple.

What he considered good news wasn't the same as what others might. Most wouldn't consider his father dying good news. To Rev, he knew it should've happened years ago. Preferably before he left and by his own hand. But back then he couldn't do it. He couldn't take a life no matter how much he wanted to. How much he dreamed about it.

Almost tasted it. But at fourteen, even fifteen, he didn't have the balls to do it, he couldn't follow through.

Now? Things would be different. So very fucking different.

What he considered bad news was the fact he'd been located. And he still didn't know how. That bugged him since he doubted his uber-religious uncle was tech savvy. Worse, he never thought one of those severed ties would be tugged on in an attempt to pull him back.

Why was he even still thinking about this? It was his past, it should stay there, even if it involved blood.

Blood wasn't always family. Blood could use the "good" word of God to be pure evil while wearing a mask of righteousness.

Sometimes what came out of one's mouth didn't reflect what was in one's heart and soul. What was on the surface wasn't the same as what was found at the very core. A piousness only skin deep.

Hypocrisy.

Deception.

Words he learned the true meaning of the older he got. When he looked back once he was free.

Now he recognized the brain-washing. The fight his parents took on to keep their children from having their own thoughts, their own beliefs. Their own free will.

Basically, their way was the only way. Any individual or differing thoughts would be beaten out of them.

With a switch, a belt, a large hand.

The "cleansings" didn't last as long as the prayer circles.

Rev didn't know which one he hated more. They were both miserable in their own way.

But it was what that bastard did to his sister that would never be forgivable. How his father took his sister's cleansing a step further.

He needed to call her. Because he needed to share this

with someone else. He couldn't keep this to himself. If he did, he might explode.

He should order Reilly to go back inside. To go back to her office. To leave him the fuck alone. To let him deal with his personal demons by himself.

To allow him to keep his secrets as just that.

But he couldn't tell her to go. Her being this quiet was a rarity since her attitude was normally larger than life. Surprisingly, that quiet strength as she leaned into him was what he needed right now.

Especially to make his next call.

He reached under the table, planted his hand on her thigh and squeezed. Her hand settled over his and they kept them there. Connected.

They both knew if someone came out and saw her arm around him, with his hand on her thigh, words would be said. Warnings given.

But at the moment he didn't give a fuck.

Everyone else could fuck right off.

He stared at the phone in front of him. He left it on the table, scrolled through his contacts with one finger and found Saylor's number. He pressed the Call symbol and then the speaker icon.

This should be a private conversation between him and his sister, but again, he didn't give a fuck. In the back of his mind, he didn't want to deal with this alone.

"I'm busy," was Saylor's abrupt answer.

"Busy doin' what? Daisy's at school." Normally, he'd give her a rash of shit about her attitude, but he couldn't muster up any right now.

However, her silence worried him.

"Busy doin' what, Saylor? You up to no good?"

"Always," she answered with a low chuckle.

He shook his head in frustration. "Don't fuck up."

"I won't."

"I'm serious, Saylor. You fuck up and Judge throws your ass out, you got nowhere to go."

"I'll just get my own place, then."

Big dreams for both a broke and broken girl. "You can't afford your own place."

"I could if I got a real job."

"Doin' what you do is a real fuckin' job, Saylor." She had only recently obtained her GED due to Cassie's insistence on it. Beyond that, and being a house mouse, his sister had no skills. At best, she'd get a job for minimum wage at some fast-food joint. At least being in Judge and Cassie's household kept her busy, gave her responsibility and, even better, two more people looking out for her.

"It doesn't pay anything, Mickey."

"Judge gives you scratch." It might not be a lot, but it was at least some spending money. Given too much, Rev worried what she'd do with it.

He did not want to find his sister OD'd in a fucking alley somewhere after snorting some hillbilly-made meth in order to forget the sins of their goddamn father.

"Yeah, like a damn allowance. Not enough to do anything fun."

"Seriously, are you bitchin' about your life right now?" Right now, it was the best she ever had. And she fucking knew it.

Her answer was more silence.

"Saylor."

A long sigh. "No."

"You got it good. It ain't perfect but you're part of a real family now. Family who cares about you *and* takes care of you. Don't shit on that."

"Did you only call me to remind me to behave?"

"Don't expect you to behave. Expect you to respect Judge and Cassie's household. Respect them."

"Whatever, brother. So, that's why you interrupted me?"

"From doin' what?"

"Watching porn."

He wasn't sure how to react to that. But Reilly slapped a hand over her mouth to muffle the noise that almost escaped. He twisted his head to see the corners of her eyes wrinkled up and tears in her eyes.

"What the fuck, Mickey!" came through the phone. "You actually thought I'd answer the phone in the middle of watching porn?" She laughed. "I was cleaning up the kitchen. And believe me, I love you, brother, but I'm not sharing my porn-watching schedule with you."

"Thank fuck for that," he grumbled.

Reilly made a cute little squeak and bumped her shoulder into his.

"Who's listening in?"

"What?"

"You have me on speaker phone, I heard a female. Did you play hooky from work today to get laid instead?"

Jesus fuck. "No." He shot another quick glance at the blonde smashed against him, her big soft tits now pressed into his arm. He did a quick check to see if her nipples were hard. "It's Reilly."

"Hey, sweet cheeks!" Saylor yelled through the phone.

"Hey, girl!" Reilly called back, now wearing a grin.

"Is my brother boning you right now?"

"No, we're at the garage," Reilly answered with an exaggerated pout. As if Saylor could see her. Rev shook his head.

"Oh, damn. I hoped you two would hook up."

"Saylor. Jesus fuck. Don't say shit like that," Rev growled.

"Why? It's true. You two would make beautiful babies."

"Fuck! I ain't havin' babies. We're not hookin' up. That's not why the fuck I'm callin'."

She laughed. "So, then, spit it the hell out, big brother.

26

Cassie wants me to put together some meal in the Crockpot—"

"Yeah, okay, don't give a fuck about Crockpots. Got somethin' more important to tell you."

"What's more important than Cream Cheese Chicken over rice? That shit is banging. Just like you two should be doing."

"Didn't know you wanted your brother to die," Rev said dryly.

"Reilly, your pussy is worth dying for, right?" Saylor asked. "I bet she's got a bomb ass pussy."

"Saylor!" Rev yelled, now avoiding looking at Reilly who was laughing so hard she was crying. "Need to tell you somethin'. Stop fuckin' around."

"Okay, what? Spill. Wait. Hey, Reilly, you need to come to The Barn tonight. We need to get smashed and then have a contest on which one of us can get more of the guys to pop boners without us even touching them."

"What the fuck," Rev muttered. "She ain't comin' to The Barn for that shit. You two ain't gettin' smashed and you better not be fuckin' with the guys like that. Especially those goddamn prospects. Don't be the reason I gotta slice one of those fuckers' throats for steppin' out of line 'cause you're fuckin' teasin' them."

"You're no fun."

Rev sucked in a long breath to cool off his temper.

"I'll text you later," Reilly said.

He twisted his head toward her. "The fuck you will."

Reilly frowned.

So did he.

"Okay, I have shit to do. What do you want, brother, if you're not calling me to tell me that you and Reilly are knocking boots?"

Rev sighed. He needed to get this conversation back on

track so he could get it out and over with. "Got a phone call."

"So?"

"Matthew called."

Dead silence followed. After a few seconds, he heard a shuddered breath. Yeah, for Saylor, suddenly this phone call was no longer fun and games. "Why?"

"Said the motherfucker's dyin'."

Reilly jerked against him and the hand covering his on her thigh squeezed tight.

His sister simply answered with, "Good."

"He wants me to go there."

"He who?"

"Matthew."

In the silence that followed, Rev could hear his own heartbeat in his ears.

Finally, Saylor asked quietly, "Just you?"

"Told them you were dead."

Reilly gasped and Saylor made a choking sound.

Rev quickly added, "They don't know you're here with me," to help prevent any panic.

It wasn't fear or panic he heard in her voice, it was seething anger when she asked, "Why the fuck would they want you there? Why would he?"

Rev scraped a thumbnail across his forehead and sighed, struggling to keep his own anger in check. "Don't know. Think our uncle contacted me on his own. Our wonderful, lovin' father probably don't know. 'Cause I can't imagine he asked for me." If he asked for anyone, it would be for Saylor. *Sarah*.

"You're not going, are you?"

He twisted a hand back and forth along the back of his neck. "Don't know."

"Well, I'm glad you told them I'm dead because there's

no way you'll catch me near that fucking place. The next time I see that bastard, it'll be in hell."

The call ended but not before he heard her sob.

Did he make a mistake by telling her? Maybe he should've left her in the dark and not drug out the nightmare of her past.

But then, maybe he shouldn't have returned Matthew's call in the first place.

Why did he?

Why?

Worse, why would he even *think* about going back there?

If he did, could he even do it alone? Without Saylor? But, in truth, he'd never force her to go. To take her back to the place that caused her nightmares.

Caused them both nightmares for years.

He had successfully put it all behind him.

Until the phone call.

If he was smart, he wouldn't go.

If he was smart, he never would have called Matthew back.

If he was smart, he would've burned that note.

Apparently, someone forgot to remind him that he wasn't smart.

Chapter Two

Reilly didn't know what to say. From where she sat, that whole conversation between Rev and Saylor was confusing at best.

She wasn't sure if she should be upset or angry. Not at him, but for him. When she had stepped outside and saw his shoulders hunched, his head hidden in his folded arms and his phone on the table next to a still smoldering pot pipe, she knew something was very wrong.

Whoever the person was whose name and number she'd written on that slip of paper had given him some sort of bad news. She wouldn't have even known that Rev was Michael Schmidt if the caller hadn't happen to mention that Michael might be using the name Mickey.

However, the bits and pieces of conversation she heard didn't give her enough to go on. So, she said the only thing she could come up with. "I'm sorry about your father."

He turned those stunning eyes—the bright blue orbs that created flutters in her belly and lower—toward her. "Don't be."

"You're not upset about him being sick?"

"Don't give a fuck about him bein' sick," he answered.

"When I came outside you looked... upset."

"Nothin' to do with him havin' cancer."

Cancer?

She wanted to keep probing but whenever she bugged the guys, they usually shut her down or shut her out. They all had their secrets, every last one of them, and usually didn't share. If they did, she imagined it was with each other and not with anyone else. Or for some of them, maybe they shared with their ol' ladies. Something she wasn't.

But she knew they didn't sit around simply talking about shit. Not like the Fury sisterhood did. In fact, when one of the guys saw the ladies gathered—especially when they were drinking—they usually got the hell out of there as fast as possible so they wouldn't get sucked into whatever the women were up to.

She imagined them screaming, "Gird your loins!" in warning as they ran away.

The longer she sat there without him saying anything else, the more she realized Rev probably wanted to be left alone with whatever was going on in his head. But usually none of them had any difficulty telling her to go away. She'd been told plenty of times to "fuck off" or "get fuckin' lost." None of that offended her since it didn't take long after coming to Manning Grove, and becoming a part of the club, to figure out that was just the way the guys were.

They not only hid their secrets, but their feelings, too.

If she wanted to have a long and *somewhat* meaningful conversation with someone of the male variety, she did it with her hairdresser Teddy from Manes on Main. That man could talk.

He could also listen. And he certainly could give some great advice. Especially on how to use makeup to minimize the visibility of her scar.

Men bent the ears of their bartenders. Women chatted

with their hairdressers. It was the way of the world. At least in a normal world.

The MC world was definitely not normal. Not even close.

"I'll leave you alone." She tried to keep the disappointment from her voice.

As soon as she got to her feet, he snagged her wrist and yanked her back down. Maybe he needed some company but didn't want to ask for it. "You know Dutch is going to have a fit. We've been outside for too long."

"He can wait."

Yes, he could. Whatever was going on with Rev was more important. Not that Dutch would know. Or care.

But Dutch's blow-ups tended to peter out pretty quickly and if they didn't, Reilly only had to teasingly tug on the man's salt-and-pepper beard and blow him a noisy kiss. That usually disrupted the gruff biker's rampage and also got her a silent thanks from the four mechanics who were usually Dutch's targets. Not only with words but sometimes flying wrenches.

She'd also stepped in plenty of times in the past year to prevent Rook and Dutch from coming to blows. She couldn't imagine how many fights the father and son got into before she rolled into town.

Okay, maybe she didn't quite roll into town. In actuality, she'd been driven by Judge to the farm from her sister's house so she could hide out and be safe from her psycho ex-boyfriend. Then after she torched the asshole to death, she decided to stick around.

Any reasonable woman would want to stay when surrounded by a bunch of hot, growly, alpha bikers. The Fury was a single woman's wet dream.

Though, the truth was, she had nothing and nowhere else. Except for her sister Reese, who was now a part of the club, anyway.

So really, Reilly belonged here. In this town, a part of the Fury family and, even better, the Fury sisterhood, even if she wasn't an ol' lady. And might never be.

She just didn't belong being a secretary in an auto repair shop.

Her sister was right. She had a business degree she was wasting, one Reese helped pay for. She needed to think seriously about doing something with it. To have a clear direction instead of simply floating along.

She had only stayed working for Dutch because it kept her busy, had put enough money in her pocket to rent a tiny studio apartment within walking distance of the garage, allowed her to score a reliable used car and gave her enough "scratch" to buy some really sexy boots.

Admittedly, she had a thing for boots. Ankle, shin, knee or even thigh-high. She loved them all.

But now? Now, she needed to get serious about her future.

Answering phones at Dutch's Garage was only her "now" and not her future. She loved the assholes, but the dead-end job wasn't challenging enough.

She was pretty sure Dutch was surprised to see her when she walked in every morning with their donuts and coffee from Coffee and Cream from the other end of town. But she figured the cash stuffed into the coffee can in the break room was better spent on decent coffee and fresh pastries than that generic ten-pound bag of beans Dutch bought at some warehouse store near Williamsport.

They could drink that crap the rest of the day but they should at least start their morning out right. However, her daily lattes and glazed crullers had widened her hips, slightly thickened her middle, and made her bras overflow.

She needed to do something about that, too.

But not this minute. Right now, she had another issue to

deal with. Reilly reined in her thoughts and studied Rev's quiet profile.

The man was hot as fuck.

Hot. As. Fuck.

While most of the Fury men were considerably hot, Rev was at the very top of that roaring flame.

Every time one of the bikers got clubbed in the head with the "ol' lady" stick—what the sisterhood called the members getting snagged and bagged—she had been relieved it hadn't been Rev.

She had a few fantasies about the other guys—how could she not?—but every time she broke out her purple Greedy Girl G-Spot Rabbit Vibrator, it was Rev's blue eyes, his tattoos, his numerous piercings, his panty-soaking raspy voice, and those luscious lips—ones she'd love to have pressed on her upper *and* lower ones—she thought about. Dreamed about. It was thoughts of Rev replacing her Rabbit that made her orgasms even more intense.

Reilly shifted on the hard wooden seat. Rev was currently having a crisis. She shouldn't be daydreaming about getting him naked and riding his cock until they both passed out.

Wait. Was that even possible? She didn't know but she was willing to try, even though he might not be.

The only sex she'd had in the past year—due to her dear sister's fear of her getting involved with another abusive fuckwad like Billy—had been with one buzzed guy while crammed in his two-door coupe behind Crazy Pete's and he'd lasted about twenty seconds, if that, and…

And a failed attempt with a Fury member.

Who was not Rev.

But they ended up aborting that mission after massive drinking, furious flirting and something tragic happening…

Fear freezing him.

Apparently, Reese, Deacon, and even Judge's looming

threat of a "blanket party" if any of the members attempted to touch one of the women on the "Don't Even Fucking Think About It" list, was enough to kill any man's hard-on.

Reilly had heard the details about what had been done to Cage. She heard about it multiple times whenever she flirted heavily with any of the guys. She could see it in their eyes. Having sex with Reilly was not worth being clubbed by the six-foot-two, two-hundred-and-forty-pound sergeant at arms.

After seeing the result of Cage's own blanket party, she might agree. But that sucked for her because it meant if she was going to have sex with anyone, it had to be some random guy who didn't wear a Fury cut and ride a "sled."

The man next to her did both.

Which sucked. It really did.

That also meant her life was being controlled by someone other than herself. Even if it was only her sex life. Because normally her sex life was a big part of her whole life. Except for now.

And she did not like that one bit.

However, she knew the guys had to agree to the by-laws and rules to remain a patched member in good-standing. She also knew she had to respect those rules and by-laws herself to also remain a welcomed part of the club.

Was she willing to give up any of that just for the opportunity to get between the sheets and sweaty with any of the single Fury members? She stared at Rev.

Yes.

No.

Shit. Maybe.

She shook herself mentally.

The man next to her was already dealing with enough shit. She shouldn't be adding to it with her desire to jump his bones.

She shouldn't.

She wouldn't.

At least, not right now.

However, if he didn't say anything soon, her thoughts would continue to spiral down a delicious but dangerous path. He needed to either officially finish this conversation by getting up and walking away or continue it since he had forced her back onto the bench. A sign he didn't want her to leave just yet.

Not sit there like Cujo had bitten his tongue off.

Men. Frustrating as hell.

"Why would you tell this Matthew, whoever he is," *hint, hint,* "that Saylor is dead?"

"To them, she is."

Them. His family? Was Matthew part of his family?

"The reason Saylor came here…" She mentally sighed when he didn't pick up on her prompt. So, she continued leading him in the direction she wanted the conversation to go. "You said they didn't want her to come home after her release from juvie because she was out of control. But you told this Matthew, whoever he is," *hint, hint,* "she's dead." She waited, mentally poking at him to explain.

"Matthew's my uncle. My mother's brother."

Finally!

Rev locked his damn irresistible eyes with hers. "Haven't told anyone this. Shouldn't be tellin' you, either, but…" Reilly hung on that last word, watching his lickable, kissable lips move as he spoke. "They wanted her to come home."

Hold on. She blinked, confused. That wasn't what Rev *or* Saylor had said. "Oh. But—"

"That was the last fuckin' place she wanted to go and, even if it wasn't, there was no fuckin' way I was lettin' her go home. Not then, not now. Not fuckin' ever."

Unfortunately, the more he talked, the more confused she got. Conversation was supposed to clear up misunderstandings, not make them more convoluted. Someone needed to tell Rev that. Or steer him in the right direction. That somebody was her. "I thought you called her so she could go with you... to wherever home is." *Hint, hint.*

"No." He shook his head. "Shouldn't have called her."

Now, instead of wanting to ride his cock, she wanted to strangle him. "But she needed to know her father—*your* father—is ill, right?"

"Why I called her."

"But you don't want her to go with you to... wherever." *Hint... Oh, fuck it.* "Where *is* wherever?"

"Reilly."

"Rev. Seriously. I was going to go back inside and leave you alone, but you forced me to sit back down. I'm thinking there's a reason for that. Am I wrong?"

He turned his gaze from her to stare out over the storage yard, which was really more of an organized junkyard, full of old vehicles, stray cats and rats. Mud, too. She couldn't forget all the damn mud.

Even under his thick, but short, dark blond beard she could see his jaw clenched tight.

"I'm not wrong," she whispered, turning on the bench until her thigh was pressed against his. She brushed her fingers over the short wiry hairs covering his tight jawline. "I can't sit out here forever, Rev. Dutch is probably throwing things right now. Especially if the phone is ringing off the hook in the office and I'm not there to answer it."

"Go inside, then."

"You didn't want me to go back inside," she reminded him softly. "You wanted me to stay. I'm here. I'm listening."

His eyes squeezed shut. "Can't fuckin' think straight." He opened them and jerked his chin toward the slip of paper. "Don't ever take a call from that man again."

"Okay."

"He calls, you hang up."

"Okay."

"No. First tell him to fuck off, then hang up."

"I'll do that." She stared at him a few more moments while he worked through whatever emotion was crossing his face. "What are you going to do?"

He scrubbed both palms down his face to wipe that emotion away and sighed. "Don't know."

"What do you want to do?"

"Don't know."

Maybe she should ask questions he knew the answers to, to make it easier for him to process whatever he was attempting to process. "Where do they live?"

"Outside of Coatesville."

Coatesville. Coatesville in Chester County?

Reilly blinked.

Coatesville was not far from where she lived prior, before moving in with Reese all those months ago. Where she lived when her former boyfriend almost killed her.

When her former fucknut of a boyfriend scarred her face.

Before she slammed the button on the furnace with her former abuser inside.

Still alive. Still breathing.

Until he wasn't.

Her heart kickstarted in her chest and began to thump heavily.

Every time she was reminded of that day—even though she avoided talking about it, even though *everyone* avoided talking about it—she relived it like it only happened five minutes ago.

Her shoving past Deacon, her eyes focused only on that red button.

The whoosh of the burners lighting. The muffled screams.

Then feeling nothing but relief.

The sense of freedom washing over her. Filling every cell in her body.

The tension gone.

The fear gone.

The abusive asshole… *poof*… gone.

Unable to make anyone a victim again.

With one simple push of a button a rabid animal had been reduced to a pile of worthless ash.

She jerked back to the present. To Rev. Where were they? *Oh yeah.* "Are you even considering going?"

"Don't know."

He was. For whatever reason.

"If you do, you shouldn't go alone."

"Saylor ain't goin'."

"Then, don't go, either. I see you're torn. That means there's a reason to be torn. Leave the past in the past. Like Elsa, just let it go." She stood up. Her work here was done.

He frowned. "Who the fuck's Elsa?"

She rolled her lips under. Even if she told him, he wouldn't know. And then she'd have to admit why she watched Frozen a half dozen times with his sister and Cassie's daughter Daisy.

"Nobody you want to know," she murmured. She smiled down at him, once again plucking at the spiky dark blond hairs on the top of his head.

He kept his hair short but used a lot of gel to spike it at the top. While she preferred the shorter hair on him, some of the other guys could rock the long-haired look. Like Shade. And Easy.

Even Cage's longish, disheveled hair fit him perfectly. During one of the sisterhood's "Wine and Whine" get-togethers, Jemma drunkenly confessed one night it was the perfect length to grab ahold of and manipulate his head for certain activities.

That confession made Reilly drink even *more* wine, since

she was feeling sorry for herself for having no one to partake in those "certain activities."

Also, unlike the rest of the guys, Rev had several barbell piercings in both ears and a hoop in his left nostril. The only other Fury member who had piercings like that was her sister's ol' man, Deacon.

She dropped her gaze to Rev's chest when she realized she'd seen his cock plenty of times, even his naked ass cheeks—which, if anyone asked her, were a solid fifteen on a scale of one to ten—as he had sex with sweet butts back at the farm, but she'd never seen him without his shirt on.

Huh.

It was on the tip of her tongue to ask whether his nipples were pierced. But that would be a weird question to ask while they were discussing whether he would go home to visit his dying father.

She tucked it away for the future. Deacon had his nipples pierced and Reilly had all kinds of questions that neither Reese or Deke would answer. However, she'd caught her sister touching them over top of Deke's shirts when she didn't think anyone was watching.

She took that to mean Reese liked them and Deacon *really* liked them.

Rev wrapping an arm around her hips and his hand squeezing her waist fished her mind back out of the gutter, where it tended to do the backstroke for laps at a time. Probably because she was so damned sex starved right now. She could ride a freaking lamp post and think it was the best sex ever.

"Know you don't talk about it and don't expect you to. But… Know how you wanted to ensure that motherfucker was dead?"

That motherfucker?

Ah, shit. Her fingers stilled in his hair. He not only fished her out of the gutter, she was now flopping around fighting for breath on the sidewalk.

"Kinda want the same thing. Ain't upset he's dyin'. Hope to fuck he's sufferin'. And truth is? I want to be there to witness it."

"Rev."

"You don't even know, Reilly. Ain't even gonna go there. But trust me, if you knew, you'd see why I'm sayin' what I'm sayin'."

Shit.

She had hated her parents—both of them—for abandoning her and Reese. Her mother might have lived in the same house, but she was never present. She wasn't a mother. She was only a living, breathing object they had to step around when she was passed out drunk.

But she never once wished her parents dead.

The only person she did was Billy Warren. And not until he'd almost killed her.

Twice.

Okay, maybe she wanted some of the Shirleys dead for all the shit they'd pulled with the club. But right now, she wasn't going there. And right now, things were quiet for them. For good reason.

More importantly, right now, she was trying to understand a hatred for a parent that ran so deep that made someone want to visit that parent just to watch him suffer before he took his last breath. "I don't think that's healthy."

"Might not be healthy but thinkin' it's needed. Some kinda goddamn closure."

"So, you're going to go."

He tipped his head up to her. "Yeah. Gonna go. You helped me decide."

Oh sure, lay a guilt trip on me. Thanks for that free ride, Rev.

"You shouldn't go alone, Rev. Especially for the reason you're going."

"Saylor ain't gonna go."

"Not Saylor. Take someone else."

"Ain't takin' anyone else. This ain't a trip for me and my bestie. That's women shit. Just gonna go down, see it done, and get the fuck outta there."

See it done.

Like help it along? Shove his father to the end a little quicker?

"When are you going to go? You'll have to give Dutch that news. You know he won't be happy about you just up and leaving like that."

"Gonna have to get over it. Just gonna pretend that I give a fuck about my sperm donor instead of hatin' his fuckin' guts, then Dutch can't say shit. What boss won't let an employee go see his dear dyin' dad?"

None. Even Dutch.

"When?" she asked again. She needed to know because a plan was already brewing in her head. All she had to do was smooth out some of the rough details.

One of them being Dutch, who took that moment to fling the back door open and bellow, "What the fuck! Think I'm payin' you two to sit out here and watch the fuckin' weeds grow? Get the fuck back inside, or you're fired."

Reilly bit her bottom lip in an attempt to hide her grin. "Told you."

"Didn't need to tell me how grumpy that asshole is." Rev didn't hide his grin.

Holy shit, it was as beautiful as the man himself.

If Dutch wasn't glaring at them, she'd be tempted to tuck her fist under her chin, bat her lashes at Rev and sigh dreamily.

Snort. Rev would probably think she bashed her head on a corner of a raised car lift.

"You supposed to be touchin' her like that?" Dutch

shouted. "I don't get to touch her, you fuckin' don't get to touch her."

The door slammed shut.

Rev chuckled, which was nice to see.

Reilly snorted out loud this time. "Like I'd let him touch me."

Rev released her and stood up, stepping from between the bench and the table. He offered his hand to help her step over the bench, too.

"Never know. The man's got snatch droppin' at his feet left and right. Must be a reason for it."

"And you don't?" The sweet butts and the hang-arounds practically got into fistfights over him some nights.

Reilly would like to know what they were fighting over.

"I do all right." He grinned and his blue eyes held a sparkle.

She rolled her own.

He went to pull away but Reilly tugged on the hand she refused to let go. He turned back to her with his eyebrows pinned together.

"Hey, I know you guys aren't big into talking, but if you need to, I'm here. Just putting that out there into the universe."

He tilted his head as he stared at her. "The universe heard it and appreciates it. Now, get inside before the old man fires your sweet ass." With that, he smacked her ass so hard, she jumped and squealed.

But damn…

What she wouldn't do for a little more of that…

To hell with "a little." She'd take a whole hell of a lot more.

Chapter Three

REILLY CHEWED on her thumbnail as she perched on Rev's bike where it sat in the long storage shed in which they parked their sleds. She'd hidden her car behind The Grove Inn and had Ozzy drop her off early this morning.

She loved The Great Oz. He was the best. And he proved that once again when he peeled himself out of bed and away from a sleeping Lizzy just to do Reilly that favor. No questions asked.

She didn't have to give him any excuses on why she needed a ride to the farm that early. Unlike most of the guys, he really didn't give a fuck what she was doing or why. His reasoning was: if you don't ask someone's business, they won't ask you about yours.

Simple.

He'd always gone out of his way for her during the many months she lived at the motel. In exchange, she'd help him out in the office when needed. While it was great having her own apartment now, she missed being around him since he'd become like an older brother to her.

Now here she was... waiting. In the dark shed.

Nervous.

Because she knew she'd get a rash of shit from Rev for being there. But she had donned her invisible armor and was ready for whatever he would dish out. She'd also gone over and over in her head what she'd say to him and how she'd get him to see reason.

He never answered her yesterday about when he was making his trek to Coatesville, but she'd overheard—okay, purposely listened in—him talking to Dutch about it.

Dutch grumped a whole lot but reluctantly let him take the days off. Rev, not knowing when his father was going to "peacefully depart"—Reilly almost choked when she heard that description—left the date open for his return to work. She'd also kind of eavesdropped on his conversation with Trip just to confirm Rev wasn't leaving until this morning and not late last night.

Before Ozzy rode away earlier, she made sure Rev's sled was still inside the shed. She was relieved when it was. She didn't expect him to leave at the crack of dawn, so that was when she had Ozzy drop her off. Just to make sure she caught Rev before he left.

She promised the older biker lots of coffee and fresh pastries from Coffee and Cream when she returned. He only grunted in response and rode away, the deep rumble of his sled deafening in the quiet pre-dawn, mid-April morning air.

She'd hidden in the back corner of the shed behind some boxes while everyone but Rev had stumbled in, got their bikes and left for work. She wanted to avoid all the questions that would be asked—and didn't want to answer —if she was spotted.

So, one by one, sleepy bikers rolled in and rolled out. Not surprising, not one of them was a bright and chipper morning person.

One hour, eighteen minutes and thirty-four damn seconds after she arrived was when the door finally opened once more. She hoped like hell it was Rev and no one else this time because she was done hiding.

If it wasn't him, she was heading over to the bunkhouse and dragging him out by his hair. She couldn't imagine anyone was left in there except for Rev and maybe a couple of the prospects. But it was the risk of being seen by those prospects that made her stay put instead.

Some of the tension drained from her as she recognized his very familiar silhouette coming through the open doorway. As he hit the automatic door opener on the wall to lift the double garage door in front of his sled, she yelled out, "Don't open that!"

His whole body jerked, his hand automatically went to where he kept a knife on his hip and his head twisted toward her. "What the fuck?" he grumbled. "What the fuck you doin' in here?"

He didn't sound or look happy to see her. No surprise.

"Close the door before anyone sees me."

"I saw you."

"Not you, doofus," she clarified. "Anyone else."

He slammed his palm on the garage door button and the door grumbled its way closed again. "Why the fuck are you hidin' in here?"

All the overhead LED lights in the shed turned on when he hit that switch next. She squinted and raised a hand to shield her eyes from the blast of the cornea-burning brightness.

"I'm not hiding," she said with feigned innocence.

He glanced at her from where he stood and simply cocked an eyebrow.

She shot him a *whatever* face. "Just hear me out."

"Reilly," he growled.

"Just hear me out," she shouted, "before you go all alpha asshole on me and start beating on your chest and stomping your boots." Ever since she heard Teddy call the Fury members "leather-clad gorillas" it was hard to get that similarity out of her mind. It actually fit them perfectly.

"You shouldn't fuckin' be here."

"And you shouldn't go alone," she countered.

His expression turned hard. "What the fuck, Reilly!"

She sighed and weaved around the few sleds left in the shed to approach him, since, apparently, he was frozen in place.

When she got there, she tipped her face up to his and said, "You're not taking your sled."

His eyebrows shot so high up his forehead, she couldn't tell where they ended and his hairline began. "Wanna clue me in on when I started takin' orders from you?"

"It's not an order, it's a… strongly worded suggestion."

"All right, then. That's much better," he said way too agreeably. He stared at her for a few seconds, then bellowed, "Who the fuck d'you think you are?"

She winced. "Someone—"

"I musta drank way too much whiskey and smoked way too much Kush since I certainly don't fuckin' remember claimin' a woman at the table last night."

"I—"

"Also don't remember givin' a fuck about your strongly worded suggestions. I'm takin' my goddamn sled and goin' by myself."

She planted a hand under his cut and against the waffle-patterned dark gray thermal shirt he wore underneath it. The muscles under her fingers were so tense it was like touching a rock wall. "No, you aren't."

He shoved a finger in his right ear and wiggled it. "My hearin' must be fucked up."

"You heard me."

He tilted his head back, stared up at the shed's ceiling, barked out a single dry laugh, dropped his head back down, shook it, then tipped it the rest of the way down to her. His mouth opened, a hiss escaped, he snapped it shut again and stepped around her, heading to his Indian Dark Horse.

It was a sweet ride and a badass bike that she'd had the pleasure of straddling a couple of times, unlike its owner.

She decided to follow him.

He dropped his backpack on the concrete floor, then toed her own bag with his boot. "What's this shit?"

"My stuff. It's what I'll need for the next few days."

His nostrils flared as he stared at her backpack that seemed to be a lot fuller than his. Unlike him, she couldn't wear the same underwear, socks and shirt for days at a time. She also used a lot more than a squirt of gel for her hair.

"For our trip," she added. That came out a little weaker than she intended.

"Reilly, this ain't *our* trip."

She stiffened her spine, and lifted her invisible shield, prepared for battle. "It wasn't, but it is now."

"No, it ain't."

"Yes, it is. I understand why you don't want Saylor to go. But someone should go with you."

"And you think that someone is you."

She lifted her chin even higher to let him know she wasn't backing down. "I know it is."

"No, Reilly."

"Look, I know I'm maybe not the best choice for this, but I'm your only choice. Do you have someone better?"

"Yeah. No one."

"I'm not going to let you go by yourself."

"Reilly, ain't up to you."

She ignored that and pushed on. "So, you're not taking your sled. We need to take your Bronco, instead."

His brow furrowed and he did not hide the annoyance in his eyes. "Why the fuck would I drive my Bronco? Would cost me a fortune in fuel."

"Since I need to go that direction, anyway, I figured we

could split the cost." Okay, that last part might be a bit of a fib. Even though the guys knew she liked to pay her own way, none of them would ever take money from her, so she was counting on that since she didn't have much.

Normally, if she offered them money, they got insulted, cursed at her, turned their back on her and walked away, shaking their head. The same thing happened when she offered to pay a fair price for the used car Dutch sold her and the repairs it needed to be in tip-top running order. The garage owner just about bit her head off and took about half of what the car and the repairs were worth.

While she appreciated it, she also wanted to be independent. She'd been dependent on her sister for far too long. She had wanted to change that once she relocated to Manning Grove. It was time for her to be her own woman, to be responsible for her own decisions and her own mistakes. Especially after almost being killed by Billy Warren. So, that was what she set out to do.

He jerked his chin back and repeated, "You need to go that direction, anyway? Are you fuckin' crazy, woman?"

She shook her head. "Crazy smart." She tapped her temple. "Now that I have my own apartment, I need to get the rest of my stuff out of the storage unit. Reese has been paying for it this whole time and I can't let her do that any longer. But I'm never moving back there, so there's no point in keeping it. This is my home now."

"So, go get your shit yourself. You got a cage now."

"It's not just the point of saving on gas, I really could use the help. Plus, all my stuff won't fit in my car, anyhow. Think of it like this, I help you and you help me."

"How the fuck you gonna help me?"

Besides being there for emotional support? She knew that answer wouldn't fly. Instead, she said, "I'll keep you company on the three and a half hour trip. If you want, I can sing. Or tell jokes. Or we can listen to one of my really hot audiobooks."

"Or you can just be quiet the whole fuckin' way."

She smiled. "I'm not sure that's possible."

"Ain't that the fuckin' truth."

The other truth was she was starting to win this conversation. Persistence was paying off. "So... that means we're carpooling?"

"You're somethin' else," he muttered, plugging his hands on his hips, dropping his head and staring at his boots.

"Thank you."

He lifted his head. "Ain't a compliment. You clear this with Reese and the rest?"

The rest. He meant Deacon and Judge.

She rolled her lips under.

"You're gonna get my ass kicked, woman."

"Nah," she scoffed.

"Right. Gonna be gone for as long as it takes," he warned her.

She had already expected that. "I'm okay with however long it takes."

She assumed his uncle wouldn't have reached out unless Rev's father was at the very end of his illness so it would give Rev the time and opportunity to see his father while still alive. She also assumed it was so Rev didn't have any regrets afterward of not seeing his father one last time.

"What excuse d'you use? 'Cause I didn't see your cage parked out there. That means you hid it somewhere, didn't you?"

The man was not dumb.

She shrugged. "Maybe."

"Where?"

She gave him a look that he read clearly.

"Fuckin' Ozzy. You told him you're goin' with me?"

"Nope. He didn't ask or care."

"Fuckin' Ozzy. He shoulda asked." He shook his head in disbelief. "So, what'd you tell the others, the ones who *would* care enough to beat me silly with a fuckin' club?"

She gave him another look.

"Christ," he muttered. "Spill it. Or I'm leavin' you standin' here and takin' my sled without you. It better be a good fuckin' story, too."

It was actually pretty good, if she said so herself. "Well…"

He groaned. "You want me dead, right? That what you want?"

"I told Reese I was driving down to hang out in Philly for a few days with a couple of girlfriends from college. And, great friends that they are, they offered to help me clear out the storage unit while I was there."

He stared at her for the longest time before mumbling, "You and a coupla other college girlfriends. Would like to see that."

Of course that was the part he picked up on. "Girlfriends as in friends who have girl parts. Not girlfriends who squatted over my face while I licked their pussies."

Rev groaned and turned away for a moment. Or two. When he finally turned back, his voice cracked when he asked, "And Dutch?"

"I'm sure Dutch would love to get in on that action. Oh wait. You mean… I told him the same thing as I told Reese."

"And he wasn't pissed you're leavin'?"

"Believe me, he's surprised I still show up at the shop at all."

"He ain't the only one."

"Well, I'm kind of attached to you assholes, believe it or not."

She expected him to reply that they were kind of

attached to her, too. He didn't. Instead, he asked, "You got a trackin' device on your cell phone?"

All signs were now pointing to him relenting and letting her go along. Even if reluctantly. Now she only needed not to screw it up. "I don't know, do I?"

He held out his hand.

She plucked her phone from the outer pocket on her backpack and, after unlocking it, handed it to him. Once he swiped through the five million other apps on her phone, he found the one he was looking for and screwed with it before handing it back.

"Hate to tell you, you ain't as smart as you think you are. We all got those *find-your-ass* apps on our phones for a reason. Wouldn't be good to have both of us popping up in the same location other than Manning Grove."

"Well, I guess someone is smarter than I thought." She never would have thought about a location finder app. Something she forgot Judge required everyone to install on their phones during all the trouble with the Shirleys.

"Ain't too smart if I'm considerin' you goin' along."

She bounced on her toes, grabbed his shirt and shook it. "You won't regret it."

"Oh, I'm gonna fuckin' regret it. Already know it."

She grinned. "You'll enjoy my singing."

"Prefer road head to keep you quiet."

"Hard to give you road head on a sled."

"Easy in my Bronco."

She grinned.

He grinned.

Wait. Maybe he was serious.

"Havin' your head bobbin' in my lap won't only keep your trap shut but will keep you outta sight when we drive off the farm and outta town. Don't need you bein' spotted in my Bronco." He grabbed his backpack. "Get your shit. Ain't carryin' it for you. Gonna go out and make sure the coast is clear before you climb into my cage and wrap your lips around my dick."

She chewed on her bottom lip.

He leaned in and whispered, "That's it, get those lips warmed up, babe. Can't wait. 'Cause this ain't gonna be a free ride."

With that, he slapped her hard on the ass and walked out of the shed, leaving her standing there wondering what she just got herself into.

And whether she wanted to get herself back out of it or not.

———

THEY RODE in silence for over three damn hours because every time he turned on the satellite radio he'd installed last year in his custom '68 Ford Bronco 4x4, she sang along. After changing the station three times from classic rock to heavy metal to even rap, she tried to sing to whatever song played no matter if she knew the words or not.

He quickly hit the power button and put an end to that before he killed her and dumped her body alongside the road.

Truth was, she couldn't sing for shit. It was even worse when she made up the words.

She also sucked at telling jokes.

And while he made her duck down while leaving the farm, and then town, she did not give him road head. Not that he didn't want her fucking lips wrapped around his dick sucking his nuts dry, he did. But that wasn't going to happen.

Ever.

Because if she sucked him, he'd end up fucking her after that and then he would die.

Or be severely maimed.

54

And maybe even have his colors stripped.

No pussy was worth that. Not even the blonde sitting next to him, most of the trip turned in her seat, staring at him like some lunatic.

"Will you knock it the fuck off?"

"Why'd you get your ears and nose pierced?"

"This ain't gonna be a Q and A session, woman. Just sit there and shut up."

"What else is pierced?"

"My taint."

"No, it isn't. I've seen your dick and taint plenty of times and I know it isn't pierced."

"Why were you lookin' at my dick?"

"It's hard to miss when you fuck anyone who bends over in front of you not wearing panties."

He cocked one eyebrow and turned his eyes from the road to her for a second. "Not anyone."

"Anyone who doesn't have a dick," she corrected.

That might be true.

"And who doesn't wear someone's colors," she added.

That was definitely true. He would never touch an ol' lady. Or even someone's regular.

Even Lizzy, who was a sweet butt. She wasn't officially Ozzy's regular but those two were always doing their thing together since Ozzy preferred her over the rest of the sweet butts. Because of that, it would just feel weird fucking her. Unless him and Oz were double-teaming her, then he got over any guilt pretty fucking quickly.

Hold up.

He turned to glance at Reilly again. "All that time you stayed at the motel, did you join Oz and Lizzy in his bed?"

Her expression remained blank when she answered, "That man sure likes his threesomes," while staring out of the windshield.

That man sure likes his threesomes? She used the same

matter-of-fact tone as if she'd announced, "That man sure likes maple syrup on his pancakes."

Nope. That answer wasn't going to fly. "Yeah, he does. But you didn't answer what I asked."

She twisted her head toward him. "Why would it matter if I did?"

Why would it matter?

Why the fuck would it matter?

Because... It just would.

She arched one perfectly shaped eyebrow. "Have *you* joined them in a threesome?"

He pursed his lips and turned his attention back to the road.

"I'll take that as a yes since I know for a fact that you aren't opposed to them. I've witnessed you doing one too many."

In truth, there was no such thing as one too many threesomes. Even foursomes.

His rack in the bunkhouse might not be big enough for three women to join him, but there were other ways to make it work...

"Still waitin' on your answer."

"I'm not into other women," was her non-answer.

"Most women don't gotta be into women to have sex with them. Straight women don't mind shovin' their face in another woman's cunt if they're horny enough. Or drunk enough. Unlike men who got a problem with goin' down on another man or lickin' his asshole if they ain't into givin' or takin' dick."

"That's because we have less hang-ups than men. And most women know how to please another woman better than a man does."

His head spun toward her. "You speakin' from experience?"

She gave him an exaggerated eye roll. "I went to college, remember?"

"What the fuck does that gotta do with anything?"

"If you went to college, you'd know."

Maybe he should've made more of an effort and found a way to go to college if that was the kind of shit that went on. "College girls gone wild, huh?"

"Are you getting hard?" she accused, eyeing his lap.

"How the fuck can I not? You talkin' about shovin' your face between another chick's thighs and lickin'—"

"I did *not* say those words. That's just your horny imagination."

"You never ate pussy?" *Christ.* He *was* getting hard.

"You just said this wasn't going to be a Q and A session."

He sighed. That he did. *For fuck's sake,* he should've kept his damn mouth shut and let her just talk. He might have heard some great stories instead.

He frowned. "Fine."

"Fine," she huffed.

He needed to get his mind off Reilly and back to their destination. They were only about fifteen minutes away from the house he grew up in. He needed to prepare himself for what they'd be walking into.

It wouldn't be a teary reunion full of hugs, kisses and claims of missing each other. It would be more of a "I'll try not to smother your fuckin' face with a pillow after I spit on you," just to make sure his old man took his last damn breath.

He figured they'd head straight over there, check out the situation, see how long his asshole sire had to live and then find a motel. Because he certainly wasn't planning on sitting at his father's bedside to hold the fucker's hand.

He also wasn't planning on forgiving him, even if the

JEANNE ST. JAMES

man asked for it with his last dying breath. His father didn't deserve even an ounce of forgiveness. Not one.

Closure. That was what he was going for.

Nothing but closure.

Once the man's evil soul left his body, the man could be forgotten for good. *Have a nice trip south, dearest Dad.*

"Hey, why did the Harley fall over?"

Oh Christ, here she went again with lame jokes.

"Because it was two tired!" she shouted, then slapped her knee and laughed.

He groaned.

With her tracking device off, he could dump her body anywhere and she'd never be found again.

That might be for the best.

Chapter Four

REILLY SAT in the passenger seat and studied the plain, two-story house in front of them. The white paint on the wood siding was faded and peeling. It needed a fresh coat at least ten years ago or to be updated with vinyl siding. The house wasn't falling down or anything, it just needed a facelift.

The Bronco's engine still rumbled since Rev had put the shifter into neutral as he also stared at the house. He hadn't even engaged the parking brake yet, almost as if he was weighing his options.

His expression was unreadable but his stiff body and the fingers white-knuckling the steering wheel said it all. This was not a joyous homecoming.

He was dreading it.

That made her wonder, for the hundredth time since yesterday, why he wanted to come back here at all. He said he wanted to make sure his father was dead. Simply reading the obituary would give him that. So would getting another phone call from his uncle once his father passed.

He didn't need to put himself through turmoil just to witness it.

She wanted to say something but didn't know what.

Whatever she said he probably wouldn't appreciate right now. Instead, she sat quietly—a struggle in itself—and let him work out whatever he needed to work out in his head.

Most likely whether to stay or go.

The problem was, if he didn't say something soon, words might simply explode from her like a drunk unable to contain his vomit. She dug her nails into her palms in a desperate attempt to keep herself quiet.

She could do it. She could be patient. The whole point of going along was to be supportive and, if he needed her to keep her mouth shut, she'd do her best.

Staying quiet wasn't her strong suit, so she hoped he appreciated the effort she was taking. She tried to concentrate on their surroundings instead, like… The fact that his parents didn't live in a neighborhood. It wasn't a farm, but the house was situated along a country road with other homes within view but not close enough to be on top of each other like in the suburbs.

She also noted that three vehicles were parked in the stone driveway. All plain, boring four-door sedans.

The lawn seemed—

Reilly jumped when he stomped on the parking brake and shoved the shifter into first gear before shutting off the engine. He yanked the keys from the ignition and stuffed them deep into the front pocket of his jeans.

For some weird reason, her heart began to pound. She wasn't nervous about meeting his family. She was nervous for Rev.

She'd known and worked with him for a year now, and the way he was acting was not normal for him. *Hell*, it wasn't normal for most people visiting their parents.

But she could understand it. She would feel the same way if she had to visit her own. In her case, though, she'd never do that, even if they were dying. Neither deserved her time or attention. Neither deserved even a second of thought. She had never been their priority, even when she was in her mother's womb, so why would she ever make them hers?

What she was taking away from Rev's words and behavior was that his parents didn't deserve his time or attention, either. They had done something to severely damage their relationship with him and Saylor. She doubted it was anything minor. Maybe whatever it was was even heinous.

That made her thumping heart quicken.

"Rev," escaped from her, even though she hadn't meant it to. But the dread thickening the air of the Bronco's interior had begun to seep into her own chest. "We should just leave."

He turned his head, his blue eyes hard when they met hers. "No."

The tension in the Bronco's interior ratcheted up a notch or two. "I don't think this is a good idea."

"Told you not to fuckin' come. Once again you forced your way in the middle of somewhere you don't fuckin' belong."

She caught her grimace and smoothed it out. He was striking out and she just happened to be conveniently close. She understood that, too.

She would give him a pass. This time. "Now that we're sitting here, I know it was the right decision for you not to come alone."

"Don't need you or anyone else."

She pressed her lips together in her attempt not to snap at him for being a dick. That was not what he needed right now.

Her heart seized when the front door of the house opened wide and a tall man stepped out. He didn't look ill or feeble so it couldn't be Rev's father. The older man was dressed in a plain black suit with a black button-down shirt and a white clerical collar. As he walked down the porch steps, he did not turn toward the parked vehicles, instead he took long strides right toward the Bronco.

"Fuck," Rev muttered under his breath.

It wasn't a good sign if the visit was starting out with a muttered curse in reaction to a man of the cloth. Or whatever they were called. Reilly had no idea. The only time she'd ever stepped into a church was when a friend got married a couple of years ago.

She rated that experience a one out of five stars. *#WouldNotRecommend.* The wedding service was endless, and she didn't understand why they kept standing and sitting and kneeling over and over... Especially when Reilly was wearing a short dress.

"Fuck," Rev muttered one more time as the preacher, pastor, *whatever*, stepped up to the open driver's side window.

At least Rev hadn't closed the windows and locked the doors.

Reilly had no idea how long it had been since Rev had last been home, but the gray-haired man in the crisp clerical collar didn't have any problem recognizing him. But then, Rev did have a face that was hard to forget.

"Brother Michael. It's been far too long." Not a friendly greeting, but actually quite icy. An unexpected tone from someone she figured was a church leader.

"Not long enough," was Rev's grumbling answer.

Shit.

Without any kind of reaction to Rev's insult, the man glanced past him to her frozen in the passenger seat. He pointed a stiff, plastic smile in her direction that was nowhere near genuine but only because it was expected. "I see you brought your wife."

What? "I'm—" Her words were interrupted when Rev's hand shot out and clamped on her knee. He squeezed it almost to the point of pain.

"Yes, my wife decided to accompany me in this trying time."

She blinked. *Say what?* Why was he speaking like that? Like he had a stick up his ass and wasn't a carefree biker who dropped his pants and whipped out his dick every time the wind changed direction.

The man turned his gray eyes back to Rev. Reilly noticed the way his cold, narrowed gaze slid from the barbell piercings in Rev's right ear to the hoop in his nostril and then over to the barbells in his left ear before coming back to settle on Rev's face with an expression that looked like he'd just sucked on a lemon. Or a whole orchard full of lemons.

"It's a dark time for our congregation, Brother Michael. Your father is such a pillar of our community. A leader to look up to. A perfect example of a God-fearing man whose life's work is to serve the Lord. His loss will leave a gaping hole that may not be possible to fill."

Rev's fingers twitched painfully on her knee. She grabbed it and gave it a little squeeze of her own so he wouldn't unintentionally pop off her kneecap in his simmering rage.

Reilly didn't know whether to laugh or throw up at that description of Rev's father. Even with the little she knew so far, she could guess that was all a bunch of bullshit. To say that to the man's son was even more insulting. Obviously, it was said with a purpose.

The purpose wasn't to console Rev, it was to make a damn point. A very sharp one jabbed in Rev's chest.

"You receive his deathbed confession yet?"

The man made a sharp *tsk-tsk* sound. "Brother Michael, you know our order doesn't do last rites or take confessions. A man's sins are solely between him and God. No one else."

"How 'bout their victims?"

The creases at the corners of the pastor's mouth deepened when it became tight and his shoulders stiffened. "Your father has always been an upstanding member of our order. Since you lost your way and left our community, he's also become an elder who is revered and respected."

"'Hear now this, O foolish people, and without understanding; which have eyes, and see not; which have ears, and hear not.'"

Reilly's eyes went wide as she stared in shock at the back of Rev's dark blond head since he still faced the preacher. Or pastor. Or whatever the fuck the man was.

Did the cursing, pot-smoking, fuck-anyone-with-boobs biker just quote some sort of scripture?

She ran those words over again in her mind and realized what he said held the same meaning as "none so blind as those who do not see." But for some reason he did not choose that simple and effective reminder, he recited that particular passage for a reason.

These two were verbally sparring with backhanded insults.

Maybe Rev was more complex than she ever thought.

She slid her gaze from him back to the clergy's face. The older man no longer hid his now very unfriendly and unwelcoming expression. The religious leader no longer hid his disdain at Rev's presence.

Reilly wasn't liking this. Not at all. Something was very, very wrong. Had they stepped into some Stephen King or M. Night Shyamalan movie? Were things only going to get worse from here?

"Did you only come home to make trouble, Michael? Have you not outgrown that stage in your life and become a man? Or are you still a stubborn, petulant child who did nothing but create problems for your parents and steal your sister's innocence?"

Rev's whole body jerked, then his chest inflated so slowly that Reilly tightened her hand over the one he still had pinned to her knee so he wouldn't swing at a man wearing a clerical collar.

Though, maybe she should let him. The condescending asshole deserved it.

When he tried to tug it free, she put her other hand on top and put her weight into it, too. "Don't," she whispered just loud enough for him to hear.

He didn't even bother to glance at her but turned his face enough so she could see his jaw working and a muscle jumping in his cheek.

He needed to start the truck and they needed to get the hell out of there. Whatever this was, it was not going to get any better. She'd seen these types of movies, they never ended well.

Finally, Rev managed, "Not here to be judged by you or anyone else."

"How about God?"

"Only here to say my final goodbye."

"Did they ask you to come?"

"Brother Matthew did."

"Then Brother Matthew made a mistake," was the last thing the man said before turning and going to one of the dark sedans. Rev, with his nostrils flared and his lips now an angry slash, tracked his movement.

He breathed slowly, deeply and steadily like he was trying not to blow a gasket as he watched the sedan carrying the pastor drive away.

"Time to go," she whispered.

With a single nod, he shoved open the driver's door, yanking his hand from her knee.

"That's not what I meant."

He stood just outside the Bronco and ducked enough to look inside at her. "You stay in the truck. Doubt I'm gonna be long." He slammed the door shut.

Oh no. No. He was not going in there alone.

She scrambled to open her door and climb out of the raised four-by-four. She almost twisted her ankle in her heeled boots as she jumped down, but she caught her balance and hurried after him. Only almost face-planting once along the way.

She caught up to him at the porch. "Think about this, Rev."

"Nothin' to think about."

She stood at the bottom of the steps and sighed, watching him take determined steps to the front door. She expected him to pound on it, but he didn't, he just turned the knob and flung the door open, going inside.

"Shit," she muttered and jogged up the steps, across the porch and into the house before he could slam the door in her face.

She caught the door and closed it behind her, then turned and froze.

Yes, she knew only too well how these types of movies ended.

With desperation, destruction and, ultimately, death.

———

HE FELT her presence at his back. He heard her shallow breathing. "Go back outside."

"No, I'm not letting you do this by yourself."

She was so fucking stubborn and always had to wedge herself where she didn't belong.

"Don't need you, Reilly." Complete fucking lie.

While he'd never relied on anyone before, for some reason he was relieved she was there. Now was not the time to figure out why.

Matthew stepped out of the room to the right and into the hallway. He stopped when he saw them. "I thought I heard voices." His lips moved like he was trying to force a smile but couldn't quite manage it.

His uncle approached them and when he got within a few feet of Rev, he jutted out his hand. While his voice wasn't cold, it wasn't warm, either. "Welcome home, Brother Michael."

He ignored the outstretched hand. "Name's Rev. You don't wanna call me that, call me Mickey. Haven't been Michael since the day I walked out that door behind me."

In reality, he didn't walk out that door. He snuck out the back in the middle of the night with only the clothes on his back and a few things tossed into a brown paper bag.

Matthew dropped his hand and his brow furrowed. "Rev? Like reverend? Have you continued on the path of serving God?" The man actually sounded hopeful. Rev was about to smash the shit out of that.

"Fuck no. Short for revenge."

A nervous laugh bubbled out of Reilly. She pressed a hand to the small of his back and stepped to his side. "Rev like rev an engine since he's a mechanic."

Matthew's eyes fell on the woman by Rev's side. "And this is?"

Reilly chewed on her bottom lip for the second she glanced up at Rev, then extended her hand to his uncle. "I'm Reilly—"

Rev dropped an arm around her shoulders and pulled her into his side, tearing their clasped hands free. "My wife."

Matthew's eyes went wide. "Oh, your parents will be pleased to hear you've settled down." Rev's jaw shifted as his uncle's eyes dropped to Reilly's full hips. "Any little ones yet?"

Motherfucker.

"I keep her busy. Four, so far." He dropped his arm from her shoulders and patted her ass. "She's a good little breeder." Reilly choked and he lifted his hand from her ass to pat her on the back. "You good, babe?"

Reilly nodded with one hand on her throat, still unable to talk. A fucking miracle in itself.

"And you didn't bring them along?" Matthew asked, surprised. "I'm sure your parents would appreciate seeing their grandchildren."

"Wouldn't bring my babies around here. They're safer at home." Rev lifted one eyebrow. He didn't give a fuck if his uncle picked up on his meaning or not. In fact, he hoped he did.

"Well… Your mother's in the kitchen and your father has been in the sitting room ever since he's been confined to a hospital bed. Who would you like to visit first, Broth… Michael?"

Neither.

"Mickey or Rev," Rev reminded him.

Matthew tipped his head. "Yes… well. You'll always be Michael to me. It's a good strong name."

Rev leaned in closer and lowered his voice. "Don't give a fuck what you think about that name. It's no longer mine."

Matthew went pale and he cleared his throat. "So, um…"

Rev ignored him and glanced around. Nothing had changed. Not one thing since the day he left. A large wooden cross was the only decoration that hung in the narrow hallway that led to the back of the house.

He curled his hand around Reilly's hip, gave it a little squeeze and guided her past his uncle and down the hallway that ran along the stairway to the second floor.

They might as well deal with his mother first. He didn't even know if his parents knew he was coming.

"You tell them?" he asked over his shoulder as he continued toward the back of the house.

"No, I... wasn't sure if you'd show up. I didn't want to disappoint them if you didn't."

Rev doubted they'd be disappointed if they never saw him again. They probably thanked God every day since the day he disappeared.

Since they weren't expecting his arrival, this would be a surprise family reunion.

Perfect.

When they stepped into the kitchen, his mother was at the stove, he swore wearing the same apron she wore when he was a kid. Her dark blonde hair, now with a few strands of gray, was pulled up into a tight bun and her back was to them.

"Sister Rachel," Matthew called from behind them.

Rev stood frozen in place, his fingers tightening on Reilly's hip as the mother he hadn't seen in about twelve years turned and looked at him. With those few strands of gray hair and the wrinkles lining her make-up free face, she looked a lot older than her forty-six years.

It shouldn't be a surprise that the way his parents lived their lives had aged them faster than normal. Or at least his mother.

It took her a full second before recognition filled her face. As soon as it did, it turned hard. And about as welcoming as Pastor Thomas's.

Her blue eyes landed on her brother, who pushed past them to act as a buffer between mother and son.

"What's the meaning of this?" she asked sharply, wiping her hands on her apron.

Yeah, this would be no loving family reunion. Not even close.

No smile. No tears. Just a frown marred her face. "Why is he here?"

From the corner of his eye, he saw Reilly's face tipped

up toward his and her eyes flicking back and forth from him to the woman who gave birth to him.

"I figured it was time for everyone to make peace," Matthew said to his sister. "It's time for things to be settled between you all."

"Didn't come here to see you," Rev announced, shooting his uncle's peace-making efforts to shit.

"Where's your sister?"

Not "You look great, son," or "Thank God, you're alive. We've been worried," or "We've missed you so much."

Nope. That might mean they cared.

Matthew stepped between them, turning to face Rev. "I didn't get a chance to tell them yet."

"Sarah's dead." No lie was told when he spouted that out without bothering to soften the blow. Sarah had been dead for a long time. It was Saylor who lived in her place now.

He waited for his mother's reaction to the knowledge that her only daughter was dead. Again, nothing. No tears, no gasp, not even a look of surprise.

She didn't even ask how Sarah died.

His mother was emotionally frigid. She always had been. But then she'd been married to a man who had controlled her and her thoughts since she was seventeen. Women in their religious order were only allowed to serve God, their fathers and then their husbands. And, of course, bear children.

That was it.

They did not work outside of the home. They did not drive. They didn't have one damn unique thought.

And sex was not supposed to be enjoyed, it was to be endured only for procreation. A woman who enjoyed sex was a whore. Even though, as many times as Rev was forced to read the bible, he never read anything in the "good book" that said a woman couldn't enjoy sex.

Because the men sure did. Even with their daughters.

Seeing his mother reminded him what life Saylor would've lived if she hadn't found a way to escape on her own. By acting out and committing crimes.

Though, Rev would've done his best to get her out of there as soon as he could've. But when he finally escaped at sixteen, he couldn't raise his baby sister.

So, she did things to get herself out of the situation by stealing, fighting and anything else she could think of that would get her thrown into juvie over and over. She'd hardly be out for a week before she would do something to get thrown back in. A week home was probably too long. *Hell*, a day was probably too long.

Finally, she made sure to do something that would keep her locked up until she was eighteen. With what she did, she was lucky she wasn't charged as an adult, skipped juvie and went right to prison.

Once she was released that final time, Rev brought her to Manning Grove—using the excuse she wasn't welcome at their parents' home—because there was no fucking way she'd ever go back to Coatesville, this house and their father.

Over Rev's dead body.

He'd felt guilty leaving her behind in the first place. But his parents never would've tolerated him taking Sarah with him. He would've ended up charged with child abduction and, once found, she would've been delivered right back into their hands.

His hands.

The hands that doled out punishment for every minor infraction. Even imagined ones. The hands that doled out different punishments to his daughter than his son.

Rev struggled to breathe as he stared sightlessly across the barren kitchen. Nothing was ever left out unless the item was in use. The counters were clear, the table was empty, the walls were bare except for another cross. None of the crosses in the house were the kind with a crucified Jesus. None were fancy. They consisted of only two strips of polished wood.

The house was not full of knickknacks or decorations. No family photos. No drawings or crafts made by their children were displayed. Plain curtains were used only to block the sun or to give the family privacy. Or to be pulled to avoid seeing what her husband was doing to her son in the backyard.

Was it to fight the temptation to go out and stop him? Or was it because she believed Michael was getting what he deserved?

Or was it because if she intervened, she would take his place and receive the lashes instead of him? Of course, with some additional strikes added on to the number for stepping out of her place.

He wondered how many times his father had made his mother bare her back so he could paint stripes on her skin with a switch. All with the excuse to remind her on how to be a good wife.

Or did she marry him already trained to serve him? Trained by her own father like Michael's father had been "training" Sarah?

Everyone in their church seemed to look the other way when it came to things like that. Like it was normal. When it wasn't.

None of it was normal.

It was all fucked up.

All of it.

He made fun of the Shirleys and their cult-like ways, but in truth, he had grown up in a community no better than theirs.

Unlike the Shirleys, they did not hide and keep to themselves, they walked among the greater community. Their secrets hidden in plain sight.

Their children constantly complimented for being so well-behaved.

Until they weren't.

Until they acted out. Until they fought the chains that bound them.

Until they fought to be free from the restraints forced on them by their parents, grandparents and the members of their order.

Those disobedient children were prayed over.

And when that didn't work, they were punished.

Brought to heel.

The rod was not spared but instead used generously.

It was also highly encouraged.

Rev squeezed his eyes shut and simply breathed as a hand pressed to the center of his back, grounding him. Bringing him back to the situation at hand.

Which was his mother. Stepping closer. Inspecting him. Seeing the multiple piercings in his ears. The hoop in his nose.

The forbidden tattoos that covered his hands. He had worn a long sleeve T-shirt but it was impossible to hide the tattoos that spilled past his cuffs and onto the backs of his hands.

She would probably drop to her knees and ask for God's forgiveness if he whipped off his shirt and she saw what was underneath.

Not scars from his father's punishment. But different types of markings. More of what was already revealed. What she only got a glimpse of. The marks his father left behind on his back now mostly gone and the very bold statement of who he was, where he now belonged, in their place.

He chose not to join the fellowship his parents groomed him for, but instead a fellowship of another type. A brotherhood that stood stronger together than apart.

Also full of secrets. But nothing like the secrets kept within this house.

Within their church.

Within their minds.

She did not hide her disgust, or the fact that she was judging him, when she said, "Leviticus 19:28, Michael. Have you forgotten by accident or by choice?"

Ye shall not make any cuttings in your flesh for the dead, nor print any marks upon you.

"On purpose, Mother mine."

Her mouth tightened and her blue eyes narrowed. Yeah, there was no doubt where he got his eyes from. Only his weren't so damn judgmental.

"You are not welcome here, Michael."

He shrugged "Ain't a surprise."

"So then, you will leave."

"No, I won't."

"Brother Matthew, see your nephew out," she ordered.

"I won't, Sister. I had a purpose when I asked him here."

"To create problems. John doesn't need this stress right now. His passing over should be peaceful."

Rev hoped to fuck it was anything but. The real reason why he came. Why he was putting himself through this. Bringing himself back to a past he'd left far behind.

She turned and headed back to the stove, clearly dismissing them.

Reilly tugged on his arm. "Maybe we should go, Rev."

"Rev?" His mother spun back around, a wooden spoon in her hand, her face now showing some emotion. Disbelief. "Are you a Reverend now? What church allows all those tattoos and piercings?" She pointed the spoon in his direction and waved it up and down. "The marks of the devil."

"His wife said it's a nickname since he's an auto mechanic, Sister." Matthew still trying to be the Schmidt family whisperer.

"Rev your engine," Reilly explained weakly next to him, still gripping his elbow.

"That's not an appropriate name," she said sharply. "What kind of name is that?"

"One I chose and you did not."

Her head snapped back and her words became extra crispy, just like he liked his fucking fried chicken. "We gave you the perfectly good name of Michael, the archangel. The great protector and leader of God's army to defeat the forces of evil. But you have become one of them, haven't you?" Disappointment filled his mother's face. There was the mother he used to know and tried to love. "You have chosen the wrong path. I always knew you would. I knew you would never grow up and be worthy of that name." She sniffed. "Maybe it's better you don't use it."

He hadn't used it since he was ten. He insisted all his friends call him Mickey. Only his parents, his extended family and the members of their church used the name Michael. Or Brother Michael.

He hated it. He even stopped answering to that name in school. The teachers finally relented and began to call him Mickey, too.

He kept that name until Trip rolled into town and resurrected the Bloody Fury. When he became a prospect, they called him Mouse, a stupid play on the name Mickey. And once he was patched in, he got to decide for himself. Dutch said the name Mickey was for a pussy and he needed a more manly road name.

One day at the garage he was revving an engine and Dutch decided to bitch about it. The more he bitched, the more Rev gunned the engine. That was when the idea to use the road name Rev popped into his head. Rev not only liked it but knew it would annoy Dutch, so it stuck.

"The devil has always been inside you. We tried to remove you from his clutches. We tried to help you but you resisted us at every turn. Starting when you were very young. If I told you to look up, you looked down. If I told you to turn left, you turned right. If I told you to keep your Sunday clothes clean, you purposely got them dirty. Pure evil."

Reilly's grip moved from his elbow to his wrist and she tugged. "We should go, Rev."

"Didn't do what I came here to do. Not leaving 'til that's done," he murmured, not taking his eyes off his mother and the item in her hand.

Instead of asking about his intentions, his mother rushed back across the kitchen with the wooden spoon, making Rev's head snap up, his spine stiffen and his breath seize.

He couldn't help but close his eyes as he braced to feel the pain associated with that familiar tool of punishment. Usually used when he said something out of line in the kitchen while she was cooking. Or when he wasn't moving fast enough while setting the table or washing the dishes. Or when he tried to sneak some food.

But instead of feeling the impact of the spoon, Reilly's grip was torn from his arm. He opened his eyes to see his mother tightly holding Reilly's left hand.

He saw what his mother saw. No wedding band on Reilly's finger.

"Traveling with a woman who's unmarried. Who also bears a mark." His mother dropped Reilly's hand and swept her hair away from her scar, staring at it for far too long. "The devil's mark."

Reilly yanked her head away, pulling her hair free from his mother's fingers. "That's right. That mark was made by a devil. One who died for his sins," Reilly said sharply.

Rev grabbed her hand and intertwined their fingers, pulling her back into his side. "Didn't bring her here for you to insult her."

"You shouldn't have brought that jezebel here at all. You

have dishonored us and this home by allowing an unclean woman into my house. Uninvited."

"We were invited," he said through clenched teeth.

"Sister, he says they're married and are blessed with four children."

"Then she bore those poor children out of wedlock. I see no commitment band on her finger. That means she's available for any man. She's not committed to her husband."

It was laughable, judging children who didn't exist. Judging Reilly and Rev's relationship when there wasn't one.

"It's what you don't see that matters most," Rev said, making a point that his mother probably wouldn't pick up on.

"You always thought you knew better than your parents. But the truth is, if you did, you wouldn't have come here. You would've stayed wherever you came from."

"I'm happy to see you, too, Mother. And now I will go see the person I came here for."

Rev spun on his boot and tugged Reilly with him out of the kitchen, hearing his mother's words in his wake. "He doesn't want you here, either."

"Go sit in the truck, Reilly," he growled as he took long strides toward the sitting room, dragging her along.

Her hand tightened in his. "No. You're outnumbered."

"Nothing new."

"Brother Michael," Matthew called from the end of the hall.

Rev spun back toward him. "The words you said to me on the phone were not the truth."

Matthew's lips thinned out. "I thought they were, nephew. God forgive me, clearly I was wrong."

Clearly.

Chapter Five

Rev stopped just inside the doorway, Reilly's fingers slipping from his.

The light in the sitting room was dim, the curtains drawn. Only one small lamp in the corner lit.

Rev sucked air that held the heavy scent of impending death into his flared nostrils as he took in the hospital bed set up against the far wall. All of the simple furniture he remembered that used to be in this room was gone. The room now only consisted of a small side table and a few wooden chairs set up in a semi-circle around the bed.

He'd recognized those chairs. The ones used for visitors.

Or prayer circles.

It was hard to see the man of his childhood nightmares under the pile of white blankets. The big chested man with broad shoulders and powerful arms seemed to have disappeared. What looked like a skeleton took his place. Blankets and bones were all Rev could see.

The room smelled like sickness. Puke, shit and piss.

John Schmidt's power was gone. Stripped from him by an evil the man couldn't beat into submission.

Rev dug deep to see if he felt empathy or even sympathy.

Nothing. He couldn't drum up anything for his sire except loathing.

A slender woman sat by his father's bed, her head tipped down as she read from a well-worn bible, her mouth moving but no words escaping. Her dark hair was pulled back into a tight bun like his mother's, but she looked a lot younger than Rachel Schmidt.

Maybe even younger than Reilly.

"Patrice," Matthew called from behind Rev, making him take an involuntary step deeper into the room.

The woman's head lifted. Her gaze sliced over Rev, then Reilly, and finally landed on Matthew, who still stood behind them.

"Come, give my nephew some time with his father." A hand clamped on Rev's shoulder. "I'll introduce you to my wife another time."

With an obedient nod, the woman rose and Rev saw her dress fell all the way to her ankles. Not an Amish-type dress, but one similar to his mother's, a style the women from their order wore for modesty. No cleavage or skin showing below the high neckline. The dresses always reminded him of something between what the Amish and Mennonite women wore. However, unlike the Amish and Mennonites, the women of his parents' church did not wear any kind of head coverings—what Rev called sin sifters—except in church on Sundays.

Rev guessed that their religious order broke off from either the Amish or Mennonites a very long time ago, though he never cared enough to ask. The groups were all similar in some aspects but not exactly the same.

Even so, all of them had problems with abuse. Either with domestic violence, sexual assault, even incest. But rarely were those secrets shared outside of their community. Rarely did the pigs get involved. Those closed communities tended to handle their own problems.

Or simply sweep them under the rug.

Or accept it as God's will.

"Hello," Patrice said softly to each of them with a slight nod as she passed.

"Hello," Reilly returned the greeting, glancing over her shoulder to watch them walk back down the hallway toward the kitchen. She then lifted her face to his and bugged out her green eyes.

He didn't give a shit about Matthew or his wife. He was here for one person and one person only.

He walked through the room, turning on more lamps so his father could see him clearly. So his father would know who was here to visit him. So his father would have no doubt who it was that stood over him in his weakened state.

When Rev was done lighting the room, he moved closer to the hospital bed and glanced down at the man with the pale, paper-thin skin. His eye sockets were shadowed in dark purple, his cheeks hollowed, blue veins visible just below the skin like rivers on a map. Only a few dark strands of his formerly thick hair remained.

This was not the man Rev remembered. His father was now the shell of the man who had ruled his family and this very household. It used to be that Rev was the weak one, unable to overpower his father. How things had changed.

Reilly stepped up behind him, not quite touching him, but close enough he could feel her body heat mix with his. Making her presence and support known without words.

Since stepping into this house, she hadn't said much. Definitely not normal for her, but then maybe she couldn't find anything to say. She couldn't understand the undertones of the house, of the past, of the people who had lived under this roof. Of the people who still lived under it now.

But he was sure she would ask too many fucking questions later.

That was her nature. To be curious, to constantly be

chattering, to be involved in whatever was happening around her, whether it was welcomed or not.

It was both cute and fucking annoying. Normally, more of the second than the first.

He hadn't wanted her to come along, but at this very second, as he stared down at the man who used to be his father, he sure was fucking glad she had elbowed her way along on this trip. Her presence helped keep him from doing what he suddenly wanted to do.

Rev's fingers twitched with the urge to wrap them around the man's thin, fragile-looking neck and squeeze until the rattling breath that filled the room went silent.

He wondered how much time his old man had left and whether it would be worth shortening that time or not.

No. Not with Reilly here. Or Matthew and his young wife. Even his mother.

They would be witnesses and strangling always left bruises behind.

Even though his father had cancer rotting away at his insides, to Rev, the man could never suffer enough. Taking his life would only shorten that suffering.

And that wasn't why he was here.

He was here to witness karma to the very end.

More importantly, while the good pastor didn't want to hear deathbed confessions, Rev did. Rev wanted to know why the man had violated his sister's trust. Violated his sister, period.

While he hated every punishment his father doled out to him, he hated every time he heard his sister's door close and lock even more.

The man's breath caught and Rev moved even closer, until his body was pressed against the metal side rails, until he was staring straight down into his father's face.

"Wake up, old man," Rev ordered. "Wake up and face me."

His father's thin, pale lips parted and a weak hiss escaped. His eyelids fluttered a few times before they opened.

Father and son were nothing alike. Rev was blond with blue eyes. John Schmidt's hair, when he had it, had been a very dark brown that matched eyes neither Saylor or Rev inherited.

His sister also had their mother's blue eyes, even though Saylor was born with brown hair. Not as dark as their father's, but certainly not dark blonde like their mother's or Rev's.

Their eyes tied mother, son and daughter together. While neither looked like their father. *Thank fuck.* Because if he had to look in the mirror every day and see his father looking back at him, he wouldn't have made it to his twenty-eighth year.

"Who are you?" The man's voice was weak and not as booming or intimidating as Rev remembered.

"Don't know your own son?"

A flicker of recognition filled his bloodshot and watery brown eyes. "I don't have a son." The man tried to pull himself up to his elbows but failed and his head flopped back onto the pillow. He managed to turn his head enough to narrow his eyes on Rev. "Get out of my house, Michael." His effort to sound commanding, even menacing, failed.

How the mighty have fallen.

"Make me," Rev said. "And the name's Rev, not Michael. Michael is dead and so is Sarah Schmidt." He leaned over and put his ear to his old man's ear. "Soon you will be, too. Ain't leavin' 'til that happens."

"Why would you… come back here… somewhere you're not… welcome?" When he started hacking uncontrollably, Reilly grabbed the cup of water with a straw on the nearby table and offered it to him.

His father weakly slapped her hand away. "Sarah?"

Reilly was blonde with green eyes and looked nothing like Saylor.

"Just like you don't have a son, you don't have a daughter, either. You lost her a long time ago."

"Your loss... was not a hardship," he croaked, "but Sarah... belonged to me." It sounded like it hurt his throat to talk.

"A young girl can't belong to a man. A daughter can't be owned by her father."

John Schmidt forced out a weak huff. "You have always... been argumentative, child. Always. No matter how many times... I tried to teach you," he took a rattled breath, "you refused to learn the ways... You know a man's daughter belongs to him... until the moment he gives her... to her husband." He wheezed as he struggled to take his next breath. "A worthy man... of the father's choosing. Just like your mother belonged to your grandfather... until she was given to me." His skeletal hand, transparent skin over bones, flopped onto his chest. "A daughter faithfully serves her father... until the moment she exchanges hands... from father to husband."

That was what their church taught. But there was either an unspoken meaning behind that lesson or his father had heard what he wanted to hear and interpreted it to fit his own personal agenda.

"What does your precious bible say about a father lyin' with his own daughter? What does your preacher say?"

"He tells us... to teach our daughters well. I cannot find a good husband... for my daughter if she isn't worthy." He struggled to take another noisy breath. "Sarah was a wayward child... Like you... She needed to learn how to serve... her future husband well. Otherwise, if she failed to do so... she would be an embarrassment to me... to your mother... She would be proof... of our inability to raise our children according to our beliefs... If we failed her... we would fail God."

Bullshit. Utter fucking bullshit. Rev's teeth were clenched so tightly he thought they might shatter.

But his sire wasn't done spewing that verbal diarrhea. "You were a bad influence on her... Encouraging her to act out... to be an ill-behaved child. It was *your* fault she needed... to be punished so much."

The pressure in his chest swelled to the point he thought his skin would split open. "Oh no, old man, don't you fuckin' dare blame me for your sickness. For what you did. Don't even fuckin' go there." He needed to get the fuck out of there before he up and killed the man anyway. Because he was seconds away from doing just that. From stopping the bullshit and lies. "Are you gonna die today?"

"You would like that... wouldn't you?"

"It can't come soon enough."

"Agreed. It'll be glorious... to feel the arms of God surrounding me... as He welcomes me into His Kingdom... You will never feel that."

Rev leaned over the bed and growled, "Neither will you."

He stepped back, bumping into Reilly. He grabbed her arm to keep from knocking her over and tugged her behind him as he took long strides from the room.

He didn't go to the kitchen to say goodbye, instead he went directly to the front door, slamming it behind them. He didn't stop until they reached his Bronco. He went around to the passenger side, yanked open the door and helped Reilly into the seat before slamming that door shut, too.

As he was rounding the front of his Ford, he heard, "Michael!" shouted from the house.

He paused with one hand on the driver's door handle and glanced back over his shoulder.

Matthew stood on the porch.

Rev couldn't take much more today. He was already teetering on the edge of a cliff. It wouldn't take but a small breeze to knock him over.

And if he began to fall, he was taking everyone inside that house with him.

"We'll be in the area. You got my number now. Text me if you think he's about to take his last fuckin' breath. Wanna witness it."

"But—"

"Make sure to text me, Matthew!" he shouted. "You don't, you'll regret it."

He flung his door open, got in and slammed it shut. He couldn't get the fuck off that property fast enough.

Stones shot from the tires as Rev gunned the Ford in reverse and backed onto the road.

"Rev—"

"No." He shoved the shifter into first gear, the tires chirping as the Bronco surged forward.

"Rev," she tried again.

"Ain't talkin' about it right now."

Her chest had been tight the whole time she listened to the exchange, not only with his mother but his father, as well.

She'd been right. Stepping into that house was like stepping into a whole other world or dimension. Or something.

It was freakishly weird. And nothing what she'd expected.

Rev clearly did not fit in that household. Neither did Saylor. That family was just as messed up as the Shirleys were. And she didn't think that was possible. She had been wrong.

But, *holy hell*, how was Rev not fucked up? How did he not turn out to be some sort of serial killer? She didn't even know most of what he and his sister dealt with but the little she heard so far…

No wonder Saylor acted out and ended up in a juvenile detention center for all of her teen years.

To escape that house. To escape that life.

To escape whatever her father did to her, most of which Reilly could only assume without knowing all the details.

Truthfully, she didn't want to know the details. She could only imagine what they were and that was bad enough.

Reilly glanced around as he sped down the curvy country road and into town. She had to hang onto the dash and the door to keep from being tossed around, even though she wore her seatbelt. When they approached a strip mall, the knobby four-by-four tires squealed like a poked pig as he turned sharply into the parking lot.

After pulling the Bronco into an empty spot in front of Fine Wine & Good Spirits, he threw the shifter into neutral, jammed on the parking brake, left the engine running, climbed out of the truck and growled, "Stay here," before slamming the door shut.

Well, then.

Without his cut, he looked like every other Joe Citizen entering the state-run liquor store. Every other citizen who was pierced and tatted up, at least.

Maybe he was a bit hotter than most of the men walking through the parking lot.

All right, a lot hotter. Actually blistering.

Holy shit, his ass in Levi's was just…

Wrong time, Reilly. The man is in the middle of a crisis and ogling his ass is not appropriate right now. Nor is drooling.

She swiped a hand over her mouth and sighed.

Not even five minutes later, his long legs were eating up the pavement between him and his truck. He jerked the driver's door open and shoved the bag at her as he climbed in.

She glanced inside it and saw three bottles of Jack Daniels.

Three bottles of Jack.

"Um…Three?"

"They were on sale."

She pulled the receipt from the bag. No, they weren't. She glanced over at him with a raised eyebrow. "If you're going to drink this much booze, food would be a really good idea, too. Don't you think?"

The problem was, he wasn't thinking. Right now he wanted to drown out his anger and memories and whatever else he was dealing with.

Three bottles of whiskey would certainly do that. Three bottles might also put him into a damn coma.

"Food, Rev. And I'm hungry, anyway," she lied. She still was kind of sick to her stomach after dealing with the Stephen King house and family.

He scanned the strip mall, then once again growled, "Stay here." He repeated the whole mouth-watering performance over again, but instead of going in the liquor store, he disappeared into a pizza shop two doors down.

Of course, Reilly had a hard time not watching his ass the whole time. Because not watching just wasn't humanly possible.

She sighed at her weakness and noticed she hadn't been the only one staring at it. The woman standing by her car three spots closer to the strip of stores had also been appreciating everything that was Rev.

The stunning eyes, the short spiky hair, the neatly trimmed beard, the badass tattoos and piercings, the denim-clad perfect ass and those damn, powerful thighs that Reilly had seen at work every time he pumped into a sweet butt on the farm out in front of anybody and everybody.

The man had no shame, but then none of them did.

That was just the way the guys were. They liked sex and didn't care who watched them have it.

Sometimes they didn't care who they had it with, either.

Sometimes they didn't care that they were also getting sloppy seconds.

Or thirds.

Yuck.

If she was smart, she'd find a nice guy to be—what the guys called— her regular, who didn't wear a cut and the act of fucking him wouldn't cause an issue with her sister or anyone else. Also, a guy she hadn't watched have sex with a bunch of other women. Not just fucking, but getting head and giving it, too. The "giving it" part being cunnilingus and not sucking another man's cock.

Though, that might be kind of hot...

No. She didn't think any of the Fury members were into that and if they were, they certainly weren't open about it.

The guys didn't mind having sex together as long as they had a female as a buffer between them. No sword play allowed.

She might have to use two of the guys "accidentally" discovering each other as one of her future fantasies while using her Rabbit.

Yes, she would.

She eyed the woman still standing at the rear of her minivan, loading her groceries into the back with a slowness that reminded Reilly of a vibrator with dying batteries. As in, the woman was too busy keeping her eyes on the door to the pizza shop than worrying about her Rocky Road melting in the warm mid-day, mid-April temperatures.

But then, Rev was much tastier than Rocky Road. And eating a healthy helping of Rev wouldn't cause a woman to put on a few extra pounds like ice cream might.

Sorry, lady, if anyone is jumping his damn bones tonight, it isn't going to be you. You better save your ice cream before it turns to soup because that's the only snack you're eating tonight.

The woman's spine suddenly snapped straight, her breasts pushed out and manicured fingernails fluffed her hair around her shoulders.

Reilly pursed her lips and debated whether to watch Rev coming back to the Bronco or the woman.

The woman. Who just happened to drop an item, then do some exaggerated movements, including bending over and wiggling her track pants-covered ass, to catch Rev's attention.

Rev was too busy beelining back to the Bronco to even notice. His hands were full with a six-pack of Coke in plastic bottles, a large bag of chips and what might be two large submarine sandwiches.

Yep, the woman could have been naked and slapping her own ass and he wouldn't have noticed. He had too much other shit clogging up his brain matter right now.

Like murdering his father. Maybe even his mother, too.

What a damn mess.

He opened the driver's door and the smell of the freshly baked hoagie rolls filling the interior made her mouth water. Not as much as Rev's ass, but damn close.

She pouted when she saw the chips were BBQ flavored instead of sour cream and onion, but she didn't dare complain. Not in the mood he was in. She'd like to keep her head attached to her neck.

However, six sixteen-ounce bottles of Coke were *not* enough to mix with three 750 ml bottles of whiskey, that was for damn sure.

"Are you sure that's enough soda?"

He squinted at her. "That shit's for you, not me." He threw the stuff behind the driver's seat and finished climbing inside. "Anythin' else, princess?"

Princess?

He thought she was acting like a princess because she suggested food to add to his liquid dinner?

"You know—"

Her mouth hung open when he cut her off with a sharp, "No," like she was Cujo and Rook was scolding his four-legged terror for taking a shit on the shop floor.

She snapped her mouth shut and stared at him with pursed lips, debating whether it was worth wasting good whiskey by cracking one of the bottles over his head.

Her conclusion was that it wasn't.

"Fine," she huffed.

He gave her a sharp look and a cocked eyebrow before releasing the parking brake and shifting the Bronco into Reverse.

They drove in complete silence—no radio, no talking, nothing—until he located a motel at the other end of town that advertised vacancies in red flashing neon.

She anticipated his growled, "Stay here"—since that seemed to be today's theme—and he didn't disappoint her. He left her in the Bronco to go into the motel's office alone.

The place reminded her a lot of The Grove Inn, an older, but well-kept, motel. The differences were the office was on one end instead of the middle, and there seemed to be rooms in the front and the rear of the one-story building.

And she was pretty sure there wasn't a smoking hot biker like Ozzy behind the front desk.

She wondered if Rev was getting one room or two but that was answered when he got back into the truck with three key cards in his hand.

Three.

That was an odd number for two rooms. He tossed one plastic card into her lap and slipped the other two into his back pocket. As her brain processed that, he pulled the Ford around to the back of the motel where the rest of the parking spots were empty.

"Hold up, you have the key to my room, but I don't have the key to yours?"

She received silence as an answer. Unacceptable.

"Rev..."

He pulled in front of the room at the end farthest from the office. After shutting down the Ford, he turned to her. "Yep."

"Why?"

"'Cause you're property of the club and since you're with me, it's my job to protect you."

Oh.

But wait. "That still doesn't explain why I don't have a key to your room."

"'Cause you don't need one."

"But I want one."

"Don't always get what you want, Reilly. Though, I know you think you should. My trip. My rules. You didn't have to come along."

"After what I saw today, I'm glad you didn't come by yourself," she muttered.

That made his mouth get even tighter than it had been since the moment they pulled into his parents' driveway. "Coulda done it without you."

She wasn't so sure of that.

"Get whatever you need outta the truck before I lock it up."

"If you're going to get smashed on whiskey, how are you going to protect me?" She had air-quoted the word "protect."

"Once you're in your room, you ain't leavin' it."

"But—"

"My trip. My rules," he repeated. "You could be back in the Grove doin' your own thing. So, buckle up, buttercup. You insisted on comin' along."

Buttercup? She wasn't sure if that was better or worse than princess. "You keep reminding me of that."

"'Cause you keep forgettin'. You think I wanted you to see that shit you saw? Think I wanted for you to hear that shit you heard?"

No, probably not.

"Don't want anyone to know that shit. That's my shit and no one else's goddamn business."

"Saylor."

"Leave her out of it." His tone cut her like sharp glass.

It was hard to leave his sister out of the equation since they had the same parents and she dealt with the same things as he did. Maybe even worse.

"She's my friend, Rev. She's like my sister, too. Do you think I don't care what happened to her?"

He stared at her for a couple of breaths. "She talk to you about that shit?"

"No."

"Then it ain't your business. Know you struggle with this, buttercup, but everything ain't your business."

She wasn't liking this whole "buttercup" thing. He'd never called her that before and he wasn't doing it to be cute, he was doing it because anger was seething just under his surface.

Right now, he was annoyed at the world. He needed to decompress.

He thought whiskey was going to help him do that. Reilly doubted it would. However, she was pretty damn sure he wasn't only going to be hitting the bottle tonight. He'd also be hitting a joint or smoking a bowl.

Hopefully he wouldn't go on the prowl to hit up a woman like the one doing her mating dance in the parking lot of the strip mall.

With one look, one crook of his finger, he could probably

get most women to drop at his feet. Maybe they wouldn't want anything more than one night with the biker bad boy, but they'd at least want a little forbidden taste of him.

Maybe he'd be a checkmark on their bucket list.

She'd seen nasty cat fights between female hang-arounds over getting one of the guys to themselves. Usually, whoever it was solved it by disappearing with them both after the nails were retracted and the blood stopped flying.

Someone needed to club her over the head if she ever got to the point that she thought any man was worth fighting over.

When it came to the Fury sisterhood, if any of their ol' men stepped out of line with another woman, they already made it clear to them, they'd simply walk away. They weren't putting up with that shit and they also weren't going to fight another woman over him.

And what did that do?

It kept those men on a short leash without them even being aware of it.

You stray, you pay was the silent code the women followed. And it was damn effective.

No nagging, no arguments and no having to keep tabs on their men. It was an easy and tidy way to keep their relationships loyal and solid. It simply worked.

"Grab your shit," he grumbled, getting out of the truck and going to the back hatch. When she got out and joined him, he handed her her backpack, the soda and one of the subs.

He grabbed the rest of the stuff, locked up his vehicle and headed to the room on the end.

"Which one is mine?" she asked with her arms full.

He jerked his chin toward the room next door and disappeared inside.

His door slamming shut jerked her into motion and she

went to her door, managed to open it without dropping anything and went inside the dark room.

She couldn't see shit but at least it smelled clean.

She made her way to the bed, dumped everything on it, then went back to close the door, lock it and turn on the lights. Once she did, she turned and noticed something.

Another door on the right.

He'd gotten them adjoining rooms.

She immediately went over and unlocked her side and was faced with a closed door on his. She tried the knob but it was locked. She sighed, closed hers but didn't bother to lock it since he had a damn key, anyway.

Truthfully, she had no reason to keep him out. If he wanted to come visit her during the night and ravish her, she certainly wasn't going to push him back out the door.

A whole bunch of hot, sweaty sex and exchange of fluids —besides whiskey—might help release some of the irritability he was struggling with.

They were in Coatesville, PA. Far, far, *far* from Manning Grove.

No one had to know.

Hell, no one even knew she and Rev were together. In the same town, in the same motel. The two of them knocking boots would just be one more secret in a club full of them.

All they had to do afterward was pretend it never happened.

That could work.

It could.

Couldn't it?

She stared at the door that connected the two rooms and chewed on her thumbnail.

No. He wanted to be alone. To wallow in his misery. She needed to respect that. He was always telling her she was sticking her nose where it didn't belong. And if she pushed her way into his room, she would be proving him right.

"Damn it," she whispered.

She'd leave the interior door unlocked and she'd let him make the first move, if that was what he wanted.

She glanced at her phone and saw it was only a little after five and way too early to call it a night. She removed her boots, jeans, bra and top and pulled on the comfy silky shorts and camisole set she slept in. Once settled on the bed with pillows propped behind her, she grabbed the remote, found a decent movie, sucked down the bottle of warm generic water that came with the room, and ended up scarfing down the whole ham, cheddar and bacon sub by herself.

After getting up before the crack of dawn and now with a full belly of carbs and processed meats, the movie became a distant memory as sleep pulled at her, dragging her under until it spit her back up hours later.

The drone of the TV filled her ears before she blinked open her eyes, taking a few seconds to remember where she was and why. She wiped the saliva away from the corner of her mouth, brushed breadcrumbs off her chest and sheets, then glanced at the time on her cell phone again since it had to be the middle of the night.

She groaned. It was only nine. She'd slept away the last three hours.

If she tried to go back to sleep now, she'd never sleep through the rest of the night.

What was the solution? Whiskey. Maybe a few hits of pot.

But did she have any? Hell no.

Did she know who had some? Hell yes.

Now, was he willing to share?

She didn't know, but it couldn't hurt to ask, now could it?

Chapter Six

AFTER SPLASHING water on her face, running a brush through her snarled hair, and tugging a few strands forward to cover the scar along her temple, she glanced down at what she was wearing. Without a bra, her breasts hung a little lower but they were still damn perky for their size. Her nipples were punching through the thin, silky royal blue fabric, but it wasn't like Rev hadn't seen nipples before.

He'd seen plenty. He just hadn't seen hers yet.

Yet, being the key point.

She went back to the doors connecting their rooms, opened hers and saw his was still closed. She put her ear against it to hear voices and music droning on his side.

Instead of knocking, she tried the little knob and blinked in surprised when it turned easily within her fingers.

He'd unlocked his, but he hadn't opened hers? Had he checked on her while she was sleeping?

Huh.

Or maybe he had come in with the intent to ravish her, found her asleep and decided otherwise. *Damn.* Did she cock-block herself? That would be her luck.

She nudged the door open and tentatively peeked into

his room. It was dark except for the ebb and flow of colorful light and shadows caused by the television.

She immediately glanced at the bed. He was sitting up against the headboard with a half-empty whiskey bottle in his hand.

Damn. He'd hit that hard. How he was still sitting upright, she had no idea. The room also smelled like pot. She hadn't checked to see if their rooms allowed smoking or not. Most likely not. Not that Rev would give a shit.

But it wasn't only the amount of liquor and the lingering smell of quality bud that caught her attention, it was the fact he wore nothing but jeans.

His denim-clad legs were stretched out with the ankles crossed and his feet bare. The waistband of his jeans was unbuttoned right at the bottom of a dark blond happy trail—she would have to inspect it closer to make sure she wasn't seeing things in the funky light. That meant he was completely shirtless.

The light of the TV flickered off something reflective on his chest.

Something reflective on his chest.

Much smaller barbells than what were in his ears divided each nipple.

Holy shit.

Holy… fucking… shit.

He had pierced nipples just like Deacon. Not that she ever saw Deacon's—she hadn't—but she knew he had them because Reese had mentioned it a couple of times. And it wasn't a secret.

No one ever mentioned Rev's. And if they had, that information had never been spilled around her. This important information she should've known! Who the hell was holding out?

Because… *Daaaaamn.*

Even in the uneven light of the TV, she could see his upper chest was covered with a huge tattoo, too, that blended into both inked sleeves covering his arms. Of course, she'd seen him wear short-sleeved shirts plenty of times, but she wasn't kidding when she said she'd seen his ass and cock more times than his torso. Which was a big, fat zero.

"Problem, buttercup?"

Yes! He had been hiding some very important information. "I don't get the whole buttercup thing."

"Not for you to get." His voice was low, slow and held a touch of a slur. The whiskey and pot must be doing their job.

"I'd have to argue that point since you're calling me by that name."

"Ain't a bad name. Fits you." Oh yeah, his words were a bit fuzzy around the edges. She bet his vision was, too.

"It does?" She didn't think so.

She stepped farther into his room as he lifted the bottle to his lips and she focused on his Adam's apple smoothly sliding up and down as he took a long swig of whiskey.

"I have so many questions," came out on a breath.

"Nothin' new." She waited for a drunken hiccup to be the exclamation point on that statement.

It didn't come.

"Did you check on me?"

He swiped his hand over his mouth before answering. "Yeah. You were droolin' and snorin'."

She gasped. "I was not!"

"The fuck you weren't, buttercup." The alcohol in his system made the word butter sound like *budder*.

"I was exhausted," seemed like a valid excuse.

"Yeah," he said softly.

"I won't be able to sleep now." *Especially, now that I want to touch those nipple piercings!*

"So, don't." He lifted the bottle in her direction. An offering.

She'd like to think it was more than just an offer to get drunk with him but a peace offering of sorts.

She wrinkled her nose and glanced around the room. She spotted an unopened bottle and one of those flimsy plastic cups sealed in plastic provided by the motel. She rushed back to her room to grab the soda and returned before he could close the connecting door and lock her out.

He was up and out of the bed in an instant and pushing her away from the tiny counter where she planned on mixing her drink. She wasn't going to fist a bottle like he did. Plus, she preferred to keep the lining of her stomach intact. Drinking whiskey straight from the bottle tended to make her insides burn. A lot. She didn't care if she seemed like a wimp and needed to mix it with soda.

She stopped him from pouring the whiskey from his bottle and handed him one still sealed.

His lips might have actually twitched the slightest bit. That was a good sign that he wasn't so angry anymore. "Afraid of a little backwash?" he murmured close to her ear, causing her to shiver and her nipples to peak painfully.

His own nipples were now right within reach. Her fingers wrapped tighter around the six-pack of soda to avoid reaching out and giving them a twist. "I have a feeling there's more than a little in that bottle."

"No worse than swallowin' a man's cum. You done that, right?"

She took a step back and stared at him. "Is that a way of asking me if I spit or swallow?"

He turned away from her and unwrapped the plastic cup, poured it half full of whiskey from the fresh bottle, cracked open a soda and finished filling it to the brim.

He stuck his finger into the drink and swirled it around, then inserted that finger between his lips and sucked it clean.

Holy shit.

Her nipples were not only aching now, but her breasts suddenly became a lot fuller.

He handed her the overfull cup and she was careful not to squeeze the easily crushable plastic too tightly. She hissed at the strength of the drink after taking a sip.

Turning toward her, his eyes took a slow stroll over her from top to toe.

Well now, add a pussy twinge to the reaction of her breasts. Especially after he topped that heated look with a lick of his lips.

What the fuck? Was he trying to make her self-combust right there in a motel in Coatesville, Pennsylvania?

Her heart skipped a beat when he suddenly moved. Not toward her like she hoped. He went directly to where his backpack sat on the floor, dug inside it and pulled out a T-shirt. He threw it at her.

She caught it but not without spilling a little of her drink on her hand. She licked the drops of Jack and Coke off her skin and when she looked up, he was watching her way too intently.

Well, that caused another intense pussy clench. *Damn it.*

"You gonna be in here, put that on."

She glanced down at the shirt in her hand. "What's wrong with what I'm wearing?"

"My trip. My rules."

She was about to shove that response down his damn throat.

She took another sip of her drink to prevent it from spilling again, put it down and tugged his shirt over her head. The worn, soft cotton fell just past her crotch and smelled like Rev. She resisted fisting the fabric, pressing it to her nose and inhaling. She might sneak a sniff when he wasn't watching.

As he moved around the small room back to his side of

the bed, her eyes were glued to the flex of his back muscles under the club's colors inked onto his back.

It was rare she saw any of the Fury members without shirts. Occasionally she would on the farm when the weather was warm, either around the bunkhouse or during one of the parties. She knew most of them, if not all, had shown their dedication and loyalty to Trip and the club by having the rockers and insignia permanently tattooed onto their back, so it didn't surprise her that Rev had it done, too.

She took another long sip of her Jack and Coke and watched his perfection climb back onto his side of the bed and get comfortable. He paused while lifting the whiskey bottle to his lips and jerked his head toward the other side of the bed.

She smothered the hiss that would've relieved some of the heat starting to gather in her center. He wanted her to climb into bed with him and just chill?

Okay, then. She put her drink down and did so until their shoulders were close but not touching.

He tossed the remote onto the bed between them. "Change it if you want."

She glanced at the TV, then him. "Does the TV have Netflix?" She rolled her lips under.

He snorted and took a long pull on the bottle, then twisted his head to face her. His normally vivid blue eyes were now glassy and bloodshot between the mix of booze, dope and most likely mental exhaustion.

"Why? Wanna Netflix and chill? Think that's smart? Got enough fuckin' problems right now without addin' fuckin' you into the mix."

"I'm not a problem."

He threw his head back and laughed so loudly, she winced. When he was done, she was good and annoyed.

"Fuckin' you would be a problem, buddercup," he said seriously.

"You might have a problem fucking anyone tonight with the amount you're drinking." She leaned toward him and glanced at the open tin on the nightstand. "And also with whatever you smoked. Little Rev might not be revving to go after all that."

He grabbed his crotch over his jeans and shook it. "Got no problem gettin' it up."

"Yes, I know. I've seen you hard plenty of times. But not after putting away so much whiskey. Did you do anything else?"

One of his eyebrows lifted but it listed like it was drunk, too. "Whadya mean?"

"Like any hard shit. The shit Trip doesn't like to see around the farm."

He shook his crotch again. "Got somethin' hard."

She rolled her eyes. "You know what I mean. And don't offer something you aren't willing to give. That's just being a tease. Now light one of those fatties and *puff, puff, pass*."

He grinned at her, shook his head and put the bottle down to remove an already rolled joint from the Altoids tin he carried. Most of the guys carried some kind of small container for their dope unless they preferred to smoke a pot pipe. But the guys who smoked tobacco found it more convenient to carry both types of hand-rolled in a tin.

He lit a joint, took two puffs and passed it over to her.

"We probably shouldn't be smoking in here," she murmured.

"Shouldn't be in my bed, either."

"You or me?"

"Both. Same bed. You wearin' that shit. Temptin' me."

"I'm wearing your shirt."

"Meant what you got on under that."

"PJs."

"That ain't no PJs. That shit's whack-off material."

His speech was getting thicker and his *S's* were getting

drawn out. Soon they'd turn to *Sh's* and spit might accompany them.

Say it, don't spray it.

She snorted and took another long hit off the joint before passing it back to him.

"*Whasho* funny, buddercup?"

Bingo.

Watching the Fury members get totally smashed during pig roasts was entertaining. Usually, the sisterhood got a little tipsy, too. However, they had more fun sitting around watching the guys party. Then they'd round up their ol' men, drag them home and put them to bed.

Unfortunately, Reilly always went to bed alone. The club's "do not touch" rule extended to even the damn hang-arounds. And it wasn't like Manning Grove had a hopping singles scene. In fact, it had a completely dead dating scene. Unless you liked rednecks who still lived in their momma's basements, or married men.

Occasionally a cute tourist would come into town. But it was hard to tell who was truly single and who was lying about it.

She was lucky to find that one guy she humped in the back of his car behind Crazy Pete's. Maybe not so lucky, since he sucked at it.

Being a part of the club had both its positives and negatives. The biggest negative being that her sex life was pretty much non-existent due to being "property" of the club.

Maybe she needed to set up an online dating profile and do some distance dating. After Billy Warren tried to put her six-feet-under—twice—she was in no rush to get back into the dating scene. It wasn't like dating and sex always went hand in hand. Sometimes a woman wanted a good sweaty sex session without any bullshit afterward. The same reason the guys used the sweet butts.

They got their rocks off and didn't have to worry about

being tied down. At least when they weren't hooking up with Billie—the sweet butt Billie, not her burnt-to-a-crisp ex— then they got tied down, tied up and wrung out. She had seen a few of the guys have trouble walking after a night with that sadist.

She glanced over at Rev and let her gaze slide down to his nipple piercings. She pursed her lips, wondering what damage Billie could do with those.

Rev was staring straight ahead, not concentrating on the TV, not concentrating on anything. Probably deep in his head. Maybe even reliving what happened earlier at his parents' house. Possibly even reliving his youth.

She glanced at the lit joint in her fingers and took another small hit before once again offering it to him. She nudged his arm with hers. "Here."

His eyes did a slow roll down to her hand and he took the joint, took another hit then pinched out the end.

"You look thoroughly baked," she told him. His face was relaxed, his body appeared boneless and his eyes unfocused.

"Feel baked," was his delayed response.

She smiled. She was not into guys who liked to get falling down, sloppy drunk or who turned into abusive monsters, like Billy Warren had. But Rev was pretty chill when he drank. She also understood his need to calm the turmoil deep inside him.

She wanted to ask him about the cause of that turmoil, but tonight was not the night. She had a feeling they'd be in town at least a few more days. Especially if he kept to his word about wanting to be at his father's side when he passed.

She didn't understand it but it wasn't for her to under-stand. They had both had shitty parents. It was true, having shitty parents deeply affected their lives. But how they dealt with it might not be the same.

She assumed he had just forgotten them, put that life

behind him, just like she had hers, until he got that damn phone call. If she had only known, she would've thrown the message away and spared him all of this.

She grabbed her drink off the nightstand next to her. "Rev?"

"Yeah?"

"For tonight, let's just say 'fuck the rules.'" She lifted her plastic cup between them and tapped it lightly against the bottle he was drinking from.

She took a long swig of her Jack and Coke and smiled. No, that wasn't quite right. She took a long swig, hiccuped when the strong whiskey hit her gut, *then* smiled.

"Yeah, buddercup, lesh juss get fucked up in… shtead."

He was already standing on that precipice. It wouldn't take much more for him to tumble head first to the bottom. But she'd stick around and help cushion that fall for as long as he needed her. Whether he'd admit he needed her or not.

During that time, if he wanted to talk about anything, she'd be there to listen.

The guys complained she talked too much but she was pretty damn good at listening, too.

They'd taken her in like she was family. Well, after some strong-arming on her part. But even before she was deeply entrenched in the club, whenever she needed help, they stepped in. Like when it came to the whole dangerous mess with Billy Warren.

So, it was only right she help Rev, or any of them, when they needed it.

Rev being shit-faced after dealing with his family was proof this was the time he needed that help the most.

Chapter Seven

WITH THE ENGINE shut off and the keys already stuffed deep in his pocket, Rev sat in his Bronco.

He was in agony this morning, even after stopping at a convenience store for a large black coffee and a bottle of aspirin. His head pounded, his patience was paper thin and he had the damn shakes. He was pretty fucking sure every cell in his body was pickled and he most likely smelled like it, too.

He normally didn't drink that much and, *fuck*, if he'd be drinking that much again any time soon. He'd just about kicked that bottle. By himself. Because of that, he passed out sometime in the night.

Earlier, when he finally pulled himself free of his alcohol-induced coma, he'd found himself flat on his back in the middle of the queen-sized bed, still wearing his unbuttoned jeans, with Reilly's warm, soft body curled around his.

She was knocked out cold and snoring softly since she must have overdone it, too.

Unfortunately, he didn't have much memory of it. Things had gotten a bit fuzzy after she'd joined him. Of course, she had to come into his room wearing that blue silky shit, trying to make it even more difficult for him to resist her.

Even worse, while she slept, the T-shirt he insisted she wear had pushed up enough he could see her long, bare legs. And, even as fucked as his head was from his hangover, he could not forget the way her hard nipples had pressed through that damn thin fabric the night before.

He'd rubbed a hand over his own nipples, causing a pleasurable pull from his barbells all the way to his toes and also made his morning wood flex in his jeans.

He continued sliding his hand down his chest, his abs, and then over his hard-on. If he was still wearing his jeans, and Reilly his shirt, he could safely assume they hadn't had crazy drunken sex last night.

Thank fuck.

Because if he was going to break that particular rule, he, at least, wanted to remember it.

Her mouth was parted and her long, messy blonde hair covering most of her face. After sweeping a few strands away until he exposed the scar along her temple, he lightly traced a finger over it.

It didn't take away from her looks at all but he knew it reminded her of the mistake she made by letting a violent fuckwad named Billy Warren into her life.

The motherfucker had tried to kill her twice. Rev had just missed witnessing the second attempt. He'd been on a damn test drive when the psycho ex-boyfriend showed up at Dutch's Garage with a bat.

Thank fuck for Rook. Though they didn't talk about it, Reilly owed her life to him. He'd been out back getting stoned, while Whip had been out in the yard looking for a used part, when the fucker tried to hit a home run using Reilly's head as the baseball.

While Rev hadn't been the one to make Billy Warren pay, he now wished he had been.

Rev remembered Warren's cocky laugh even though the guys had him on the ground, on his knees and surrounded. The asshole was so fucking arrogant he hadn't shown any fear, even though every one of Rev's brothers wanted to kill him when he kept running his mouth.

"This is why you got to teach them a fucking lesson. Teach them obedience. It's what they want. In the end, they thank you for it…"

Unfortunately, Billy Warren wasn't the only man who believed that females should learn to be obedient.

He stared through the windshield at the house he grew up in. Inside was a man who followed very similar thinking. The same belief that a woman should serve her man. It surprised Rev that Warren had the misconception that Reilly would be one of those women.

Even though he had showed up to kill her, that day she hadn't been scared of him, either. Not one fucking bit.

Her being that kind of woman was the reason he almost killed her the first time. For refusing to curl up into a ball and hand over everything she owned and worked for to the grifter.

Hell no. Reilly would not simply roll over and let him win that easily. Which was why she ended up in the hospital beat to fuck. It was also why she ended up with that scar she fussed with.

That day at the garage, Rev had been holding Reilly back from attacking Warren when she hissed, *"What the hell did I ever see in you?"*

"My big dick. You liked it in your mouth and in your fucking ass."

She had actually snarled like a feral cat and began to struggle to get free by clawing at Rev's arms hard enough to draw blood. Even as feisty as she was, he'd managed to keep hold of her. Barely.

"I hope you get fucked up the ass in prison, asshole!"

That might have been the exact moment Rev began to lust after her.

Warren then blowing her a smart-ass kiss had been the final straw that turned Reilly into an out-of-control, hissing, spitting wild woman.

Knowing if he let her go, she'd run over and kick Warren's ass had actually made his dick begin to chub up. At least until Warren threatened, *"I'll just find you again when I get out, baby. I look forward to getting a piece of that tight ass again. And next time you might remember the lesson I taught you about sharing what's yours with your man."* Warren was lucky Rev's job was to hold onto Reilly, otherwise, he would've kicked in that bastard's teeth.

As it was, they made sure there was no "next time" and definitely a "never again." The Amish unknowingly tilled Warren's ashes into one of the fields on the farm. *Hell*, he and his brothers probably ate some of the produce fertilized with his ashes.

Circle of fucking life.

The man inside the house Rev was now parked in front of had also given him life. And, really, Rev should be the one to take his. But John Schmidt would get his karma soon enough. Rev just needed patience and to let nature take its course. Waiting for the cancer to do its job would keep Rev out of prison but, in the end, the result would be the same.

He needed to remember that, no matter how much his old man baited him. No matter how much Rev wanted to strangle the fuck out of the man who created him. No matter how much Rev wanted to smother him with a fucking pillow.

He pulled in a long breath through his nostrils and blindly reached for his coffee and, as he took a long pull of caffeine, he kept his eyes glued on the house. Nothing moved inside, nothing moved outside.

He fuzzily remembered Reilly mentioning last night about how the house and the people inside reminded her of a B-rated horror flick. Also, that she and Rev had reminded her of a young couple in one of those movies, going into the house and never escaping alive.

He was pretty sure she was drunk by that point. But drunk or not, she wasn't far off.

Staring at the house now, stuck in the driver's seat, dread was swallowing him whole. He wasn't sure if he could deal with going back inside, seeing his disapproving mother and his dying father. But he couldn't assess his father's health and how long he might have left without doing so.

Plus, he wanted to give the dying man a memory to take to his grave. Rev's face watching karma do its job.

This morning, only one vehicle was parked in the driveway, so he doubted that Pastor Thomas or Matthew was around. At least, not yet.

Out of all of them, Rev could probably stomach dealing with Matthew. Though, he couldn't stomach how submissive his uncle's wife seemed to be. Submissive women were a big turn-off for Rev. He couldn't imagine fucking a woman who didn't have any fire inside her.

Like Reilly did.

Or hell, any of the Fury women. Once Red had broken free of her trance-like state and her true personality had been exposed, she wasn't nearly as quiet as they all originally thought. It only took a bit for the cracks in her shell to begin to seal themselves up and for her to become close to whole again.

In truth, she had to be a strong woman to deal with Sig and his easily-ignited temper.

He could only imagine that fucking Matthew's wife was like fucking a half-deflated blow-up doll. Without lube.

No, a good fuck involved fast and furious skin-slapping, sweat dripping, hair pulling, biting, scratching and plenty of loud vocal encouragement. If a woman didn't make him struggle to keep from popping a nut within a minute or two, then he had no interest in fucking her a second time.

He needed to stop thinking those kind of thoughts while sitting in front of his parents' house. Now was not the right time to get a damn boner. He couldn't put off going inside much longer and he'd prefer to do that erection free.

Especially since the last time his mother saw him with one was when Michael was in Sarah's bed all those years ago. A natural response from him turned into a very unnatural, unforgiving response from her. One he'd never forget.

That was also the day he began plotting his escape.

"Fuck it," he muttered and climbed out of the truck. He needed to suck it up and get this over with, then head back to the motel to check on Reilly.

He strode to the front door and, when he tried the knob, found it locked. Cupping his hands around the sides of his face, he pressed it to one of the narrow windows alongside the door. Like earlier, he neither saw or heard movement inside.

His parents used to be early risers. He couldn't imagine they weren't up yet since it was now late morning. Maybe his mother was in the kitchen at the back of the house doing her "wifely duties."

He *could* knock, but...

Fuck it.

He jogged down the porch steps and rounded the house to the backyard.

And immediately froze in his tracks.

Nothing had changed. Not a damn thing.

It was just how he remembered it in the days before he rushed out the back door for the last time and into the night.

Just how he remembered it all those times his father dragged him out into the backyard to punish him for whatever wrongdoing Michael did that day. Whatever rule he broke. Whatever transgression he committed.

In an attempt to "cleanse" Michael of his sins.

Bed sheets hanging from the clothesline fluttered in the

morning spring breeze. But it wasn't hearing the snap of the damp cotton in that gentle wind that made his heart pound in his throat.

It was the white wood posts buried into the ground with the cotton rope tightly stretched between them.

The eyebolt was still there. Toward the top of one of the posts. It was now rusty from either time or lack of use. Or both.

He turned slowly and spotted the witch-hazel shrub. Of course, it was now overgrown since no one had to cut any of the branches any longer. Or at least, not as often.

With his chest tight and his jaw set, his vision narrowed to the point of only a pin prick as he stared at that fucking bush. His memories started to rush in and take him back.

To a place he didn't want to go. To a time he didn't want to revisit.

This was why he shouldn't have come home. To avoid reliving all that he left behind. He should've known coming back would be like picking off the scab of his childhood and making it bleed all over again.

He had so many memories of this backyard. Not one of them good. Not of him playing catch or having fun by running through sprinklers. Not of playing hide-and-seek or being pushed high into the sky on a swing.

None of that.

Instead, they consisted of that damn bush, of that wood post and of the knife his father would hand to him. Every time he was handed that sharp blade, he would stare at it and consider using it on his father, or on himself, instead.

He never did.

Because he was weak.

Those were the rare instances where, to lessen the damage, he did what he was told. In truth, he had no choice. If he didn't follow his father's orders, things would only be a lot worse. The punishment, his anger, his degrading words.

The only good that came out of it was if his father was busy with Michael that meant he wasn't focusing on Sarah. At least, for a little while.

"The longer you wait, the more I will add to the number. You must learn to be obedient, Michael. When I give you an order, I expect you to do what you're told without hesitation. You have always been an obstinate child, no matter how many times I've tried to rid you of that behavior."

Words like that would snap him out of his head and he'd force his feet to move toward the shrub his father called the "switch bush."

Part of Michael's punishment was he'd be forced to cut his own switch and strip the leaves from the stick in preparation. From past experience, he knew the thinner branches cut deeper. They hurt less in the beginning but more later on because they split the skin. The thicker ones hurt more in the beginning and less later on. They usually didn't split the skin but left welts and bruises behind.

He had to decide which of the two he wanted to deal with.

When Michael was done, he would be forced to say, "Thank you, Father," with his gaze tipped to the ground as he handed over his carefully chosen switch.

Rev hadn't realized his feet had moved him closer to the shrub and he now stood in front of it. He ran his fingers lightly over the yellow, orange and red spidery blooms.

Yeah, the shrub was much fuller and healthier now that it wasn't constantly being stripped.

The colorful plant wasn't the only thing in the backyard that had been stripped.

Once Michael handed over the instrument of his punishment to his punisher, he was forced to strip down to his boxer shorts. No matter what the weather.

That night—the night his father came home from work after his mother found him in Sarah's bed—it had gotten dark early and the temps had dropped to barely above freezing.

When his arms were bound over his head and attached to that eyebolt, when he was only wearing his loose cotton boxers, he began to shiver. He had to be careful he didn't accidentally bite his tongue from his teeth clattering violently together or from clenching them every time his father raised his arm and dropped it again, causing a searing burn along his skin from the long, thin switch.

Once it started, Michael always lost count. There was no point in counting anyway. It was over when it was over and not a second before.

He never made excuses, as that only added to the number.

He never begged to be spared, as that only added to the number.

He never cried or whimpered, as that only added to the number.

It was best to simply think of something else. Anything but what was happening.

When it was over, when he was released and given permission to move, he had to thank his father again. Even if the words were forced through tightly clenched teeth and a whole lot of hatred.

Even though his breath was hard to catch due to the pain.

As always, his father asked, *"Have you learned your lesson?"*

As always, Michael answered, *"Yes."*

And, as always, that was a lie.

"Your mother has drawn your bath."

The bath.

"It'll help finish the cleansing."

He wanted to argue that she had forced him to bathe

early that morning, to scrub his skin clean with the harsh brush. But this bath was different.

Salt was added to the cold water.

The only good part about those baths was when he was done soaking in it, he could hardly feel the pain anymore since he was so numb.

At least for a little while...

Rev struggled to pull in his next breath, to shake that memory and the rest of them.

By reliving them, he was handing control over his life back to his father. Michael had stolen that control the night he ran away. He took it and ran as fast and as far as he could.

He never regretted leaving and the struggles to survive that followed. He only regretted leaving Sarah behind.

In truth, he deserved to be tied to that post again and whipped with a switch until nothing but bloody strips of flesh remained of his back.

Because he failed her.

He ran because he was too weak to stay.

But now, he was no longer weak.

His father was.

Rev forced himself to climb the two steps to the small back porch. He forced his fingers to wrap around the metal knob. He forced himself to turn it.

Both surprise and unease filled him as the door opened without resistance.

Did his mother believe that if she locked the front door he wouldn't go around to the back?

Was she foolish enough to think he would simply go away? Leave them in peace?

He didn't give a fuck about their peace, only his own. Only Saylor's.

And they wouldn't achieve theirs until he knew with

certainty his father was gone. Then that peace would finally be within reach. Wouldn't it?

Didn't he finally deserve his own with everything he went through when he was Michael? Didn't Saylor deserve hers after everything she went through when she was Sarah?

The kitchen was empty. Quiet except for the ticking of the clock above the sink.

The counters were perfectly clean. Not a dirty dish in the sink. The dish towel hung perfectly straight in its place.

At first glance, you'd think the kitchen was never used. That the table was never sat at. When he knew for a fact Michael had sat at it more times than he could remember.

They couldn't eat until his father came home from work. Starting at the scheduled dinner time, which was six, he and Sarah would have to sit quietly at the table, waiting.

Waiting to hear the front door open, waiting to hear his footsteps coming down the narrow hallway.

Waiting for their father to kiss their mother on the cheek before settling into his spot at the head of the table.

And with all that waiting, especially when his father was late, his stomach would growl and twist in pain as he stared at the cooling food on his plate.

Sometimes he was so hungry he couldn't resist taking a bite before his father blessed the food and thanked God for providing it. When Michael would reach out, his father would slap his hand away from his plate and send him to bed without dinner.

If that was his only punishment for that infraction, he didn't care. He went willingly to his room. Because buried deep within his closet he had hidden a shoebox full of snacks that he'd stolen from the store in town.

Every time he was sent there on his bike with a few dollars to pick up an item for his mother, he'd pocket something. A candy bar, a granola bar, a pack of cheese crackers, anything that would fill his stomach. If he could, he'd take two. One for him, one for Sarah.

Rev moved through the kitchen and, instead of going directly to the sitting room, he moved up the back steps. The narrow stairway was designed for the hired help when the house was originally built in the mid-1800s.

The Schmidts never had hired help since they couldn't afford it. Even if they could, his father didn't want strangers in his house. The only people allowed in their home were family and the members of their religious order. People with the same beliefs.

It was easier that way. Safer.

No questions asked. No comments made.

The steps creaked slightly as he moved up them slowly, carefully. The narrow walls closing in on him the higher he climbed. To prevent himself from a full-blown panic attack, he focused on the door at the top of the steps and, once he got there without stumbling, he opened it and stepped out at the end of the upstairs hallway.

He sucked in air and hesitated for only a second while his vision restored. Then, instinctively, he headed to the first room on the left. The door was closed but not locked.

When he opened it, the disturbed dust and the stale air filled his nostrils. He struggled not to sneeze.

The curtains were drawn but he didn't need light to see what he expected.

Sarah's bedroom remained unchanged. It was exactly as he remembered. Almost as if they expected her to come home at any time and step directly back into her youth, prior to that first time she was sent to the detention center.

He stared at the single bed. The bed he had curled up on with his sister too many nights to count, holding her and trying to soothe her when all she could do was cry.

He always had left before morning.

All except that one time when he made the mistake of

falling asleep. When what he was doing wasn't seen as something good, but something bad instead.

A worn spot on the wood floor by Sarah's bed caught his attention. She knelt in that exact spot to say her prayers before bed. After doing it night after night and year after year, it had worn away the paint on the wood.

The bed was crisply made. No items left out. Sterile and neat. Nothing to indicate it was a little girl's room. No dolls. No toys. No hair bows or barrettes. No pinks. No purples. No bright colors at all. All muted whites. The color of purity.

He stepped back out and closed the door behind him, then walked the few steps farther to his room. Again, the door was closed.

He held his breath as he slowly opened it with his heart trying to escape his chest.

The air in his old room wasn't dusty or stale. This room was currently used. It was not waiting for him to return home.

Nothing was the same except for the spot in the middle of the room where he, too, had knelt every night. Where he, too, had settled his elbows on his mattress and pressed his palms together. Where he bowed his head, closed his eyes and mouthed the words that were expected.

Words that were hollow.

Unlike his sister's old room, his did not remain frozen in time. Proof that they never expected or even wanted him to return. Most likely relieved he left.

His mother had turned his old bedroom into a sewing room. A sewing machine was now stationed in front of the only window. The room was also full of neatly organized bolts of fabric and all the other shit needed to sew clothes, quilts and what-fucking-ever else she made from scratch.

Unlike his friends from school, his bedroom never had a television or even a radio. He wasn't allowed to listen to music or watch a sitcom. Comic books were forbidden. So were cell phones and the internet.

Nothing secular was allowed in this house. They did their best to prevent their children from becoming wayward.

Though, they tried so hard that it caused them to fail.

He stepped farther into the room and opened the closet to see if his hidden goodies were still there. The closet no longer held the clothes Michael left behind but more miscellaneous sewing supplies.

Every evidence of Michael's existence was now gone.

His shoebox of snacks had been discovered and probably thrown away. Or maybe Sarah had found them and hidden them for herself. If she had, Saylor never mentioned anything to him.

If they would've been found, his father would have seen that as another offense and would've taken Michael out to the backyard, made him choose his own switch and then tied him to the post where anyone walking or driving by could witness his punishment. *If* they were paying attention.

He wondered how many people saw it happening and decided to look the other way. Decided it was none of their business. Decided it wasn't worth the hassle of becoming involved.

Reilly only survived Warren almost beating her to death because of her neighbors getting involved. If they hadn't…

Rev sucked in a slow breath, beating back the anger beginning to bubble up from his gut.

It wasn't only from what happened to Reilly, it was from his memory of how differently their father punished his son and his daughter.

His father never took Sarah outside. It would happen in her bedroom. With the door closed.

Sometimes he would use a belt, sometimes his hand, but never a switch. He didn't want to risk breaking Sarah's skin like he sometimes did with Michael's. Most likely he was afraid of scarring her and those scars eventually reducing the chance of Sarah finding the right husband.

A girl who had to be whipped often wasn't an obedient one. And if she wasn't obedient, she wouldn't make a good wife.

It was the way.

Michael could hear everything in the next room because the walls were thin. He could hear the strikes of the leather or his father's palm. He could hear Sarah crying.

But then those cries would become muffled when a large hand covered her mouth and a different kind of punishment commenced.

Michael would cover his ears and let his fury drown out the sound. He would think of other things and try not to imagine what was happening in his sister's room.

He would also flay himself with an imaginary switch for not being brave enough to break down Sarah's door and stop the man's punishment.

His mother would be down in the kitchen humming. Sometimes even singing a hymn. She never stopped her husband, the father of her fucking children, from those types of lessons.

She never comforted Sarah afterward, either.

That was why Michael did.

Until he ran away and no one was left to comfort Sarah at all.

Rev squeezed his eyes shut, his fingers curled into fists and he left the room of his youth to head back downstairs.

Back then, his father had been larger than life. Now? Now he was just a shell of a bitter, abusive man.

Waiting for his end.

An end that better happen soon.

Chapter Eight

REILLY GROANED AND ROLLED OVER, swiping at both the wet and dry drool clinging to the corner of her mouth.

She was never drinking that much again.

Eeeeeever.

Her head pounded, her tongue had turned into a wad of cotton and, apparently, her eyes had remained wide open during a sandstorm. On the bright side, she had slept like the damn dead.

Only moving her eyes—because everything else was on strike—her gaze swept the empty bed.

Rev's bed.

She shot up so fast, she groaned again and slapped a hand to her forehead to keep her brain from spinning like one of those old rotor rides at a carnival. The kind of ride that spun the hell out of you, the centrifugal force sticking you to the side before the floor dropped out.

Yeah, that one. Where you risked losing a limb.

That was what her head felt like. Only, she wouldn't lose a limb, she might lose her cookies.

If she had any. Her stomach was a deep, empty pit. Food would be a good idea to help with the hangover. Especially a big greasy breakfast like they served at Dino's Diner. Unfortunately, they were about three and a half hours from Manning Grove and Rev was nowhere to be found.

Wait.

Did they have drunken sex last night?

She glanced down, relieved—okay, maybe not so relieved—to find she was still wearing his T-shirt over her sexy, silky PJs. Her effort to get him to break last night was foiled by his insisting on her covering up with the plain, boring cotton shirt. Along with them both getting stoned and drunk out of their minds.

She not only needed food to sop up the alcohol still surging through her veins, but a gallon of water to relieve her dehydration.

But first…

She slid her hand under Rev's T-shirt and into her silky shorts to find herself bone dry down there, too.

She glanced around, looking for any empty condom wrappers.

None.

She didn't know whether to be pleased he didn't take advantage of her or disappointed. But then, if they had sex, she wouldn't have remembered it. That in itself would've been disappointing. Because the first time she had sex with Rev, she *definitely* wanted to remember it.

That was right, she thought it: the *first* time. If it was up to her, it was going to happen not only once, but maybe a few more times before leaving Coatesville.

Doing it here, away from home, they could have a little fun without the risk of getting caught. And nobody had to know.

Only the two of them.

The problem was, she had to get Rev onboard with her plan. That meant tonight couldn't be a repeat of last night, where both of them ended up passed out.

Moving as slow as a turtle, she leaned over, snagged her phone and hit the side button to light it up.

It was almost freaking noon! No wonder she was hungry.

She frowned at the flashing indicator that told her she had a text message. Opening up the text app, she saw she had several text messages. One from Tessa. One from Saylor. Two from her sister, but only one from Rev.

She read his first. *B back L8R*

Be back later?

That was sent around nine this morning.

"Oh shit," she whispered. Did he go back to his parents' house without her? Without someone along to keep him from committing murder when his dad acted like a dick and treated his only son like he was an unwanted nobody?

She typed a text back: *Where are U?*

Staring at her phone, she waited. Nothing.

She texted again. *R U out getting food?*

"C'mon, Rev, answer. Please don't say you're back at that house by yourself," she murmured.

After a few more minutes without an answer, she sighed and tapped her phone on her bare thigh while she considered her options.

Besides showering. That was a given. Brushing off the fuzz that grew on her teeth overnight, too. That was a guarantee.

But between her cotton mouth and her hunger pangs, she really needed to grab something out of the vending machine by the office to at least tide her over before her body started eating itself. However, she couldn't do it the way she was dressed. And without shoes or money.

When she stood, she threw her arms out for balance and waited until the room stopped rotating before heading back to her side of the connected motel rooms.

She yanked on his interior door and it didn't budge.

He'd locked it. She unlocked and opened the door, then tried her side and that was locked, too.

Huh.

She frowned. She left both doors open last night. Why would he lock them?

She grabbed her room's keycard, flipped the hinge-y lock-y thingy to keep the exterior door in Rev's room propped open an inch and to keep from getting locked out, and hurried over to her own exterior door.

She inserted the card into the slot and it blinked red.

What the hell?

She tried it again. Flashing red.

Did she have his room card by mistake?

She went back into his room and glanced around, not finding any other keycard. But what she did find was her backpack was no longer in her room where she'd left it. It was now sitting on the floor next to his. In *his* room.

In her stupor, did she grab it sometime during the night? Had she needed something out of it?

She unzipped it and dug through her stuff to find everything still where she packed it, along with the toiletries she had placed in the bathroom next door.

Someone had stuck all of her products, including her makeup, back in her bag.

Was that someone her?

No. Couldn't have been. If she was so drunk she couldn't remember doing it, how could she actually do it?

She stood, pursed her lips and stared at her bag for a few minutes while scratching the back of her neck.

So damn strange.

Unless…

She hurried back outside, leaving that metal hinge-y thingy in place again so she didn't get locked out and tried her keycard in Rev's lock this time. The light turned a solid green.

Son of a fucking bitch.

Had he taken her keycard by mistake and left his?

She stood on the threshold, only wearing her PJs covered by Rev's T-shirt and stared inside the room, trying to determine what all of that meant or if it meant anything at all. Maybe it was just a simple mistake.

Speaking of his T-shirt... She fisted the cotton and shoved it against her nose.

Shit. Whiskey and pot. That could be the scent for any of the guys. Whiskey, beer, pussy, pot, leather and tobacco combo made up the typical Fury fragrance.

Her fingers loosened on the cotton and she let the shirt drop back into place as Rev's Bronco pulled around the side of the motel and into the spot in front of his room.

Had he caught her sniffing his shirt? *Damn it.*

The engine cut off, she heard the unmistakable sound of the parking brake being engaged, then the driver's door was flung open.

He climbed out of the truck and went around to the passenger side, opening the door, leaning in—unfortunately, from where she stood, not giving her a good look at his ass —and then shutting the door with his knee since his hands were now full of bags.

His face actually looked haggard, much older than his twenty-eight years. Likely due from a lack of real sleep, drinking too much, and, if he spent time in *that* house this morning with *those* people, he was probably emotionally worn down again.

He paused in front of her and whatever was in the bags smelled like heaven. Food! *Hot* food! Not vending machine shit.

"You look like a goddamn deer in headlights standin' out here. And you don't got any fuckin' pants on." He pushed past her and into the room.

She blinked, hurried after him and shut the door behind her. "You took my keycard. I'm locked out of my room."

"Yeah," was his only response, his back to her as he set the bags down on the tiny table in the corner.

She planted her hands on her hips and when he turned to face her, his expression was unreadable. "What do you mean, '*yeah*?' I need to get in my room to shower and change."

"You can do it in here."

Her brow furrowed. "Why would I do it in here when I have a perfectly good room next door?"

His mouth twisted and suddenly she knew exactly what he was going to say before he said it. "Decided no point in payin' for two rooms. Gonna share one."

Her eyebrows launched to the top of her forehead. "We are?"

"Yeah. We are." He tipped his head at the other queen bed in the room. The one that was still perfectly made. "Got two beds in here. Last night proved we can sleep in the same room without fuckin' up."

It did?

They had both passed out!

But, wait… She shouldn't argue this turn of events. Not at all. This might actually help her plan.

She rolled her lips under.

He frowned when he read her face. "You in that bed. Me in the other."

"Okay."

His bloodshot eyes narrowed.

She smiled.

He jerked his head toward the bathroom at the back of the room. "Go shower."

She had no idea what he bought for breakfast or lunch, or whatever, but it smelled way too good to wait. "I'll shower after I eat."

He wrinkled up his nose. "Gonna shower before we eat."

She lifted her arm and sniffed her own pit. "I don't stink."

"Thought a fox always smells his own fuckin' hole first. Guess that's wrong. Shower. Then eat."

"But I'm dying of starvation!"

He cocked one eyebrow and looked her up and down.

She rolled her eyes. "Are you saying I'm fat?"

"Didn't say shit."

He didn't have to. "I know I need to lose weight. I've done nothing but put on the pounds since working at the shop. We eat like shit. Donuts, snacks—"

"Shut the fuck up, woman. You don't gotta lose even one goddamn pound. Any weight you put on was needed and it all went to the right places."

"Yeah, my fat ass." She slapped one hand on each of her ass cheeks, then shook the junk in her trunk.

His blue eyes became more intense as he watched her. "Men like to smash an ass like that."

She grinned.

"Men who won't die doin' it," he corrected himself.

Her lips flattened out. They would have to have a discussion about that once she showered, changed and her stomach was no longer complaining.

"Do you happen to have aspirin in your bag?" she asked, hopeful.

"In the Bronco."

Oh, thank fuck. She needed a handful. "I guess you needed some, too."

"Go shower, Reilly. I'll grab the aspirin and set out the food. You take too long, I'm eatin' without you."

———

AFTER HER SHOWER, she was glad she hadn't put on her jeans. Instead, she pulled on cotton shorts she had shoved into her backpack. She was thankful that she did since her stomach now felt twice the size after stuffing herself on the smorgasbord he had set up on the table during her quick shower.

A whole cheesesteak hoagie and a few fries later, all washed down with a large bottle of water, she couldn't even glance at the food on the table that still remained uneaten.

She placed her hand on her gut with a groan and stared at the movie he had turned on. She guessed it was an old John Wayne movie, but wasn't sure. It certainly wasn't something she would watch if given a choice.

With the aspirin and carbs kicking in along with the drone of the TV, she was starting to nod off. And here it was only early afternoon.

She glanced at Rev propped up against the headboard on "his" bed, his eyelids also getting heavy. His fingers were laced together and his hands planted on his belly. He was barefoot once again but he still wore his jeans and today's choice of T-shirt, otherwise she might have been tempted to eat him instead of the cheesesteak.

Less calories, hopefully more satisfying.

However, if they remained in this room—in separate beds—both of them would soon be asleep, then wide awake tonight. "Maybe we should head down to my storage unit today." At least that would get them out and moving. She paused. "Unless you're afraid to go too far from your parents' house."

He'd said nothing about his visit there earlier, but she could tell it was eating at him. Just like it had yesterday.

And, of course, he had to have smoked at least half of a joint while she showered.

She didn't bother taking a hit or two since she had already been ready to gnaw off her own arm. Smoking pot would have made her inhale that damn cheesesteak even faster. She had to force herself to slow down so she wouldn't choke as it was.

His words were a little sluggish but nothing like last night. This time it was only exhaustion and weed causing it, not copious amounts of alcohol. "That stubborn old fuck ain't gonna die today. Doubt it'll be tomorrow, either. Thinkin' we go get your shit tomorrow mornin' since it's forty minutes away. Matthew's got my number, he can call me if anythin' changes. No point in puttin' off emptyin' your storage unit, 'cause as soon as that motherfucker's black heart stops beating, we're headin' home. Already sick of this place and we've only been here two days."

Not even two days. Just a little over twenty-four hours. And even that short amount of time was taking a toll on him.

But she understood his impatience to go home and put this all behind him. What little interaction she saw yesterday between Rev and his parents couldn't be healthy for him. And he was even out of the house and grown. It had to be so much worse when he'd been too young to leave.

Reilly was damn lucky she had Reese to step in place of their shitty mother. Even though that was a burden a young child should never have to bear. But Reese sacrificing her childhood to raise her baby sister was what helped Reilly survive and become a functioning adult in society.

Yes, sometimes Reese still acted like her mother instead of her sister and, yes, it could get extremely annoying, even smothering at times, but Reilly knew she only did it because she loved her, and it was all Reese had done since she was only eleven years old.

Reese became Reilly's "mother" at eleven.

She wondered how often Rev had to step in to help his baby sister. He didn't even hesitate to bring Saylor onto the farm and into the club once she was released from juvie.

While she was eighteen—and, legally, an adult—he could have easily told her that she was on her own and not taken that burden on himself.

But he did. He made sure his sister was set with a roof over her head and a job. He also ensured she was welcomed into a better family than the two people who were supposed to be their parents.

She smothered a yawn, quickly losing the fight to keep her peepers open.

If he didn't want to head out and get some fresh air, then maybe she should go walk laps around the motel.

Yeah, that wasn't going to happen.

But she needed to do something to stay awake and if he wasn't willing to get naked... *yet*... then they needed something to occupy their time until she could convince him to risk doing some horizontal dancing with her.

She had no idea if he'd answer any of the many questions floating around in her head, but it couldn't hurt to try. She only hoped he didn't clam up and shut her out completely. Her plan was to start out by lobbing softball questions and slowly work her way into the more complex ones.

"How old were you when you left?"

"Sixteen."

Shit. She didn't realize he'd been that young. He must have run away since she doubted he went through any kind of legal emancipation process. "That made Saylor how old?"

"'Bout seven."

"I mean, I won't lie and say your parents seem like lovely people because clearly they're complete whack jobs, but why? Why did you leave when you were so young? Besides the fact they act like they've stepped out of a M. Night Shyamalan series about religious freaks."

Well, that went from zero to sixty in two-point-five seconds. *Good job, Reilly.*

"They were strict."

"I'm finding that hard to believe," Reilly teased, her effort unfortunately falling flat. "But most kids think their parents are too strict."

"Yeah, but most parents don't make a kid cut their own switch, string them up practically naked in their backyard and whip them 'til they bleed."

"What?" she whispered, unable to close her mouth or even breathe. This whole conversation just went from sixty to one-hundred-and-sixty in half a second. "They did what?"

She thought parents using switches on their children was a thing of the past. Nobody did that nowadays, did they? They'd most likely be arrested for abuse.

Rev surged from the bed. He went directly for the whiskey, unscrewed the top, tipped up the bottle, dropped his head back and guzzled a good amount.

"Uh... Rev."

Maybe they shouldn't talk about this. She did not want a repeat of last night where they both overdid it and suffered the next morning because of it. Plus, she wouldn't doubt some brain cells were killed last night by drowning.

She hadn't drunk that much since college and she was surprised she didn't end up hugging the toilet and retching her guts out.

He slammed the bottle down on the table and wiped his mouth with the back of his hand. Without even a slight pause, he reached over his shoulder, grabbed a fistful of cotton mid-back and ripped his tee over his head. Totally exposing that mouth-watering, well-defined terrain.

Was he doing it to distract her from asking questions? If so, that was an effective way to go about it.

"Didn't notice this last night, did you?"

Honestly, last night she'd been kind of distracted by his chest and nipple piercings and the room had only been lit by the television. So no, she hadn't noticed whatever he was indicating.

Good God, he actually had dimples above his ass. She thought those were a myth. How had she missed those all the times she saw his jeans halfway down his thighs? Maybe because she was always focused on the flex of his naked ass instead...

But those sexy-as-fuck dimples couldn't be what he was pointing out. What the hell *was* he pointing out?

Besides those muscles—honed from whatever routine he did in the club's tiny gym on the farm to counteract all the garbage he ate and booze he drank—she only saw the club colors inked on his skin, mostly in black and gray except for the red blood that dripped from the skull's eyes and mouth.

"C'mere."

He didn't have to tell *her* twice. She scurried off her bed and got nice and close.

"See it?"

See it? She wanted to touch it. All of it. Every inch, trace every valley. But she still had no idea what he was—

"*Ooooooh shit*," Reilly breathed.

The Fury rockers and large center insignia covered most of them, but in the negative space, where the skin wasn't touched by ink, she could see them. Faded fine lines, barely visible, crisscrossed his back.

If he hadn't pointed them out, she might not have noticed. Maybe even thought they were a trick of the light.

"Those were done by a switch?" She'd never seen a switch in real life but she had an idea of what one looked like.

"Yeah."

"Why?"

"You mean what did I do to deserve them?"

"No. Nobody deserves that. Okay, maybe pedophiles and rapists… And some select others. But what *child* deserves that? Who would do such a thing?" She sighed. "That was a dumb question. Your parents did—"

"Father."

She tilted her head to the right. "Your father did that. What reason could he come up with that warranted that type of punishment?

"Plenty."

"Name one," she insisted, reaching out and lightly tracing her fingertip over the thin, barely visible lines.

His skin quivered under her touch. "Touchin' my sister."

Reilly froze and her chest tightened. "You touched your sister."

"Hugged her."

There had to be a lot more to that story than those two words. Her mouth opened and it took a few seconds for her to repeat flatly, "You hugged her." Her brow furrowed. "You weren't allowed to show your sister any affection?"

"No."

"No one could?"

"Not in the way normal families did."

Normal families. Yes, the description of *normal* didn't seem to apply in Rev's family's case. "I'm confused."

He spun around and her eyes dropped immediately to those damn shiny barbells. She curled her fingers into her palms so she wouldn't reach out and touch them. The time had to be right and now was not it.

She needed answers first.

"We were always in training."

"For what? Sports?" Every answer he gave made her want to ask so many more questions. This conversation was like opening Pandora's Box.

"To be Godly, most of all. Also, to be obedient. For both of us to become good members of our congregation. For me to become a worthy husband. For Sarah to become a worthy, submissive wife."

Sarah.

"Who's Sarah?" Did he have another sister he'd never mentioned before?

"Saylor is Sarah."

He wasn't clearing up her confusion, he was creating more. She did a little shake of her head and, once again, forced her gaze from his chest to his face as he began to explain.

"Hated the name Michael 'cause of what was attached to it. Saylor hated the name Sarah for the same reason. We both wanted to be free of that life and start new. In school, I began to tell people my name was Mickey and refused to answer to Michael. Once Sarah freed herself from their grip, she changed her name to Saylor and took the same last name I was usin' in an effort to scrape off the remains of this life."

"But to be free of one prison, she had to be locked up in another," Reilly murmured.

Holy fucking shit. That was heartbreaking. Saylor had never talked about her childhood. Not once. All the times they'd hung out together, either with the rest of the sisterhood or even on their own, she only talked about stuff currently happening. On a rare occasion, she'd bring up an entertaining story from her time spent in a juvenile detention center.

"Yeah."

"That's fucked up."

"Yeah," he agreed.

But wait, she needed to circle back. "So, those scars are from when your father punished you for touching your sister?"

"And other things."

"Worse than touching your sister?" Because a brother

touching a sister in an inappropriate way was pretty damn bad.

"Nothin' worse in his eyes than me touchin' Sarah."

"And did you?"

He sucked on his teeth for a second, took a deep breath and lifted his bearded chin a notch. "Not in the way they thought."

She was almost afraid to ask, "What did they think?"

The slow roll of his Adam's apple caught her attention. She could see he was on the fence about continuing this conversation or shutting the whole thing down.

While she didn't blame him for not wanting to talk about it, she also needed to know what the hell had gone on. Not only to be supportive for Rev while here and back at home, but for her club sister Saylor. Even if Saylor never found out that Reilly knew, Reilly could still know the truth and respond appropriately to a situation, if needed.

However, she would never spill any of Saylor's secrets. If Saylor wanted to share them with others, that would be her choice and her choice alone.

Maybe that was why Rev hesitated. Because they weren't only his secrets, they were Saylor's. Their secrets were intertwined like a knotted shoe lace.

Holy shit, she hated to even ask this, because it was not the Rev she knew. "Did you... touch your sister inappropriately?"

She made sure the question was soft and not accusatory because she definitely didn't want him to cut this conversation short. If he did, she would never stop wondering and questioning who the real Rev was. Who she thought he was.

But, *holy hell*, this trip was barely two days old and had been enlightening. And not in a good way. Worse, it wasn't even over yet.

"You think I'd do that?"

Guilt washed over her for even asking if he would. "No,

but... I mean, I assume you were young. Young kids don't always know the difference between what's wrong and what isn't. We learn that from our..."

"Parents," Rev finished for her when she didn't. "Never molested my sister. I only ever tried to soothe her when she was upset."

"They thought you were molesting her when you were actually consoling her?" *For shit's sake*, now she hated his parents even more!

"Yeah."

Again, the story had to go deeper than that. A simple hug was not sexual. A brother hugging his sister was not sexual, *damn it!*

"But why did she need so much consoling?" she prodded gently.

"I'm pretty sure someone else did."

"Did what?" Reilly sucked in a sharp breath. "Molest Saylor?"

"Sarah," he corrected.

God, this separation of two children into four hurt her brain. She understood their need for that coping mechanism, but for her, it was like dealing with people who had two separate personalities or were two separate people. However, this was different than a personality disorder they couldn't control, it was a choice both of them decided to make.

"Who molested Sarah?" she repeated with the correct name. Her pulse was racing because she already knew. There was no need for him to confirm it.

She now knew why Saylor wanted nothing to do with her family, why she kept committing crimes to get pulled from the household, why she didn't want to go home after juvie, and why she changed her damn name.

Why Rev didn't want Saylor to come "home" with him to visit their dying father.

Reilly forced herself to swallow the rage that had rose out of her chest and into her throat. "Do you know for sure he did that to her?"

Holy shit, the man needed to die. No wonder Rev wanted to see his father's end through.

"When I was punished, I was taken outside. When she was…"

Reilly held her breath.

"He only ever did it in her room, with the door closed and she'd cry for a while afterward. He never used a switch on her. He'd…"

The breath rushed out of her as his face twisted and his hands clenched into fists.

"What else would make her cry like that? When I was whipped, I wasn't allowed to cry without addin' to the number of strikes. But she cried every fuckin' time after he left her room. Every damn time. I'd go into her room once they went to bed, once it was safe. I'd crawl into her bed and hold her. I'd beg her to tell me what was wrong, what he did and she never would."

Why did he look guilty? How was any of this his fault? "He probably threatened her not to tell."

"Or he brainwashed her into thinkin' whatever he did was normal. 'Cause to him it fuckin' was. I think it was accepted among all of them. However, it was never fuckin' talked about and since I wasn't a female, it didn't affect me like it did her."

"Shit," she whispered. "Why would it be accepted?"

"It was—probably still is—a father's job to prepare any daughters he had to be obedient to her husband. This way he could hand her off to a worthy one. No man would want her if she acted out or wasn't submissive."

"The way Matthew's wife looked."

"Yeah."

"This… church… it's more than a church, isn't it?"

"Yeah."

"It's a damn cult, almost like the Shirleys," she concluded.

His tattooed chest rose and fell. "Yeah."

"Jesus Christ, how many fucked up groups are there like this in the world?"

"Bet more than we know."

"That's scary," she whispered.

"Ain't it?" He shook his head. "Think about it. Wouldn't be hard to take a brotherhood like the Fury and twist it into something darker, like a cult. Wouldn't be hard at all."

"Which is why Trip is careful not to let the club turn back into the Originals."

"Part of the reason. Though, the Originals were never into incest that we know of. Were they the best parents? Fuck no."

"No," Reilly agreed, "but from some of the stories that are told, they were into some other fucked up shit."

"Yeah, the stories that are told. Sure there are much worse ones buried somewhere."

"But the Originals are now gone," she stated.

"Not all of them," he reminded her quickly.

Right, Dutch and Ozzy were Originals and even wore the patch stating such. Trip and Judge, and some of the others, were positive more were out there, they just hadn't been or didn't want to be found.

Also, a few of the Fury members, along with some of the club sisters, were products of some of those Originals. Most with secrets as deep as Rev and Saylor's.

When she got back to Manning Grove, she was going to give Saylor a bone-crushing bear hug. She'd just have to find a good excuse for it, so Saylor didn't guess that Reilly knew the truth about her past. Or figure out that Reilly went with Rev to Coatesville.

Unfortunately, this trip would be one more secret thrown onto the ever-growing mountain of Fury secrets.

"I'm sorry," she finally said, because she didn't know what else to say to help take away the horrible memories from his childhood. "After you left, did you have any way to stay in touch with Saylor?" She grimaced. "Sarah, I mean."

"Not really. When I could, I would go to her school and check on her there. Wasn't often since I was barely survivin' on my own. Once I turned eighteen, I could visit her at juvie without the threat of bein' caught as a runaway, so it was a little easier."

"When she was in school why didn't you report to them what your father was doing?"

"Had no proof. I never saw what he did. I only could guess. And like I said, I was a runaway and didn't want to be taken back. Anyway, who would believe me over adults? Saylor has never spoke of it. Not once. She acts like it never fuckin' happened."

"She's probably repressed it. Hidden it away in her mind. It's a coping mechanism."

"The same as you?"

Chapter Nine

"WHAT DO YOU MEAN?" Reilly asked him.

She never talked about it. No one did.

Rev hadn't been there. *Thank fuck.* That was the kind of shit that made nightmares. And Reilly had been the one to engage the actual button on the incinerator to do "the deed." She had shoved past Deacon and slammed her palm on it to ignite the burners.

To burn a still conscious, breathing human being to death.

Did that motherfucker deserve it? No fucking doubt.

Still… It was disturbing.

He wondered if she had nightmares about it. About hearing a man scream as he was being incinerated.

But like Saylor, Reilly acted like it never happened. Maybe it was repressed memories, like she mentioned. "That day—"

She interrupted him. "Just because I don't talk about it, doesn't mean I don't think about it. I think about it every damn day." Her cheeks had turned a dark shade of pink. It wasn't from embarrassment.

They found it difficult to embarrass the woman. No

matter what was said by any of the guys, even when they busted her non-existent balls, she never was offended or embarrassed. She could take ball-busting as good as she could give it.

That attitude made him a little lusty over her, too. More than a little lusty.

"Not what he did to you. What you did to him," he clarified.

"I didn't do anything to him. He caused that himself. But if you want me to say something about *that* particular incident, then I'm glad I took the burden off Deacon. Nobody but me should've done it. And, as we all know... Paybacks are a fucking bitch."

Normally, he'd grin at that last part but he got caught on the fact that she wanted to kill the motherfucker herself, so it wouldn't be anyone else's burden.

"I got everyone into that whole mess, so I wanted to be the one to get us out. I appreciate how everyone stepped in to help me even though you all hardly knew me."

"Yeah, but Deke didn't wanna make that motherfucker pay just 'cause of you, it was for what he did to Reese, too." Warren hurt both sisters. He had also hurt other women in the past and would've hurt others in the future if he'd been allowed to keep breathing. He was that much of a fucking piece of shit.

"Reese is *my* sister." She slapped a hand to her chest, drawing his eyes to her tits for a brief second. Or two. His gaze rose when she finished with, "And I handled it for both of us."

She certainly did. Like a fucking boss, too. Even so... "I shoulda killed that motherfucker. Shoulda fuckin' killed him even before Deke and the others got there. As soon as he swung that fuckin' baseball bat in your direction. Shoulda grabbed that bat and smashed his fuckin' brains in. Just like he wanted to do to you."

Then the fucker would've been dead and no one would've had the "burden" of pushing that button while he was still alive. Throwing the asshole into the furnace would've been only about getting rid of any evidence that Billy Warren ever existing. The same way they got rid of the Shirleys when any of his brothers pulled one off the mountain. Or used to.

That Shirley situation was currently in limbo until the feds did what the feds were going to do with them first.

"You weren't there when he first showed up, remember? Rook and Whip were. Rook saved my damn life. Maybe I should've given him a thank-you blowie for that..."

A thank-you blowie?

"Are you fuckin' serious?" he growled. She better not be fucking serious! It was bad enough when Rook got to be the one to hang all over her while taking the Instagram photos to draw Warren out of hiding. They had pretended to be hooking up and acted like it, too. Rev had to walk away every fucking time Rook had his hands all over her "for the camera."

She rolled her eyes at his reaction. "I'm kidding. Rook would never get head from me because he's an asshole. I've had my fill of those after dealing with the dead douchebag. Assholes are permanently off my blowjob list."

She had a blowjob list?

She tilted her head and her blonde hair fell to the side. "And, anyway, what if you'd been arrested for bashing his head in? Saylor would be on her own right now. You're her family, Rev. She needed you, she still needs you. You're also the only one—well, besides me now—who knows about her past."

Her past. He should've done something to stop that "past" back then. "Failed her."

"No you didn't. Kids shouldn't be forced to make adult decisions. Reese was forced to do that and so were you." She planted a hand on his stomach and he automatically sucked in his gut at the contact.

Her touch on his bare skin felt electrically charged. Like she could control his pulse with simply a touch. That same pulse started to pound somewhere it shouldn't. Just from her warm, soft hand planted on his skin. From her big green eyes tipped up to his.

From her sinking her teeth into her plump, bottom lip.

He mentally groaned at how fucking tempting she was.

He thought if he could resist her last night when he was drunk, he'd be strong enough to resist her when he was sober. But maybe moving her into his room had been a bad idea. Because, as they stood that close inside the small motel room, his lust for her was spilling over into something more. Even though it shouldn't, since the topic they were discussing should be a turn-off for anyone with a normal brain.

But, *for fuck's sake*... Knowing she'd never been fucked by any of his brothers and he could be the only one to do so... was starting to fuck with his judgment. And his dick.

"You weren't the only one with shitty parents. Our father deserted us because our mother was a damn drunk. He didn't only leave her, he selfishly left his two daughters, too!"

Her words solved his fucking dilemma. They had the same effect as if he'd soaked in Morton Salt dissolved in a tub of ice-cold water.

"He was so fed up with her drinking, especially when she was pregnant with me, he simply decided to say fuck it and forget we ever existed. What kind of dickhead father does that? Decides to leave a bad situation but leaves his daughters behind?"

Rev had done the same damn thing... "I left Sarah behind."

"You were sixteen, Rev!" she shouted, practically in his

face. "How the hell were you supposed to take care of a seven-year-old? *And* do it without being caught and charged with kidnapping? How? I'm sure if you could have, you would have. Unlike you, my father was an adult who wanted us until he decided he didn't. Then Minnie wanted nothing to do with me after I was born because she blamed me for her man leaving. Me! While I was in her damn womb. When it was she who was drinking while I was just floating helplessly in a sack of fluids inside of her."

He cringed at that description, but it also pissed him the fuck off.

"Reese called our mother Minnie, or Minimum Mom, for a good reason. The woman had done the bare minimum to keep us alive. And once we were older, she stopped making the slightest attempt to do even that. Reese did *every-thing*. If she didn't know how to do it, she figured it out. Did she screw things up? Yes, but at least she tried. Because of her sacrifice, I owe her everything in return. *I* am the reason Reese never had a childhood."

"No. Your goddamn mother is. Your father, too. Ain't your fault."

"Just like it isn't yours that you had to leave Saylor," she shook her head and released a cute little snarl, "*Sarah* behind."

Her fingernails dug into his flesh and she stepped even closer, until her bare toes were pressed to his. He held his breath because he was having a hard time not grabbing her hair right now and throwing her onto the bed. No matter who or what the fuck they were talking about wasn't helping that urge.

"Reese did what she had to do for us to survive. You did what you had to so you could survive to be able to help your sister later, when you could. To me, you did the best you could, Rev. Be happy you have each other."

He was struggling to stay on track, to cling to his anger at his parents. At hers. At that Warren motherfucker.

Instead, he was focusing on the way her mouth was shaped, the way her tongue darted out and moistened her bottom lip. The way her pupils had become wider. The heat of her body. The way she filled the cotton shorts and snug T-shirt she now wore. He was tempted to feel the contrast between how soft that cotton was and how hard her nipples were.

Just a touch. No one would know.

He needed to feel the weight of her breasts in his hands. The softness of her mouth on his. He wanted to draw a groan from deep down inside her until it filled his ears.

"This whole thing with your parents… You're not upset or pissed, or whatever, over what you *lost*. You're upset over what you *never had*."

What? He shook himself mentally.

"I didn't lose good parents. I never had them," she continued. "Neither did you. You can't miss what you never had but you can be mad you never had it to miss."

Christ. She was making too much sense, even though he was struggling to follow what she was saying. And why the fuck was she still talking about people he hated?

He didn't want to think about her parents right now. He didn't want to even think about Saylor. He sure as fuck didn't want to think about how his mother was a cold bitch to him this morning and disappeared as soon as she'd seen him in the house. Or how his miserable, asshole father was still fucking breathing.

Fuck no.

He wanted to think about the woman who stood so close he could smell her citrusy-scented body wash and see how flawless her skin was, all except for the scar she tried to hide.

He could see her chest rising and falling as she took

deeper and deeper inhales. He could see her lips parting to release those breaths.

Her palm slipped a little on his stomach. He had no idea if it was by accident or on purpose, but now the tip of her thumb was pressed to the top edge of his waistband.

"Rev."

"Heard everythin' you said," he murmured, right now not even giving a flying fuck about anything she said. Unless it had to do with getting naked with him and sliding down his now-throbbing dick.

"This conversation shouldn't have made you hard."

No fuckin' shit.

"Wasn't the conversation, buttercup." She'd noticed how hard he'd become, but did she notice he was hard enough that his zipper was trying to tattoo a pattern into his dick?

Her hand was still there, now pressed to his lower stomach, only a few inches from his hard-on. All she had to do was slide her hand down. Just a little.

Slide it down, Reilly. Touch me 'cause I can't touch you.

"We're not supposed to," came out on a ragged breath.

"But you wanna," he said.

Jesus Christ, woman, say no. Say you don't want me. Say it so I stop bein' tempted. So you stop temptin' me.

Her eyebrows rose. "You don't?"

Reality cracked him upside the head. "You know I fuckin' can't," he practically growled, wanting to punch a goddamn wall.

"You know what? I'm tired of being a pariah in the club. The untouchable one when all I want for you to do is touch me."

That wasn't what he needed to hear. He needed to pack his shit tight so he could resist. "Me? Or any one of us? Is it me 'cause I'm the one here right now, the one who's available? Or me, 'cause you only want me?"

"Does it matter?"

His head snapped up and his nostrils flared. His rough words came from the back of his throat in what sounded like a strangled growl. "Yeah, woman, it fuckin' matters. It sure as fuck matters. If I break this goddamn rule, it needs to be for a good reason and not just to empty my fuckin' balls. I can do that anywhere where I don't risk getting maimed. You get me? And I ain't here just to get you off, either. This will be a huge violation of the rules. A violation that has a worse punishment than what my father could ever give me. Also, don't think I'm gonna fuck you, then turn around and watch you fuck another one of my brothers. Or anyone else, for fuck's sake. That shit ain't ever gonna happen." He dropped his head until they were practically nose-to-nose. "So, yeah, it fuckin' matters."

He fisted her hair, yanked her head back and pressed his mouth to her ear. He brought his voice down an octave lower. "Want my tongue in your mouth, my dick in your pussy, my fingers in your ass. Wanna fill you up with my cum, want you to soak my dick and balls. Wanna feel you pump me 'til I'm empty and you're full."

Her shuddered breath escaped her in a rush and her shiver left goosebumps behind in its wake.

Fuck yeah. Her nipples now had to be diamond hard.

"Never done what I've been told. Never followed anyone else's rules but my own. 'Til the Fury. To keep my home, to keep my brotherhood. But, fuck, babe, you're one rule I wanna break so goddamn badly."

When another shuddered breath rushed from her, it almost sounded like a sigh. Her hand fisted the waistband of his jeans and twisted it tightly. But, still, she said nothing.

No words were needed, he could see everything he needed to know on her face. In her eyes. In the way she breathed.

"Know you want this. Know that's why you came into my room last night wearin' that shit. But not sure if givin' in to what I want, what you want, is worth losin' everythin'. It'll stir shit I don't want to fuckin' stir."

"No one needs to know."

He huffed out a breath. "Yeah, right. No one needs to know. We'll know. *I'll* fuckin' know. Once I sink my dick inside you, once I taste your pussy, ain't gonna be easy to forget."

"You might be giving me more credit than you should."

"It's risky to find out."

Her sigh this time was nothing like the previous one. "I love this club and you guys but I hate the rule that includes me. It's not right or fair."

"Bein' a part of this club means rules. And it's one way your sister's lookin' out for you."

"She's done that my whole life. She can stop at any time now."

"She ain't ever gonna stop, Reilly. You know that. She might be your sister but she raised you like a daughter. Wants the best for you. That's what *true* family wants for each other. Good shit, not bullshit."

"But a Fury member is good enough for her. What a fucking hypocrite."

Sighing, he straightened and stepped back, giving the two of them space. This turn of conversation was quickly killing his erection and he needed to think more clearly, anyway. "Difference is, Deacon's her ol' man. She wears his cut. That right there means a lot. She don't want anyone usin' you like a sweet butt. Don't want anyone disrespectin' you. I get it. That's exactly why Saylor's on that same fuckin' list. She don't need to be ridin' a different dick every night. You don't, either."

"Why don't you let us make those decisions for ourselves?"

"You can. You can ride as many dicks as you want." Lie. "Just ain't gonna be Fury dicks." Truth. "That's something

Reese can control. Anyone not wearin' Fury colors, she can't."

"That's why I had to—" Her lips pressed together and she turned away. She walked the few steps over to the window and peered out between the closed vertical blinds.

Out back, there was nothing to see but a parking lot and a privacy fence. The motel wasn't full. The clerk had assured him that the rooms in the rear of the motel weren't normally used until the front rooms were first filled, so they'd get plenty of privacy.

Why she was glancing out the window, he had no fucking clue, unless she was simply trying to avoid finishing her thought.

"Had to what?" he prodded, stepping behind her and confirming nothing was out there to cause any interest or concern.

She continued to look outside at nothing when she murmured, "Find some elsewhere."

He stared at the back of her head, of all that blonde hair falling loosely around her shoulders, doing his best to ignore what she just said.

But he couldn't. He couldn't ignore that, just like he couldn't ignore her. No matter how hard he tried.

It shouldn't fucking bother him because she was a hot fucking chick in her mid-twenties. She was no prairie dress wearing virgin waiting for a husband before spreading her legs. He knew that.

He. Fucking. Knew. That.

But he had always wanted to ignore that she might be finding dick elsewhere.

The same with Saylor.

Jemma, Reilly, Saylor and Tessa, the prez's sister, went out a lot together since they were all closer in age. He was pretty fucking sure, being Cage's ol' lady, Jemma wasn't trolling for dick. But the others?

He set his jaw. Manning Grove didn't have a singles' scene but tourists, Mansfield U. students, and others with functioning libidos were always coming to town and even hitting up Crazy Pete's for bands, pool tournaments, and all the other shit Stella scheduled at the bar to bring in more customers.

He pursed his lips. The women went there a lot for karaoke…

For fuck's sake, maybe they only said they were heading to Pete's and, instead, hit up Mansfield or even Williamsport, where there were plenty of bars or clubs to find a random hookup. And where no one would notice, like Dodge or Stella.

Though, Stella would never spill that info anyway, since there seemed to be some sort of code of silence in the sisterhood. That alone should pucker the assholes of all the men attached to those women.

"Wanna say that again?"

She let the blinds fall back into place and turned to face him. "This stupid ass rule is why I have to find dick elsewhere." As his mouth opened, she threw up a hand to stop him. "Don't you fucking dare. Don't you say one fucking word. Not one. You all stick your dicks anywhere you damn well please—"

"Not anywhere—"

She ignored him and plowed on. "And no one blinks a damn eye. I'm supposed to watch you all getting your rocks off—front and center, I might add—and I'm supposed to go back to my place and be satisfied with my Rabbit or my own hand."

What the fuck was a rabbit? Besides the furry animal with big ears.

"That's just bullshit. I'm a living, breathing woman who has *needs*. Just like you guys have needs. I'm an adult and not a damn child. I can make my own damn decisions of whose cock I want to ride or suck." She frowned. "Close your damn mouth. It's hanging open like you have a damn brain injury or something."

He snapped his jaw closed. "What's a rabbit?"

She bugged her eyes out at him and sighed. "It's not dick, that's what it isn't. While it gets the job done, it's lonely. Sometimes you just want the weight of a man crushing you as you come, or you want to hear his deep grunts in your ear as he pumps his thick dick in and out of you, or you want to watch his face twist up when he finally blows his load. Your mouth is hanging open again." She stepped closer and pushed it shut with her fingers.

"Reilly…"

"I love sex." She raised a finger. "*Good* sex. I liked it before the dead douchebag and it's been kind of okay afterward, but nobody has knocked it out of the park recently. In fact, it's been rushed and unrewarding. A back alley—"

"What?"

She kept talking. "—fuck in a backseat of a cramped car isn't always satisfying."

"You need to shut the fuck up now."

She planted her hands on her hips and glared up at him. "Why? Because you can't imagine me having sex? Or you don't want to?"

Both.

No, the second one. Because the first one he could. As long as she was having that sex with him. He squeezed his eyes shut and pressed his fists to the sides of his thighs because if he didn't, he was going to grind them into his eye sockets to wipe away the vision of her having sex with anyone else from his head.

She kept talking anyway because that was who she was. "So, what's wrong with me wanting to have sex in a damn bed with someone I trust, to actually take our time and make it good? I could really use a good fuck."

When those last two words came out huskily, his eyes opened.

"And no one has to know," she finished.

"Had that discussion already," was all he could manage.

"Yes, well, *we'll* know." She threw her hands up and yelled, "Who the fuck cares? Fuck me and forget about it. Then, once we go home, you can go back to your man-whore ways."

She was trying to make what she wanted seem more simple than it was. Most of his brothers would jump on that offer and not even think twice. In fact, before she had even been done talking, they would've had their dick out and in their hand, impatiently waiting on her to stop running her mouth and wrap it around their hard-on instead.

But it wasn't any of them standing in this room, it was him. "You ain't gonna say shit if you see me railin' one of the sweet butts?"

Her brow dropped low.

Yeah, he didn't think it would be that easy. It never was with a woman.

"No. Why would I?"

Hold up. That meant... "You're sayin' you only wanna use my dick temporarily."

"Yes, why not?"

Why the fuck not? he wanted to repeat in a scream.

"That whole to-do list you growled into my ear earlier— which made me wet, by the way—proves to me that you want to fuck me. Am I wrong?"

"You're not wrong."

"Well, then..." She shrugged. "I just decided what we'll be doing to pass the time the rest of this afternoon... Instead of watching one of those boring black-and-white movies."

He stood frozen in his spot by the window as she moved toward his bed. While she did so, she ripped her T-shirt over her head, reached behind herself to unclip her bra, letting it drop to the floor, and then she paused with her back to him. She snagged the elastic waistband of her shorts, bent over and shoved them—and whatever panties she'd been wearing —down her legs until they dropped to her feet.

What.

The.

Fuck.

This was not a fair fight. Not a fair fight at all.

How could she just do that and...

He needed to go get her room back from the front desk, then he needed to go over there and take an ice-cold shower.

Because his dick now had its own heartbeat. It also had its own opinion, too. It was screaming at him to not look a gift horse in the mouth. To take the damn gift and say, "Thanks."

Be appreciative.

Stop being a pussy.

She was right. No one had to know.

Coatesville, Pennsylvania could be the new Las Vegas.

What happened in...

Yeah, yeah, yeah.

But what happened in Manning Grove once they got back could be far from fun. What happened here might not matter, but what happened there would.

He wasn't Rook, who thought he could fuck Jet out of his system. He was mistaken, of fucking course, because that was a complete failure.

Rev wasn't stupid. He was smart enough to know that if he fucked Reilly, he wouldn't be able to shake her afterward, not because *she'd* be clingy, but...

He could do this. He could fuck her without wanting anything afterward. Right?

He did it all the time with the sweet butts and randoms.

The only problem was, he'd have to see Reilly almost every day. At the garage, out at the farm. On the runs, at parties.

Stop bein' a pussy. She's offerin' you hers. Take it.

Why was he having a conversation with himself when there was a naked blonde in his room, climbing onto his bed?

All that damn smooth skin, the weight of her tits rocking and rolling as she moved, the tips puckered into tight rose-buds, the curves of her bare hips and ass. *Christ*, she hadn't faced him yet, but he was dying to get a good look at what he was only getting glimpses of while she moved to the headboard.

His headboard.

While she was completely *naked*. And she had already waved the green flag, giving him the go-ahead.

Of course, fool that he was, he still remained frozen in place, his conscience fighting with his ever-increasing thirst for her.

What he'd been fantasizing about for the past year could actually become a reality. All he had to do was fucking move!

"Reilly," he choked out. His dick was now so goddamn hard, his balls so damn tight, the discomfort almost unbearable.

He was trying not to stare at her, so he could think clearly and make the right decision, but…

He was only fucking human.

Chapter Ten

"WHY DO you look like a damn deer stuck in high beams? It's almost like you've never seen a naked woman before."

Rev's Adam's apple popped up, stuck for a second and then dropped like a rock. "Seen plenty of naked women."

"Then you know what to do with one," she huffed as she settled onto his bed.

She was now buck naked, and he was only wearing his jeans. There was no reason they weren't already sweating, panting and exchanging body fluid.

Okay, yes there was. His resistance.

Damn stubborn men with their fears of being bludgeoned to death! *Fsst.*

"Don't make me feel self-conscience now." She sat on the bed and waved a hand down her body. "Like this isn't good enough for you. I know I got a little softer—"

"Ain't nothin' wrong with what I'm seein'."

"Well, there must be since you're still standing all the way over there."

"Reilly…"

"Rev… Look, let's make a pact. Oh, I know! We could do a pinky swear and we'll swear we won't tell anyone. That whatever happens between us won't leave this room." She jutted out her hand, curled her fingers and thumb into her palm and stuck her pinky straight up in the air.

His brow dropped low. "A fuckin' what?"

"A pinky swear. Didn't you ever... Never mind. Just come here. I'll show you."

"Said the spider to the fly," he muttered under his breath.

"I'm not a black widow."

"Maybe not directly. But if anyone finds out, you could be indirectly responsible for my demise."

"That's what the pinky swear is for," she explained. "Nobody will find out. *No one* breaks the sanctity of a pinky swear." She rolled her lips under to keep from laughing at how ridiculous this whole thing was. If she laughed, he'd never agree.

But he looked so damn conflicted. His erection was raging in his jeans, but he looked about ready to puke. That wasn't giving her the warm fuzzies since what he was looking at was her naked on *his* bed.

Time to get out the big guns.

She sighed and dropped her hand, then rolled off the bed and to her feet. "I guess if you don't want to fuck me, I'll get dressed and go find someone else who will."

One thing she learned in the last year of being around bikers was they were possessive of their women. Like crazy possessive and protective. She might not be Rev's "woman," or ol' lady, but she worked with him, had ridden on the back of his sled many times and spent a lot of time around him.

She already knew the response she would get to her "threat" and, of course, she wasn't disappointed.

"Don't you fuckin' dare." His order was so gruff, so alpha, it made everything on and in her clench tight.

With long, determined strides, he advanced toward the

bed, his expression hard, his eyes clearly shouting that his orders were not to be messed with.

Finally.

As he closed in on her, she jutted out her hand for a pinky swear again. A noise so guttural came from deep within his chest, it made her lose her breath for a second. She lost it again when he grabbed her wrist, yanked her forward, shoved his hands into her hair and slammed their mouths together.

Fuck the pinky swear. This was so much better.

Finally, finally, finally!

She'd been wanting this for a long time, but figured it might never happen, not at home, and certainly not with Rev's concern about getting jammed up because of it. They had skirted around each other for months.

Months!

She'd noticed his reaction when she and Rook had pretended to be involved for social media pictures to draw the dead douchebag—undead at the time—out of hiding. She saw his reaction when any of the other guys did *overly*-friendly flirting with her. Even if it was only in fun.

She truly didn't want him to risk his brotherhood, or even his life, just because she wanted him. Because of that, she was serious about no one having to know what happened, or would happen, in this room. Okay, yes, she tended to blab a lot, but she also knew when to keep her mouth shut.

She would do it about this. He shouldn't worry at all.

And—

Holy shit, the man could kiss. She'd never seen him kissing any sweet butt or hang-around. None of the guys did. The women's purpose was for one thing and one thing only and it was not getting intimate.

His hands were now fisted tightly in her hair, holding her in place as he took total possession of her mouth. *Total* freaking possession with his lips *and* tongue. Her breasts ached, her nipples peaked painfully, her pussy was crying tears of arousal for his attention.

Holy shit, this was really going to happen, wasn't it? He wouldn't change his mind and then just leave her hanging, cold and wanting? He better not…

She grabbed the back of his head to hold on, too. She was not going to let him have second thoughts. Not even for a damn second.

Her thighs quivered, her breathing slowed, her pulse quickened and she pressed her taut nipples into his chest. A groan came from deep within him and she captured and combined it with her own.

She dug her hand between them and hurried to yank open the button on his jeans and slide down his zipper. As soon as she did, she dug her hand into his boxer briefs and grabbed the hot, solid length of him. Delicate silky skin encased his thick, pulsing cock, and her thumb found the drop of precum at the slit and smoothed it around the crown.

He ripped his mouth from hers, pressed his forehead onto the top of her head and thrust upward into her palm with a loud moan. "Fuck, babe."

He rarely called her that at the shop, or even on the farm, but when he did… *holy hell*, it was a huge turn-on for her. It was another word the guys tended to throw around like "baby" or "woman" out of habit, normally without any deep meaning.

But she never heard him call anyone else babe. Not once. Only her. And now that she thought of it, when he did, it was never within earshot of anyone else. He seemed to reserve that endearment only for her. Why hadn't she ever noticed that before?

Her voice was thick and slightly husky when she said, "I've seen you fuck other women, too many times to count, now I want to watch you fuck me."

He pressed his cheek against hers, thrust into her palm again and put his mouth to her ear. "You ain't the same."

"Prove it," she demanded on a shaky breath. "Do everything you said earlier and more."

"Fuck, Reilly…"

"No. It's only me and you in this damn room. That's it. You disabled my locator app, so no one knows I'm with you. It's just us. And now I'm going to confess something I haven't told you before."

He pulled back and his eyes were flickering blue flames as he stared down at her. "What?"

She tugged gently on his cock, loving the way the hot skin rolled up and down his steely length. How his hips followed the movement slightly, how every pull drew more silky fluid to the tip.

He gritted his teeth and closed his eyes, a hiss escaping him as she began to milk his cock more rigorously. More determined than ever for them to keep going and for him not to think twice and bring everything to a screeching halt.

"I've wanted this," her heart did a little dance in her chest as she revealed, "wanted you for a while now."

She had never made a big deal out of it before and had flirted with him the same as the rest of the guys, so she doubted he knew.

His eyes opened and he curled his fingers around her wrist, stopping her action. "How long?"

"Does it matter?"

His fingers squeezed her wrist and he peeled her hand from his searing hot, pulsing cock.

"You don't like what I'm doing?"

"Fuckin' like it. Just don't wanna come like this. And you touchin' me like you are ain't makin' it easy to keep from doin' that. What I also want is an answer."

"Months." She wasn't ashamed to admit it.

"Months? While you were climbin' on someone else's cock?" he growled.

"Same number of months I think you wanted me, too, but were sticking your dick in anyone with tits who bent over and offered."

"Ain't so easy, Reilly."

Wasn't that the damn truth? She sighed. "I know. That's why I tried not to let it bother me. It's also why anything I did shouldn't bother you, either."

He stared down at her and she could see him considering her words.

"Yeah," he finally said softly.

Well, look at that, he didn't go all jealous gorilla on her. "How about we take this opportunity to make the impossible possible."

He cupped her face and dropped his until his lips were directly above hers. "And then what happens after?"

That answer was easy but unfortunate. "The possible becomes impossible once more." She wasn't going to kid herself that it wouldn't.

She also couldn't forget they were currently stuck in the middle of a Stephen King or M. Night Shyamalan event. The bizarre shit with his parents still existed and, back in Manning Grove, rules still remained that Rev couldn't break.

But for right now, they could both ignore the things they couldn't control and concentrate on what they could.

"Rev," she whispered, strumming her thumb over his left nipple, finally getting to touch those metal barbells. It was only a teasing exploration, she'd get more serious with them soon. The thought of playing with them made her giddy. "News flash. I'm naked. You're not. We're standing here when the bed is only inches from us."

His face tipped down to watch her brush her thumb over his right nipple. "Ain't tellin' me nothin' I don't know."

"What are you going to do about it?"

"Jesus, babe, bad enough I'm so fuckin' hard I'm about to explode but if you keep touchin' those with me already hangin' by a goddamn thread, I'm gonna shoot my load way sooner than I wanna. And it ain't gonna be where I aim to put it."

His words pulled a shudder from her at the thought of him coming deep inside her. Even with a condom. She reluctantly dropped her hand from his chest. "I can't help it. I've been wanting to play with them since I saw them last night."

"Christ, woman," he groaned.

"Well, that's what you got them for, isn't it? They're meant to be played with, right? Same as some other things on your body, too." She grinned.

"*Fuck.* Gonna make your body my playground."

That made her grin widen into a full-blown smile. "About damn time. Get those jeans off and let's get to it. Since I'm the only one naked, it seems like a lopsided situation."

He stepped away from her and, instead of peeling off his jeans, she worried he might fasten them.

"Face the bed, hands on the mattress, spread your feet and bend over. Show me what you got."

Holy shit. Goosebumps broke out over every inch of her flushed skin as she did as she was told.

The fan of the HVAC unit under the motel's window blew cool air over her heated skin and caressed her swollen lips as she bent over, planted her palms on the mattress, widened her stance and tipped her ass up.

Doing that made her whole body burn with need and impatience.

He moved only enough until he faced her, until he could see everything she was offering him.

Even facing the bed, she could feel him exploring her

with his eyes. She was about to complain and return to a stand so she didn't feel so exposed since he only stood there, but the jingle of the chain attached to his wallet made her stay put.

Then a strip of three condoms landed on the bed right next to her hand. Even better, she heard the slide of denim down his long legs before they hit the floor. In anticipation, her veins became rivers of scorching lava.

Anticipation wasn't the only reason. It was also need, want and definitely lust.

"Rev," she forced up her tight throat.

"Yeah," he answered on a breath.

"What are you doing?"

"Just appreciatin' you, babe. Seriously wanna fuck the shit out of you right now, just pound that pussy 'til it's beat the fuck up and we both can't do anythin' but blink afterward. But, shit, I need to do somethin' else first."

Before she could ask him what, the air moved around her and his long, calloused fingers were spreading her inner thighs even wider. "Open up."

She could argue that she was already open, ready and willing, but didn't bother when he pulled her slick folds apart and unceremoniously pressed his mouth to her waiting pussy. And, *holy shit*, that beard...

"*Ooooooh, shiiiiit*," she groaned, clutching the bedding so tightly she didn't give a damn if it ripped. It would be worth the cost to replace it.

She took a gulp of air and threw her head back, releasing a long groan as his tongue did all kinds of wicked, but wonderful, things to her. He left nothing untouched, as he used his tongue to worship her from the top of her ass crack all the way to her clit. It wasn't just his tongue, either. He ate her with a gusto that she'd never experienced before. And she didn't want it to stop any time soon.

He used his lips to suck, his tongue to flick and fuck, his

teeth to nibble and bite the tender flesh. All of it making every nerve stand on end and her cry out. She couldn't get enough of what he was doing but he was driving her to the point where she wanted and needed more. She wanted to face him, to taste him, to experience him fully.

In a minute...

Maybe two.

Because as much as she wanted to wrap her lips around those barbells and play with them, as much as she wanted him to fill her pussy, as much as she wanted him to play with her nipples, too, she wanted to come with only his lips on her. She'd never climaxed with just a man eating her out before and without a toy or his fingers to assist.

He was a great kisser, but his mouth was put to better use right where it was. Because her orgasm was building...

"Make me come," she begged. "Make me come, Rev. Make me..." Something shot out of her mouth and it could've been the devil fleeing during an exorcism... She didn't know. She didn't care.

But *holy, holy, holy hell....*

She shoved her face into the bed and smothered the scream from how intense the climax was that he caused. He didn't let up, he continued to lick, suck and nibble until she couldn't take any more. Until her clit was so sensitive and swollen, she whimpered and begged him to stop. As soon as he did, he took a fistful of her hair and guided her to a stand, spun her around and glued his lips to hers one more time.

She had not been expecting that. Her own taste on her tongue, on her lips. He kissed her until they were both forced to break free and gasp for air. He grabbed her under her arms and lifted her just enough to toss her onto the bed where she landed in the middle with a bounce.

He stood at the edge, his erection now an angry color and protruding straight out from his body like a javelin.

She took in his glistening lips, his shiny whiskers and his *cat-who-ate-the-canary* smile. "You are now my favorite meal," he announced, then swiped his mouth and chin with his hand.

"Better than Dino's loaded fries?"

"Never heard of them," he teased but in a serious tone, putting one knee on the bed, then the other, the mattress rocking as his weight shifted.

She couldn't pull her eyes from where his fist pumped his almost-purple cock.

"Spread your legs and bend your knees."

Everything inside her quivered at that order. He wasn't being dominant, but he *was* being demanding.

And she liked it. No, she fucking *loved* it.

Holy hell, she should've kidnapped him months ago and dragged him to some motel where no one could find them! She'd been going without him, without this, for *months* while he fucked sweet butts and other randoms!

Gah! The best sex she'd had in over a year was with her damn Rabbit! More than a year, because before that she had been dealing with the undead douchebag and all of his douchebaggery.

What. The. Actual. Fuck!

"Twelve!" exploded out of her mouth.

He paused while ripping open a condom wrapper and his brow wrinkled. "Twelve what?"

Oh my God, she hadn't planned on releasing that into the universe. "Just... Just carry on."

He didn't. Instead, he narrowed his eyes on her. "Twelve what, Reilly? Twelve cracks upside my head with that damn club if anyone finds out about this? Yeah, you're probably right."

"No. Not that."

"Twelve what, then?" He cocked an eyebrow, ignoring

the latex disc now in his fingers. He would probably continue to ignore it until she explained.

"Orgasms. You owe me twelve."

His other eyebrow joined the first one high up on his forehead. "How the fuck do I owe you twelve?"

She flapped a hand around. "Just hurry up and put that on."

He glanced down at the condom in his hand, then back to her face. "Ain't doin' shit 'til you explain."

She squeezed her eyes shut and sighed. Then she realized if her eyes were closed, she couldn't see his delicious body. And, *for shit's sake*, it was damn delicious. She was hungry for it. Starving, in fact.

"One orgasm for every month I went without."

"Without what?"

"Having sex with you. Just... Ignore me. Well, don't ignore me, ignore my random outburst." She reached up, grabbed his nipple and tweaked it. His body jolted in response and his cock flexed.

At least that got him moving. He quickly rolled the condom over his cock that looked ready to burst open like a can of breakfast biscuits. "Gonna take it slow at first, 'cause I'm already ready to bust a fuckin' nut—"

"Less words, more action," she urged, then bit her bottom lip as he moved to settle between her thighs.

"You're fuckin' tellin' *me* to talk less?"

She giggle-snorted. This was no time for jokes. Hell no. Not with him settling his weight between her thighs and putting those nipple piercings within range of her mouth.

And fingers.

The hot crown of his cock poked her inner thigh. She shifted her hips in encouragement.

"Gonna take it slow, babe. Tellin' you now... Been waitin' for this far too fuckin' long..."

He had?

She smiled up at him.

He frowned. "You owe *me* twelve fuckin' orgasms. And I expect to collect."

"I like to pay my debts," she assured him, her smile turning toothy.

"Good. 'Cause you're gonna pay. Might collect some interest, too."

"I can work off the interest. I'm good with my mouth."

"Better if you shut up now, woman."

She could do that, all she needed was his nipple in her mouth and she'd gladly stop talking. "I've got one more thing to say…"

"Christ…"

"Fuck me."

His irritation quickly changed to relief. "Was plannin' on it."

Her hips shot up when the thick crown bumped against her sensitive, slick flesh. Then his hand drove between them, sliding the head back and forth, nudging her open, finding *the* spot.

She held her breath and his blue eyes held hers.

"We do this. Ain't no goin' back," came his unnecessary warning.

Seriously? He was *right there!*

"Yes, you're right, we should rethink this," she said dryly, lifted her hips and speared herself on his cock.

Something in his face changed. Surprise maybe? Whatever it was, she wasn't going to worry about it right now. Nope, not right now. She had better things to do.

Like appreciate how full and complete she felt with him inside her.

"Fuck, babe," he breathed, his face going soft and his eyelids lowering halfway.

"Don't close your eyes," she begged, desperately trying not to throw her head back and close her own.

"Fuck no. Wanna watch you."

"Watch me do what?"

"Come."

"You need to do a lot more than just pump into me once for that. The way you're constantly pumping into those sweet butts, you'd think—"

He slapped his hand over her mouth and gave her a warning look.

She blinked once in a silent signal that she hoped he recognized as her accepting his warning and wouldn't bring up those women again. At least not right now while he was inside her.

He stared at her a few more seconds before removing his hand. "Not a fuckin' word, Reilly. Not one. Or I'm pullin' out, puttin' you over my knee and spankin' your ass."

"*Oooh.* Can we do that later?" she whispered, excited at that prospect.

"That was supposed to deter you from sayin' shit. Shoulda known nothin' will shut you up but my dick in your mouth."

"Add that to the list," she said, trying not to laugh.

"How 'bout I do this, instead?" He dropped to his elbows, stole her mouth, and began to move his hips in a slow, rolling rhythm.

Wrapping her legs around his hips and digging her heels into the backs of his thighs, she tilted her pelvis to drive him even deeper, so he hit all the right spots. It was sensory over-load with the way his cock was filling her, their tongues were mating and his bare chest brushing against her peaked nipples.

She groaned into his mouth, lifting her hips to meet each of his thrusts with one of her own. Her hands grabbed his ass, feeling the firm muscles flex beneath her fingers. She curled them and scraped her nails over his heated skin, then up his back and neck. Grabbing the back of his neck with one hand, she wormed the other between the press of their bodies to find the warm metal dividing his pebbled nipple.

She flicked at it with her finger, wondering what he liked the most. Wondering who else had experienced them. Since she'd never seen him with his shirt off, she guessed he only removed it when he was in private, when he wasn't doing the deed in the middle of The Barn or out in the courtyard.

She wanted to know when he got them and why. Had he liked his nipples played with before getting them? Or only now that he had them?

His moan erupted into her mouth when she got a good hold of the left barbell and twisted it hard. His hips surged and stuttered, then he began to power up and into her faster and more frantically. She released his neck so she could concentrate on both of his nipples. Twisting and teasing, flicking and tugging.

Every one of his reactions to her manipulation causing a reaction within her.

He broke his mouth free and turned his head to the side, closing his eyes and panting. "Supposed to be goin' slow."

"You *were* going slow," she complained. Too damn slow.

"Need to not play with them right now."

Damn. She was like a child about to have her toy taken away. "Can I add that to the list, too?"

He sighed and jammed his cock inside her harder, making her body rock. "Yeah, add that to the fuckin' list," he pushed through gritted teeth.

"That list will keep us busy for a while."

"Not if I strangle you first." When her mouth opened, he growled, "Ain't addin' that to the fuckin' list. Ain't into that shit."

"Good. Me neither."

His hips stilled and he pushed himself up, holding her gaze with a tight, unhappy expression. "Someone strangled you?"

She didn't even need to answer, it only took him a few seconds to figure it out on his own.

"Fuck," he whispered, his jaw going rock solid. He drew in one long inhale, then another.

"Dead douchebags aren't allowed in this room right now."

He closed his eyes and muttered another, "Fuck."

He dug his elbows back into the mattress and used both hands to brush her hair away from her face as he stared down at her. She noticed when his eyes flicked briefly to the scar at her temple before they landed on her lips for a second, then he met her eyes again.

"Eleven more orgasms might take a while," he said seriously.

"I have faith in you."

"Least someone does," he whispered.

"Wait a sec… *Eleven* more? No, twelve! You're not cheating me out of an orgasm."

His jaw softened and he shook his head slightly. "Then let's bang some of them out, buttercup."

"Oh yes, let's."

And that's what they did. He managed to give her two on her back before rolling them both until she was on top. She straddled him, his cock as deep as it could get, and stared down at him.

He was so fucking beautiful, but it was his eyes that made her heart swell. They could say so much without him even speaking a word. She could read it in his face that he'd wanted this almost for as long as she had. This was not how he looked when he was bending a sweet butt over a bus bench or a picnic table or even The Barn's bar. He looked at her differently.

If she didn't know better, she'd think it was a mix of respect and awe. She was glad he respected her, which is why he held out from fucking her at first. But the second one… The awe part she didn't understand.

She also didn't understand how he didn't turn out to be some lunatic with how he was raised. If anyone knew psychos, it was her. Billy Warren had used his fake and practiced charm to draw her in and once he got his claws in her, he showed his true self. His monster was released.

It reminded her of being coaxed into a trap and, once you were lured in and the trap snapped shut, it was about impossible to get free.

Death was one way. And she'd come close to it twice.

But right now she was very much alive, and Rev had just given her one awesome orgasm with his mouth and two more with his very awesome cock, proving he was no selfish asshole like the dead douchebag.

Only ten orgasms to go.

"Why you smilin' like that?"

"Maybe it's because you have a nice cock."

His lips twitched slightly. "You seen it before."

"Too many times to count, but seeing it and experiencing it are two different things. I'm lucky…"

"Ain't you that's lucky, babe."

She sat still, loving the satisfying stretch and the occasional impatient flex of his cock inside her. "I don't know," she murmured, "I'm thinking I got the better end of this pact."

"Then you're seein' it through the wrong eyes. Should see what I'm lookin' at."

That was the kind of stuff the dead douchebag would say to make her think he cared when he didn't. It was all an act. A way to suck her in and put his foot in the door, and for her to let her guard down. In reality, he only cared about himself and draining her accounts dry. He was an expert at fleecing women and then abusing them when they didn't cooperate. Something she didn't know until she found out firsthand.

But Rev had no reason to lie. He'd worked with her for a year, he knew what she went through, he was there the last time Billy tried to kill her. *And* he knew only one word from her after this could risk his life and everything he had.

He meant what he said. While she needed to resist falling from lust into something deeper with him, his words still made her feel very wanted and more than worthy.

"Where have you been hiding, Rev?" she whispered.

He frowned. "What d'you mean? Hidin' what? My scars?"

"No."

"My past?"

"No."

"Then what?"

"That little bit of sweetness you keep sprinkling on me like powdered sugar."

"Christ," he muttered, but the corners of his eyes crinkled like he was fighting a smile or an annoyed grimace. "Ain't sweet. Now, you gonna ride my cock so we can scratch that off your fuckin' list?"

"Can I twist your nipples now?"

"Don't do it 'til you're ready for me to blow."

"Got it. They're like launch buttons."

"Woman…" He grabbed her hips and his whole body shook beneath her, which meant his cock vibrated inside her, almost pulling a groan from her.

She rolled her eyes. "Oh, all right. I'll fuck you if I must." She pressed the back of her hand against her forehead and bemoaned, "Such a freaking chore!"

"Gonna find yourself on your back again in a damn second." His grumpy growl was clearly fake.

She dropped down and brushed her lips over his, then paused as they shared a breath. She moved on, kissing down his neck, circling his Adam's apple with her tongue and then sucking at the hollow of his throat.

She moaned against his heated skin. "Why do you taste so damn good?"

"Cheap motel soap."

She peppered kisses down and across his tattooed chest, pressing kisses as light as a butterfly landing on a flower to the very tips of his nipples.

Using her tongue, she flicked one platinum barbell and then the other, causing everything on him to quiver, including his buried cock.

The man was so fucking sexy she almost couldn't stand it.

She wrapped her lips around his right nipple and sucked it into her mouth, using the tip of her tongue to play with the piercing.

"What'd I tell you?" he groaned.

"I'm not twisting them," she insisted, her words muffled around the flesh now gently caught between her teeth.

"Reilly…"

She gasped when he grabbed both of her nipples and did exactly what she wanted to do to his. He twisted them. Hard. That sent a bolt of lightning straight down to her clit and beyond. She began to rock, grinding it into his pubis, still toying with his hardware with her tongue.

"Jesus fuck," he grunted.

"I want to come one more time, then—I'm warning you now—I'm twisting the fuck out of those bad boys."

He grunted again as she rocked back and forth and then ground in circles. She put her hands over his and encouraged him to twist her nipples again. Her breath shot out of her as she rose and then slammed down on top of him, making his torso lift and his knees rise to the point where he almost folded into a V.

He rolled both of her nipples between his fingers and

murmured, "That's it, babe, come all over me. Goddamn wrap…"

As much as she hated having that between them, too, at this point, there was no way they were going without one.

"I'm close," she whispered. "So… close…"

She fell forward again, dislodging his hands from her breasts and claimed his lips, sweeping her tongue through his mouth, while reaching down and nabbing his nipples again. She was so close to her third and final destination that she knew she'd come the moment he did.

With the metal bars between her fingers, she cranked them. His back bowed off the bed at the same time she slammed down on his cock.

Rev shouted a loud, "Fuck!" as his face twisted and his muscles turned to concrete. Knowing he was about to come shoved her right over and she cried out his name when a grunt exploded from him and they both did a freefall at the same time. Her pussy gripped him firmly and didn't want to let go as his latex-covered cock pulsed inside her.

For a second she thought she was having an out-of-body experience and she was floating above their bodies. Because, *phew*…

Four damn orgasms. A record for her.

She could easily get used to that. But then, at only twenty-eight, Rev still had a lot of gas in his tank.

She collapsed like one of those red, inflatable dancing tube men after someone pulled the plug, and melted into him, his damp, heaving chest a pillow for her cheek. She smiled when his arms wrapped around her and he planted his hands possessively on her ass cheeks, kneading her flesh gently. His quick, ragged breath stirred the hair by her ear.

"Okay, that was much better than my Rabbit."

Using his fingers, he pulled damp strands of hair away from her face. She tipped it up so she could see his more clearly.

"Much better than my fist. Kinda gettin' an idea of what a Rabbit is. Would like to watch you use it on yourself."

"No, you don't. I promise, it's not a pretty sight. But it gets the job done when there's no one else to do it."

He made a noise deep within his throat.

"Am I crushing you?" she asked. She hoped not since she liked being sprawled on top of him like that. Still connected. Rising and falling with each breath he took.

"No."

"You're still hard."

"Yeah."

"You won't be for long."

"Won't take me long to recover. Never does. We could knock out a few more of those orgasms I owe you before the night's over. Then you can work on givin' me my dozen. I got some ideas…" He gave her a lazy grin.

"I might need some pizza first."

"Pizza and pussy. Sounds fuckin' perfect." He paused. "Reilly…"

"Yeah?"

"Gonna make it clear right now… You ain't sleepin' anywhere but in my bed 'til this is over."

Until what was over? "This trip?"

"Yeah. The time we got here. 'Til we gotta go."

Ah, yes, until they were back to reality. Right now she was in no hurry to get back there, but reality rushed in when he began to slip from her.

He rolled her back over, finished pulling free and quickly removed the full condom. He knotted the end and tucked it into a take-out napkin on the nightstand. He shifted back into place and stared down into her face.

"I need to clean up," she whispered.

"In a few. Like where I am."

"I like where you are, too, but we *could* share a shower. Do you feel dirty?" She wiggled her eyebrows at him.

"So fuckin' dirty," he teased back. "But no point in cleanin' up yet, you're gonna get messy again soon."

"With pizza crumbs?"

He snorted. "Gonna feed you somethin' and it ain't pizza."

Her eyes went wide. "Garlic knots?"

He sighed and rolled off her, snagging his phone off the nightstand. "Christ, woman, let me get you fed before you chew off my damn limbs."

"It doesn't mean I'm not hungry for a certain appetizer before the main meal's delivered."

He stopped scrolling through his phone and glanced up. "Was gonna pick it up, but you just changed my mind."

"Delivery has its perks."

"Sometimes you're all right, buttercup," he said as he continued his online search for a local pizza joint. "You might be worth takin' a couple clubs over the head."

"Just a couple?"

"Gonna re-evaluate after I get my dozen orgasms."

"Hopefully you don't expect them all tonight since you only have two more condoms."

"Don't need wraps for some of what I got planned." He lifted his head, shot her a grin, then put the phone to his ear and ordered pizza.

Hours later, their bellies were full, they were sexually sated and had plans to stop for more condoms on their way to Media the next morning.

The man was like a damn Energizer Bunny. In a short amount of time, he not only paid his debt, he began to bank interest.

Chapter Eleven

AFTER STOPPING for a big breakfast and a large box of wraps, his Bronco was now backed up to a small storage unit located in Media, about forty minutes from the motel. Reilly had been abnormally quiet for the whole ride and now stood staring at the front of the blue roll-up door with the key in her hand.

She'd been standing there ever since he opened the rear of his truck, so they'd be able to easily load whatever she wanted to keep. Luckily, the storage place had dumpsters to unload anything she deemed not worth hauling home. But with the size of the unit, he couldn't imagine she had a lot of shit to begin with.

She turned the silver key over and over within her fingers and her bottom lip was crushed between her teeth. Rev plucked the key from her hand and unlocked the padlock.

She blew out a loud breath behind him. "It feels like I'm stepping back into a past life."

To him, it was simply a storage unit. Unfortunately to her, it was more. "Ain't a magic door, babe. Ain't a portal. That fucker will never touch you again. You never got to even say his name. This is just one last piece to deal with so you can finish movin' on."

This morning, over coffee and two orders of the Belly Buster Breakfast Special, she had told him that she'd never gone back to her apartment after her hospital stay. Her sister had hired movers to pack up Reilly's personal shit and put it in storage. Reese had only grabbed some basics from her place before shuttling her off to Mansfield the second Reilly was discharged.

Reese was fucking smart to get her sister the fuck out of the area. Especially after that dangerous fucknut made bail and then ghosted.

It was bad enough the motherfucker had almost snuffed out Reilly's life, but he'd also stole the little money she had managed to save. She didn't have much to begin with but after Warren was done, she had nothing. Her bank accounts were scraped clean and her sole credit card maxed out. Since Reese moved Reilly into her house to hide her and keep her safe, Reilly also lost her job and her apartment.

Reese had stepped in and taken care of everything, but then, Deacon's woman had tight control of her own life and taking care of Reilly wasn't anything new to her. Reilly might get annoyed at Reese's smothering sometimes, but her older sister had been there for her from the moment she was born.

She did for Reilly what Rev had wished he had done for Saylor. Taken her from birth and raised her on his own. While Reese had no other choice, Rev had two "functioning" parents and didn't know things weren't "normal" until much later. When it was already too late.

"Okay, you can open it now." She pulled him from his thoughts.

Rev rolled up the door and revealed the interior. He expected it to be packed solid since it was such a small unit. It wasn't. Besides a few appliances like a toaster oven and a microwave, most of the contents were boxes. *For fuck's sake,* none of those fucking boxes were marked.

"Would say we'll just load everythin' up, then you and Reese can go through them once we're back in Manning Grove but all that shit ain't gonna fit in my Bronco. So, if you want this to be once and done, gonna need you to figure out what you want and what you don't."

He couldn't imagine she would want to return a second time since Media was almost four hours from home. That would be a hell of a haul for a few more knickknacks.

Reilly also wanted to empty the storage unit today and turn in the key so Reese was no longer obligated to pay that monthly bill.

"I didn't have much since my apartment came furnished. Some of the stuff I might be able to sell at the consignment shop back home to get a little extra cash to give to Reese, but there's no point in hauling things home if they need to be thrown out."

It would help if they got a system in place. "How 'bout you go through each box, then tell me to either load it up or take it out to the dumpster?"

She considered the stacked boxes and nodded slightly. "Okay."

He stepped in front of her, forcing her to look up at him. He grabbed her hands and held them to his chest. "Babe... Let's just get it done and over with, then once we shut that door, it's fuckin' shut for the final time, if you know what I'm sayin'."

She nodded again; her face paler than normal. "I do."

"If it's easier, I can throw all this shit out and you don't have to touch any of it."

She glanced past him into the unit. "No, I have clothes and boots... My books and electronics... Stuff I've been without for the past year."

"But you've borrowed or bought other shit. You've done without anythin' in this unit for the last year."

"Not by choice. I won't let that dead douchebag steal anything else from me. And by dumping everything I own, that's what he'd be doing. Even from beyond the grave."

Rev didn't want to remind her that the asshole didn't have a grave. He'd been plowed into the dirt and the only thing left of him was her memories.

He turned and considered the contents of the unit. "Any clothes you're keepin', right?"

"Yes, as long as I still fit in them." She sighed. "I might not."

"Ain't gonna try everythin' on now. Any clothes you find, we'll take. If we run outta room, we'll get pickier. Yeah?"

She nodded. "I can always donate the clothes to a shelter after we get home."

He clapped his hands together sharply once just like Trip sometimes did to get everyone's attention. "Okay, let's do this. Wanna stop at the house on the way back to the motel later. Check on that fucker's progress."

Matthew was supposed to text him if things seemed close to the end, but Rev didn't trust the man to do it now that his uncle knew why Rev had come home.

He probably regretted ever tracking Rev down.

They made fast work of the boxes at the front of the unit. Reilly was moving quickly, opening and digging through them, pulling out shit she could toss and even combining some boxes.

She would finish with one and say "toss" or "keep" and he'd either take the shit to the dumpster or his Bronco. His Ford had a decent amount of space, but not as much as a full-sized pickup and the cargo room it did have was filling up fast.

Fitting the boxes inside the back was like a fucking puzzle. He found a spot for a box of kitchen shit, then turned, "Babe, you gotta be more selective, gonna run out of space."

With her face ghost white, she was squatting next to an open box at the back of the unit, staring inside.

What the fuck?

"Reilly," he called out as he zig-zagged through the remaining boxes in the unit to get to her. Stepping up to her back, he glanced down and just about lost his fucking shit. "What the fuck! Your sister didn't make sure that stuff was thrown the fuck out?"

"She told them to pack everything but the furniture. She was too busy taking care of me… Like normal," she said in a flat whisper.

With boxes blocking him, he couldn't get around her to block her view of the contents, so he leaned over, grabbed her under her arm pits, hauled her to her feet and pinned her to his chest. Without releasing her, he took a few steps backward until they could no longer see the bloody items in the box. Shit that had been splattered with her blood during the beating had been tossed into a box instead of being cleaned or thrown away.

She was stiff in his arms as he held her with one arm supporting her just below her breasts and the other across her belly to make sure she didn't collapse.

Reilly was a strong woman, but having that reminder thrown in her face, especially when she wasn't expecting it, had to fuck with her head.

"Let's go," he whispered, backing out of the unit, careful not to trip.

"We're not done." Again, her voice sounded flat. Lost.

He turned her around in his arms and saw her eyes were just as dead as her tone.

"You're done here," he insisted.

"No—"

"Yes, Reilly, you're fuckin' done." He had no idea how

many more boxes had bloody items in them, or even if one contained the object Warren used to create that scar, whatever fucking knickknack he used in an attempt to bash in her brains.

For all he knew, it could've been more than one object.

No matter how many boxes contained tainted items— even if only that one—she would not be forced to go through them. He'd do it on his own. *Fuck that shit.*

"Let's go." He shuffled her out of the unit and into the passenger seat of the Bronco. He leaned in and latched her seatbelt for her, slammed her door shut and ran to the rear of the Bronco to secure both it and the unit before getting her the fuck out of there.

Then they drove the forty minutes back to the motel with only road noise, the rumble of the engine and the satellite radio playing rock filling the Ford's interior.

The whole way, he kept sneaking glances at her, but she had her face turned toward the passenger side window, watching the landscape pass by as he took the roads leading back to their motel.

It was early enough that he could drop her back off at the room and head back down to the unit to finish. If he threw out shit she needed, oh fucking well, she could buy new shit. Putting her through the trauma of her seeing her own damn blood on her own damn possessions was completely un-fucking-necessary. He'd deal with it and spare her that.

It was too bad that motherfucker was already dead, because he really wanted to fucking kill him. He'd squeezed the steering wheel tightly, wishing it was Warren's throat. He couldn't stop imagining him being the one to punch the man unconscious that day at the garage instead of Deacon.

Deacon had struck Warren using his right hand for what he'd done to Reese and his left for what he'd done to Reilly.

It wasn't until Warren was unconscious and Deke's hands were a raw, bloody mess that he stopped.

Rev had missed most of that since he had been inside the garage with Reese and Reilly, keeping them from going out back, getting in the middle of it and killing Warren themselves.

But, in the end, Reilly had been Warren's judge, jury and executioner instead of Deacon. Rightfully so, since the bastard had broken her arm and nose, cracked open her face and head, plus left behind a permanent reminder she had to see in the mirror every damn day.

That was enough to make her *just a bit* pissed about it.

Only right now, she wasn't pissed. She was being swallowed up by the past. He knew it bothered her that she had allowed a piece of shit like Warren into her life and let him take advantage of her when she was not that type of woman.

Maybe that affected her more than the violence itself. That might be one of the reasons she avoided talking about Warren at all. It embarrassed her when it really fucking shouldn't.

Either way, she shouldn't dwell on hindsight. They all could get caught up with wishing they'd done or seen things differently before it was too late.

Unfortunately, life wasn't that fucking easy or clear. It was a deep mud puddle that sometimes sucked your boots in so deeply, it was a struggle to get free.

Warren had the skills to suck Reilly in. He had honed those skills with many women prior to her.

He shuttled her into the motel room—relieved the housekeeper had already been in their room for the day—stripped her down to her panties, tossed one of his T-shirts over her head and tucked her into bed.

All without a fight from her.

That was not like her. No words? No spark? Definitely not her normal Reilly-self.

It worried him. And not just a little bit.

Worse, he couldn't call the one person who might be able to snap her out of it. Calling her older sister would cause a lot of grief and then turn a mess into a complete disaster.

Hopefully, she'd soon snap out of whatever shock she'd fallen into.

He'd never seen her this down. That made him wonder how deeply she'd been burying what happened that day in her apartment.

"Why don't you just sleep for a bit?" he suggested. "We were up most of the night, you're probably exhausted." He tucked the bedding around her and leaned over to brush a kiss across her forehead.

As he pulled away, her hand shot out and grabbed his wrist, stopping him. "Where are you going?" Her question held much more panic than it should.

"Back to the unit to finish goin' through the boxes and load them in the truck."

"Don't leave!"

Fuck. He didn't want to leave her, either, but… "Need to get that shit done, babe. Not sure how long we're gonna be here. If I finish it today, we can hit the road as soon as my father bites it." Which he hoped was within the next couple of days.

"I don't want you to leave," she whispered.

The bed dipped when he sat on the edge, grabbed the remote and turned on the TV. He flipped through the channels, bypassing anything with blood, guts and gore and found some sappy-assed, kissy-face movie. Some chick flick.

He knew what else might help her. Normally he kept that shit in his cut, but he hadn't worn his cut once since leaving Manning Grove. One reason being, he was driving a cage instead of his sled. He also didn't want to wear it at his parents' house and get questions he wanted to avoid. Because it had a "Manning Grove" patch right on the front, it might also give them an idea on where to look for Saylor.

It was bad enough Matthew had found the info where he worked. He did not want them, none of them, trying to contact her.

But another important reason was, a Pagans MC support club had territory in the southeast of Pennsylvania and he did not want to step on any other club's toes, possibly causing issues. Especially since he'd be a lone Fury member versus a club of rivals. Out of courtesy and respect, most MC members gave a heads up before entering another MC's territory whenever possible.

If another club rolled into Manning Grove and didn't keep moving, Trip would have a problem with it. They all would. It was one thing to simply be riding through, it was another to stop and stay any length of time without permission. Doing so could be considered a threat.

Since the Blood Fury, Dirty Angels and Dark Knights MCs controlled all the territory on the western side of the state, and were allies, they were careful about who else might be in the area. Territory grabs were a real threat. The DAMC had way too many issues with a former nomad club called the Shadow Warriors. A decades-long war all three allies would like to prevent in the future.

She made a sharp noise and grabbed his wrist tighter when he stood up. "Ain't goin' nowhere," he said softly. "Just gonna run out to the truck and grab somethin' that's gonna help." He didn't want to leave it in their room while they were gone, so he had removed it from his backpack and hid it in his truck.

He was out and back within a couple of minutes with his tin full of hand-rolled cigarettes, a small baggie of quality weed and a metal pipe in his hands. Her green eyes followed his every movement as he removed his boots, climbed onto the bed with her and sat up against the head-board. As he packed the pipe, she curled up against him, laying her head in his lap.

Christ, she looked way too good there. Like she belonged in and owned that spot. In a bed, wearing a shirt that smelled like him, blinking those green fucking eyes up at him filled with all that damn trust.

He suddenly saw what could be if she wasn't who she was. If she didn't have a red warning label slapped right in the middle of her damn forehead.

If he could, he'd strip down and join her under the sheets, but he really wanted to get the storage unit dealt with so she could put it out of her mind. And he wanted to get the fuck out of Coatesville as soon as he could.

He lit the bowl and took a long hit, letting the smoke fill his lungs before blowing it up and away from her.

"C'mere, babe," he murmured, pulling her up by her elbow to face him. He took another hit, not inhaling this time, but filling his mouth. He cupped her face with his free hand and pushed their mouths together. She opened hers automatically and when he sealed his to hers, she stole all the smoke, inhaled it and managed to hold it for longer than he expected.

He'd take one hit, share the next, until they were both a hell of a lot more relaxed and zen-like. Rev was also ready for some cold, leftover pizza from last night. He was pretty damn sure it had turned to cardboard but he might be willing to gnaw on it for a while like a dog with a bone.

When they were done with the bowl, she settled back down onto her side, using his lap as a pillow again. He stroked her hair until her eyelids got heavy and finally closed. He didn't stop until she went totally limp and her breathing became deep and heavy.

Just listening to her made the sleep pull at him, too.

They'd spent half the night fucking and making each other come in a variety of really fucking fun ways. Because of that, he could use a few hours of solid sleep, too.

But it could wait. He'd head back down to Media, then come straight back. To fuck with checking in on his father today. If the fucker died before tomorrow morning, then so fucking be it. Reilly came first and with his asshole sire's death, at least that part of his life would be over with, too.

Two doors closing. For him, on his youth and for her, her time living near Philly and her past with Billy Warren. Once those doors slammed shut, neither had to step through them ever again. The past would remain the past and they'd have nothing but the future to look forward to.

They just wouldn't have a future with each other.

He lightly traced the thin scar that ran along her right temple by her eye and barely missed her cheek. Her face she saw as flawed wasn't, to him the now soft and relaxed face framed by blonde hair was flawless. Perfect, even.

She'd find someone else. Someone not tied to the club, and he'd...

Continue doing what he'd already been doing.

Fucking randoms.

Fucking sweet butts.

And waking up alone every morning.

The last two mornings were the only times he'd woken up with someone else in his bed. Not counting the morning his mother dragged him out of Sarah's bed by his hair.

He grabbed the motel-branded notepad and pen from the drawer and scribbled out a note, telling her he'd be back ASAP. He left a full pipe on the nightstand, along with a spare lighter from his backpack on top of the note.

He quietly tugged on his boots and headed out the door.

He wanted to get this shit done as quickly as he could and get back to her. Preferably before she woke up and found him gone.

—————

Rev steered his Bronco into the parking spot in front of their room. He was fucking exhausted and really wanted to just eat, then sleep. But Reilly was in his bed again tonight, so he wasn't sure if that would happen. He might have to just dig deep if she was in the mood to do a repeat of last night.

He hoped she was. He didn't want to miss out on even one night of getting naked with her, but, more importantly, it would mean she was out of her funk.

No light could be seen through the narrow gap in the wide vertical blinds, but he could see flashes, which meant the TV was still on.

He opened the driver's door, turned sideways in his seat and took a last couple puffs on his hand-rolled before flicking the remainder of the cigarette out into the dark parking lot. He blew the smoke up toward the night sky and stepped out, glancing back at his now packed Bronco.

He'd stuffed his truck to the point where he could no longer see out over the boxes in the back seat and would have to use his side mirrors to see behind him when he drove. He'd taken whatever he thought she could use or anything that he guessed might mean something to her and sorted out the rest.

He was fucking shocked at just how many items he found with blood splatter on them. Her apartment had to have looked like a murder scene by the time she was hauled away by the EMTs.

Thank fuck it ended up only being an "attempt" instead of an actual successful murder.

If he knew where her old apartment complex was located, he'd head over there, knock on her neighbors' doors and thank them for stepping in when they could have easily ignored it like a lot of people would.

Thank fuck good people did exist in the world. It gave him some hope.

His life had begun to look up when he landed the job at Dutch's Garage, then got to prospect for the newly resurrected Blood Fury MC. Manning Grove, the fucking snow and frigid temps in winter aside, was a great town. Great for him and even better for Saylor.

This shit with Reilly, though…

Yeah, it would only be a temporary thing.

Would it have to be? Would he want something more? Could he feel out Deacon and Reese about it? See what their reaction would be?

Or would that cause a bunch of suspicion and him getting fucked up the ass and not in a good way?

The problem was, he'd only fucked her one night. He also had to work with her, at least for now until she decided to move on to a bigger, better job, one in which she could put her college degree to use.

To approach Deke and Reese, there would have to be more between them than only a casual hookup. At this point, he wasn't sure if he was ready to take that step. Not because of Reilly, but because of him. One nut-draining night with Reilly didn't mean he was ready to claim her at the table, either.

Getting naked with her had been fun. For both of them. Maybe it wouldn't ever go any farther than that.

A fun, friendly fuck.

Friends with bennies.

Reese might not have such a shit fit about him fucking Reilly if Rev offered her sister his cut. Then she would be the only woman on the back of his sled and also in his bed. He couldn't imagine Reese could argue that, especially since she let Deacon claim her. Otherwise, she'd be a fucking hypocrite.

But they'd need to be serious.

They weren't serious.

Yeah, they'd had the hots for each other and the sex had been banging. But right now, that was all it was. A forbidden, secret fling in a motel in Coatesville, Pennsylvania. The second he pointed his Bronco north, it would be over and need to be forgotten.

He stared at the motel room door with his keycard paused over the slot.

Because, *fuck that*, he wasn't ready to settle down. He bet Reilly wasn't, either.

With her at only twenty-five and him at twenty-eight, they both had a lot more exploring to do before getting tied down.

He unlocked the door and slipped inside, surprised to find her curled up under the covers with her eyes still closed. The TV volume so low it was being used as white noise.

He stepped over to the nightstand and saw the pipe's bowl still full. But the bottle of water he left for her was half empty. That meant she hadn't slept straight through.

He sat on the spare bed and blindly unlaced his boots since he was too busy staring at her while she slept. Once he had them kicked off and his socks tucked inside, he stood, yanked his T-shirt up over his head and quietly dropped his jeans.

He slid in next to her and curled his arms around her, pressing his nose into her hair, just enjoying her heat and softness against him.

She pulled her head back and opened her eyes. "You're back," she murmured, sleepily.

"Yeah, it's done. Emptied the unit and gave the key back to the office. No reason to ever go back there again."

She stared at him for a few heartbeats then, with her lips slightly turned down, whispered, "Sorry."

Christ. This was *not* Reilly. Not her at all. "For what?"

"For letting it get to me. I just wasn't expecting… It was stupid."

"Wasn't stupid. Can't help how it made you feel. Own it, recognize what it is and then scrape it off. You're allowed to let that shit bother you, babe, just don't let it drown you. And, anyway, it would bother anyone. Truth? It fuckin' bothered me and I wasn't even there."

"If you were, it never would've happened."

If he was, she never would have been with Warren in the first place. "Yeah, well… Can't go back in time." He wished he could. He would've done a lot of shit differently.

She probably would have, too.

"What a fucking idiot I was to trust him. I was wary of him at first. I kept resisting but he kept coming into where I worked and… working me." She covered her face with both hands. "Damn it!"

Holy fuck, was she going to cry? He hoped like fuck she wasn't going to cry. He'd never once seen her cry. Not once. She couldn't do it now. He wouldn't know what to do.

"Don't cry," he urged in a panic. It was bad enough when he had a hard time getting Sarah to stop crying. In fact, he usually failed. His sister would only stop once she fell asleep in his arms and it broke his fucking heart every damn time. It also made him feel helpless.

She dropped her hands and blinked at him. "I'm not crying."

Oh thank fuck.

"I'm pissed at how damn stupid and foolish I was. He made me his mark and I let him."

"He was a fuckin' pro at it. You weren't the only one he did it to, Reilly. You fit his M.O., that's all. And, of course, you caught his attention 'cause you're hot as fuck."

"But after that, Reese felt the need to go back to mothering me. Or *smothering* me. It was like she revoked my adulthood. It didn't help that I decided to stay in Manning Grove and work at the garage."

"She don't think it's good enough for you."

"Not for me. For my degree. One she paid for, mind you. I disappointed her in a couple of different ways."

"Need to make your own mistakes."

"I know she realizes that but I guess when your sister was close to being bludgeoned to death and sitting in a hospital bed hooked up to machines…" Reilly sighed.

"Yeah, the mother of all motherly instincts kicked in."

"I was all she had… Well, until Deacon."

"'Til all of us," he corrected her.

"Yes, that's probably one reason why she relented to me staying in Manning Grove, becoming a part of the club and working at the garage. She realized how much of a tight family the Fury was. Something we never had before since we only had each other. Okay, I had her. She never really had me to help her. I was a burden."

"Jesus fuck, woman, not once have I ever heard Reese say you were or are a fuckin' burden and you know that woman's opinionated as all fuck and not afraid to say shit. She fuckin' loves you. 'Cause of that, she's protective of you. She's like a momma lioness protectin' her damn cub." He blew out a breath. "What the fuck, I can't believe I'm defendin' her, but it's true. Everybody sees it and gets it. Here's the thing, we all gotta take care of each other. Blood or not. For some of us, the club's all we got. Someone needs somethin', we gotta step up and step in."

"Now you know why I insisted on coming along with you, why I didn't want you to do this alone. When someone we care about needs something, we need to step up and step in to help."

She just snared him with his own goddamn words, proving why he shouldn't have fought her coming along.

She was so much smarter than him. He was sure plenty

of people assumed by her being a hot, young blonde that she was some sort of airhead. She was far from that.

She was the complete fucking package and some man, someday, would be lucky to get stuck with her.

"It's also why you went back to the storage unit to finish what I couldn't."

"You could've done it, Reilly, but there was no point in puttin' you through that if it ain't necessary. But push come to fuckin' shove, you woulda buckled down and got it done. Got no fuckin' doubt about that."

"I'm glad you think so," she murmured.

He tucked a thumb under her chin and lifted her face until their gazes locked. "Don't think so, know so. Known you long enough now. Seen you in action. Know what you're capable of. You ain't stupid and you definitely ain't foolish."

"There you go sprinkling me with that powdered sugar again." She grabbed his cheeks between her fingers and squeezed them together. "Too damn sweet."

"Woman, I ain't fuckin' sweet! Stop sayin' that shit," he growled, jerking free of her grasp. He quickly smothered a smile when she laughed. He was relieved she was no longer in that weird funk.

And now she wasn't, they could move on. To other things…

Like much more pleasant shit.

But first, she might be hungry. He sure was. For her and for food in his stomach. "Wanna know if you're up for eatin'."

"When am I ever not up for eating?"

When you're in a zombie-like state, he answered in his head. But now that sass was back. "What are you in the mood for?"

She smiled up at him. "You."

"Well, ain't that funny. Hungry for you, too. But we're

gonna need real food sooner or later. Ain't eaten since breakfast."

"Hard to resist the delicious meal before me."

He ran a hand down his own chest. "That's right. Ain't no snack, I'm a satisfyin' meal that'll fill you up."

She rolled her eyes. "All right. Let's not go too far now."

In response, he rolled over her and took her mouth. It was a while before they both came up for air.

And for food.

It was all worth another sleepless night.

Chapter Twelve

REILLY WIGGLED against the hot steel pipe pressed into her ass crack. She had no idea what time it was but knew Rev hadn't gotten enough sleep since she had slept the afternoon away and he had not. After banging one out after he returned yesterday evening and then pigging out on takeout from a local Chinese restaurant, they spent a couple more hours taking their time with each other.

Sleep-deprived or not, Rev seemed to be revving to go again.

Reilly groaned as she stretched her tired and sore muscles, then rolled over to face the naked, ready man next to her...

Whose eyes were closed.

She gently nudged him to his back, slid over top of him and pulled the sheet over their heads, creating a cocoon around them.

Whether he was faking sleep or not at this point, she didn't know and, honestly, didn't care. This morning she was going to give back what he'd given to her. Quite a few times. And very satisfactorily, too.

Stretching up, she started at his left ear, running her

tongue around the outer shell and over the metal piercings that dissected it. After. sucking on his earlobe briefly, she continued on her journey. Her nose traveled along the short, wiry hairs covering his jawline, her eyes catching the glint of the small hoop in his nose.

He and Deacon were the only ones with nose piercings and both of them had it done before joining the Fury, so she had to assume it wasn't typical biker hardware. She guessed neither were their nipple rings.

She'd say Rev's nipples were her favorite part of him, but, truthfully, his tongue and his cock were hard to beat.

She paused over his parted mouth, her warm breath kissing his lips. Then she moved on again, keeping the sheet covering them both as she shifted down his body, forging a path with her tongue and lips. Tasting and teasing.

She took her time with one nipple, then the other. Not cranking or yanking them like he enjoyed when he was really worked up and ready to blow, but gently toying with his pierced flesh. Enough to stimulate but not enough to launch his rocket.

During all of this, his breathing hitched and changed slightly, but he said nothing, nor did he move. The few glances she snuck at his face showed his eyes still closed. She traveled down his abs, circled his belly button, then kissed along the happy trail of dark blond hair leading to her final destination.

His erection was hard, thick and rested on the heated skin below his navel, where a string of precum connected the crown of his cock to his lower belly. She collected the tangy, silky fluid on her tongue and kept going, skipping what he probably wanted her to touch the most and heading lower instead.

She wedged herself between his spread legs, kissing a line from one knee up along his lightly furred inner thigh, ignoring the apex, and back down his other thigh.

His cock flexed a couple times, almost as if beckoning her. She'd get there, it and the man attached would need a little patience. She had one stop to make first.

She nuzzled the soft, delicate skin of his sac, inhaling his now familiar and very manly scent, amazed at the heat radiating off him. With the sheet still tented over them both, the heat almost became too much, but she liked the coziness of their cocoon and the intimacy.

The idea that this was how it could be—waking up on a lazy weekend morning with a lover and taking time to appreciate each other—didn't go unnoticed.

Only this morning, she was taking the time to concentrate solely on him. She was sure he'd "appreciate" her later.

Taking his sac fully into her mouth, her tongue played along his balls as she lightly sucked. A low groan filled the enclosed space under the sheet. Without releasing him, she lifted her eyes to see his blue ones were now open and focused on her. On what she was doing.

"Fuck," he whispered huskily. His rough, unused morning voice sent a ribbon of heat swirling from the top of her head to the tip of her toes.

She mouthed his balls one more time, then released them, licking up the thick ridge on the underside of his cock. It flexed again and another drawn-out groan filled her ears.

"Fuck, babe."

A quick swipe of her tongue captured the ivory pearl that had begun to fall. She swirled her tongue around the rim of the bulbous head and circled the tip before shifting up and taking him completely into her mouth.

His breath shuddered and a noise caught in his throat as she swallowed him as deep as she could before wrapping her fingers around the base and squeezing. His fingers wove into her loose, messy hair, pulling tight, making her scalp sting, as she drew him in and out of her mouth. Only pausing to suck on the tip, then taking him as deep as she could all over again.

After a few more strokes, his hips began to rise and fall, following her rhythm, and the grip on her hair tightened to the point of making her eyes water, but she didn't slow down. She didn't stop.

"Fuck... babe... *Fuuuuck...*"

She took him even deeper until the head of his cock bumped the back of her throat and she managed not to gag, though her eyes watered. She could take him that deep two more times before she had to give herself more breathing room. Otherwise, she might not be able to finish him off.

He slipped from her mouth, slick and shiny, and she licked along the underside again, tracing the thick ridge. Down to the root, up to the rim. Down. Back up. He held her head still, bumped her lips with the slick crown, demanding entrance, and when she opened wide, he thrust inside as far as he could.

She did her best to stay with him as he continued to thrust upward, doing what the guys called face-fucking. He grunted each time he went deep, pulling her head down to meet each thrust.

She wasn't sure she'd be able to do much more, worrying she might have to tap out, but after a couple more times, he growled that he was about to come.

When his body bowed off the bed, thick, hot fluid painted the back of her throat and she managed to swallow it all down and suck him clean before he pulled free.

She took a few seconds to catch her breath and it took him a few more to loosen the fingers locked in her hair and for him to melt back into the mattress. She climbed up his body again, letting her peaked nipples brush along his heated skin, until they were face to face.

She blinked down at him and he blinked up at her.

After a few more seconds, he whispered, "Christ, woman."

She wanted to smile in triumph at his surprised but satisfied expression. She managed to keep an innocent, straight face. "Did you like that?"

"Loved it. Also hated it," he said seriously, "'cause I can't fuck you right now."

"I think you got your dozen."

"Yeah? And you got two dozen."

"I did?" She unleashed her smile. "Some of them are just a blur."

"You sayin' they weren't worth rememberin'?"

"We've just crammed a lot of fucking in a short amount of time." It was one marathon she hadn't minded being a participant in.

His lips twitched. "Yeah, we did. But we ain't done yet."

He brushed the hair away from her face. And once again, whenever he did that, his eyes flicked to her scar and his jaw tightened for a split second. If she wasn't looking for it, she would have missed it.

"Wanna fuckin' kiss you but not into tastin' my own cum."

"Pineapple."

"What?"

"Fruit is your friend. Especially pineapple," she explained. "The woman on the receiving end will thank you."

He cocked one eyebrow at her. "And you know that how?"

"This ain't my first rodeo," she said, keeping her tone serious. "Just so you know, women who like to go down on men talk about these tricks with each other. I'm surprised the sweet butts don't set out fruit platters around The Barn and the bunkhouse."

He lifted his head. "Say fuckin' what?"

"I said I'm surprised the sweet butts don't tell you guys about that trick as many times as they've had your dicks in their mouths."

"No, not that fuckin' part. The other."

"About women talking?" she repeated, purposely being obtuse.

"Nope. Not that, either."

"Then what?"

"The other part... About women who like to go down on men."

"Oh, that part."

"Yeah, *that* part."

She cocked her head, struggling to keep the amusement from her face. "Did it seem like that was my first time?"

He blinked.

"Hmm?" she prodded, doing her best not to burst out laughing at his expression.

"Woman," he growled, flipping her over and getting in her face.

Her smile finally broke free and she pinched his cheek. "Do you like getting your dick sucked?"

He frowned. "That even a question?"

"Then why can't women like sucking them without judgement?"

"Ain't judgin' you if you wanna suck my dick."

"No, you'll only judge me for sucking other men's dicks."

"So fuckin' done with this fuckin' conversation."

"Wait. You don't have a problem with sweet butts sucking your dick after sucking everyone else's, right?"

His jaw shifted.

"But you have a problem if I do?"

"Whose dick have you sucked?"

"In my lifetime?" She shrugged, lifted a hand in front of

his face and started ticking off her fingers one at a time. "Well, the first time was back in high school and—"

"No," he barked sharply. "Just fuckin' no. Don't need a fuckin' count and commentary to go along with it. I meant, who in the Fury?"

"Holy shit," she whispered, giving him wide eyes. "You know I'm 'off limits' and you want me to narc on one or more of your brothers?"

"One *or more*? Are you fuckin' serious?"

His face was now red and his blue eyes blazing.

"Wait. Are you jealous?"

His nostrils flared, his anger quickly doused and his expression closed up like a clam.

"I've seen you fuck so many women. *Sooo* many…" She lifted a *don't-even* palm in front of his face. "You know what? I'm tired of the double standards. If I want to suck someone's dick, I'm going to wrap my lips around it and blow it to smithereens. I've had to walk by you double-teaming Lizzy with Ozzy, or Angel with Whip. Or watch Brandy, only wearing thigh-high socks, on her knees sucking you off. I can't even keep track of the women I've seen you boning or blowing your load down their throats. So, you don't even have a right to say one fucking word. Not one." He opened his mouth, but she stopped him with a sharp noise at the back of her throat in warning.

His mouth snapped shut.

"Not one," she cautioned him. "And I certainly would never throw one of your brothers under the bus if it was reversed."

"Woman…"

"Don't you fucking *woman* me. You're right, this conversation is done and over with. Now, what are we doing for breakfast? Are you hungry?"

His mouth opened again, hung there for a good five seconds catching invisible flies before snapping shut once more. A few reactions she couldn't read raced across his face.

After a few more seconds, she raised her eyebrows in question. "Breakfast?"

His expression smoothed out. "I could eat." With that, he pulled the sheet over them, putting them back in their cocoon, slid his hot, naked self down her body and landed between her legs. A few seconds later, his mouth filled with something other than food, and he ate.

Breakfast started with a very explosive bang.

And then it all went to hell from there.

———

HE HATED that she insisted she come along to the house today. He would've preferred it if she had stayed at the motel while he checked on his father's progress.

Of course, she wasn't having it. And when Reilly wasn't having something, she dug in her damn heels and became an unremovable, irritating splinter.

Most of his brothers had learned it was easier to give in to her than to keep fighting. The woman could be fucking exhausting.

Did he want to come back here today? Fuck no.

Did he keep coming back to this house as a form of self-flaying? Possibly.

If so, why did he feel the need to punish himself? If he was sane, he'd take Reilly, and all of her shit, back to Manning Grove and forget the parents who lived in this fucking house. Pretend they no longer existed.

To him and Saylor, they already died. So, why did he feel the need to stick around and actually witness it?

He didn't have that answer.

Maybe he'd feel better once he knew John Schmidt was truly gone and was on his way to becoming only a distant memory. Maybe then Rev could shed some of the guilt that still hounded him from leaving Sarah behind that night.

But he was here now, in Coatesville, in the house he grew up in, and he might as well see it through to the end. Afterward, he could go home, assure Saylor the bastard was dead and she could live the rest of her life in peace.

He wasn't sure that would work, but it was worth a shot.

At least it would be a guarantee that their father could never search for or possibly find her. The risk that he'd be hiding around the next corner to take her back would be down to zero.

Whether his sister could also extract the man from her nightmares, he didn't know. He sure as fuck hoped so.

He didn't have too many nightmares from his youth still haunting him but then, what happened to him and what happened to her—from what he could guess, even though she never admitted it—were two different things.

He could never begin to understand what she lived through. He could only be there for her, be supportive of her, if and when she needed it. It was the best he could do. Though, it would never make up for him running away without her.

To his knowledge, she never once held that against him. If she did, she never said a word. Maybe it was just one more thing she kept hidden and buried deep.

As soon as he and Reilly had entered the house a few minutes ago, his mother had caught sight of them and went out to the backyard to hang laundry without a word. Not even a greeting.

Surprisingly, she also didn't demand they leave. Most likely she knew it wouldn't do any good and didn't even want to waste her breath.

He now stood at the kitchen sink staring through the window above it, watching the woman he wished had been a loving mother pin pants and shirts to the clothesline, keeping her back to him.

Shunning the "sinner." Ignoring his very existence.

Reilly stood pinned to his side, a hand tucked under his shirt and planted on the bare skin of his lower back. Her touch grounded him. Made him aware she was being supportive. Reminded him she would remain there even when he wished she wouldn't.

He really didn't want her to witness the fucked-up relationship between him and the people who brought him into the world. He also didn't want to subject her again to the bitter motherfucker who was supposed to be his father.

On the other hand, if anyone understood shitty parents, she would. Nothing she would see or hear would shock her.

"This house seriously gives me the creeps," she whispered, bumping her hip against his.

"The house or the people who live here?"

"Both. There are no decorations, nothing to make it seem like a home. It's very sterile and unwelcoming. I can't imagine being a child and your childhood being white-washed like this."

"Whitewashed is a damn good way to describe it. 'Cause it definitely was that in more ways than one."

"Did they even hang any of your art on their refrigerator? Did they read you bedtime stories? Did you and your sister play games? Was laughter even heard in this house at all?"

He turned his head, pulling his gaze from his mother, a lifeless shell of a woman wearing her laundry apron full of clothes pins and stiffly hanging the wet laundry, and settling it on the very full-of-life woman he'd spent all morning making sigh and moan in pleasure. Not to mention, leave a huge wet spot on the bottom sheet.

Reilly's face had been a work of art as she came during their adult games, he could easily read her mood, and he could still hear her laughter when he touched her somewhere that tickled.

Fun and passionate. Vocal and open. Totally opposite of his childhood.

"Do I need to answer that?"

"No. If this house looked the same when there were two children living in it as it does now…" She sighed, using the hand on his back to turn him toward her. She blinked her big green eyes up at him. "I don't know how you didn't turn out to be some sort of cardboard cutout of a man."

"I left."

"Yes, but not before some damage had already been done."

"Instead of groomin' me for the life they wanted me to live, their actions showed me what I didn't want. I didn't want this fuckin' life. The submissive wife. The obedient daughters I was expected to 'ready' for their husbands. Didn't want any of this fucked-up shit. Didn't wanna be the one to continue the cycle of what I consider fuckin' madness."

She turned her gaze back outside to his mother. "Madness is a good word for it. I've only seen the very tip of the iceberg. I can't image the rest." She shook her head. "Honestly, I don't want to. It breaks my heart for you and Saylor, it really does. I still don't understand why you needed to come back here, but it's not for me to understand. If it's something you need, then it's something you need and this is why I'm here with you."

He wasn't stupid, he knew coming along to clear out her storage unit had only been an excuse.

"Woman," he breathed. She was wedging herself under his fucking skin without even trying. Like that damn splinter.

She glanced back up at him and squeezed his waist. "Can we just get done what you need to so we can get the hell out of this place? I'm worried that the house will start shifting wildly or we'll see ghosts, or some monster will slither out of the cellar."

"A monster will slither out of my jeans later," he assured her.

She rolled her eyes. "Uh huh." She pulled her hand from under his T-shirt and patted his cotton-covered stomach. "I should have added: Let's leave before we both start having delusions. I guess we're too late on that one." She went up on her tiptoes and pressed a kiss to his lips.

He hooked an arm around her waist and pulled her into his chest, deepening the kiss for a brief moment. When he pulled back, he noticed how soft her eyes had gone.

Fuck.

Yeah, she might be burrowing under his skin, but he was afraid he was getting under hers, too.

And that was a problem he didn't know how to deal with. *Hell,* maybe it wouldn't be a problem. Maybe once they got home, they could easily go back to the way it was.

Or, *for fuck's sake,* maybe he could stop lying to himself. He knew bullshit when he heard it, even if it was his own lie and only said in his own head.

No matter what, he needed to push that problem aside for now and deal with the one at hand.

John Schmidt.

"All right. Let's go see if we need to stick around or we can head back to the motel where I can unleash my monster."

A soft smile curled her lips even though her words didn't match it. "I just want this over for you and Saylor."

You and me both. But when this is over, we're over and that's gonna suck.

She peeled away from him and turned to head back to the sitting room, where his father had been sleeping when they first walked through the front door.

The asshole had probably been faking it to avoid him.

But Rev would sit at his bedside all fucking day if he needed to.

"Hey," he called out softly, stopping her from walking out of the kitchen by nabbing her wrist.

She paused and glanced back over her shoulder at him.

"Thanks for bein' a fuckin' pest."

"You can thank me properly later." She tipped her head toward his crotch. "By unleashing the Kraken."

Fuck yeah. "Reilly Porter, slayer of monsters."

"Oh, I like that title. Maybe I need a whip and a sexy leather outfit to go along with it." She walked out of the room with a smile.

He stared at the empty doorway in the direction she'd disappeared, unable to get the image out of his head of her wearing a badass leather outfit that hugged her curves and showed off her tits, while brandishing a bullwhip and slaying both monsters and men's hearts.

Yeah, she could be a huge problem for him.

He unfroze his feet and quickly followed her, not wanting her to face his father alone. When he caught up with her, she was already standing by the medical bed, her smile a distant memory. Her mouth was tight and her expression closed as she glanced at him entering the room.

Her eyes weren't the only ones glued on him. His father was awake and his normal loving self, though his voice was weak and raspy, like he was struggling to breathe. "See you brought your… whore with you again… You insult me … and sully my home… by bringing her… here, Michael." Every few words he had to stop to take a rattled breath. He was definitely getting worse by the day. "Why did you come back? … I told you not to…"

"Just seein' if you're dead yet."

"Sorry to disappoint… you."

"You can't die soon enough, old man. I'd make it

quicker for you, but I'd prefer you suffer 'til you can't suffer no more."

"You were always... a horrible, horrible child."

"How about that. You were always a horrible father. You reap what you sow, old man."

"Couldn't even beat... the petulance out of you... no matter how many times I tried."

"A man reaps what he sows. The one who sows to please his sinful nature, from that nature will reap destruction," Rev quoted.

"Don't you dare... throw scripture at me... you wretched, unrepentant brat." His father lifted his bony, pale hand to weakly tap his own temple. "Figured out why... you are who... you are."

"We already discussed why. You sowed the fuckin' spoiled seeds."

His father continued as though Rev hadn't spoken. "You have issues due... to who your parents are." He sucked in a wheezing breath, his chest barely rising under the pile of blankets.

"Ain't tellin' me nothin' I don't know, old man."

His father smirked. "Oh, yes... I am, boy... I figured it all out."

"Figured what out?" His father was playing games Rev didn't like and wouldn't stand for, for much longer.

"You came back here... for nothing." The man's thin lips almost curled into a smile. Almost. But John Schmidt had never smiled once that Rev could remember so he probably didn't know how. "After you were born... no matter how many times... I tried to get your mother with child... I failed." He paused to suck in another noisy breath. "Went to the physician... without telling her... found out I had no fertile seed... Turns out neither of you... ungrateful, sinful children were mine."

Rev snorted in disbelief. "You're delirious. That cancer's rottin' your brain."

"No." The man managed to drum up enough energy to sneer. "Your grandfather…"

Rev leaned forward, waiting. His heart began to pound like a bass drum.

"Gave me your mother… when she was already… with child."

Chapter Thirteen

THIS HAD to be a sick joke. One last twist of the knife in Rev's back before the motherfucker died. "What the fuck you talkin' about?"

"He sowed... your rotten seed... Not me."

Rev stared at him, not comprehending the words that just spilled from the dying man's mouth.

Reilly barely smothered a gasp next to him. When he shot a quick glance at her, she was staring wide-eyed at the man in the bed, her face paler than normal, proving Rev hadn't misheard him. He turned his attention back to the bed and the man who was *not* his father.

That was what he'd heard, wasn't it?

He couldn't wrap his head around it. It had to be a lie. His father—No, the man who he had thought was his father—had to be lying, right? A way to torture his son with words since he no longer had the strength to do it physically?

Was it possible that he...

"Wasn't Sarah's... either."

Those three words didn't quite sink in, because right now, Rev's brain was on overload.

Yeah, this was all a sick joke.

All of it.

His whole life. A damn sick joke.

He would never stop getting punished for being born. With a hand clamped on his forearm, Reilly's nails drilled painfully into his skin. "Who's Say— Sarah's father?" she asked in a pained whisper.

"Doesn't matter now... does it? ... Since she's no longer... on this Earth."

Rev pressed himself against the side of the bed and leaned in until his face was just above the man who no longer was anything to him. Not a fucking thing. They didn't even share a drop of blood. Not one. "Who's her fuckin' father?"

"Had to beat the truth... out of her... Your mother not only lied... to her husband... about coming to me pregnant with you... but she was unfaithful, too."

"With her own father?" Reilly squeaked.

He couldn't think straight enough to ask the questions Reilly was asking. Something had broken inside his brain. It felt scrambled and wouldn't function properly. He couldn't grasp what the fuck was going on.

None of this made any damn sense.

He needed to slam the brakes on his spinning thoughts.

"Was she unfaithful, or was she forced?" Reilly grilled his father, one hand still gripping Rev's arm, the other white-knuckling the bed's metal side rail.

No, not his *father*. Not any longer.

The man with one foot in the grave, and about to finish falling into it after Rev shoved him there, ignored Reilly. He only had cloudy eyes for Rev, and they held revenge and pure hatred in the dull brown orbs.

"Who's Sarah's father?" Rev demanded since he refused to answer Reilly. He clenched his fingers to prevent himself from strangling the man before he could get the answer he needed. He wanted to know the truth about his sister first. Even if it was a truth he never told Saylor.

He couldn't ask his mother. She was the type of woman who would take a secret like that to her grave simply to remain being seen as holy and pious. While the man she married preferred to cause pain. And a fuckload of it. He generously sprinkled that shit around like salt on a bland meal.

If anyone was going to tell the truth, it would be him. For exactly what Rev saw in his eyes.

Spite.

"Who?" Rev shouted and slammed his hand on the metal side rail causing the whole bed to jolt sideways and the living, breathing skeleton to rock under the blankets.

"The man who sought you out... without my permission... I told him no... he did it anyway."

The man who sought you out.

Matthew.

Rev couldn't breathe. His lungs simply stopped functioning. His heart thumped in his throat, trying to break free, while his ears rang at a deafening volume.

It couldn't be.

Was that why Matthew hunted him down? In an attempt to find Sarah? Maybe he didn't even give a shit about Rev coming to see the dying man they thought was his father. His uncle was using John Schmidt's illness to try to ferret out where Sarah was, or he hoped Rev would have brought Matthew's niece home along with him.

No...

Christ!

Rev's eyes squeezed shut and a bolt of pain speared through his chest and down his arm because he was gripping the bed rail so tightly.

Saylor wasn't only his niece…

Jesus fuck. His niece *and* his daughter.

That couldn't be it, could it?

That couldn't be the reason that motherfucker called him? Did Matthew know the truth? Did Matthew know Sarah was his? If so, how long had he fucking known?

But that meant John Schmidt didn't share any blood with Rev's sister, either. They weren't related at all.

"Did you know this before or after you touched her?" Rev asked, his words sounding like they came down a long, narrow hallway. A corridor closing in around him. Like he was on a bad acid trip.

"I don't answer to you… I only answer to God."

Bullshit! A muscle ticked in Rev's jaw and he snapped free from the mental quicksand he'd been bogged down in. "Before or after you touched her?" he roared into the dying man's face.

It didn't matter. It made no difference. John Schmidt was still a pedophile, just not an incestuous one.

"Go away, boy… you don't belong here."

"The moral hypocrisy in this family makes me fuckin' sick." He slammed the bed rails with both palms, wanting to choke the dying breath out of him.

Reilly grabbed his shirt sleeve and tugged at it. "Rev," she whispered.

He glanced down at her. Her eyes were focused toward the room's archway and she lifted her chin slightly in a silent message.

He turned, expecting to see his mother…

Instead, he saw Matthew standing in the opening.

That motherfucker.

His head began to pound when he realized his uncle was also his first cousin. His grandfather also his father. His mother his half-sister.

Was that right? Was any of that right?

Holy fuck, him and Saylor were both born from incest. If he hadn't come back, he would've never known. That secret would have died with his parents.

He never should've come back. He would've remained in the dark. Clueless that they were inbred like the Shirleys. Born from incest. Born from lies.

Born from deep, dark secrets.

He was called a sinner. Over and over.

He was not the sinner. He was the product of a grave sin.

He and Saylor... They weren't even full brother and sister.

They were... half-brother and -sister and... cousins? Was he Saylor's uncle-cousin-brother? He didn't even know. He was struggling to wrap his head around all of his jumbled thoughts. Trying to straighten out their twisted and fucked-up family tree.

He couldn't deal with that shit right now. He needed to deal with the man standing there with a worried look on his face.

He should be fucking worried.

His asshole should be puckering tight right about now. Especially if he overheard any of the conversation.

Cursed be anyone who lies with his sister, whether the daughter of his father or the daughter of his mother.

How about the daughter of both?

Rev rushed toward Matthew and shouted, "Did you know?"

Rev could see the tremble in his uncle's hand as he held it out in front of him like a stop sign. A useless, ineffective shield. "Let's step outside, Brother Michael."

Brother was right. Matthew was his actual half-brother.

His pulse pounded painfully at his temple from all the

mental gymnastics. "Yeah, let's, brother-uncle." Grabbing a fistful of Matthew's button-down shirt, Rev dragged him the few strides to the front door and flung it open.

"Rev!" Reilly called out, rushing after them and sounding more than a bit panicked.

"Stay in the house," he ordered over his shoulder.

He continued to yank the older man along with him, making him stumble down the porch steps and into the yard, where Rev flung him to the grass.

"I'm not staying in this house alone! It creeps me out."

"Reilly," he growled, not in the mood for her to be a pain in his ass right now. "You don't step off that porch."

He had no idea if she argued or not because he blocked her out. Instead, he concentrated on the man before him in a heap on the ground, cowering in fear. The blood had drained from Matthew's face, making his blue eyes more noticeable. The same blue eyes as his. As Saylor's. He wasn't dark blond like Rev's mother, or Rev himself. Or even his grandfather... No... *father.*

What the fuck! He didn't even know how to label his grandfather anymore. He was so damned confused.

No, Matthew's hair wasn't blond at all, it was the same color as Saylor's.

Brown.

Like his grandmother's. *Wait.* Was his grandmother still his grandmother? *Christ!*

His brain hurt. All he wanted to do was jam the heels of his palms into his eyes and collapse to the ground until everything stopped spinning around him. Until things made sense.

Or he woke up from this nightmare.

He didn't. Instead, he reached down, grabbed the man's wrinkled shirt again and hauled him to his feet.

"God help me. Don't hurt me," Matthew pleaded.

Rev sneered at him. "Did you fuckin' know my sister was your daughter?"

"It's… It's a woman's duty to bear children. A wife who can't bear her husband any children is seen as a failure. We didn't… We… She couldn't go to anyone else. We had to keep it a secret. We had to keep it in the family."

Apparently. They took "keeping it in the family" to a whole other level. A sick and twisted one.

"But women will be preserved through the bearing of children—"

"Don't spout that shit at me. Don't wanna fuckin' hear it. You're all fuckin' hypocrites. Wanna know why you fucked—"

Matthew winced and cut him off quickly. "It's also a man's duty to create a family. *Children are a heritage from the Lord—"*

"Said I don't wanna hear that bullshit. Want the truth."

"Your mother couldn't get pregnant. She asked me for help…"

Rev's eyebrows just about launched free of his forehead. "And that's how you helped her? By knockin' her up 'cause her husband couldn't? What kind of sick motherfucker are you? This whole fuckin' family's whacked. Christ!"

"Don't take the Lord's name in vain."

His head was about to explode off his neck. "That's what you're worried about? Me takin' the Lord's name in vain when you fucked your own sister?"

"No one was supposed to know. Not even your father."

"Who isn't my fuckin' father! More fuckin' family secrets!" he roared. "Does your wife know you had a child with your own fuckin' sister, just so she wouldn't be blamed for being a failure? How she appeared to her congregation was more important than getting pregnant by her own brother?" Maybe getting knocked up by her father hadn't been a choice but fucking her brother sure the fuck was.

"It wasn't like that!" Matthew exclaimed.

"Oh, okay, it happened by accident, then. You just accidentally busted a nut in your sister."

Matthew's face became dark and stormy. "*If we confess our sins, he is faithful and just to forgive us our sins and to cleanse us from all unrighteousness.*"

"It's that easy, is it? Spout some bible passage, ask for forgiveness and all your sins are cleansed? This family is fucked. This whole thing is fucked. You're all fucked!" Rev shouted, his pulse pounding at his temples. He jabbed a finger toward the house. "You let that man touch your niece…" Rev shook his head. "No! Your fuckin' daughter!"

Matthew blanched. "He didn't do anything differently than what our father did with Sister Rachel. *He must manage his own family well and see that his children obey him…* He was teaching her to—"

Rev slammed his fist into Matthew's face shutting him the fuck up. The man's nose exploded under the force of his knuckles, causing blood to spurt and splatter on Rev's skin and shirt. Before Matthew could fall, Rev grabbed a fistful of his shirt again and yanked him back to his feet, released him and punched him once more, knocking him backward and off his feet. His brother-uncle landed hard on his ass in the grass.

Matthew tried to scramble away, to pull himself out of reach, but Rev was quicker than him. Standing over and straddling him, Rev leaned over to lift Matthew's torso again by the shirt with his bloody and bruised right hand. His left fist made contact with his jaw, snapping his head to the side.

Matthew's eyes rolled back, his eyelids fluttered closed and his bleeding mouth gaped open. A second later, he went limp in Rev's grasp. Rev released him and let him crumple to the ground.

"Fuckin' motherfucker. If there was a God, he woulda

struck you dead by now." Rev made sure the man was no longer conscious before straightening. His voice felt strained and raw when he continued. "You don't deserve to breathe the same air as Sarah. You don't deserve to have the same blood in your veins. I should steal your breath and drain your blood. You aren't fuckin' worthy."

I should kill him. I should kill him. I should kill him.

It would be too risky. The man wasn't worth going to prison for. Not worth the possibility of him being locked up and leaving Saylor with no one but the club.

Matthew's death would most likely be questioned and investigated, when the person's who already laid on his deathbed wouldn't.

Even so, Rev could make the man hurt and maybe regret his life choices. Rev punted him in the ribs with his boot, hoping he cracked a few while he was at it. "That's for not protectin' what was yours. Whether she was your fuckin' niece or your damn daughter. You did nothin'. Not a goddamn thing to stop it."

He was wasting his breath. Matthew couldn't hear shit. But when he came to, he would remember why he was fucking hurting so damn bad and who made it happen.

Rev decided to leave him one more reminder for when he woke up. He sucked a hocker deep from his nasal passages into his mouth and spat the thick wad onto the unconscious man's face.

He stared down at his brother-uncle, reminding himself the man wasn't worth doing a life-long prison bid. He twisted his head to see Reilly still standing on the porch where he told her to stay.

She had listened to him. Imagine that.

She was holding onto one of the wood posts and her mouth was moving.

He had no idea what the fuck she was saying. He

focused on her, trying to clear his mind, and managed to catch the tail end of whatever she said.

"—should leave."

No. He wasn't done there yet.

Before he left, the man in that house, in that bed, needed to die. He was done waiting for nature to take its course. He was done being at this house, in this town, being related to these whacked fuckers.

He needed to scrape all this shit clean. From his memories, from his future.

But the man who left physical scars on his back, the man who caused Saylor's mental scars... His time had come. Whether he stopped breathing today by force or tomorrow from his illness, it no longer mattered to Rev.

He. Was. Done.

He rushed up the porch, blowing past Reilly, who stood frozen in place, her mouth gaped open.

She had seen everything that happened so far, but he didn't want her to watch what was about to come next. She didn't need to be an accomplice or a witness who could be questioned by the pigs if it ever came down to that. He didn't want any of his fucked-up family's shit splattered on her.

"Rev!" Reilly screamed, scrambling after him.

Before she could reach the door, he slammed it shut and flipped the deadbolt, locking her outside.

"Rev!" She pounded on the door and jerked on the door handle. "Don't do anything stupid! He's not worth it, either! None of them are!"

He ignored her and spotted his mother standing at the end of the narrow hallway in the entrance to the kitchen with her hands wringing her apron.

The same way he wanted to wring her damn neck.

"Lock that back door and don't you dare let her inside if you know what's good for you." She didn't move and also didn't say a damn word. Funny how she had a lot to say to him when he was a child but now that he was an adult? Nothing. "Go lock the fuckin' door! If you let her in here, I'll kill you, too."

His mother's face paled and she disappeared into the kitchen. A few seconds later he heard pounding on the back door.

"Let me in, damn it. Let me in!"

His mother appeared again in the kitchen doorway, her face a washed-out, haggard mask, her lips pressed into a slash.

He had one last thing to say to her. "Don't you dare call the fuckin' cops or I'll tell them how fucked-up you all are. You," he jabbed a finger in her direction, "are just as guilty as them." He pointed toward the sitting room to his right. "You could've stopped it. Any of it. All of it. You didn't... May you burn in hell alongside the man you married, while you both still cling to the secrets you fuckin' kept."

He didn't wait for a response. He knew he wouldn't get one. She just wanted him to go away. Just like John Schmidt wanted him to disappear, too.

She believed he and Saylor had put dark smudges on their "pure," devout family when it was her actions that made those smudges. Her complacency. The steps she took to look like a good wife and mother and to have their family appear godly, when she and they were far, far from that.

Judge not, that you be not judged...

That was a favorite pastime of their religious order. To judge. Then judge each other for judging.

He snorted, shook his head and stepped into the front room, where his father— *Fuck!* The abusive son-of-a-bitch— lied awake, his rheumy eyes set on Rev as he approached.

The man had heard everything.

Good.

His now... stepfather?... sucked in a wheezy breath so

he could speak. "I'm ready... to meet my maker... And even better... I will never have to... set eyes on you again."

"Relieved it will also be the last time I ever set my eyes on you, you sick fuck." He stepped up to the bed, yanked one of the pillows from behind the man's head and squeezed it between his fingers.

"Do it... End my suffering."

Rev closed his eyes for a moment and remembered. Remembered every time he heard Sarah cry through the thin walls between their bedrooms. Remembered every time he had been the one to console his upset sister. Remembered every damn time he'd been called a sinner. Every time he had to pick his own switch off a bush grown for just that purpose.

And every time he'd been tied to the clothesline in the backyard.

At some point in their childhood, John Schmidt had discovered "his children," Sarah and Michael, were not from his blood. Rev had no idea when and whether that was the reason the man was quick to punish them both. Or if that even mattered.

Maybe he would've done the same if he was their true father.

Maybe he was an evil bastard at his very core and not just an angry one for being lied to. By both his father-in-law and by his wife herself. That wasn't reason enough to treat his "children" as he did. An unbending taskmaster who went far beyond simply teaching his "children" manners.

"I'd prefer you continue to suffer, but I won't make this quick, either. Just like every strike of the switch on my flesh. Just like every perverted 'punishment' you doled out to Sarah. None of it was quick. All of it unnecessary." He leaned over the bed, the crushed pillow hovering over the dying man's face. "Want my face to be the last thing you see. Don't want you to see any fuckin' bright light or get any fuckin' peace. Want you to be thinkin' about what you did to me while you struggle, about what you did to Sarah, right before you head to the place where you earned your spot. And let me tell you, it won't be up where you think it is. Hell no. Prepare to meet your maker, old man. And it ain't God."

Chapter Fourteen

"WE CAN LEAVE and go home, or stay the night since the room's paid for." Rev paced the small motel room with a restlessness he couldn't rid himself of. It was like hundreds of fingernails scratching at him under his skin.

He thought he would feel better once he lifted the pillow and saw the blank stare, gaped mouth and unmoving chest of John Schmidt.

It hadn't given him any satisfaction, especially since the man had been too weak to struggle. Rev had wanted him to fight and panic. Maybe even beg. Instead, the bastard welcomed the end with open arms.

Rev scrubbed the hand holding his hand-rolled cigarette back and forth over his hair as he took long strides across the short length of the small room.

He paused, lifted the whiskey bottle clutched in his other hand to his lips, tipped his head back and let the liquid worm its way down to his gut. He picked up his pacing again, swiping his palm over his hair for the hundredth time, unable to see anything but the man's lifeless face in his mind's eye.

By the time he had finished in the sitting room of his

childhood residence and went outside to leave, Matthew's cage was already gone and so was he. The man was smart to leave when he did, because Rev might have finished off the job if he'd gone out and saw him again.

What greeted him instead was Reilly leaning against his Bronco with her arms crossed over her chest and a very unhappy expression on her face.

Now sitting on their bed and watching him pace like a caged tiger, her mood hadn't improved.

But then, neither had his.

"I don't think you're in any condition to drive."

"Hate this fuckin' place." His feet stopped, he took another long swallow of the amber liquor and then returned to wearing a path in the carpet. "You drive, then. You drive stick, right?"

She grimaced. "No. I asked Rook to teach me."

"Rook ain't teachin' you."

"No shit since I don't know how to drive stick," she huffed.

He ignored her annoyed tone. "I'll teach you. Shoulda asked me."

"Really? I did. You blew me off."

He stopped his pacing and spun toward her. "Think I needed that fuckin' temptation so close to me when no one else is around? Both of us on some back fuckin' road, alone in a cage together? Right." He blew out a breath.

A smile grew across her face and she waved a hand down her body from her head to her toes. "You can't resist all this, huh? Hot and tempting, like a donut fresh from the fryer."

He narrowed his eyes on her. "What the fuck are you blatherin' about?"

She rolled her eyes. "Never mind. You're struggling to focus and I'm wasting my genius sense of humor on you right now."

"Ya think?" He sucked down another mouthful of Jack. The smoke from his hand-rolled swirled in a white ribbon toward the ceiling.

She held out her hand from where she sat on their bed, propped against the headboard. "Give me some of that."

"Not if you're drivin'." She probably just wanted to get the Jack away from him so he'd stop drinking.

"Listen, I know you've got a lot on your mind right now, but we just had this discussion, Rev. I can't drive stick and unless you're going to teach me in the next couple of hours, with how much you've already drank, we're not going anywhere. We're staying right here. And, honestly, I think it's for the best. You need to process what the hell went on today and also what you learned. We both do. While this doesn't have to be decided tonight, you also need to figure out what you'll tell Saylor, if anything. If we head home tonight, we'll end up going our separate ways and you won't have anyone to talk to about this."

That was a lot of fucking words jamming themselves in his already full head for her to simply say they should stay put for the night.

But, *for fuck's sake*, she was right. He'd already downed a third of the Jack Daniels in the bottle he carried like a security blanket. He needed to smoke a bowl and, once his thoughts stopped ping-ponging around his brain, wrap his head around all the shit he learned barely over an hour ago.

Like the fact he had tainted blood. Both he and Saylor did. It might not be anything he could change but it was something he could forget.

He hoped to fuck he could. He didn't want this haunting him for the rest of his life. He didn't need the reminder that his twisted blood wasn't any better than the Shirleys, those redneck motherfuckers who used to live up the mountain and probably would return as soon as the feds were done processing their compound.

Those goat fuckers weren't his problem right now. He needed to figure out what to tell the most important person in his life. Saylor.

It might be best not to say anything at all. What would be the point other than to take a bad situation and make it a million times worse. He wanted to spare her any more pain. And finding out their uncle was also her father might send her spinning out of control like a hubcap falling off a vehicle while speeding down the highway.

Since arriving in Manning Grove and settling in with Judge and Cassie, she'd been doing really well. They were the best thing that ever happened to his sister and he'd hate to see that change. For once her life had been traveling a steady and smooth path instead of a crazy, bumpy roller coaster.

No, this was a secret he should take to his fucking grave. But he needed Reilly to keep it, too. She couldn't say a fucking word to anyone.

"Ain't gonna tell anyone about this, Reilly. Don't even need to decide what to tell Saylor besides that our 'father' is now dead. It's better she don't know the truth. That means you can't say a fuckin' word."

He paused and turned toward the bed, tucking his cigarette in his mouth and flooding his lungs with quality Amish tobacco. Just smoke and the booze wouldn't do the trick. He was still wrapped as tight as a rubber band ball. One that was ready to snap and then explode into a thousand tiny pieces.

"I agree. She doesn't need to know. It won't change anything. I assume if it didn't affect her, it shouldn't affect her future children…"

He blinked. Future children? "Yeah, since we don't plan on repeatin' history with the brother-sister fuckin' thing, I'm thinkin' her kids will be good."

"So will yours."

He blinked again. "So will my what?"

"Kids," she answered, sounding exasperated. Like she was tired of talking to a two-year-old.

"What kids?"

She shot him an irritated look. "Your future kids. Holy shit, Rev. This is why we're not going anywhere tonight. Your mind is a fucking mess!"

"No shit," he muttered, taking another pull off the bottle and chasing it with a deep draw on his hand-rolled.

He never thought about having kids before because he'd first need to get himself an ol' lady who'd be willing to have them. He was in no rush to claim an ol' lady, either. He had plenty of time before he would even think about settling down and having only one woman in his bed.

Not only one woman, but the same one. Over and over.

He'd need to find one who wouldn't annoy the fuck out of him. Or bore him, either.

One who liked to fuck. Was loyal. Would be a good mother to those non-existent snot monkeys.

He shook his head at his stupid thoughts and took another swig of whiskey to wash them away.

"You need food in your stomach if you plan on drowning your problems."

"Yeah. Later," he said distractedly. His gaze sliced from her to the drawer of the nightstand. Within two long strides, he was there, ripping it open and pulling out the motel-provided pad of paper and pen.

He went over to the counter that doubled as a desk and sat down, plugging the cigarette between his lips and planting the bottle on the countertop, keeping it within reach. "You know how to pack a bowl?" he threw over his shoulder.

He jumped when her voice came from behind him. "Not like you guys."

He shook his head. "Grab the shit and bring it here."

"That sure didn't sound like an ask. That sounded like a demand."

He glanced up from the blank pad of paper before him. He twisted in the seat, snagged both of her hands and pulled her between his spread thighs. She extracted one hand free of his and combed it through his hair, her expression switching from annoyed to soft in a second flat.

"I understand your world just got flipped upside down, but don't take it out on me," she said softly.

He closed his eyes and gently squeezed the one hand he still held before lifting it to his mouth and brushing his lips over her knuckles.

"I'm sorry this is happening to you," came out of her on a wispy breath.

"Sorry for bein' a dick."

"You're not being a dick, your brain is just on overload. I get it. My worry is that if I wasn't here right now to stop you, you'd be driving home drunk. Or trying to, anyway."

He had no idea what he'd be doing. Reilly being with him was one reason he had kept a tight grip on his fury. If she hadn't been, he might be in custody of the pigs right now because, in his rage, he probably would have massacred everyone in that house. If his grandfather was still alive, he also would've gone over to that motherfucker's house and done the same to him.

Not his grandfather. His father. *Jesus fuck*, his grandfather-father.

He wrapped his arms around Reilly's waist and buried his face against her stomach, taking a moment to simply breathe. She smelled like a combination of her citrus body wash and whatever detergent she used to wash her clothes. But breathing her in still dulled the razor sharp edge slicing through him a notch.

One hand played along his hair, while her other stroked his back and he realized at that very fucking moment, he'd never been comforted like this. He'd never been held or hugged before this trip with Reilly.

Then he realized maybe Saylor hadn't, either.

Having sex with someone was just that. Bodies slapping together, plain and simple, until all the parties involved got off. But holding someone because they needed to feel comforted, wanted or even understood… It was an entirely different thing.

He'd been missing this kind of contact his whole fucking life. The only time he'd had anything similar to this was when he snuck into Sarah's bedroom and held her until she stopped crying. But every time he went in to help settle her to sleep, it made him more annoyed and filled him with even more hatred because he shouldn't have been the one to do it. Even worse, it shouldn't have needed to be done in the first place.

He would go in after the fact desperate to fix what John Schmidt broke.

He sucked another long breath in through his nose, trying to inhale Reilly the same as he would pot. To share her calmness and let it wash over and through him.

Once he got home, whether Saylor wanted it or not, he was grabbing his sister and hugging her so fucking hard. He needed to remind her that he was there for her no matter what. He also needed to show her instead of just saying the damn words.

Words spoken could be empty. They could also be full of lies.

When Reilly's cheek pressed to the top of his head, he tightened his arms around her, pulling her into him even closer.

He had no idea how long he clung to her, but she never got tired and pulled away. As long as he was holding on, she remained holding on to him. There was something so goddamn healing about it.

Now he wished he'd held Sarah a lot more before he ran away. Once he left, she didn't even have that. She had nothing.

He left her with nothing.

For fuck's sake, he never should have left.

He should have stayed. For her. Then figured out a way to get them both out of that situation.

He fucked up. His fuck-up fucked her up even more. He was partly to blame.

Reilly cupped his face and lifted it to hers. She kissed him lightly and when she moved to pull away, he stopped her and took her mouth even deeper.

He wanted to hold her again, but while he was inside her. Not just to fuck her, but something more. Unfortunately, his head wasn't there yet. He needed to get it there by smoothing out his jumbled thoughts first.

He ended the kiss and she pressed her forehead to his. "Wanna fuck you," he whispered.

"Same," she whispered back. "But that's not going to happen if you get trashed." She went to move away again and he let her go this time. "I'll grab your pipe."

"In a minute, help me figure this out. Sit."

"There's nowhere to sit. There's only one chair."

"My lap makes a good seat."

She gave him a soft smile, wrapped an arm around his shoulders and settled on his lap. "Yes, you're right, when nothing is poking me, it does."

"Makes an even better seat when I'm hard."

"When we're both naked."

"We're both gonna be naked soon. Think I want you to ride my dick in this chair."

"You think it can handle that action? It's a cheap motel chair."

He shrugged. "We break it, I'll pay for it. Might be worth the cost."

"Might not be worth the hurt if it breaks and we land hard on the ground."

"We'll figure it out. Need to figure this out first so I can try to put that shit outta my head… for now."

"Do you think writing it down will help it make sense?"

"None of it will make fuckin' sense." But seeing it spelled out in front of him might help him wrap his head around it.

"True," she murmured, her fingertips strumming the back of his neck.

That kind of touch shouldn't make him hard, but it did. Despite his messed up head, he couldn't ignore the fact he wanted her. More now than ever.

He curled his left hand around the pen so he could write one name on each rectangular sheet he tore free from the rest of the pad.

"I never realized you were a lefty before. Is Saylor?"

"Think so."

"You don't know?"

"She was still pretty young when I left, and I never paid attention if I saw her write."

"How about when she colored with crayons? You should've noticed it then."

He lifted his face to her in answer.

That was all it took for her cheeks to darken in anger. "You weren't even allowed to color?"

If they wanted to do anything normal kids did, they had to do it away from the house, usually at school. Like when he got a chance to play baseball. He really wanted to play on a team, but that had been forbidden.

Once he had all the names written on the slips of papers, he lined them up along the counter. One name he omitted was John Schmidt since the bastard had no blood tie to him or Saylor. The man didn't deserve one more thought.

He slid the paper with his grandfather's name, Lorne, to the top edge of the counter. Under that he placed two more each with the names Rachel and Matthew. "Father, son and daughter."

"That would be simple if those leaves on that family tree remained that way."

"Yeah," he murmured, moving both sheets with the names Michael and Sarah under his mother's name. "This is what it should look like. Ain't what it ended up bein'."

He took the pen, drew an arrow from Sarah's name to their mother's name, then drew another arrow angled toward Matthew's name, Sarah's real father. He also drew an arrow pointing from his own birth name to Rachel. Then another arrow pointing up toward Lorne, Rev's grandfather who also was his father.

He stared at those sheets, knowing he wasn't finished. That more arrows needed to be drawn. But he couldn't.

He fucking couldn't. Instead, he took the pen and scribbled angrily over the names until the pen snapped and ink began to leak. "Fuckin' motherfucker!" He threw the pen across the room and surged from the chair, forcing Reilly to her feet so she wouldn't tumble to the carpet.

With his back turned to her and the counter, he scrubbed at his forehead.

Seeing it laid out before him didn't make it better, it made it so much fucking worse. It was impossible to straighten out a crooked branch without breaking it.

And he was about to break.

"Grab your lighter," she suggested from behind him.

Yeah, good idea since he really needed to get baked. He strode over to the nightstand, snagged his tin, pipe and lighter and when he turned, he saw her gathering the slips of paper from wherever they landed and stacking them together neatly.

She tipped her head toward the door. "Outside. Just bring the lighter."

She headed out the door, leaving it open with an obvious expectation for him to follow. A few seconds later he forced himself outside, not bothering to close the door behind him. Most likely because she wasn't wearing any shoes, she only went as far as the edge of the concrete sidewalk, where she squatted down and crumpled up the sheets of paper. Once it was in a ball, she held her hand up, not bothering to look behind her.

Once he placed the lighter in her hand, she flicked it until a flame ignited and she held it to one edge of the crumpled ball. A few second later it caught and began to burn.

When she rose, he stepped up to her and she moved to stand next to him, snaked an arm around his waist and leaned her head into his side. He wrapped one arm around her shoulders and pulled her close.

She had been his rock these last few days. Solid and supportive. Understanding and, for the most part, patient. Having her lean against him while he held her felt... *right*. Like they did it all the time and it was normal between them.

He couldn't imagine anyone else but her coming along on this trip.

Thank fuck she had insisted on coming along.

Thank fuck she was a pushy, stubborn smart-ass.

Thank fuck she understood how fucked up parents could be.

They stood watching the tiny fire until it burned out and nothing but ashes remained. A light April breeze eventually blew the flaky ash away and they watched it disappear.

"There," she finally whispered. "Gone for good. Both of our evil pasts are now reduced to ashes. Never to be thought about again. Deal?"

Never to be thought about again.

Once again, she was right.

He needed to forget what he heard and never think about it again.

He needed to move forward and leave this all fucking behind him and never look back again. Never return. Whether physically or mentally.

None of those people who used to be family were worth one more fucking moment of his time or effort.

Unlike the woman pinned to his side.

He turned her in his arms and tipped his head down to her. "Fuckin' love you, woman."

Whoa.

He blinked and his heart began to thump.

What the fuck did he just say? Was he that drunk already? Did that really come out of his mouth?

For a moment, he thought—and hoped—she would act like he never said it. That she would ignore how fucking asinine that unexpected declaration was.

Unfortunately, she didn't ignore it. Instead, she sighed softly, patted his stomach in a patronizing way, and said, "That's just the whiskey and messed-up emotions talking, Rev. You don't mean that."

Fuck him, she didn't ignore it but blew it off, instead.

As she headed back into the room, he stood frozen on the spot and watched her disappear inside.

It hit him right then and there like a two-by-four across his forehead that she was wrong.

So fucking wrong.

What he said wasn't because of the whiskey or his fucked-up head.

It wasn't because of that at all.

Holy.

Fuckin'.

Shit.

Chapter Fifteen

HE DIDN'T MEAN IT.

He couldn't.

They'd only spent five days in the same room, in the same bed. They've known each other and worked together for a year, but still...

It *had* to be the whiskey talking.

For the rest of the night, they both managed to ignore the words he spilled *by accident* and pretend it never happened.

Instead, they both shared a bowl, pigged out on delivered take-out and spent half the night naked, sweaty and writhing in the sheets. And on the sheets. *And* on the desk chair, that miraculously managed not to break.

During all of that, the L-word wasn't mentioned again. By accident or on purpose.

Because it wasn't love.

Was it?

Alcohol *could* act as a truth serum. When drinking heavily, sometimes things could be blurted out when least expected. Or when the timing was bad or awkward.

Maybe...

No.

Could he…

No.

It didn't make sense.

Yes, they'd been attracted to each other for the past year and flirted on occasion—okay, more than on occasion—but she flirted with him no more than any of the rest of the guys. Right?

She was an equal opportunity flirt. They all knew that. They were all used to it.

None of them took it seriously since she was planted firmly on the "do not touch or you die" list…

Flirting and ball-busting were one thing, but love?

Nah.

The sex had been great and she would miss it, for sure, now that they were driving through Manning Grove and would soon be parting ways.

If she was being honest with herself, she wouldn't only miss his cock but the man attached to it.

Of course she would see him regularly at work, but it wasn't the same. Working with someone and rolling around naked in the sheets with that person were two different things.

And, yes, she had noticed the difference during the sex last night from the previous nights. Something had changed. It wasn't just two people having sex, it was more.

Damn it, could those words actually be true?

No, he had been in emotional turmoil. For good reason, of course. That was all it had been.

Even if he did mean them, what could they do about it?

Perhaps she could have a serious sit-down with Deacon and Reese and explain to them that she would do what she wanted to do with anyone she wanted to do it with and they'd have no say in the matter. None. Done. And all that crap.

Then demand the club take her off the "no fly" list.

Suuuure.

Simple.

Just like everything always was when it came to dealing with Reese. The older sister who morphed into an overprotective mother-figure whenever she thought her baby sister might get hurt or make a bad decision.

Reilly got it. She understood her sister's attitude, especially after Reese witnessed Reilly bed-bound and battered in the hospital, plus dealing with all the shit afterward.

However, she didn't like it. She didn't like not having one hundred percent control over her own life. Not only because of Reese, but also by being under the club's protection.

She was considered Fury property.

Yes, *property*.

She snuck a glance at Rev's profile as he drove. Today, he looked older than his twenty-eight years. He looked mentally and physically exhausted.

Not just from a lack of sleep.

She reached over, squeezed his thigh and he planted his hand on top of hers for only a couple of seconds before he had to use it to downshift when he pulled onto her street and then backed into her assigned spot in front of her studio apartment.

It was late afternoon since they hadn't rushed back from Coatesville after taking their time having sex again this morning and stopping at a diner on the way home for breakfast. The problem with it being late afternoon was he could be spotted with her at her place. Even worse, with his Bronco stuffed full of her storage unit contents.

How would they explain that one?

Unfortunately, her apartment was on the second floor with stairs that ran along the outside of the building. It would take some time for them to unload his Ford and carry everything up those steps. The only good thing about where her apartment was located was it faced an alley rarely traveled by anyone but residents who lived along it.

If they hurried, they might avoid getting caught.

However, neither of them was in good enough shape to quickly haul boxes up a whole story for what she swore was fifty times. Both were out of breath, sweating and hurting by the time they were through.

Her heart was still sprinting in her chest after dropping the last box on a stack of them filling up a complete corner in her studio apartment. "Holy shit," she breathed, wiping away the beads of sweat from her forehead and temple with her palm.

"No fuckin' shit," he muttered, also breathing hard and glancing around her small apartment.

She realized he'd never seen it before. None of the guys, except for Deacon and Judge, had. Like her, she was sure her place had been declared off-limits.

She sighed. "Nothing like climbing those steps over and over to prove how out of shape we are."

He came over and pulled her into his arms, holding her tight. His body was boiling hot—not the sexy kind of hot—and normally she'd pull free since she was a bit overheated, too, but she didn't want to let him go.

Not yet.

Instead, she settled her chin on his pumping chest.

"We're both sweaty already and that bed over there's empty. Should take advantage of it," he suggested.

"Do you really want your Bronco parked out front for that long? It's a custom classic and unique," she reminded him. "Everyone in town knows who it belongs to."

His mouth went tight and the spark left his eyes. "Yeah. Right." He released her. "Still gotta drop you off at the motel to get your cage."

This was it. Once he dropped her off at The Grove Inn,

they would go their separate ways and have to pretend the last five days never happened.

They'd already made a pact to forget Rev and Saylor's real parentage. That info would be locked away in an invisible box and the key thrown away, hopefully never to resurface again.

So many damn secrets. Unfortunately, all of them necessary.

"Well," she started, "I want to say it was a fun trip, but... uh…" She grimaced.

"Yeah," was all he needed to say. His resigned tone pretty much covered how they both felt about the whole thing.

She tugged lightly on his shirt. He hadn't worn his cut at all during the trip and still wasn't wearing it since he was driving his truck instead of riding his sled. Soon enough he'd slip it back on in the same way he'd slip back into his life here in Manning Grove with his job and family. His *real* family. The ones who loved and respected him and also had his back.

She was happy he had that because he had gone too long in his life without it.

She was happy she had that, too.

They just couldn't have it together unless the rule hanging over her head changed.

But… Did she want that with him? Something more serious than the awesome sex they had in the motel for the past few days?

While she was property of the club, she would need to be ready to become "property of Rev" if they revealed what already happened in Coatesville and what they'd want to continue. All without him getting clubbed upside the head or getting his colors stripped first. That was key.

Was she ready for that? Was he? What did he really want with her, if anything?

Since they both had avoided that discussion, she could only assume neither of them was ready for anything further.

She stepped back, creating space between them. Right now, he had the freedom to do what he wanted, when he wanted and with who he wanted.

If they approached Deacon and Reese, she had a feeling they'd insist Rev claim her at the table and force her to wear his cut. It would be no better than a shot-gun wedding. And nobody wanted that kind of pressure. Nobody wanted to be forced into something they weren't ready for.

Any forced relationship would turn into a complete disaster.

They were in their twenties, *for shit's sake!* Neither should be ready to settle down. Even if they were, she wasn't sure it would be with each other.

Would it?

Gah. No.

He hadn't meant what he said. It had just been his emotions talking, that was all.

Because if he meant it…

Stop it, Reilly.

An unfamiliar sting started in her eyes. *What the hell?* She wasn't a crier and she certainly had no reason to shed tears in this instance.

She was tired, that was all. From the emotional roller coaster of that trip, from the long drive home and from the physical exertion of bringing the boxes up to her second-floor apartment.

The exhaustion was getting to her. She simply needed a nap.

A perfect and easy solution.

She blinked back the welling tears and managed to say through a thick throat, "Can you take me to the Inn now?"

His brow dropped low as he stared at her. She quickly turned away to hide whatever he saw. Or thought he saw.

"Reilly…"

"Rev, I'm worried someone will see your truck and get the wrong idea."

"Yeah, but it wouldn't be the wrong fuckin' idea, now would it?"

"Right," she agreed, quickly wiped the sting from her eyes and turned to face him. "And we need to avoid that. Not for me, but for you. And for Saylor."

She needed to remember that. Whatever happened to him would affect his sister, too.

"Got it." With a stiff nod and his lips pinned tight, he pulled his keys out of his front pocket. "Let's go."

———

SHE WAS ALREADY FEELING the loss of him as he pulled into The Grove Inn's parking lot and drove around back to where her car was hidden behind the building.

He parked next to it, shoved his shifter into neutral and sat there saying nothing. Only the rumble of his Bronco's V8 filled the gap of silence between them.

Maybe he was waiting for her to get out.

She sighed, pushed open the passenger door and grabbed the handle above it so she wouldn't just tumble out of the high-sitting truck and onto her ass like the klutz she could be.

Before she could escape, he grabbed her arm and prevented her from climbing out. When she turned her head to address him, she noticed something else besides his pained expression. And when she grimaced, his head turned, too.

Lizzy, in only a tiny, neon pink bikini, showing off almost every inch of her rocking bod, was now sitting up in a lounge chair where, apparently, she'd been catching rays to turn her skin a rich golden tan.

"Shit," Reilly whispered.

The blonde stood and walked over to the deck railing, showing off even more of that rocking hot bod. *Double shit.* Her smile was large and genuine as she took in Rev and gave him a small wave.

The sweet butt's normally joyous greeting of "Hey!" ended up being drawn out to a, "He…….eeeeeeey," once she realized *why* Rev was there.

To drop Reilly off at her car.

The older blonde's face twisted into a worried expression as she shot a quick glance toward the double sliding glass doors that led from the second-floor manager's apartment to that very deck.

"Shit, can she see me?" Reilly asked under her breath.

"Yeah, babe, you ain't invisible. Neither was your damn cage sittin' here for the last fuckin' week."

"Well, it wouldn't have been sitting here if I hadn't had to hitch a ride with Ozzy because you were too damn stubborn to let me go along," she almost shouted but managed to keep it to an annoyed hiss.

"Always gotta get what you want."

"Oh, you're blaming *me* for this?"

Lizzy's gaze ping-ponged back and forth between Rev and Reilly. Unfortunately, that meant she could not only see them both, she could *hear* them, too, especially since Rev had both windows rolled down.

The sweet butt's perfectly sculpted eyebrows rose but she quickly schooled her surprise and concern as Reilly sighed and climbed out of the Bronco.

Lizzy was the coolest of the sweet butts and Ozzy tended not to give a shit about much, so hopefully they could keep their traps shut. And if Ozzy hadn't run his mouth already about dropping off Reilly at the farm before the crack of dawn five days ago, then he most likely could keep this secret, too.

Or so she hoped.

Two seconds later, the Original himself sauntered out of one of the open sliders, only wearing raggedy cotton shorts and scratching his crotch. He had a hand-rolled—whether it was tobacco or pot, Reilly couldn't tell—tucked between the fingers of the scratching hand and he palmed a full beer bottle with the other.

His eyes were glued to Lizzy in that teeny weenie bikini with her breasts practically falling out as she leaned into the railing. He went from scratching to adjusting what might now be an erection from what Reilly could tell. "Bend over that railin' and—" His grey eyes flashed their way and he froze for a second when he noticed the Bronco and its occupants. He grinned and raised his beer to them in greeting. "You guys wanna watch?"

Lizzy laughed, turned and whacked his arm, her mouth moving but her voice low enough that neither Reilly nor Rev could hear whatever she said to Ozzy.

Ozzy shrugged and went to the railing to stand next to Lizzy, looking down onto the parking lot. "'Bout time you two are back. Didn't think you were gonna be gone so long, woman."

Shit.

"Also didn't realize he was the reason I dropped you off at the farm Tuesday mornin'." Oz put his hand-rolled to his lips and took a long drag. As he continued to speak the smoke escaped his mouth in cloud-like puffs. "Didn't realize you were takin' off the forbidden fuck list, either. 'Cause if I woulda known that..." Ozzy shrugged and his grin widened.

Reilly heard a guttural noise come—maybe even a growl—from deep within Rev's throat.

Shit.

"She's young and doesn't want you, old man," Lizzy sassed him with a hip bump.

"Why? Could teach her a thing or two." Ozzy grabbed his crotch and shook it.

Lizzy bugged out her eyes at Reilly, who had climbed out of the truck and now stood at the rear of it. The sweet butt hooked a thumb toward the older biker and shook her head. "I'm sure she's learned a thing or two just hanging around the barn. We all have."

"Lizzy's really good at eatin' pussy, Lee, if you wanna come up and join us."

Ozzy had called her Lee from the start. She was surprised only a few of the other guys picked up on it and began to use it, too. Rev was not one of them.

"*Lee* don't wanna come up and join you," Rev growled, quickly unfolding himself from the Bronco.

Reilly could see the tension across his shoulders and in his face. She moved next to him and whispered, "He's just fucking with you. You're giving him the answers to his unasked questions just by your reaction."

"Shit," he muttered.

Reilly sighed and yelled up to Ozzy, "I'm going to pass on that offer, Oz, but I appreciate it. And I'm still on the *forbidden fuck* list. However, since Lizzy doesn't have to abide by that list, maybe me and her can go at it together some-time. I'm not opposed to trying something new."

Rev made another noise in his throat. This time it wasn't a growl but more of a choking sound.

"Any time, beautiful," Lizzy said, playing along. "When-ever you want to get together and experiment, I'm up for it." She blew Reilly a kiss.

"If I was going to sit on any woman's face, it would be yours, Liz," Reilly answered, using the name the woman preferred and not the one the guys tended to use, then blew a kiss back to her, knowing it would drive both men bonkers.

Ozzy had an excited look in his face when he said, "You

ladies are makin' me hard as fuck," and rubbed at his crotch. "How 'bout you, brother?"

Rev ignored him, grabbed Reilly's arm and dragged her around the Bronco and to the other side, where her car was parked.

"Are you fuckin' serious?" Rev growled.

She drew a mask of innocence over her face. "Why wouldn't I be? She's hot."

His mouth opened.

"How many times have you done her?"

His mouth snapped shut.

After waiting for a few more silent seconds for his answer, she said, "That's what I thought." She clicked her key fob to unlock her car and reached for the door handle.

His "See you Sunday," made her pause and glance back over her shoulder at him.

"Sunday?" That was tomorrow. What the hell was going on tomorrow?

"Yeah. Club run. You're gonna be my backpack."

Oh shit. She had completely forgotten about it with everything else going on. "I don't think that's smart, Rev."

"Agree it wouldn't be smart if anyone knew we'd been together the last few days."

"Ozzy now knows."

"Ozzy already knew somethin' was up when he dropped you off on the farm. He don't give a fuck. He's too busy picturin' Lizzy's face planted in between your thighs."

"But he now knows who I was with these last few days. Before, he didn't."

Rev snorted. "Like I said, he probably don't give a fuck. If you walked up those deck steps and told him to get naked, he would. He'd have his fuckin' dick out so fast, it would knock you silly."

"Holy shit," she whispered. "Is it that big?" She glanced

up toward the deck where Ozzy and Lizzy still stood at the rail watching them and being nosy.

He shot her an annoyed look. "That wasn't the fuckin' point. And you've seen it. We all have."

That was true. The only cocks she hadn't seen so far was anyone who already had an ol' lady when she came to the club and, of course, Deacon's. She hadn't checked out a couple of the prospects, either, but she was sure she'd see them all soon enough.

Dutch's she'd seen too many damn times. She could probably pick it out in a boner line-up.

"Rev, I don't want to risk you getting caught for breaking a club rule."

She wouldn't be the reason he lost everything. She wouldn't be the reason he was taken out to the field behind The Barn and clubbed like Cage had been. After seeing Rev's fucked-up family, she knew Saylor, the club and the brotherhood were all he had.

She would not be the one to risk any and all of that. She wouldn't be able to live with herself. That meant until that particular rule changed, they needed to be careful.

That also meant she wouldn't be his backpack tomorrow.

Whether he liked it or not.

Chapter Sixteen

SOON REV'S teeth would be ground down to the damn roots. He'd end up a toothless motherfucking fool. Only one hour into a three-hour planned run and he almost couldn't take another fucking minute. He was about to lose his fucking mind and expose shit that they needed to keep a tight lid on. For his sake. For Reilly's sake and for Saylor's sake.

But seeing Reilly wrapped around Dodge's back...

Seeing her thighs gripping his...

Seeing her pussy smashed against the bar manager's ass, who was probably loving every fucking minute of it...

Seeing her tits pressed into a Fury brother's cut...

"Fuck!" he shouted, hoping the deep, loud roar of their sleds covered up his outburst.

Easy's head twisted toward him and he gave him a questioning look.

Rev ignored the man who was paired with him in formation, and kept his eyes on the sled directly in front of him. Maybe he should switch positions with Whip, who was riding toward the front. Then he could ignore Reilly's arms wrapped tightly around a man who wasn't him.

Sure he fucking could.

But then he couldn't make sure Dodge didn't do anything inappropriate with Reilly. Like squeeze her knee or trail his fingers up her thigh, or…

Touch her in any way.

He swallowed down his next, "Fuck!" and screamed it in his head instead.

His sled wobbled and he quickly straightened it out. If he crashed due to his inability to pay attention to anything other than Dodge and Reilly, he'd most likely take out anyone in formation behind him.

It would end up a dangerous game of dominos.

All because of his spiraling, out-of-control thoughts.

Since his parents had considered him a sinner, they had made him repeat the seven deadly sins over and over until he could recite them from memory.

Now, as he repeated each one out loud, the wind whipped it away. "Lust. Gluttony. Greed. Sloth. Wrath. Envy. Pride."

They'd insisted that by him committing any of those seven deadly sins, it would spur him to commit even more. Committing one sin would lead to another and another until his soul was condemned to eternal damnation.

Until he was forever lost and could no longer be saved.

For fuck's sake, he wasn't committing only one right now, but all of them.

The sin of lust was his burning desire to touch, taste and fuck her. He committed the sin of gluttony because he couldn't get enough of her. And he was greedy as fuck. He didn't want to share her. He wanted to keep her for himself and not let anyone else touch her.

After every time they'd had sex at the motel, once they both came, he had committed the sin of sloth by never being in a rush to move. He wanted to stay right where he was forever. Inside her and connected to her.

Wrath... *Fuck.* Right now, he was really hating Dodge, even though the Fury brother had no clue what was going on.

He was envious of Dodge because she rode on his sled instead of Rev's. Envy led into his sin of pride. Reilly shouldn't want to be on anyone's sled but his. It shouldn't have been a goddamn question. Her ass should be planted solidly behind him and her arms wrapped around his waist, instead.

According to his parents *wisdom,* he was facing eternal damnation because of the woman in front of him who tempted him. And because he realized what he felt for her was much more than simple temptation.

Worse, she had blown off his words as if they'd meant nothing. But then, at the time, he hadn't taken them seriously, either.

When they first were spoken, he thought it was a mistake. A crossing of wires in his overloaded brain. But, yesterday, after going their separate ways, he realized he hadn't misspoken. The whiskey had forced the truth to the surface.

It all really hit home last night when sleeping alone in his bunkhouse rack had fucking sucked. In the past, he'd always preferred to sleep alone. Before Reilly, the only night he hadn't was the night he fell asleep in Sarah's bed.

But last night, being a typical Saturday night, The Barn had been hopping with his brothers partying. Sweet butts and female hang-arounds did their rounds, making it known they were available. With, of course, his brothers taking advantage of that availability like normal, whether out in The Barn where everyone could watch, back in the bunkhouse or even out in the courtyard against a wall or bent over a picnic table under the pavilion.

For the few minutes he'd been sitting at the bar nursing a whiskey, he had to make excuse after excuse of why he couldn't double-team Angel with Easy or why he didn't want Brandy to unzip his jeans and drop to her knees right there on the spot.

Or why he wasn't in the mood for Billie to do what she normally did to his nipples that drove him batshit crazy to the point he'd blow his load almost instantly and he wasn't even embarrassed about how fast he came. The woman had some damn good skills and was super-efficient.

It got to the point last night where he finally went to his room, locked the door, plugged his earbuds into his listening holes and ignored the rest of the fucking world around him.

As he sprawled across his bed, drowning out everything else by blasting his favorite Spotify playlist, he went over every fucking moment of their trip. From the second he saw Reilly in the shed waiting for him, to the second he drove away from The Grove Inn yesterday afternoon.

While the run was more annoying than relaxing today, he also wasn't looking forward to this evening back at the farm when he'd have to once again sidestep the sweet butts as much as possible. With the available brothers dwindling in number, the club girls tended to hone in on the few who weren't claimed. They reminded him of buzzards circling fresh roadkill.

They'd been complaining a lot lately about the available members being slim-pickings. But until the prospects were patched in, the sweet butts couldn't touch them and, in turn, the recruits couldn't approach them for any reason other than to simply hang out. If the prospects were doing anything more than that, they would find themselves outside looking in. That was after their prospect cut was stripped from them and their ass was kicked due to breaking the rules.

So, yeah, the sweet butts were limited to the Fury members without an ol' lady. That meant they were down to only six: Rev, Easy, Dutch, Dodge, Ozzy and Whip.

And right now, Rev wasn't in the mood to do anything with any of them. Even if he was, he wasn't sure he'd want to do it in front of Reilly. If she saw him doing a sweet butt, would she get bent and take off to find some random dick out there and revenge-bang him?

Jesus fuck.

He ground a hand back and forth over his mouth, trying to stifle another loud curse.

This fucking run couldn't be over soon enough. If he wouldn't be ridden until his ass was chapped, he'd peel off and go get lost somewhere with booze and a bong. Then when he woke up from his damn stupor, it would be time to go to work and everything would be back to the way it was before...

He barked out a painful laugh and Easy frowned at him.

"You okay, brother?" E shouted over the wind and the roar of their exhaust.

No, he wasn't fucking okay.

Unless something changed, he was starting to wonder if he'd ever be okay again.

Especially since shortly after they got back to the farm and while getting ready to party for the evening, he spotted Trip and Deacon taking Reilly into the barn and up to the executive meeting room upstairs.

Rev's asshole had never been so tightly puckered in his life than at that sight.

———

REILLY'S HEART thumped so loudly in her ears, she could hardly hear what Trip was saying as he and Deacon escorted her into The Barn and upstairs to where the club officers had their meetings.

She'd only been up there a couple of times. It was rare any women went upstairs and into their "sacred" room that held the heavy scent of testosterone in the air. Unless, of course, they needed to grab something from the storage area that was tucked between the meeting room and the two apartments on the backside of the bunkhouse.

The heavy, rectangular table that sat in the middle of the space had the BFMC logo carved into the top. Whoever had hand carved it had skills. The table was worn and parts of the wood were nicked and stained since the table was as old as the club. And not the current Blood Fury old, but the Originals old since it had belonged to them. She wouldn't be surprised if the guys had lifted their legs to mark it like the dogs they could be. The chair at the end, where Trip currently sat as president, was the same chair his father Buck, the former president, had used.

Deacon, who Reilly also considered her *ol' man-in-law*, yanked out an empty chair along the side and jerked his chin toward it. "Sit down."

"What's this about?" Her pulse was now throbbing at her temples so hard, they could probably see it.

Trip, wearing his ever-present black ball cap pulled low, tipped his head toward the chair. "Sit. Got somethin' important to discuss with you."

Should she drop to her knees right where she stood and beg for leniency for Rev? Blame everything on herself? Tell them she forced him?

Throw herself at their mercy?

Offer to take his place for the blanket party?

He didn't deserve whatever they would do to him. It was all her fault. She never should've insisted on going along.

She—

"Sit down, Reilly," Trip ordered more firmly.

Shit.

"It's not what you think," she began weakly as she moved to where Deacon stood behind the pulled-out chair. As she sat, the club's treasurer rounded the table and settled in the chair to Trip's right, directly across the wide table from her.

She was afraid to look her sister's ol' man in the eye. If she did, she just might start confessing everything in hopes to spare Rev.

"What ain't?" Trip asked with a small shake of his head.

"What you think. It isn't what you think."

"What the fuck you talkin' about, Lee?" Deacon asked, his brow now wrinkled.

"Why you brought me up here. Whatever you think is wrong. It's not what you think." *Holy shit.* She was babbling like a damn fool.

Late one night, she had stumbled across a documentary on police interrogation and she needed to take a page out of that book. She should just sit down, shut up and let them do all the talking. Then she should either say nothing or simply flat out deny everything.

That sounded like a plan.

If that didn't work, she'd go back to her original plan of throwing herself at their mercy and begging for Rev to be spared.

"What fuckin' drugs have you done?" Trip asked, frowning. "You're actin' crazy."

Deacon snorted. "When has she ever been normal?"

Like *he* should talk. "None. I… Wait. Why did you bring me up here?"

"Fuck that. Now I wanna know why you got all paranoid," Trip said, pinning his dark eyes on her. "What the fuck d'you need to tell us?"

"Nothing. I… I… I just thought I was in trouble for something." She grimaced and nervously tugged her hair over her scar.

Deacon noticed the movement she did out of habit, especially when she was anxious, and scowled. "What the fuck would you be in trouble for? What'd you do?"

She sat back, drew a blank mask over her face and cheerily chirped, "Nothing."

Both Deacon and Trip cocked their right eyebrows, reminding her of synchronized swimmers.

Shit.

"If you got somethin' to share, share it," Trip ordered. "If you're hidin' shit that might hurt the club and I find out, I'm gonna be pissed."

"I'm not. I swear."

Trip sat back in his high-backed chair and gripped the armrests tightly. "Better not be lyin'."

"Is one of the prospects fuckin' with you? That Scar? Is he tryin' shit?" Deacon asked, leaning forward, holding her gaze.

Huh? "No. He doesn't even talk to me."

"Good," Trip grunted. "Stay clear of him 'til we got a better handle on him." The club president sharply clapped his hands together once. "All right. Don't wanna be up here all night. Wanna go get fucked up and then go get fucked. So, let's get this shit over with." He held his hand up. "On a side note, you know you can go to Deke about anythin', right? He's responsible for you."

What? This was news to her. "He is?" Her gaze swung back and forth between the two men. "Since when?"

"Since the second he claimed your sister as his ol' lady. And once you decided to stay, become part of the club and he made you one of the untouchables."

"About that—"

"No." Trip shook his head. "We got other shit to talk about. We ain't dealin' with that tonight."

"I don't want to be on that list."

"That's not negotiable 'til your sister says otherwise," Deacon said.

"Which will be never," she muttered.

Deacon shrugged, crossed his arms over his chest and sat back. "Work it out with her. I ain't fightin' that fight."

Trip chuckled. "Yeah, 'cause he don't want to be outside lookin' in. And by lookin' in, I don't mean her fuckin' windows."

"Ain't gonna lie. That's fuckin' true. Ain't givin' up pussy for you to get dick," Deacon said.

Reilly rolled her eyes. "Thanks for thinking of me."

"You want dick, just get it elsewhere," Deacon said with another shrug.

"*Annnnnd* thanks for that advice on how to get laid. But if we really want to get down to it, I don't need permission from anyone." She shrugged just like Deacon had and added a raised chin in a clear challenge as she stared back at him.

"Right," Trip said, his head swiveling back and forth between her and the club treasurer. "But just not with any of our brothers. Or prospects. Get it elsewhere so you ain't causin' problems."

"So... no one cares if I fuck some hobo living by the railroad tracks, but you only care if it's someone I've known for the past year because they wear a Fury cut."

"Yep," Trip agreed. "Now, we're done talkin' about your sex life and where you need to find dick and we're gonna talk about the reason we brought you the fuck up here. Don't got all fuckin' night. I'm thirsty, hungry and horny."

It was her turn to sit back in her chair and cross her arms over her chest with impatience. "Then spill whatever you're going to say."

Trip's eyebrows shot up and disappeared under his ball cap. "Damn, woman. Don't make me change my fuckin' mind about handin' you this opportunity."

She dropped her crossed arms. "What opportunity?"

"You ready to listen?" Trip asked smartly.

Reilly pinned her mouth shut and opened her ears. The word opportunity made her think this wasn't going to be an interrogation but about something else entirely. That whatever they brought her upstairs for was possibly good and not bad.

"Guess that's a yes." Deacon grinned.

"You ain't stupid..." Trip started.

What kind of conversation starter was that?

She opened her mouth and Trip lifted a hand to stop her. "You talkin' or listenin'?"

Reilly flapped her hand at him to continue.

"Like I was sayin', you ain't stupid and you got business smarts. We ain't usin' you to your full potential with you workin' for Dutch. Also like that you don't take no shit, so you'd have no problem runnin' a crew made up of possible dickheads."

"Coulda omitted the word 'possible,'" Deacon informed him.

"A crew?" she asked, more confused than ever.

Trip lifted one eyebrow and she shut up.

He continued. "You got a business degree you're wastin'..."

"Have you been talking to Reese?" she accused him with a frown.

"Woman," Trip breathed impatiently. The club president had a trigger temper and she could see he was edging toward it.

"Sheesh. All right. Go on."

Trip pulled his cap off his head, raked fingers through his hair, slapped the hat back on and blew out a noisy breath. He glanced at Deacon, shook his head and then looked back at her. "Pushin' my buttons, Lee," he warned.

"It's a bad habit."

"Tryin' to help you out here."

"Help me or you?"

Trip's mouth got tight. "Both. You wanna hear it? Or

you want me to cut this shit short and find someone else who don't backtalk?"

She stared at the club's president sitting at the end of the table. In the chair of power.

He could've told her to fuck off when she was in danger from Billy Warren, he didn't. He allowed her to come out to the farm and stay in Deacon's apartment until that asshole was gone. He permitted her to stay even after that and become part of the club when she had no blood ties to any of the members and couldn't become an official member herself. He also helped convince Dutch to give her a damn job because she was bored as hell waiting for that abusive asshole to be caught.

Trip had done a lot for her. So had the rest of the club. More importantly, her sister was deeply in love with the Viking of a man who sat across the table from her. That alone was priceless to her.

Her older sister finally found someone who not only truly loved her back, but would be dedicated, loyal and protective. Traits Reese had hoped for with her first husband, but never got. Instead, she was hurt and ended up building an even higher barrier around herself. An almost impenetrable wall Deacon struggled to scale. But he was smart about it and didn't push her. He let her begin to deconstruct her wall on her own to the point where he could finally manage to climb over it and into Reese's heart.

Reese had finally found her happy. Their relationship might not be conventional, but it was real. Because of that, Reilly loved Deacon for everything he did for and gave to Reese. Also, for his endless patience when dealing with her very stubborn older sister.

The club was her and Reese's family now. They didn't have to be. They could have shut Reilly out and told her to take her problems with the abusive asshole elsewhere.

They didn't.

Once again, her eyes began to sting with tears.

What the hell was wrong with her? First, Rev's declaration of love almost made her cry, now this. And she still didn't even know what "this" was yet.

She sniffled and nodded.

"You ain't cryin' are you?" Deacon asked, his eyes wide and his words a bit panicked.

"I'm not crying!" she exclaimed. "I never cry!"

"All women cry," Trip muttered under his breath.

"No, we don't," she insisted, rubbing the sting away.

"You and your sister are tough as fuckin' nails," Deacon said more softly. "I get it. You had to be to survive your childhood. You also had to be to survive that motherfuckin' asshole Warren. Ain't a thing if you gotta cry."

"Can we just get on with this opportunity?" she asked, wanting to change the subject.

"'Kay," Trip started. "Here it is… When we got that trailer for Cage, Dutch spent a fuckload of scratch to temporarily rent it. That got me thinkin' a similar business would be a good investment for the club. As treasurer, Deacon's been doin' the footwork to see what scratch we'd need to invest to get one started. We got the room out here on the farm to set one up and I wanna start doin' that. It's a huge investment, but it's got a lotta potential for profit, 'specially when the insurance companies are footin' the bill durin' natural disasters, house fires, or whatever reason someone would need emergency housin' for."

"Like surprise babies," Deacon chimed in.

"Yeah," Trip agreed. "Like someone stickin' their dick where they shouldn't and then wonderin' why a surprise that cries pops out months later."

Reilly planted a hand on her belly in panic for a second, then remembered they'd taken precautions. Not only with condoms but she was also on birth control. Unless Rev's sperm were mini-Transformers or her eggs were like the

Kool-Aid man crashing through a brick wall, neither were getting through those secure roadblocks.

Deacon's eyes narrowed. "Why'd you do that?"

"Do what?"

"Slam your hand on your gut like that," he answered with a curious tilt of his mohawk-braided head.

"I'm hungry and my stomach's growling," she lied and slid her hand down to her lap where they could no longer see it.

"Can we get back to business here?" Trip asked sharply. "She ain't the only one starvin'."

"Carry on," Reilly told him.

"Okay, thanks for your permission." Trip sighed. "Any-fuckin-way, want you to manage it."

What? Did she hear that correctly? "Manage what?"

"The fuckin' emergency housin' business and the crew who are gonna help you," he just about shouted like she was hard of hearing.

Holy shit! "Who will be the crew?"

"Castle and Bones for now. They're gonna get their commercial driver's licenses and then I'm gonna get them some trainin' on how to haul and set up the trailers. You're gonna need that trainin', too, so you know what the fuck's goin' on and you can ride their asses if they fuck up."

Holy shit! "Am I going to get my own office?" She was trying not to bounce in her seat with excitement.

This was an awesome opportunity, especially if she was allowed to run it herself. She could put her business skills to use. Marketing, advertising...

Trip answered, "Not yet."

Shit.

"Talked to Dutch already. You're gonna work outta his office since the business will be slow to start and it'll be a while before it starts bringin' in scratch. If you can build it to the point it takes off, gets busy and starts bringin' in enough scratch, we'll get you set up somewhere else so you'd only have to concentrate on that. Look at it as motivation to grow that business. Club's gonna buy two mobile homes to start. In six months, if we find it's worth it, we'll buy two more and so on." He leaned forward and held her gaze. "Also, after a point, you'll earn a percentage of the profits. In the meantime, Dutch will be payin' you your salary and the club will be throwin' you some extra scratch for runnin' things 'til the business is self-sufficient."

Holy shit! They were stepping in again in an effort to make her life even better. To give her the purpose she had lost along the way after graduating college and then after almost taking an unexpected, permanent nap.

"Just think, you might be able to afford somethin' better than that shithole apartment you got now," Deacon said. "In fact, your sister and I prefer you get a modular and put it near the other three so you're close."

The other three were where Judge, Cage and Rook lived all in a neat row.

"They ain't the only ones," Trip added. "You know how I feel about you livin' in town even though it's close to Dutch's place and his garage."

The only reason Deacon and Reese hadn't moved into a modular themselves was Reese refused to give up her beautiful mountain home to move onto the farm and into a small modular. Reilly didn't blame her not wanting to sell her dream home, but it was a point of contention between her and Trip, since the club president preferred everyone to live on the farm.

The only acceptable compromise they could come up with in Deacon and Reese's case was for the couple to continue to divide their time between the farm and nearby Mansfield. Deacon kept the bunkhouse apartment, so the couple could spend weekends on the farm, and weeknights at her house, so she'd be near her law practice. Deacon didn't mind the twenty-minute drive during the week to spend the night with his ol' lady.

Reilly's gaze swung between the two men. "Does Reese know about this?"

"Yeah. She's in full agreement with the plan since you'll be puttin' your degree to better use and eventually makin' a shitload more money if you make that business a success. She's already workin' on the paperwork to establish the business name, get the licenses, and all of that shit, plus draftin' the contracts you'll use for the rentals. Red's gonna do the books for you, too, so you won't have to worry 'bout that."

Holy shit!

"So, you onboard?" Trip asked.

"Hell yes!" she yelled, jumping to her feet. She barely managed to stop herself from dancing across the room. "I freaking love this idea!"

Should she hug them? She wanted to squeeze them both!

"And if the prospects give you any shit you can't deal with, you know to come to us," Deacon reminded her.

"I can handle a couple of prospects," she told them with confidence.

"Figured that," Trip said with a grin. "If anyone can snag them by the balls and keep 'em in line, it's you."

"I can snag them but I just can't suck them, right?" she teased the Fury president.

Trip dropped his head to stare at the table and shook it. When he finally lifted it, he said, "Make a deal with you. You convince Reese to take you off the list, we'll take you off the list. But don't want you causin' any fuckin' drama in the club 'cause one of 'em is bonin' you one night and bonin' someone else the next. The second you cause that drama, you're back on that list," Trip warned her. "You got me?"

She smiled. "I got you."

"But 'til Reese gives the okay, you're still stuck on it," Deacon reminded her. "Don't get a brother fucked up 'cause you want to take a spin on his dick."

She rolled her lips under and nodded.

"Good fuckin' luck with your sister," Trip said.

Unfortunately, she would need it.

But even so, this conversation had given her a lot of hope and a much brighter future.

Chapter Seventeen

Rev paused with a beer to his lips as Reilly came out of The Barn and practically bounced across the courtyard. Her movements looked like she had done a few lines of coke followed by a hit of acid.

What the actual fuck.

No one ever said she was graceful. Because she sure as fuck wasn't.

In fact, his heart caught in his throat as she stumbled and almost face-planted halfway to the pavilion.

"Jesus fuck," he muttered before taking a long draw on the can to keep from rushing over to her. When he was done swallowing his beer along with his instinct to protect her, he realized he'd almost crushed the can within his fingers.

Maybe he needed to switch over to the hard stuff.

Yeah, that woman was enough to make anyone drink. Especially him.

While he was relieved to see her so happy, it bugged the shit out of him that he didn't know why. If Trip and Deacon had grilled her about where she'd been and what she'd been doing for the last week—and with who—he doubted she'd be wearing that huge-ass smile. It only made him more curious about why Trip and Deacon hauled her, and no one else, inside and upstairs.

He'd have to pull her aside and find out. Right now, the courtyard was packed, and it would be for hours yet. He glanced around to find he wasn't the only one who noticed she was beaming and excited. It also bugged him that he wasn't the only one with a functioning dick watching her closely. He was damn sure Reilly was spank bank material for some of his club brothers.

But she was also hard to ignore since Cujo was snarling and snapping at her heels like the asshole Chihuahua he was.

Between the two of them, it was comic entertainment.

Rook yelled for Cujo, but the dog ignored him. Jet rushed over to scoop up the tiny terror so he didn't trip Reilly as she finished heading over to the pavilion where the ladies gathered.

Yeah, now was not the time to get her attention since she was surrounded by nosy eyes and ears. As soon as the sun went down, he'd have to catch her somewhere no one else would see or hear them.

It wasn't like everyone wasn't used to seeing Reilly flitting around the parties and pig roasts being over-friendly and social, but if Rev got her aside, he was going to have a hard time not touching her.

And that could cause a problem.

Not could. Would.

Because his urge to touch her involved a lot more than a friendly hug or handshake. Or casual flirting. So, it would be safer if he had an opportunity to get her somewhere private. And not in his room.

He was surprised how fast he'd gotten comfortable with her sharing his bed and sleeping by his side while in Coatesville. The best part of the trip was being able to simply roll over and slide right between her thighs whenever he wanted.

He had to turn away from watching her now because he was starting to get a semi. He needed to focus on anything other than her. Across the open courtyard, he spotted his sister talking with Chelle's daughters, Maddie and Josie.

He hadn't had a chance to tell Saylor that their "father" was dead yet. He was sure the news would put her in a better mood than she already was. She might even start bouncing around the courtyard like Reilly.

Fuck it, there was no better time like the present. Hopefully that conversation would help get his mind off the blonde now sitting under the pavilion laughing and drinking with the rest of the women.

With a few interested eyes, not only the ones in his own head, turned her way.

———

REILLY PEERED over the lip of her wine-filled Solo cup as she watched Rev swagger across the courtyard in the direction of Saylor, Maddie and Josie. When he got to the girls, he stood chatting with them, a relaxed smile on his handsome face as he sipped a beer held in one hand and occasionally took a drag on a hand-rolled held in the other.

When Saylor held out her hand for the cigarette, Reilly realized it wasn't tobacco but something stronger.

"Funny how you disappeared at the same time as Rev did," Autumn murmured. Her hazel eyes were also glued with interest to Rev across the courtyard.

Chelle's daughters appeared to be playfully flirting with him while Saylor took a couple of long hits off the joint. Suddenly the smoke shot out both her nose and mouth as she doubled over in laughter at whatever had been said.

After seeing the nightmare in Coatesville, she was glad

Rev's baby sister was happy for the most part and could laugh. It was amazing what support and a loving family could do for someone.

Reilly included.

"And magically reappeared at the same time, too," Autumn finished softly.

Reilly pulled her gaze from the small group and glanced over at Reese to see if her sister had heard Red.

"Coincidence," she murmured. She twisted on the picnic bench to face the red-headed woman who was around the same age as her. Reilly needed to change the topic and quickly. "Trip said you'll do the books for the new business."

Sig's old lady smiled. "Yes, they already added that responsibility onto my pile."

Reilly frowned. "Will it be too much for you?"

Autumn shook her head. "No. Honestly, I really don't have enough work right now. I want to keep busy *and* earn my keep. Once I got all the books straightened out for the rest of the businesses, including the garage and Justice Bail Bonds, I now only need to keep ahead of it. Luckily, Deke was good at keeping the bail bonds books up to date, Dutch, not so much when it came to the garage."

Reilly laughed. "Yeah, he doesn't give a shit about keeping track of bills and receipts and the rest." She dropped her voice low and made it gruff to sound like Dutch. "'That's all a buncha bullshit!'" Reilly then scratched her non-existent balls.

Red giggled softly. "Well, thank you for tracking down a lot of the paperwork I needed. That helped a lot. The man would keep a greasy receipt for a hamburger but not one for an alternator, an actual business expense."

"Hey, I was just happy I didn't have to do the book-keeping at all for the garage and now for the emergency housing business. I hate that side of it."

"Your sister will be happy about you running the new business. Does it have a name yet? Sig didn't say."

Reilly shrugged. "They didn't mention one. They offered me the opportunity to run it but that's about it. Reese is supposed to be handling the paperwork." She turned toward her sister who sat with Chelle and Cassie at the next table. "Hey, sis!"

Reese glanced over her shoulder at her.

"Is there a name for the new business?"

Her older sister turned on the bench seat to face Red and Reilly, a plastic Solo cup in her hand, too. "I'm working on putting the paperwork together now. Trip didn't give me a name. Did they make you the offer? Is that why they dragged you inside?"

Reilly nodded.

Reese smiled. "And? I assume you said yes?"

"Of course. But the business needs a name if no one picked one already."

"It's going to be your business for the most part, you pick," her sister said.

"It's the Fury's business," Reilly corrected her. "I'll only manage it."

"Trip wants you to run it as your own. The more money the business makes, the more you'll make."

"And the more the club makes," Reilly added.

"But it's a business you don't have to invest a dime in, Reilly. It doesn't get any better than that. It's no risk to you."

Reese was right.

"Truthfully, I'm excited. I'll finally get to put my education to use and you can stop harping on me about that."

Reese rolled her eyes. "That education wasn't cheap."

"Eventually, I'll be able to pay you back." If she did, that would be one less thing Reese could hold over her head.

"I don't need to be paid back. I've never asked that of you. I wanted to give you a solid start in life, that's all."

"And you did and I appreciate it. If I can, I want to pay you back," Reilly insisted.

"I don't need the money," Reese said with a frown.

"Then donate it to charity," Reilly snapped, unable to control the irritation at her sister's stubbornness.

"Yes!" Cassie chimed in, attempting to cut the tension between the sisters. "That's a great idea. You can donate it to the Kids Can Do Foundation."

Kids Can Do was the children's cancer foundation Cassie's late husband stole tens of thousands of dollars from. The BFMC had organized a couple of fundraisers so far to raise enough money to replace the funds the asshole embezzled from the charity. Even though Cassie had nothing to do with the crime, she still felt guilty and wanted to help Kids Can Do recover some of their loss. Not to mention, it was a worthwhile cause.

It also didn't hurt for the club to be involved in goodwill by doing charity fundraisers or helping the less fortunate in and around town. It helped settle the townspeople's fears when it came to the growing BFMC since the Originals had wreaked havoc on the town all those years ago. Havoc some town residents still remembered.

"That's fine with me," Reese answered, getting up from where she sat and moving next to Reilly.

"Then that's the plan," Reilly said.

"But with your first million, I'd like you to get out of that apartment and into a house out here."

Reilly sighed. "So my every move can be watched?"

Reese's lips pinned flat.

Stella cut in from two tables over. "Reilly, you know Trip wants everyone as close as possible. Not so you can be watched in the way you mean, but to keep you safe. He worries. Judge worries. Hell, they all worry."

Jet, Rook's ol' lady, said, "Just because the feds raided the Shirleys' compound, doesn't mean they're no longer a problem. For all we know, it might only be a temporary reprieve. We don't know where some of them went, if any of them were released from custody or if any are coming back. Even if the government seizes their land, that won't stop them from squatting up there. They live by their own laws and they don't care about breaking real ones."

"Exactly. They don't give a shit what the government does," Stella reminded them. "They think they are their own government. Just because the feds take their land doesn't mean they won't try to take it back. In fact, count on it."

"The guys are aware of that, right?" Reilly asked.

"Of course," Stella, the black-haired, heavily-tattooed bar owner answered. "They're using the prospects to keep an eye on things."

"Speaking of prospects," Jet began, "Scar isn't going to be helping you with the new business, is he?"

Jet hated Scar. She didn't trust him for a second. The feeling was mutual between former cop and the ex-felon.

"No. Trip said Castle and Bones for now." She was glad she wouldn't be responsible to keep Scar in line. Even though both Castle and Bones were recently released from prison, too, they didn't seem as intimidating as Scar. They didn't look as scary, either.

"Good. Ladies, please be cautious around him," Jet warned. "I really don't want to have to plug a .45 between his eyes because he did something stupid with one of you."

"If he does something 'stupid' to one of us, you'll never get that chance," Cassie said. "One of the guys will do it first."

"True," Jet said on a laugh.

"Does Rook regret sponsoring him?" Chelle asked, her head tipped to the side. She was wearing her glasses and would look like the school librarian she was if it weren't for the torn jeans, the curve-hugging Harley T-shirt and "Property of Shade" cut she wore. It made her look like a librarian badass, if there was such a thing. If not, Chelle would be the definition. She not only rocked the look, she was one hot momma. "He is really damn scary. I wouldn't want to be alone with him in a dark alley."

"Yeah," Jet agreed softly. "Rook's being cautiously optimistic that Scar will end up being an asset to the club. I hope he's not wrong."

"I see he started to get that teardrop lasered off," Autumn mentioned.

"That was one of Trip's requirements," Stella explained.

Jemma wandered over, carrying Dyna. She sat down and propped the ten-month-old baby girl in her lap.

"Where's Tessa?" Reilly asked, tempted to grab the baby and blow on her pudgy belly to make her laugh.

Jemma shrugged and flapped a hand over her shoulder. "Now that the run is over, I told her I'd take Dyna and she should go have fun for the rest of the day and night. She said she might have a date later and won't be home until," Cage's ol' lady shrugged, "later."

That meant Trip's sister might not be coming home at all tonight.

"With who?" Stella asked, her eyebrows pinned together.

Judge's sister shrugged. "Not my business. She's old enough to have her own life."

Reilly bugged out her eyes. "Right? Just like I am. And Tessa is younger than me."

"No one says you can't date," Reese muttered.

"Just as long as whoever I date doesn't wear a Fury cut, right?"

"Have you ever seen anyone wearing a Fury cut *date*?" Reese asked.

Reilly's eyebrows rose. "What did you and Deacon do?" Already knowing the answer was *not* dating.

Stella snorted so loudly that all the ladies burst out laughing.

Reilly turned toward the president's ol' lady. "Did you and Trip date?"

She snorted again, not as loudly this time. "No, we fought and fucked."

Jet laughed. "Same. I highly recommend it. Hate fucks are the best."

Reilly turned to Autumn. "Did you and Sig date?"

"No. We... uh... No."

Reilly turned toward Chelle. "How about you and Shade?"

Chelle's cheeks bloomed pink. "We spent a lot of time together."

"Sure you did," Reilly huffed, "in bed."

"And other places," Chelle added, the pink in her cheeks turning to a flaming red.

Reilly leaned forward. "Jemma? Cassie?"

Judge's ol' lady lifted a hand. "Keep me out of this. I think you can sleep with whoever you want to sleep with. We're all independent women who are secure with our sexuality."

"Damn right!" Stella yelled, pumping her fist into the air and hooting loudly. A bunch of interested eyes of the male variety turned their direction.

"Cage and I definitely didn't date. I didn't want anything to do with him in that way. I was treating him as if he was poison ivy." Jemma sighed. "But I agree with Cass. If you want to bang Dodge one night and Whip the next... or Ozzy *and* Easy at the same time, who am I to judge? More power to you, girl." She lifted her wine with one hand and with the other helped steady the bottle in Dyna's mouth as the baby contently drank formula. "I think it's wrong that just because we are the sisters of Fury members that we were put on some damn list in the first place. That's crazy.

That's like us putting *them* on a list to try to control who they fuck. Ridiculous. And archaic."

Reilly lifted her plastic cup high in the air. "Hear! Hear! Now someone's talking some sense. I should be able to sleep with whoever I want to. Fury member, hang-around, Joe Schmo or even the Easter fucking Bunny. Who cares?"

"I care," Reese said. "I don't want you getting hurt again."

Reilly sighed and as she lifted her glass to her lips, she spotted Amber approaching Rev from behind. He was unaware she was there until the sweet butt tucked her arms under his cut and wrapped them around his waist, pressing herself to his back. And not in a friendly bear hug type of way, either.

Reilly could only imagine what her hands were grabbing onto on the front side of the biker.

She began to stand but forced herself back to her seat. She couldn't say anything and she definitely couldn't go over there and act like some jealous bitch. She needed to remain where she was and not let any of what was normal activity between the single bikers and the sweet butts bother her.

It never bothered her before. It shouldn't bother her now.

Rev turned in Amber's arms with a frown and Reilly was right. Amber was grabbing his crotch and giving him a big smile.

And probably an offer to take care of his business for him in one way or another.

Reilly sucked air through her nostrils and more wine down her throat before forcing her attention back to the ladies.

Shit. What had they been talking about?

Oh, yeah, the list that she, Tessa and Saylor were on. And now Maddie and Josie, too. The "They're Not Virgins But Let's Pretend They Are" list.

She grimaced and peeked back over in Rev's direction again. Amber had moved on, thankfully, and he now had his sister pulled off to the side. They were having what looked like a serious conversation. Maybe he was telling her what happened in Coatesville. Reilly couldn't see Saylor's expression because Rev's broad body blocked her.

"Did you start unpacking your boxes yet?" Reese's question snapped her back to the pavilion.

"Not yet. It took forever to unload them from the car yesterday. That's one downfall of living on the second floor."

"You should've called. Deke and I would've come over to help carry them up."

"I needed the exercise."

"So, who did you visit with? Did you girls have fun?"

Suuure. We lived in a horror movie during the day and a porno at night.

"Yes, it was nice to see some of my old friends," she fibbed.

"I bet they were worried when they found out what happened to you."

"I didn't bring that up."

"Well, they're welcome to come up here to visit anytime."

"Thanks, *Mom*," Reilly said smartly.

A few emotions crossed Reese's face and none of them were good.

They also made Reilly feel awful for causing them. "Sorry."

"Me, too," Reese said softly. "I know you want to do your own thing, Reilly, I do. I also know I'm overprotective, but you know why. I'm trying to do better, I am. I'm sorry I'm failing at it. Taking care of you and being worried about you is deeply ingrained in me. It has been since the moment you were born. It's a hard habit to break."

Reilly squeezed her eyes shut for a moment because that unfamiliar sting was bothering her again. She thought about how Saylor and Rev grew up. In a totally rigid and loveless house.

Reese always tried her best, even when she didn't have to. Even when it wasn't her responsibility. Reilly never felt unloved by her. Not once.

Reese, even as a child, had done a better job at being a parent to Reilly than John and Rachel Schmidt had ever been to Saylor and Rev.

She opened her eyes and grabbed Reese's free hand, giving it a squeeze. "No. I'm sorry. I'm lucky I had you."

"You still have me. No matter what."

"And you have me," Reilly said. "Always."

Reese gave her a soft smile and cleared the thick from her throat. "That's what family is for... Anyway, I'm excited for this new opportunity for you."

"Me, too. I love you and I love this crazy, patchwork family of ours. It's crazy how we ended up here but I'm glad we did."

Reese nodded. "I never, ever could have imagined it." She laughed and shook her head. "Look at me, wearing a leather vest that says I'm property of a man."

"Hell froze over the day you first put that on. But seriously... I doubt Deke holds you to that."

Her sister's expression turned serious. "He'd like to."

"But he doesn't. I don't think he'd ever want to try to take away how strong and independent you are. He loves that about you."

"And I love that he respects that. Which is why I wear his cut on club runs without an argument. I do it for him."

Reilly wouldn't doubt Reese wore it for herself, too. Deacon made her realize there was so much more to life than burying herself in her work. Every time she donned

Deacon's cut and climbed on his sled, Reese allowed the pressures of life to fall away. Even if only temporarily.

Before Deacon, all she did was focus on her career. Reilly had been afraid she'd work herself to death.

"I'm glad you're happy."

"You have no idea," Reese breathed. She glanced around first before lowering her voice so only Reilly could hear her. The other women were now busy chit-chatting and drinking at the other tables. "But I'm also really scared right now."

Her strong, fearless sister was scared?

"What about? Me?"

"No…" She shook her head. "I'm pregnant."

"Holy shit," Reilly whispered. Her eyes landed on the cup her sister was clutching like a lifeline.

"It's iced tea," Reese answered her unasked question after again making sure no one else was listening in on their whispered conversation.

"Does Deke know?"

"Of course."

"Does anyone else know?" Reilly asked.

"Not yet. It's early and we want to wait until after the first trimester to tell everyone. I'm not old but I am older and we just want to get past that first hurdle. And… I know Trip's been working on Stella about having children, so I don't want to put any more pressure on her. Plus, Judge and Cassie have been planning, too… I'm positive Cass will announce something soon. I think they were waiting to see how the Shirley thing shook out."

"Was this planned?" Not once had Reese ever mentioned wanting children that she could remember.

"Not really," Reese admitted. "Chalk it up to birth control failure."

"Like Dyna."

"Yes. Dyna is one reason I'm not so upset about it.

Dyna's a precious gift and she started to bring out the motherly instinct in me every time I held her. Also, every time I hold her, I remember cuddling you when you were that age. I remember holding you tight and hoping... *praying* I didn't fail you. I was so scared, Reilly. I really was. After all that, I wasn't sure I ever wanted to raise another child again, even my own."

"You were eleven when I was born. Of course you were scared. What eleven-year-old can successfully raise a baby?" Reilly raised a hand. "You, of course. Because you're a badass bitch, even when you were eleven. You put your mind to something and you get it done, no matter what. Tenacious should be your ol' lady road name. I have no doubt you'll be a badass mother this time around, too. And look at it this way, now you're an expert because you have raising me under your belt."

Reese laughed softly. "I'm certainly not an expert. I screwed up so many times with you."

"And here we sit alive and well, with only a few emotional and physical scars. We survived." She smiled at Reese. "Well, I'm happy for you. And I can't wait to be an auntie. More importantly, I can't wait for Deacon to be a daddy. Holy shit, he'll be awesome at it. Daddy Deacon. I like the ring of that."

Reese's lips twitched. "He does, too."

"Having a baby might put a kink in your kink," Reilly teased.

"Having a baby will put a kink in a lot of things. Deke mentioned getting a house mouse to help out while we work, but I don't know..."

"You've got time to decide."

"There's a really good daycare the next block down from my office. Plus, there's always Lottie, though I'd hate to dump that kind of burden on Deke's mother at this point in her life."

"Again, you have time. Don't stress it. You've got a huge family here to help, too."

Reese's smile broadened. "That's for damn sure. You know, I'd hate to give that asshole Warren any credit but one good thing came out of that mess…"

"More than one," Reilly corrected, slightly tipping her head to Reese's stomach.

"True. More than one."

"And lots more to come," Reilly promised.

"Let's hope the bad times are behind us and we only have good times ahead." Reese lifted her drink and Reilly tapped their cups together.

She glanced over to where Rev stood, now by himself, leaning against The Barn, one hand buried deep in his front jeans pocket, a beer bottle hanging by his side between two fingers of his other hand. His bright blue eyes turned in Reilly's direction.

Yes, she hoped the bad times were behind all of them and only good times lie ahead.

But life had a habit of throwing them all curve balls when they least expected it.

Chapter Eighteen

REV LEANED back with his right knee bent and his boot planted on the side of the shed. He lifted his hand-rolled cigarette to his lips, filled his lungs, then slowly let the smoke roll back out of his mouth.

He had a good buzz going between drinking all evening and sharing some high-quality bud with his brothers.

He was relaxed, but not quite happy.

He had fought off the sweet butts all night, scraped off any female hang-arounds looking for some action and tried to stick near his brothers who had ol' ladies since the prowling females usually gave them a wide berth. For good reason.

One being the sisterhood, who had gathered in their pack and kept a side-eye on their men. The sweet butts knew better than to approach any of the Fury brothers who'd already been claimed, unless they were only having some friendly conversation, but some of the female hang-arounds didn't know any better.

Just like some of the male hang-arounds didn't know not to approach any of the Fury women not wearing "Property of" cuts. Right now, that basically boiled down to five: Tessa, Saylor, Maddie, Josie and Reilly.

Trip always kept an eye glued to Tessa. Shade watched Chelle's daughters like a hawk. Rev really didn't give a fuck if Saylor wanted to hook up with anyone as long as it wasn't out in the open where everyone was watching. Also, as long as she consented. Even so, he didn't tell any of his brothers that. He let them believe that he'd have a problem with them if they boned his sister.

However, Judge also had a say in what Saylor did and didn't do since she was a part of his family now and, as their house mouse, Rev's sister was responsible for Cassie's daughter, Daisy.

The club's sergeant at arms and his ol' lady had set certain rules for Saylor before agreeing to let her live with them. Not only to keep the then eighteen-year-old out of trouble and to steer her down a better path, but because Daisy was at the age where she was easily influenced by bad behavior. And Saylor, to remain free from John Schmidt, had been a pro at bad behavior.

Rev didn't argue with any of the rules Judge and Cassie came up with because it gave his sister structure, something she needed after spending almost all of her teen years in juvie and, even before that, being sheltered in what Rev now considered a religious cult.

She spent all of those years locked away from any kind of real family. All of those years separated from her older brother. A brother who couldn't even visit her until after he turned eighteen. His fear of being caught as a runaway, being returned to Coatesville and given back to his parents had kept him away.

Selfish self-preservation.

He gritted his teeth at his life's biggest regret.

He had broken the news to Saylor earlier about how their "father" succumbed to his cancer and he assured her she was safe since the man would never "touch" her life again. What he didn't tell her was that he discovered they were only half-siblings and that her real father was not John Schmidt. Or that their parentage had been another fucking lie among thousands of others.

No, she didn't need to know because that family no longer existed to them.

The bad was hopefully behind them now, and only the good in front of them.

He took another long drag on his cigarette, the end glowing brightly enough to break up the surrounding darkness, then tilted his head as he heard something moving in his direction. Footsteps. Not something, someone.

He quickly took one more hit of the tobacco, then flicked the remainder away into the shadows as the footsteps got closer.

Then he heard a stumble, a gasp, a little shuffled tap dance, followed by a muttered curse.

He pinned his lips together so he wouldn't laugh and give away his hiding spot.

His erection had already begun to push against his zipper in anticipation.

He held his breath as the footsteps continued toward Reilly's Hyundai Kona. She had parked it out of the way along the six-foot chain-link fence that contained all the vehicles Trip and Sig repo'd for Buck You Recovery. Last year, Trip had built the repo yard behind the long shed where they all parked their sleds, so the vehicles were out of sight from anyone looking for their missing ride. Also, to keep them from being tempted to take their vehicle back before actually catching up on their delinquent payments.

The only good thing about Reilly parking there was it was out of sight from anyone still lingering outside in the courtyard. Once things had wound down and everyone who still could function moved into The Barn to continue to party, or find available snatch to fall into, he had headed out to find her car and wait for her.

He knew she wouldn't stay too late since they both had to be back at work in the morning. He also hoped to fuck she had curtailed her drinking sooner than later since she needed to drive. If not, he wasn't allowing her to go anywhere until she sobered up.

When the crunch of her high-heeled boots came from right around the corner, his arm shot out grabbing hers and, with a hand securely covering her mouth, he yanked her behind the shed and out of view.

"It's me," he whispered into her ear. He waited for her to relax against him and removed his hand.

"You scared the shit out of me!" she yelled, shoving at his chest.

"Quiet. Don't need anyone comin' to check on you 'cause you're over here bein' loud."

"You could've just texted me to come meet you, dummy. Now my heart is pounding from my heart attack." She leaned away from him slightly. "Are you hard?"

"Maybe."

"No, no maybe about it. Is that why you're waiting for me?"

"Wanted to talk to you."

"Dirty talk?" She wedged her hand between their pinned bodies and slid her palm over his hard-on.

He grabbed her wrist and regrettably pulled it free. "No." Even in the dark, he could see her disappointment. "Are you wasted?"

"No," she answered, sounding insulted. "Should I be for this 'talk?'"

"Fuck no. Want you fuckin' sober." Not just for the talk but for what would happen after it.

"Uh oh. That sounds serious. Is there a problem?"

"You tell me."

She shook her head. "I don't understand."

"Seriously? I watched your ass get dragged inside by Trip and Deacon and you don't understand my concern? Been dyin' all fuckin' night to ask you about it."

"It had nothing to do with you." She paused. "Or us."

Us. "I wasn't mentioned?"

"No."

"You gonna spill? Or are you just gonna leave me hangin'?"

She reached down between them again. "Are you hanging to the left or to the right?" She squeezed his dick, even though it now wasn't as hard as it was when he first grabbed her.

"Woman..." he warned.

She sighed. "Okay, fine. Remember the emergency housing Trip and Dutch arranged for Cage?"

"Can't forget that. The trailer was a smart, quick solution."

"Yes, well... Trip decided it was not only a smart solution for Cage and Dyna but an even better business of our own."

"He's mentioned it several times. What does it have to do with you?" he asked, confused.

"Everything."

An impatient growl bubbled up his throat.

Her hand had made quick work of getting him rock hard again.

She tipped her face up to his. "Kiss me first."

"Use your mouth to tell me what I wanna know, then we'll use it for somethin' else."

She lifted one eyebrow. "You didn't get any of your itches scratched by any of the sweet butts?"

"You know I didn't."

"How would I know? I didn't watch you," she huffed.

"The fuck you didn't."

"Okay, I didn't watch you *every* second. You could've snuck off and—"

He claimed her lips and swept away the rest of her words with his tongue. When they were done exploring each other's mouths, they were left panting and his dick was throbbing. They needed to get this conversation over with so he could get on with the rest of his plan.

And hope to fuck they didn't get caught while doing it. But they *were* doing it. Because after the club run today, she needed a reminder. One he planned on giving to her.

"Want more of that?" he asked against her lips.

"Yes," she hissed softly while clinging to him.

He liked that... No, he fucking loved that. The feel of her pressed against him, holding on. Like he could be her rock when she needed it.

Not could be, *would* be. If she needed to lean on anybody, it should be him.

"Pussy wet?"

"It is now."

Music to his fucking ears. "Want my cock in it?"

"Meh. I probably wouldn't say no to that offer if it presented itself."

He grinned. "Then get talkin', buttercup. The sooner you spill, the sooner I can present the offer."

"It's not a big deal... Okay, yes it is." She bounced on her toes which made her bounce against him which then made his dick flex in his jeans. "They offered that business for me to manage. I'd get paid *and* also get a cut of the profits."

His grin flattened out. "Say what? That mean you won't be workin' for the garage anymore?"

"I will for a while. But hopefully... Eventually..."

"Eventually you'll be movin' on."

"You make it sound like I'm moving away. I'm not going anywhere. You know I wasn't going to work for Dutch forever. He helped me out by letting me work for him and I helped him get his office in order while I did so. It was mutually beneficial for both of us, but not a career move, Rev. You know that."

Yeah, but then she wouldn't be near him all day like she had been for the past year. He was torn with this decision. It was good for her, but not for him.

For fuck's sake, he was being a fucking selfish dick right now. Thinking about his wants and needs instead of hers. "Where's your office gonna be?"

"I don't know, but for now, until the emergency housing business is booming, I'll be using the office at the garage as the base."

Thank fuck.

After spending the last week together, he had a difficult time not being selfish when it came to Reilly. That was made worse since her decision to ride with Dodge had been eating at him all fucking day.

He knew it was fucking stupid to be jealous, but he couldn't stop feeling that way, no matter how much he'd drank or smoked.

She belonged in his bed, on his bike and wearing his cut.

He just didn't know how to make that all happen. But if he could make it happen, he would. As long as she wanted that, too.

The way she was rubbing his dick as if she was doing her fucking best to make a genie appear from a lamp, he was pretty damn sure she'd want what he did.

Or he sure as fuck hoped she did.

Whether she wanted a future or a "just for now," he was willing to give the "just for now" until they were ready for that future.

He cupped her face, tucked her hair behind her right ear and brushed his lips over her scar. Her last man caused the damage and he wanted to be the man to help heal it.

And that was what was bugging the shit out of him right now. Seeing her on the back of another man's sled had made him realize that had to never happen again.

Not fucking ever.

Selfish? Fuck yes. This kind of selfish he wouldn't feel guilty about.

"Now that you're done talkin', time for me to have my say. Only sayin' this once, so listen up... Fuckin' hated every damn second of that ride today. Hated seein' you pressed against Dodge like that. Never hated any of my brothers before today. Wanted to break every one of his fuckin' fingers every time he helped you on and off his sled. Wanted to punch him in the fuckin' face every time he smiled at you. Wanted to smash his sled to smithereens so you'd have to ride with me."

"Rev," came out on a breath and she shivered against him.

"You forgot somethin' important today..."

Her throat rolled as if she wanted to ask, "What?" but it couldn't escape.

He put his mouth to her ear and said it slowly enough she was sure to hear it clearly and not misunderstand the claim. "You... belong... to... me."

A ragged sigh escaped her parted lips.

"You ever ride on the back of anyone's sled but mine again..." He let that warning hang between them.

Again, her throat rolled, and her fingers twisted in his shirt at his gut. The hand she'd been stroking him with also stilled. "Give me time."

"For what?"

"To work on my sister."

Time? Bullshit. They'd wasted too much time already. "Realized it today, Reilly. Ain't a patient man when it comes to you. Got a taste of you and now I want nothing and no one else."

He hoped she felt the fucking same, though she hadn't said it yet. That was also bugging the shit out of him.

Her breath shuddered. "It's risky right now."

"A risk I'm willin' to take."

She shook her head. "No, I won't be the reason you lose everything. I promise to work on it. We just need to be careful until I succeed. In the meantime…"

"In the meantime…" he repeated, low and gruff. He was ready to act on the second part of his plan. The part where he didn't remind her with words who she belonged to, but showed her, instead. "Feel how fuckin' hard I am for you?"

"Is that you, or did you stuff a steel pipe down your pants?"

He thrust upward against her hot little palm. "It's all me, babe. It's all 'cause of you."

"I must have magical powers," she teased.

She sure as fuck did since she managed to cast a fucking spell on him. A spell he couldn't seem to break free from.

Not that he was fighting to get free from it, either.

Earlier tonight, the thought of touching a woman other than Reilly didn't have any kind of appeal like it used to.

Yeah, she belonged to him, but he now belonged to her, too.

Lock, stock and fucking barrel.

Maybe he could go to the exec committee and claim her at the table. Then deal with the fall-out afterward.

Yeah, maybe he'd do that. Fuck her trying to convince her sister. Reese was stubborn as fuck and that might be a long, drawn-out fight.

Luckily, he could be just as fucking stubborn as Deke's ol' lady. If he approached the committee, he'd show them he wouldn't back down no matter what Reese said. No matter what anyone else fucking said.

He would claim his woman and that would be that.

But until then... Yeah, they had to be careful. He needed to go to the exec committee with guns blazing, not go in there on a whimper after being beaten like a piñata.

Remembering Cage's brutal blanket party made him wish he had a blanket right now so he could take Reilly right there on the ground. He didn't, so they'd have to make due. Her cage was just a few feet away.

He'd always fantasized about bending her over a vehicle in the garage and fucking her until her screams echoed through the building. He couldn't allow her to scream tonight because of where they were, but he could still bend her over her cage and let that fantasy play out.

He grabbed a handful of her hair and tugged her head back until her face was tipped toward the sky. "Gonna bend you over your cage and fuck you."

"As long as you don't scratch my paint."

"It'll buff out."

"You scratch my paint and I'll use your balls to buff it out," she warned, pulling away from him. She pulled her key fob out of the front pocket of her jeans and her parking lights flashed when she unlocked the Hyundai.

He stood there watching her hips rock and roll as she headed toward it.

His heart stopped and he almost lunged for her when her heel got caught in some loose stone and she almost did a nose dive. "Why the fuck do you wear those fuckin' useless high-heeled boots on a damn farm?"

"Because I'm supposed to wear boots on the run."

"Not boots like that." She was going to break her goddamn neck one of these times.

She shrugged. "I like them."

He squeezed his eyes shut for a moment, waiting for the irritation about those fucking boots almost killing her to fade away. When it did, he opened his eyes and saw her sitting sideways in the driver's seat as she took off the damn things.

She chucked them over to the passenger side, then stood outside the vehicle and began to shimmy out of her skin-tight jeans.

That took a while and a few grunts from her. But eventually she succeeded in getting them rolled down, over her feet and flung onto the driver's seat.

Her ivory skin glowed in the dark and was like a homing beacon for him. He wanted to taste every inch of her flesh. Unfortunately, that wouldn't happen tonight.

Tonight was just a quick reminder of who she belonged to. That was all. They'd have to find another opportunity where they could take their time and do it the way they wanted it.

As she reached for her thong, he said, "Leave it on."

She stepped away from the cage, quietly shut the driver's door and said, "Now what?"

The head of his dick was now sticking to his boxer briefs because of precum leaking while watching her do that awkward striptease that was what. He wanted her totally naked but knew that wasn't practical out here behind the shed.

This was only supposed to be a quickie, he reminded himself.

They hadn't had sex since yesterday morning and even though it wasn't even forty-eight hours later, to him it felt like forever.

"Face the cage, lean over the fender and lemme see what you're offerin'."

Since she was barefoot, she took a couple careful steps to the front of the Hyundai and turned to face it.

He waited for her to finish following his instructions. For a second, he thought she wouldn't. That she'd be her typical Reilly-self and argue about the position and how she wanted to do it her way.

It shocked the shit out of him when she didn't say a

damn word. Instead, she stepped up to the fender, planted both hands on the hood and slowly, ever so fucking slowly, leaned over the front of her cage.

Christ. His dick now had its own heartbeat and it was pounding as if he'd just sprinted across one of the fields.

He wished the sun was out and he could see her clearly. Because he was sure it was one hell of a display in the light.

As he moved toward her, he began to unbuckle his belt, to unfasten his jeans, to yank down his zipper. He slipped his belt from the loops and placed it on the ground nearby so it not only wouldn't scratch her paint, but so it wouldn't clang against the metal giving away what they were doing, similar to a squeaky box spring.

He shrugged out of his cut and folded it inside out to prevent it from scratching her paint and placed it carefully on the hood.

When he moved behind her, he glued his gaze to the pale globes of her ass that he swore reflected the moonlight.

"Goddamn perfect," came out of him without thought.

"I—"

He cut her off. "Perfect and all fuckin' mine. No one else's, Reilly. You hear me? No one."

She sucked in a sharp, audible breath.

"Tell me," he demanded, sliding his palm over the soft curves of her exposed ass.

It took a few seconds for her to answer but when she did, she said, "Yours."

"What is?"

"Me."

Fuck yeah. "How much?"

"All of me."

"Whose sled will you be ridin' on?"

"Yours."

"Whose dick?"

"Yours."

"Whose name's gonna be on your lips when you come?"

"Yours."

Fuck yeah.

He quickly dug into his back pocket, pulled out his wallet and slipped out a wrap. He unhooked the wallet's chain from his belt loop and tossed it on the ground next to the belt so it wouldn't cause damage, either.

He shoved his jeans and boxer briefs down far enough to free his dick, ripped open the wrap and after a couple of strokes, rolled it down his length.

"Wrap ain't lubed. Do I need to use spit, or you soaked for me?"

"Find out for yourself."

He didn't even need to check. After hearing her husky demand, he knew.

"You like bein' out here, bent over, your ass and pussy tipped up for anyone to see it if they walked by? That get you excited? Or is it 'cause of me?"

"You... No. Both. Mostly you. Normally the risk would be hot but I'm more worried about you getting caught breaking a rule and paying that price."

"I was born a sinner, babe. I was born to break rules."

He shuffled closer, pulled her thong to the side and her ass cheeks apart, and slid the latex-covered tip of his dick from the top of her crease all the way down.

When he pressed it against her clit, she moaned and pressed back. "Fuck me."

He planned on it, but on his timetable, not hers. He dragged the head of his cock up through her folds and all the way back to her anus. He couldn't see it in the dark, but it puckered even tighter at the slight pressure he put against it.

He wouldn't take her there. Not now, not without lube, not without anywhere to clean up afterward, but he definitely put it on his to-do list for a later date.

That day at the garage when Warren showed up to finish the job he'd failed at—killing her—he had bragged about taking her ass. Whether he actually did or not, Rev didn't know and he wasn't fucking asking because he also didn't want to know if it was true. He didn't want to imagine that motherfucker touching her at all.

His voice cracked slightly when he put even more pressure there and asked, "Will you let me?"

"Is it yours?" Her question came out on a shuddered breath.

"Yeah," he breathed. "It's mine. All fuckin' mine."

He drew the throbbing head back down, the heat and slickness of her pussy pulling him deeper into the spell he was caught in.

He nudged the crown between those hot folds and hesitated because he needed to hear it one more time. He needed to make sure he heard it correctly when she said it earlier. He needed to know she was worth the risk. That she was worth fighting for because she was willing to fight for them, too. "Tell me again...Who do you belong to?"

"You."

He slid inside her until he couldn't go any further and paused to savor the wet heat and the tiny pulses squeezing his dick. Between that and her words, he had to take a moment and a deep breath to gather his control.

She was so damn wet, he slid easily in and out of her, taking his time, taking full strokes from rim to root, keeping a tight grip on his control. Because what he wanted to do and what he was actually doing were two different things.

He had the crazy urge to pull out, rip the wrap off and come inside her. Instead, as he began to move, he pretended he wasn't wearing one. That he was bare and nothing was between them.

The thought of that almost drove him to lose his shit as much as her saying she belonged to him. The need to mark her as his was a base instinct he couldn't shake. Almost as if, if he did it, all other men would automatically be warned off. The same as if she wore his cut.

Selfish. Foolish. But true.

He grimaced as he dug his fingers into her left hip to hold her in place while using the thumb on his right hand to tease her little, tight hole. It was so damn tempting.

The way her hips were pinned to the fender, he couldn't access her clit so easily. So, he pulled out—doing his damnedest not to rip off the wrap—turned her over, wrapped her legs around his waist and jerked her to him until her ass was perched on the edge of the fender.

Then he drove deep inside her again. This time he could see her face, her expression, even in the moonlight. It was goddamn beautiful every time he pumped into her and every time he pulled out until only the very rim of his dick remained inside her.

Her fingers dug into his bare ass trying to pull him closer, even though it was impossible.

"Who do you belong to?" he growled.

"You."

"And who else?"

"No one." Not even a fucking hesitation.

He pulled her legs even tighter around him and leaned over, brushing his thumbs over the hard nipples punching through her shirt. He licked up her neck that was arched and vulnerable, brushed his lips along her jawline, before taking her mouth.

Claiming it like he'd claimed her. As he powered up and into her, as he kissed her, he was taking what was his. What would always be his.

No one else's.

He never felt like this about any other woman before. It should scare him, but it didn't, it felt natural and so fucking right.

It seemed as if dealing with his past had pushed him into the arms of his future.

He was only twenty-eight, he shouldn't even want to be tied down to one woman. But he wouldn't allow her to slip through his fingers and into another man's hands. The risk of losing her outweighed the risk of them being caught, even the risk of losing his freedom to fuck whoever he wanted.

To know she would be his and only his gave him an undeniable primitive satisfaction. Like a damn caveman who sees a female, clubs her over the head, and drags her into his cave by her hair.

Mine.

For fuck's sake, he was devolving instead of evolving. All because of a woman. All because of some animalistic instinct to possess her.

With their mouths still fused together, he tweaked both nipples through her shirt, causing her to grab his, in turn, and twist.

Fuck yeah.

She had joked about them being his launch buttons, but that wasn't a lie. Being inside her soft, wet heat with their tongues fighting for control, and then that…

She needed to come and soon.

He pulled his mouth from hers, his breathing rapid and rough, and warned, "You do that at your own risk."

Her answer was an upward tilt of her hips as she twisted his piercings even harder. He groaned into her neck, reaching down and pinching her clit as he continued to pound her in a rush to get her to the finish line before he did.

He plucked at the swollen nub and sucked the soft skin at her throat as she continued the onslaught of his now tender and throbbing nipples. She didn't let up, so neither did he, until suddenly her mouth opened and, before the wail could escape, he clamped a hand over it. Her teeth sunk into his palm as he contained her scream.

He'd love to give her a second orgasm before he got his own, but this was supposed to be a quickie and he hated them being exposed like this. Now was not about numbers but a reminder…

A reminder for both of them.

With one last deep push of his hips, his breath caught and his dick got even harder a few seconds before he spilled inside her. Again, he wished that was true, and the wrap hadn't captured it all.

He fell on top of her, breathing hard, his dick still twitching where it was rooted deep inside her. The energy he had while fucking her suddenly gone. Both of them were now two boneless bodies sprawled across the hood of a Hyundai Kona.

He remained inside her when he planted his palms on the vehicle's hood, one on each side of her head, and rose up enough to look down into her moonlit face.

She reached up, grabbed his face between her hands and pulled him back down for a long, thorough kiss. As they did so, she squeezed his cock and he groaned.

She clenched around him once more then gradually ended the kiss.

"And what about you, Rev?" she asked softly before releasing him.

He stared down at her, wishing he could see the green in her eyes, the red of her lips and the little brush burn she got on her fair skin from his beard whenever they kissed for more than a few seconds. "What about me?"

"Who do you belong to?"

Chapter Nineteen

"WHO DO YOU BELONG TO?"

Before he got to answer, a noise had them both jerk into action. After separating quickly, Reilly jumped into the driver's seat of her Kona and shut the door as quietly as she could.

He pulled off the full wrap, knotting the end and dropping it to the ground near her tire. He quickly yanked up his jeans, shrugged on his cut and gathered his belt and wallet, putting both of those back in place. His heart beat wildly as he did his best to do it all quietly, until whoever it was moved on.

He did not want to get caught with Reilly and he damn well didn't want them to get caught together with their pants down. He could see her struggling to pull on her jeans while sitting in the driver's seat. At least with the door closed, the view of her bare ass was blocked from prying eyes.

He waited a few more seconds and, sticking to the shadows, peered around the corner of the shed, looking for whoever it was.

A tall shadow moved through the darkness only a few feet from where Rev now stood. His jaw shifted and his blood began to boil at the thought of someone spying on them.

Rev stepped out from behind the corner of the shed to confront whoever it was. "Hey!"

The dark figure stopped, not at all acting surprised someone was back there. A telling sign. "Yo," came the low grumbled response.

Scar.

Fuck.

Had he seen them? Had he seen Reilly naked from the waist down? Had he watched them while they fucked?

Rev's fingers curled into tight fists, drawing on his common sense not to launch himself at the prospect and pound him into the ground.

"What are you doin' out here?" he asked and waited for the prospect to throw the same question back at him. While it would be stupid on his part—a prospect should never question a patched member—Scar seemed to question shit he shouldn't. He tended to have a "don't give a fuck" attitude about most everything. That alone could get him in trouble with the club and law enforcement. Which was probably the reason he'd spent most of his adult life in prison.

But this time he didn't boomerang the question back at Rev. Instead, the scarred man stared through the dark at Rev for longer than necessary—or even comfortable—before grunting, "Rounds."

"What d'you mean rounds?" Rev walked toward Scar, in an attempt to draw him away from where Reilly was. He only hoped the woman would wait until Rev returned and gave her the all-clear before driving away.

"Judge wants all the prospects to take turns patrollin' the area at night."

This was news to him. He would check with Judge to make sure that was true and Scar wasn't just being a peeping fucking Tom when it came to Rev fucking Reilly on the hood of her cage.

Because then there'd be a problem. Not only with Rev breaking one of the cardinal rules but between Scar and Rev. If the fucker was lying, there'd also be a problem between the club and prospect.

Three potential issues caused by one nosy motherfucker.

Rev decided to test the water. "What'd you see?"

"What d'you mean?" the man grumbled, turning to face Rev with his hands now planted on his hips. His head was cocked to the side and if it hadn't been so dark out, Rev just bet his expression and his eyes held a challenge.

And the asshole had no right to challenge Rev. None at all.

"Exactly what I fuckin' asked." He repeated the question but slower this time speaking like Scar was too stupid to understand plain English. "What the fuck did you see?"

The ex-con's hesitation was long enough to put a bitter taste in Rev's mouth. "Didn't see shit. Heard a commotion, came around the corner, saw a Fury cut and decided whoever it was had things covered."

He was being a fucking smart ass by using the word "covered." Scar was also lying about seeing Rev wearing his cut since he'd taken it off and turned it inside out and placed it on Reilly's hood.

The problem was, if Rev made a big deal about it, Scar could run his fucking mouth and cause Rev a lot of grief. Just like when Scar kept challenging Rook about Jet. If Jet hadn't belonged to Rook—even though no one knew it at the time—the former cop might have ended up dead and buried, never to be seen again. That's how much Scar hated pigs. His hatred for law enforcement ran a lot deeper than most of the Fury members. It probably burned in his gut like acid.

But right now, Rev didn't give a fuck. The man needed

to go chew a Tums and get the fuck away from the shed before Reilly revealed herself.

"You got orders, then carry on with them," Rev said quietly, but firmly, making sure the older biker knew who had the upper hand here. It wasn't Scar.

The prospect had already crossed the line a few times. So far, those infractions had been forgiven. However, they hadn't been forgotten. It wouldn't take much more to get his prospect rocker stripped and send him on his merry way.

Problem solved.

But that didn't mean Scar wouldn't try to take Rev out the door with him. He could try to use the fact that Rev was banging someone on the "no fuck list" as leverage.

Fuck.

It was best to try to keep things between them civil. At least for now. Once he successfully claimed Reilly at the table all fucking bets were off.

If Trip assigned prospects to work with her in the new business, one of them better not be Scar. There was no fucking way she was working closely with that asshole.

He waited until Scar crossed the driveway, the courtyard and then disappeared into The Barn before turning and heading back to Reilly.

When he returned to her cage, she was fully dressed and outside the Kona, leaning against it, her arms crossed over her chest.

When he got closer, she asked, "Who was it?"

He considered lying to her and telling her it was no one so she wouldn't worry but decided that might not be the smartest idea. "Scar."

Her eyes went wide. "Shit. Did he see us?"

Now he needed to lie. "No. Said he was doin' rounds."

"Rounds?"

"Yeah, said Judge has the prospects now doin' rounds to keep an eye out."

"For what?"

Rev shrugged. "Shirleys? Someone breakin' into the repo yard? Feds? Sasquatch? Probably anythin' out of the ordinary."

"Like someone on the 'do not touch' list getting bent over a car and fucked by someone who is supposed to be respecting that list. Do you think he saw me naked?"

"Doubt it. My bare ass was coverin' yours. Unless he knows your cage, he wouldn't even suspect it was you."

She blew out a soft breath. "I hope not. Like I said, I'll work on Reese."

In the meantime, he'd make a plan to skip all of that and go directly to the source to plead his case. But for now, she could work on her sister until he could try his method. Her sister relenting would be the easy solution, him busting in on an exec meeting to confess to breaking a rule would be the more difficult and dangerous one.

He reached behind her and opened the driver's door for her. She pushed off the rear of the car where she'd been leaning and before she could climb in, he stopped her. "Reilly…"

She hesitated and glanced over her shoulder.

"Wasn't a mistake."

"What wasn't? The sex we just had?"

No, not the sex. The other thing. The words he'd said to her. The words she thought he said because he was drunk.

"All of it," was how he answered.

She nodded, got into the Kona, started the engine and shifted into Reverse. Before she removed her foot from the brake, she powered down the window and poked out her head. "Hey, Rev."

He lifted his head since he was busy buckling his belt. He hadn't finished doing that in his rush to get dressed.

"In case you want to know… I feel the same."

Then she drove away.

———

Rev swung the ring of keys around his index finger as he strode through the parking lot of Dutch's Garage and stepped through the open bay door. The truck's test drive proved he repaired the problem the customer had complained about. Now he needed to drop the keys off in the office and help Reilly write up the invoice so she could call the customer and Dutch could get paid.

One more job down for the day. He had a state inspection on another vehicle to do yet, as well as an oil change, then he'd be caught up with the job orders on his clipboard.

As he had approached the garage, he noticed two older sleds—one formerly owned by Dutch—parked out front. When he headed toward the office, he heard male voices inside along with Reilly's.

He paused just outside the office door, and out of sight, so he could listen for a few.

Castle and Bones.

He'd been relieved when he heard they'd be the prospects to work with Reilly on the new business and not Scar. At least, he wasn't involved *yet*.

Reilly was sitting at her desk discussing the business plan she had written up and going over the training the two prospects would need once they both obtained their commercial driver's licenses.

That was the first step. If they couldn't pass their CDL tests, then they wouldn't be able to help her by delivering and setting up the emergency housing wherever and whenever it was needed.

A couple of weeks ago, Rev had read over her business plan. He'd been impressed with how detailed and extensive it was, proving that she was smart as fuck and Trip had made the right decision to drop the new business into her lap.

Her being intelligent wasn't a surprise since her sister Reese was wicked smart, too. Their parents might have sucked at actual parenting, but they'd given the women something worthwhile. Their smart genes.

Reese had filed all the paperwork required for the new business and two mobile homes the club financed were being delivered out to the farm in the next week.

Trip had the Amish come in, level the ground and spread stone to create a lot in a corner of one of the far fields to park the trailers until they were rented. He hoped to eventually fence it in to keep the empty trailers safe, but until they knew how many they'd end up with, he didn't want to spend the money and have to turn around later and move or expand the fence line.

Yeah, Trip had a good head on his fucking shoulders when he wasn't losing his damn temper. He'd also left the naming of the business up to Reilly. She decided to name it Shelter from the Storm after the Bob Dylan song, since it fit. The housing could be used after storm damage, fire, flooding, hurricane or a Godzilla attack. Or even to house a family while building a new home or renovating an old one. The prospects would drop it off on the property, set it up and go. Then the money would begin to flow.

Reilly was also looking to partner with an outfit that would provide furniture rental. In the meantime, she was working on getting much needed smaller household items, like linens, pots and pans, and more, they could rent for an extra fee. She eventually wanted to provide some furnished trailers so they could charge a higher monthly rent.

She had all kinds of good ideas and most of them she talked about late at night when they were both naked in her bed.

The enthusiasm for the business was catching and he was happy she was happy to be given something of her own to control. Shelter from the Storm was now her baby to raise. Trip handing over the reins to her showed his complete trust in her decision-making abilities.

The Fury president was right to trust her. She had a huge heart and was sharp. Between the two, she'd definitely make the business a success. When you scratched beneath the surface, she was almost as driven as her older sister. She just wasn't so rigid about it.

He was proud of her.

So was Reese.

However, with Reilly getting caught up in getting the business off the ground, she hadn't had time, or the energy, to work on Reese the past few weeks. That meant every time he went over to her apartment it was a gamble.

A monthly executive meeting was coming up, so if Reilly didn't make any headway with her sister before that, Rev was stepping in and throwing himself on the committee's mercy. He'd rather take that chance than getting discovered by accident and getting called out.

But he hadn't warned her of his intentions yet. He put it off hoping she'd be successful with persuading Reese first.

Either way, something had to happen and it had to happen soon. Before the next club run, for sure. He would not go through another three- or four-hour long ride watching his woman plastered to another man's back.

That was damn well never happening again.

He stepped into her office and all eyes turned his way.

"Do you need something, Rev?" she asked, keeping her expression neutral. Though, she casually raked her gaze over him from head to toe, with a slight rise of one eyebrow.

Yeah, he needed something. Her. That very minute, naked and bent over her desk.

Unfortunately, that wasn't going to happen.

"Yeah. Got a sec? Need you to check somethin' in the break room." He lifted one of his eyebrows slightly, too, in a silent message.

She rolled her lips under for a second, then turned her attention back to the prospects sprawled in the two chairs facing her desk, doing the typical "manspreading."

"Be right back," she murmured.

Both Castle and Bones watched Reilly with more interest than Rev liked as she stood and came around her busy desk. He tossed the keys in his hand onto her desk and waited right inside the door, his eyes now on both men as Reilly stepped out.

Rev didn't miss either of them focusing on her ass as she moved. He cleared his throat sharply, catching their attention, then stared at them both for a moment with his head tilted. "Don't forget she's gonna be your boss. Also don't forget who the fuck she is and who you are. Right now, you ain't even at the level of Cujo's dog shit stuck to the bottom of her boot."

Castle grinned, not taking any offense. "Can't help but appreciate good rock-n-roll. Always been a music lover."

Rev had no problem reading into the man's words. "You can appreciate it but don't fuckin' disrespect it. Got it?"

Castle tipped his head in understanding. Rev glanced at Bones. "Yeah?"

Bones replied with a shrug. "She's hard to ignore."

"Don't ignore her orders but do your fuckin' best on the rest," Rev advised as he walked out of the office and into the break room behind it, where Reilly made the pots of coffee that fueled everyone in the shop all day long and also where she dropped off the fresh donuts daily.

What the fuck were they going to do once she moved her office elsewhere?

How the fuck were they going back to stale M&Ms and black tar for breakfast after that? They all might die.

She couldn't fucking leave. He'd need to convince her to remain in Dutch's office instead of moving into one elsewhere. He'd help Dutch do an expansion to the building, if needed.

Keeping her close meant he could keep an eye on her.

It was selfish as hell, but he really didn't give a fuck.

She was leaning against the little counter, both palms planted on the edge behind her. Her doing that pushed out her tits, making it more difficult to keep his hands off her than normal.

These last three weeks, it had been a struggle not to smack her ass at work every time she bent over, not to grab her by the back of the neck and pull her into him for a kiss, not to whisper dirty words into her ear in passing. They had to act like they always had prior to their week in Coatesville. That meant Reilly rode him just as hard as the rest of the guys by busting his balls and being her typical smart-ass self.

In turn, he rode her hard later at night in her bed.

"What do you need?" she asked again, this time with a wicked grin.

"You," he answered simply. He leaned forward, grabbing one of the remaining donuts, and whispered in her ear, "Keep your door unlocked tonight. I'll be over after dark."

He really didn't need to tell her that since she probably already expected him to show up. However, he needed a minute alone with her.

Again, selfish as fuck, but he was over it in a flash.

He tucked the donut between his teeth and grinned around it. He took a bite and then murmured around the sweet mouthful, "Think Bones got a boner starin' at your ass."

She reached up and wiped away some glaze caught on his lip with her thumb. He groaned when she tucked the thumb into her mouth and sucked it hard with her eyes locked on his.

"Gonna tap that ass tonight, so when you sit down tomorrow you remember who it belongs to," he warned.

She slowly pulled her thumb from between her lips and reached up to pinch his cheeks together. "We'll see, stud."

"You betcha you'll see," he promised. "Wanna see that pretty little plug I bought you winkin' back at me when I get there. I want you naked and ass up when I walk through that door."

He'd bought her a jeweled butt plug. The jewel was green and matched her eyes. He surprised her with it, a little worried she'd get pissed and shove it up his own ass.

Instead of getting angry, she got excited when she opened the box. The way she acted, he would've sworn he had handed her an engagement ring.

Now every time he thought about her lubing it up and inserting it in preparation of him coming over, he instantly got hard.

Imagining her naked, on her knees and ass up with a green gem reflecting the light had already got him rock solid and ready to call it a day. Fuck the inspection and oil change. Those customers could wait.

He checked to make sure no one was sneaking around near the break room before saying, "Tonight's gonna be the night I'm pullin' that plug and replacin' it with my dick. So be ready."

Her breath caught and the hardening of her nipples became obvious through the fabric of the sleeveless blouse she wore while goosebumps swept over her skin.

"Rev," she half-whispered, half-groaned.

He leaned closer again. "That's right, babe, that's the name you're goin' to be screamin' later."

Normally she'd roll her eyes, or even throw something at him, when he said shit like that. But this time her pupils expanded and she drove her teeth into her bottom lip. She was as turned on as he was.

Fuck yeah.

"Now, get outta here to gimme a sec so I can get my own

hard-on under control." He wasn't sure he'd be successful since, for the rest of the work day, he would be distracted by the anticipation of what they'd be doing later.

He headed over to her apartment most nights and had been doing so ever since they'd returned from their trip. He'd park his sled at the garage after hours and hoof it on foot the short block to her place.

To avoid a recognizable pattern of behavior, they sometimes met in an abandoned parking lot at the other end of town or in a secluded wooded area off Copperhead Road. For the past three weeks, not one day had gone by where they hadn't been together in some way or another, whether in her bed, in her cage, or even in a back room at the garage after hours.

But it was time to stop sneaking around. They'd been lucky so far but their luck wouldn't hold out forever. He wanted to get ahead of any future problems.

Especially since he preferred not to become a piñata that didn't spill candy and delight children when cracked open.

Chapter Twenty

Rev tagged his jeans from the floor and yanked them up his legs as he moved toward the front door of Reilly's studio apartment. He paused just long enough to slip a twenty from his wallet to give to the pizza delivery guy or girl.

He was fucking starving. His sexual appetite had been satisfied and now he needed some grub to sate his other hunger. And after that, he planned on sharing a bowl with Reilly before they both watched Netflix and chilled, then probably shared a container of Rocky Road once they both got the munchies.

He slid the chain free, twisted the deadbolt and yanked open the door.

The twenty fluttered to the floor as he slammed the door shut again, quickly flipping the deadbolt to relock it.

Total silence rang on both sides of the door for a few heart-thumping moments.

"Holy fuck," he whispered. "Holy… fuck."

"God, I'm starving!" Reilly came out of the bathroom only wearing his T-shirt and rubbing her eye. "Hey, I think you shot cum in my eye."

Rev turned in slow-motion toward her.

She glanced up, blinking quickly, then her eyes—one watery and irritated, one normal—dropped to the twenty-dollar bill on the floor at his bare feet. Her brow furrowed in confusion. "Where's the pizza? Don't tell me they screwed up the order!"

She jumped when a pounding on the door loudly filled her tiny apartment.

"Open this fuckin' door right fuckin' now!"

Rev didn't realize her eyes could get that big until that very moment. Her mouth formed an *O* and her gaze slid to the door. All color fled from her face.

He was pretty damn sure he wore a similar ass-puckering look.

The knob turned freely back and forth, but the deadbolt kept the door secure. *Thank fuck.*

"Open the goddamn door, Rev!" Deacon shouted through it, still pounding.

"Reilly!" Reese called.

Her eyes slid back to him. "Oh shit," she breathed. "Oh shit. Oh shit."

Three "oh shits" weren't apparently enough since she continued to chant those words. He agreed.

He winced at the flashback of how Cage looked after his "blanket party." Wait. Maybe that was actually his life flashing before his eyes.

Was touching one of the women on the "do not fuck" list even worse than knocking up an Amish chick? No, it couldn't be as bad. Trip had been more pissed about Cage almost destroying the club's relationship with the Amish. That was the reason, right? Not because he accidentally knocked up one of their virgins.

He squeezed his eyes shut for a second. *Yeah, right.*

For fuck's sake, at least Reilly wasn't pregnant. So, there was that silver fucking lining.

"We ain't leavin' 'til you open the damn door," Deacon warned loudly.

Reilly turned her ghost-white face from the door to him. "Do we open it?"

"Do you want me to die?"

"Open the goddamn door!" Deacon bellowed.

"Someone's going to call the cops if we don't open the door," she warned. "I can't have him out there bellowing like an annoyed bull moose. And I doubt they're just going to go away."

"No, we're not leaving," Reese confirmed through the door. "So, you might as well open it."

"Shit," Reilly whispered then chewed on her bottom lip. "I don't want you to die."

"You ain't the only one. But it ain't the dyin' part I'm worried about. It's the part that happens before that."

Reilly grimaced. "Open it."

Rev sucked in a deep breath, then held it as he flipped the deadbolt and stepped back.

A split second later the door banged open and Deacon came into the apartment with Reese on his heels.

Once they were inside and the door slammed shut behind them, everyone stood frozen for what to Rev seemed like forever. The only thing that moved were their eyes as they took each other in.

Both Deacon and Reese focused on Rev's bare chest and he knew exactly what they were noticing. It wasn't his tattoos.

When Reese turned toward her sister, her brow suddenly dropped low and she rushed over to Reilly, grabbing her chin and turning her face toward the light. "Why are you crying? Did he hurt you?"

"What? No!" Reilly jerked her chin free and stepped back. "He... uh... I was chopping onions."

Reese's gaze swept the counters, which were onion-free.

"Earlier," Reilly added weakly. "Why are you here?"

"One, you're my sister and I wanted to see you. Two, we wanted to invite you to Dino's with us for dinner. Three, to see if you needed our help unpacking the storage boxes."

"Looks like Rev unpacked her box already," Deacon mumbled.

"No! He just came over to... uh... fix... my plumbing. His clothes got wet from the leak. I threw them in the dryer."

Reese shot Reilly a look that said *yeah, sure, Jan* loud and clear. "Let me point out a few holes in your story. One, you have a landlord who takes care of your repairs. Two, you don't have a dryer. Three, you're wearing his shirt and, I'm going to assume, nothing else." Reese pushed past her sister and pointed toward her bed. "Four, you always make your bed and your sheets are..." Her words faded away and she grimaced as she spotted the damp circle in the middle of the bed.

Deacon wandered closer to the bed and sniffed. "Sure smells like someone was laying pipe. Just not under the sink. And that leak must be comin' from the roof," he glanced toward the ceiling and scratched the back of his neck, a feigned dumb-founded look on his face. "Better get that checked."

Reese whacked him in the gut with the back of her hand and Deke laughed.

Rev wasn't finding any of it funny.

First of all, his woman was only wearing his tee and nothing else, just like Reese said. Second, if they didn't quickly do damage control, Rev might die before his time. Third, and most importantly... Reilly was only wearing his fucking T-shirt without anything else in front of Deacon.

Before he could tell her to go put something on, another knock came at the door.

No one moved.

He only hoped it was the actual pizza this time and not another surprise visit from more of his club brothers.

Deacon tilted his head toward the door. "Go on."

Rev cautiously went over, hoping it wasn't a trap, picked up the twenty off the floor, opened the door and exchanged the scratch for the hot pizza with the delivery guy.

When he shut the door with his foot and turned with the large pizza in his hand, Deacon said, "Just like you live here." The club treasurer came over and plucked the box out of Rev's hands and took it over to the counter. "Proves this ain't the first time you've come over to fix her leaky plumbin'. Or whatever made that wet spot." He flipped open the cardboard box and grabbed a slice. "Gonna let Reese handle this one. Normally, I'd eat popcorn while I watched entertainment like this, but the pizza will have to do."

He went over, sat on the edge of her unmade bed and took a bite of the slice, wincing when the hot sauce and melted cheese hit his mouth.

Good. Rev hoped he burned the roof of his mouth.

Reese sighed. "This new? Or have you two been sneaking around for a while?"

Reilly's green eyes slid to him in a silent plea. He could see she wasn't sure how to answer that.

"Ain't new," Deacon answered for them, taking another bite of the pizza. "She's wearin' his shirt, he's answerin' her door, buyin' her dinner—even though it's cheap-ass pizza— his nips look like mine after you're done crankin' them and," he hooked a thumb over his shoulder, "he's makin' her leave wet spots the size of the Pennsylvania Grand Canyon."

Reese scrubbed her hands down her face and Rev braced, waiting for her to lose her shit.

"Please tell me you're being safe," Reese asked, way too calmly. Rev didn't trust it, he still expected her to let loose and freak out.

"Of course. You know I'm on the pill—"

"What?" escaped from Rev before he could stop it.

Deacon snorted. "Yeah, they forget to tell you that, right? They don't want you raw-doggin' it 'til *they* decide it's time."

Reese shot him an irritated look.

Deacon raised both palms. "Not the time. Got it." He grinned, got up and snagged another slice of pizza out of the box. "Baby, you want a slice? It's pretty damn good and I don't think they're gonna be enjoyin' it any time soon." He leaned back against the counter, tipped his head back and lifted the slice up above his face, then lowered the tip into his mouth to take a large bite.

"Glad you're fuckin' enjoyin' it," Rev grumbled.

Deacon turned and threw the partially-eaten slice back into the box. "Just like you've been enjoyin' somethin' you were told to not touch. It was a damn clear rule that you broke. And you know what the fuck happens when club rules are broken. You fuckin' knew it 'cause you saw the result and you still fuckin' did it anyhow."

"She ain't just a fuck."

"I sure hope to fuck not," Deacon answered. "But you didn't go about it the right way. Shoulda approached me and Reese before the first wet spot was even made or those barbells were ever twisted. You didn't. 'Stead, you went behind our backs and took the wrong path."

"And I'm the wrong path," Reilly said. "Isn't that up to us to decide? We're both adults and can decide who we…"

"Bang," Deacon supplied helpfully.

"And who we don't," Reilly finished.

"He's just a detour, " Reese said. "Working at Dutch's was the same way. A temporary detour before your life got back on track. I wanted better for you than what our mother wanted. I wanted to prove we could pull ourselves up from a bad situation and make a good life. Now Trip has given you a direction."

"There's nothing wrong with this life. I'm happy. Or I was until you busted in here. Now I'm not happy because Deacon will run to the committee and make Rev pay for something he shouldn't. It isn't fair and I'm calling bullshit." When Reese opened her mouth, Reilly threw up an *I'm-not-finished* hand. "What you need to explain to me is... How is it okay for you to be with Deacon but not for me to be with Rev? Or whatever Fury member I want to be."

Hold up.

He had a lot to say about the last thing she said, but before he got a chance, Reese said, "My life was already in order when I met Deacon—I only met him because of your mess, I might add—yours is not. Is it getting there? Yes, but—"

"Her life's in order just fuckin' fine. Just 'cause it ain't like yours don't mean it's not. Stop treatin' her like a fuckin' child. She hasn't been one for a long fuckin' time." His pulse was now pounding in his ears and not for the reason it originally was. He was no longer worried, he was pissed.

"Brother," Deacon warned.

Reese ignored both men. He could see she believed this was strictly between her and her sister. She was dead wrong. It involved Rev. Because he was who Reilly was with, not any of his Fury brothers.

He was staking his claim, not anyone else. So, yeah, he had things to say.

"And when he's in your bed today and tomorrow a sweet butt is crawling into his, then what?" Reese asked.

"That what you think of me?" Rev asked, crossing his arms over his chest and tilting his head to lock a hard gaze with Reilly's older sister.

But before Reese could answer, Reilly spun toward

Deacon. "How many sweet butts did you fuck after meeting my sister?" She lifted a palm again. "How many sweet butts did you fuck after she *left* you and went back to Mansfield without even talking to you first? Even though I pleaded with her to do so? You had every right to fuck each and every one of them. But you didn't, did you?" She turned back to Reese. "I was here when you weren't, Reese. Deke could've taken any of them to bed after you left him, but you know what? He didn't. Not one. And it wasn't like they didn't make themselves easily available."

"Our situation is different," Reese said softly.

"Not thinkin' it is," Deacon answered her in a murmur while staring at Rev.

Rev faced his club brother and confirmed, "It ain't."

"Damn," Deacon murmured. "Hear that, baby? He's not tappin' her ass because she's available, he's—"

"Yeah," Rev just about shouted to shut Deke up.

Everyone stared at him and no one blinked.

Fuck.

Reilly suddenly snapped back into motion. *Thank fuck.* "Reese, I want what you and Deacon have. Let me have that."

Reese was still staring at him, which made it worse when she asked, "With Rev?"

Why did she sound surprised? Did she believe he wasn't good enough for her sister?

"I…" Reilly made a noise of frustration in her throat. "Does it matter with who?"

"Yeah, it does," Rev answered Reilly's question. "'Cause you're mine, so it really does fuckin' matter."

Reese turned wide green eyes to Rev. "This isn't just a… a hookup?"

"Even if it is, stop trying to control my life. If I want to bang every Fury member, a different one every night, then I should be allowed to do so."

"Yeah, that ain't happenin'," Rev growled.

Deacon snorted.

"You know what I mean." She turned back to Reese. "Look, I appreciate everything you've ever done for me. All of the sacrifices you've made. But let... me... go. Be my sister and not my mother. Be happy for me when I'm happy. Be there to hold me when I'm not. And I'll do the same for you. But let me have this and stop smothering me."

"Reilly," Reese started.

Reilly interrupted her with, "Trip said he was leaving it up to you."

"Fuck that," Rev muttered. It was time for him to take control of the situation. He'd heard more than enough. This was his life. Reilly's life. Their potential life together. "You ain't askin' your sister's permission for shit. You don't have to. You ain't a child. I appreciate everythin' you did for Reilly, too, Reese, but you ain't her mother and even if you were, I'd be sayin' the same shit right now. She's my woman, I'm takin' care of this and *nobody* got shit to say about it."

"Oh, somebody's gonna have shit to say about it," Deacon warned. "You forgettin' about the exec committee?"

"No. And that's how I'm gonna handle it."

Deacon whistled softly. "Yeah, you got it bad. Enough to stand in front of that table and admit you broke a club rule."

"If that's what I gotta do, that's what I'm gonna do. Don't need your ol' lady's permission to claim mine. Just need the exec committee's permission for that."

When he was done speaking, the apartment was completely silent. He took one breath, then a second and turned to Reese, expecting to see her fuming.

Her expression was actually surprisingly soft and her eyes oddly glistened. Was she going cry?

What the hell was wrong with her?

He frowned. "You okay?"

"Pregnancy hormones," Deacon said as if that explained everything.

Reese was knocked up? Should he congratulate her? He wasn't sure what to fucking do when it came to Deacon's ol' lady. She wasn't like the rest of them.

Rev glanced back at Deacon for help. He only shrugged.

Reese wiped at her eyes. "Answer me one thing, Rev."

He hoped he didn't regret this… "Anything."

"Do you love her? I'm assuming you do since you're willing to do what you plan to do. We know what happened to Cage and I assume that bullshit will happen to you, too. You sound willing to go through that to have my sister. So, tell me, do you love her?"

Of fucking course Reese asked the one thing he wasn't willing to tell her. No fucking way. Not when the only time he'd told Reilly was when he was blitzed.

"Ain't tellin' you that," he answered Reese and moved to Reilly until their bare toes met. He cupped her face and tipped it up to him.

She was wearing his shirt and soon she'd be wearing his cut. Even if he had to take a beating to give it to her. "But I *will* tell her." He put his mouth to her ear and whispered, "How soon can we get them the fuck outta your place? This way I can show you how much I love you instead of only sayin' the words." He pulled back and she blinked her big green eyes up at him.

A huge smile crept over her face. Without breaking their eye contact, Reilly said, "He loves me, sis. Just as much as I do him."

———

REILLY'S HEART pumped a mile a minute, so much so, she could hardly hear through the wood door at the top of the rough-cut steps. She sat at the top, her ear to the door and tried to hold her breath so she could hear more clearly.

Tonight was the monthly meeting of the exec committee. Deacon and Reese had agreed to keep their mouths shut and let Rev handle informing the club's officers of breaking one of their rules.

What Rev was now calling "The Big Sin."

He'd been punished by his father in the past what his parents considered sins, even minor ones, and he said he was used to paying for them with physical pain. He was willing to stand and accept whatever punishment the officers decided to dole out.

But what he wouldn't accept was them not allowing Rev to claim her and make Reilly his ol' lady.

However, the committee hadn't expected Rev to burst into the room shortly after they all settled in their seats.

Rev didn't even know Reilly was there. She had shown up as support and was going to wait downstairs until he was done, but her nosiness got the better of her. She quietly climbed the steps to the second floor in the barn so she could eavesdrop.

She told herself she had every right to do so since what would be discussed involved her and also her future ol' man.

Ol' man.

That meant she'd be limited to riding on the back of Rev's sled from then on out. Not a sacrifice on her part at all.

That was *if* Rev survived and got to keep his colors.

Out of the risks involved—a blanket party, getting his colors stripped or losing Reilly—he told her that losing her would be the hardest to deal with. But he was determined to keep her, keep his colors and hope Judge didn't strike too hard when he used "The Punisher," the nickname for the wood club that hung downstairs in The Barn as a visual reminder.

Reilly heard a murmur of male voices through the door but couldn't make out what they were saying until she heard Rev speak up.

"Came here 'cause I got somethin' to say. Somethin' to confess."

"This might be a fuckin' church but it ain't that kind of church," Trip said. "You also didn't approach any of us and ask to be heard, did you?"

"No. But it couldn't wait any longer."

"Must be important." Judge's deep voice was easy to decipher.

"Really fuckin' important," Rev confirmed.

"We givin' this asshole the floor?" Trip asked.

Another murmur of voices rose.

"'Kay," Trip said next. "Got five minutes to spill your fuckin' guts. Start talkin'."

"Here to claim Reilly."

A chorus of loud voices rose around the table and Reilly had no idea whose belonged to whom. None of it sounded friendly, though. It sounded more like an angry mob.

Someone—she assumed Trip—slammed the gavel on the wood table several times to quiet everyone down.

Once the room went silent, Rev continued, "I want her. I'm claimin' her and if you need to beat my fuckin' brains out so I can have her, willin' to take it like a fuckin' man."

Oh shit! He had given her no indication he was going to say that. Not that it surprised her, but still...

That was a huge sacrifice to throw out there.

Reilly smashed her ear tighter against the door. Why was there so much silence?

She finally breathed again when Trip spoke next. "How 'bout that? We were just discussin' with Deke here the fact that Reese asked to have her cut from the list. She was lettin' her free. But apparently, she ain't free 'cause she already belongs to you. That right?"

Reilly's heart was now pounding in her throat as she waited for Rev's answer. When it came, it was loud and confident. "Yeah, that's right."

"Curious 'bout when that happened? Since you don't got a time machine to go into the future after she's removed from the list or even to know she *was* bein' removed from the list. That means you two already had to be hookin' up and hidin' it. That also right?"

"Yeah."

Reilly clenched her teeth together and pressed a hand to the door, wishing she could burst in there and make her demands. Rev had warned her to stay out of it and that he would handle it, but it was a damn struggle not to get involved.

This involved her future. Her relationship. Everything.

"Means you broke a club rule while it was still in place," Judge grumbled.

"Yeah. And it was fuckin' worth it. Whatever I gotta do to pay for breakin' that rule, I'll do it. What I won't do is accept anyone not allowin' me to claim her. The woman's gonna wear my cut, whether you want it or not."

Someone whistled low. Maybe Ozzy, she wasn't sure.

"Damn." That sounded like Deacon even though he already knew this was going to happen tonight. He was the only one sitting at that table already aware of the situation.

"You got some fuckin' balls, brother," Cage, the road captain, said.

"If you even *have* a cut for her to wear after this," Sig, the club VP, reminded him.

Trip took over again. "You weren't fuckin' lyin' when you said you've been hookin' up with a woman and spendin' a lot of time at her place. Just forgot to mention who that woman was." He didn't sound happy. He actually sounded like he was getting more pissed by the minute. That wasn't a good sign. Both Sig and Trip had really short fuses and it didn't take much to ignite them.

She stared at the doorknob, tempted.

As she stood and began to reach for it, she jumped when she heard a footstep behind her.

She swung around and tried to put on her best innocent face. She almost bent over in relief when she saw it was Whip. She was afraid it might be Scar sneaking around. She could see that prospect grabbing her by the collar and dragging her inside the meeting room to tattle on her.

Asshole. Being an ex-con he should know the code: Snitches get stitches!

Whip would never rat her out.

"You supposed to be here?" he whispered.

She put her finger to her lips and made a face.

"Ain't smart."

"Why are you up here?" She was getting anxious because talking to Whip meant she was missing out on the conversation happening inside that room.

"Why *you* up here?"

She grimaced. At this point, there was no reason to lie to Whip. Especially since they worked together. "Because Rev and I are... And..."

Whip grinned. "No shit. Already knew that. Ain't hard to see how you two look at each other ever since you both returned from your trips. Or should that be singular since you both left and returned at the same time?"

"Did we?" she whispered.

"Also hard to miss that every time you bend over at work, Rev's watchin' and then sportin' wood afterward."

"He is?"

Whip shot her a look that clearly said, *I ain't buyin' your bullshit act.*

"And you didn't say a word?" She grabbed his face and planted a kiss on his cheek. "You're the best, Whip."

He grinned, then got serious. "Now, get the fuck off these stairs before your ass gets caught and it causes more headaches for your ol' man."

"Like I said… the best."

As she reluctantly moved down the steps, she heard Whip open the door at the top of the stairway and go inside, closing it behind him.

She wondered briefly why he was being called in front of the executive committee but that wasn't her business.

Not your business, Reilly, she reminded herself.

She finished descending the stairs and walked across the first floor of The Barn and directly to the bar.

Easy was casually leaning against it, smoking a hand-rolled cigarette and drinking a beer. He shot her a surprised look. "Why the fuck were you upstairs?"

"I wasn't," she answered, going behind the bar.

Easy's eyes slid over from the stairway she just came down back to her. "I'm pretty fuckin' sure those steps lead up to the second floor."

Reilly shrugged. "They do, but I wasn't up there."

He blinked, then finally said, "Got it," before taking a long pull from his beer.

She finished making herself a Jack and Coke and came around the bar to sit next to where he was leaning.

She sucked down a third of the super strong drink.

Easy jerked his chin at the cup in her hand. "That to celebrate, or drown your problems?"

"Guess I'll know soon enough."

"Jack's good for either occasion," Easy said, lifting his beer bottle. She tapped her plastic cup against it and they both took a drink.

Her phone vibrating had her putting down her cup and scrambling to yank it from her back pocket.

She read Rev's text: *Where R U?*

She quickly texted back: *Downstairs at the bar.*

She heard the heavy footsteps rushing down the thick, rough-cut wood stairs.

When he hit the bottom, it looked like it took everything he had not to sprint over to her.

But The Barn was full of the brothers who weren't on the committee, some of the prospects and even a couple of sweet butts. Mostly playing pool, throwing darts, drinking and smoking.

The atmosphere was relaxed, unlike Reilly.

Even though he didn't run to her, he power-walked and almost didn't stop even when he practically knocked her off the chair. He grabbed a handful of her hair and used it to tip her head back before giving her a long, deep kiss.

He was claiming her right there. He'd done it at the table, now he was doing the same in front of everyone else. Whistles, hollers and hoots came from several directions.

When they both came up for air, he whispered, "Now you're fuckin' stuck with me."

She wasn't worried about that part. "And?"

"And hope you don't regret it."

She wasn't worried about that, either. "No, the rest."

Rev shrugged. "Don't know. They're gonna discuss it. Told me to get fuckin' lost and they'd let me know."

"What? My stomach is already in knots! And now we have to wait?"

"It is what it is, buttercup." He grabbed the drink from her fingers and downed half of it. He blew out a breath when he was done and cocked an eyebrow at the cup. "Damn that's probably fifty-fifty."

"Something like that."

"Don't worry, long as they don't strip my colors, we're good."

She tugged at his T-shirt under those colors. "We're good even if they do."

His bright blue eyes hit hers and held. "Need to fuck you right now."

"Right now? Like right here?" Her lips twitched. "You *really* want to claim me in front of your brothers, don't you?"

"Yeah, no. Not right here. Got a better place."

She wrinkled her nose. "Not your gross room."

"It's got a bed."

"Mmm hmm."

"And a bathroom."

She grimaced. She knew what the guys' rooms looked like. Not too many of them cared enough to be neat. Or to clean. Most of the time they had to get one of the prospects or sweet butts to do the work for them. And that wasn't often enough.

"I'm going to take a big ol' pass on that. Especially since you probably haven't changed the sheets since you last did a sweet butt in there."

"Haven't done a sweet butt in…" He rolled his eyes toward the ceiling in thought.

"Right. And how long ago have you changed your sheets?" She faked a gag.

"Not a conversation I wanna be havin' with you, anyway."

She nodded. "Ditto."

He grinned. "Gonna burn those sheets."

"All right," she patted his gut, "but until you do, we can go check my apartment for a leaky roof."

He abandoned her drink on the bar and snagged her hand, yanking her off the stool. "Think I got an idea where the leak's comin' from."

Having listened to their whole conversation and not giving a shit they knew it, Easy asked, "Since when did you become a plumber?"

"Didn't you know he's a master plumber?" Reilly winked at E.

Rev snorted, gripped her hand even tighter and dragged her out of The Barn before Easy could respond. "You sayin' I got skills, woman?"

"You have some master skills, yes. Some others you need to work on."

"Practice 'til perfect."

"Great minds..." she whispered.

Once he walked her to her car, he hooked her around the waist and turned her into him, dropping a quick kiss on her mouth. "Meet you at your place. Parkin' out front tonight." He wiggled his eyebrows. "Might even park in the rear, too."

As he pulled away, she grabbed his arm and pulled him back. "Rev..."

He paused.

"Are you sure you're okay with giving up your freedom?"

He grinned. "Ain't givin' up shit. Just takin' you along for the ride. How 'bout you?"

"Ain't givin' up shit," she echoed. "Just taking that ride along with you."

"It's gonna be one helluva ride," he said and walked away, heading toward the storage shed that held his sled. "Buckle up, buttercup!" he yelled into the dark.

"Buckle up," Reilly whispered. She got into her Hyundai and went home.

The leaky roof was never fixed.

Funny how her roof happened to leak at her new place, too...

Had to be fate.

Epilogue

AND IT CAME TO PASS

"THE NEIGHBORHOOD'S GONE TO SHIT."

"Judge said the same thing when you two assholes moved next door," Rev told Cage, who stood next to him with his baby girl perched on his hip.

Cage, Rev, Reilly and Rook watched the flurry of activity on the newly prepared lot. Two tractor trailers held both halves of Reilly's new modular home as a large crew scurried around to get them set into place on the poured concrete foundation.

Reilly's new place.

Not Reilly and Rev's. Just Reilly's.

For now.

Because that was the "deal" he struck with Reese. He didn't like it but he agreed since waiting was part of his "punishment."

It would be fucking torture. But it was better than being clubbed upside the head multiple times by the bearded Un-jolly Green Giant.

His eyes narrowed on Dyna's tiny T-shirt that read, "My Grandpa Tastes the Colors of the Rainbow," with a rainbow painted across her chest, each stripe of color outlined in gold glitter.

"What does that mean?" Rev asked. "Never seen Dutch eat Skittles."

Cage laughed. "Means none of us will ever live up to being the legend who is my old man."

Rook snorted.

Reilly wrinkled her nose. "Don't any of you ever ask me to drop off anything at his house again. My corneas are permanently damaged after that, just so you know."

"Nothin' you ain't seen before," Rev reminded her. "Hell, nothin' we all ain't seen before. Too many fuckin' times."

Dyna let out a giggle and everyone stared at her.

"Did she understand that?" Rev whispered.

Cage sighed. "She's not even a year old, yet, dumbass."

"She'll learn soon enough what a stud her pop-pop is," Rook said. "Probably in ways no one hopes she learns."

"Well, anyway, what I saw wasn't normal…" Reilly sighed, closed her eyes and twisted her face. "Just no. Find some other fool the next time something needs to be dropped off there."

"Just leave it on the porch, ring the bell and run next time," Rook suggested.

"Ding dong and dash," Rev agreed.

"Ding dong and dash?" Reilly asked. "Isn't it Ding Dong Ditch?"

"Damn," Cage whispered.

Reilly's brow furrowed. "It's Damn Ding Dong Ditch?"

Rev then realized Cage hadn't been responding to Reilly. His attention was caught elsewhere.

All eyes turned toward a trim figure heading in their direction. Long black hair was bound in a braid down her back, crystal blue eyes were focused on their little group and she was dressed like a hot as fuck badass.

Jet wore black tactical pants, a shiny skin-tight, black short-sleeved shirt, a loaded shoulder holster *and* a hip holster. All in black.

A real Lara Croft, right there.

"Lookin' hot as fuck, Jet, now that you ain't wearin' a real badge," Cage called out.

She lifted the shiny badge that hung around her neck on a chain as she joined them. "This is a real badge." She touched each of her handguns. "Real guns, too. Don't make me use you for target practice."

Rook snorted and, when she came within her ol' man's reach, he roughly grabbed the back of her neck and slammed her into his chest. He crushed his mouth to hers and, once he was done, he murmured something into her ear the rest of them couldn't hear.

Jet smiled up at him for a long... *very* long minute.

Rev could only imagine what those silent looks said. He and Reilly shared a lot of those while working at the garage. Usually her nipples popped up like turkey timers just like Jet's just had.

After a few more seconds, Jet cleared her throat. "I just came over to check on the progress." She turned toward Reilly. "I'm going to go clean up and get ready for the shower."

She was there and gone that quickly. Rook's eyes were glued to her as she strode away. He wore a grin on his face that every man with a dick knew what it meant.

Rev wore that same grin often, too. Especially when Reilly strutted naked to the bed where he waited, also naked, but hard as fuck.

"If I manhandled Jemma like that, my nuts would be hangin' off my chin," Cage announced to no one in particular.

Rook turned toward his younger brother. "Why you're a pussy and I ain't."

"You're no longer bigger than me. You can't kick my ass anymore, asshole."

"Wanna bet? If you weren't holdin' my niece…"

Cage held Dyna out to Reilly, who rolled her eyes and refused to take her. "You're both assholes and no, I'm not holding Dyna so you two can scrap. If Dutch finds out you two got into a fight, he'll crack you both upside the head with a lug wrench. All right. I gotta go, too," Reilly announced, going up on her tiptoes and planting a kiss on Rev's cheek. "Are you going to stay and supervise our house being put together like a puzzle? Make sure they don't screw up, Master Plumber."

"Ain't our house," Rev corrected, his hands gripping her curvy hips. "Your house."

"Oh, right," Reilly gave him an exaggerated wink, "*my* house."

"Wait. Where the fuck you goin'?"

Reilly shook her head. "Didn't you hear what Jet said?"

"Yeah, she's goin' to take a shower."

Cage laughed. "You sure you wanna be stuck with this dumb motherfucker, Lee? He might pass his dumb-dumb genes on to your babies."

Rev turned toward him. "Ain't that what she said?"

Reilly whacked him in the gut with the back of her hand. "She's getting ready for Reese's *baby* shower."

"Why d'you think I got Dyna instead of Tessa?" Cage asked, pressing a kiss to his daughter's forehead.

"Da! Da! Da!" his daughter yelled and pounded on her father's bearded face with fists and a huge smile.

"Where's it at?" Rev asked Reilly.

She grinned and wiggled her eyebrows. "It's a secret location."

"Why the fuck is it secret?"

"So you animals don't crash it."

"No men then?" he asked, not liking the sound of the women being at a location no one else knew about.

Reilly huffed, "It's a baby shower." Like that should tell him everything. He didn't know shit about baby showers. "But…" She rolled her lips under.

He didn't like that, either. Rev's eyes narrowed. "No men allowed, right?"

She shrugged innocently. "Just strippers and Teddy."

"Strippers at a fuckin' baby shower?" Rook asked, his eyes now narrowed, too. "What the fuck?"

"Only because it's also a surprise bridal shower for Stella. She didn't want us to throw her one, so we're combining them without her knowing. She's going to hate it!" She laughed. "But she's the first ol' lady to actually tie the knot among us, so we decided to do it, anyway, despite her threats."

"Make her wear some stupid sash and tiara," Cage said.

"Oh, don't worry, we have them for her." Reilly giggled and Rev got caught up in the sound of it.

"Take shitloads of pictures of her wearin' those, too," Rook said. "Never know when we'll need it as blackmail."

"Still can't believe your sister's pregnant," Rev muttered.

"I can't fuckin' believe one of Deacon's swimmers penetrated one of her iron-clad eggs," Rook said. "It probably argued a case with the winnin' sperm before it would let it penetrate."

When they all laughed, Dyna did, too.

"You sure she can't understand what we're sayin'?" Rev asked.

Cage turned Dyna to face him and asked his daughter, "He's a dumbass, ain't he?" Then he nodded.

Dyna nodded, too, and smiled.

"Huh. Maybe you're right," Cage said, "she can understand just fine."

Reilly tapped Rev on the cheek. "She's only reacting to

everyone else, Rev. It's what babies do. All right, I have to go." She turned and headed to her cage.

"Text me when you're home. And don't you fuckin' touch any strippers."

She waved a dismissing hand over her shoulder.

"Unless they're women strippers," he yelled out. "Then take video."

The crew working on their modular home all stopped in place and turned toward Rev. Then their collective gazes turned toward Reilly as she got into her Kona.

The crew member closest to Rev gave him a grin and a thumbs up.

"Fuck," Rev muttered.

Rook bumped Rev's shoulder. "You just gave them their whack-off material for tonight. Just think, they're all gonna be fantasizin' about your woman lickin' some stripper's snatch." He made a V with his fingers and wiggled his tongue between them.

Rev shoved him away. "Asshole."

"She likes to lick asshole, too? Damn."

Rev shook his head and studied the way the four modular homes were set up in some semblance of a neighborhood along a stone lane leading directly off County Line Road. A narrow tree line also separated the houses from the rest of the club compound.

The former fallow field was turning into a little private neighborhood. Between that and the lot Trip had built to store Shelter from the Storm's trailers, the Amish would be farming quite a bit less land.

"Can't believe how fast they got that lot prepped and the house here." Rook, now standing with his hands on his hips, was taking in the exact same sight as Rev.

"The green stuff makes shit happen," Rev muttered. Lots of scratch made it happen. Scratch that Rev or Reilly didn't have.

Reese had paid cash for the modular to expedite its delivery. Her and Deacon wanted it set up and Reilly moved out of that studio apartment as soon as possible. One of her demands in exchange for fronting the money was that he and Reilly take it slowly and not move in together right away.

But in the few weeks before they got caught, Rev had gotten good at sneaking in and sneaking out. He planned on continuing that. Especially since all he'll have to do was walk from the bunkhouse across the courtyard and through the line of trees to get to her house. Easy fucking peasy.

"Can't believe she forked over that wad of scratch," Cage said, handing Dyna over to her uncle, who took her without hesitation.

Dyna bounced with happiness in Rook's arms and yelled, "Ook, ook, ook!" her name for Rook.

She called Cujo, who was off running around sniffing and lifting his leg on anything that didn't move, Jo. *Jo, Jo, Jo,* she would squeal whenever the nasty little fucker came within eyeshot.

"Only 'cause I agreed to let Reilly live there by herself for a bit."

Rook snorted. "So, you're sayin' you'll need some empty boxes, then, to pack up your shit from your room and move it over here."

Rev grinned and shrugged. "If I move outta my room, it'll open up a spot for someone from one of the visitin' clubs to stay in durin' the weddin' blow-out weekend. The more places we can provide, the less tents will be needed."

That was his story and he was sticking to it. The wedding was a good excuse to free up his room and start sleeping in Reilly's bed every night. Since the wedding weekend was only two weeks away, that should give him the "time" Reese demanded he wait until he moved in with her.

He thought two weeks was perfectly reasonable. She

probably wouldn't. But, surprisingly, her pregnancy had softened her up enough that they hardly recognized her.

Besides some of the empty rooms in the bunkhouse, The Grove Inn reservation book had been closed to outside visitors for a few days before the wedding and a few days after. The two emergency trailers Trip bought for Shelter from the Storm had already been temporarily set up and available for anyone coming with their kids.

The two visiting clubs, the Dirty Angels and the Dark Knights had been invited to stay as long as they wanted. Trip was also planning a sit-down between all three presidents, vice presidents and sergeant at arms. The Fury prez hoped that inviting those clubs to celebrate him getting hitched would help strengthen the alliance between them.

"Gonna be like Woodstock," Rev murmured, trying to imagine how crazy that weekend would be.

"Without the fuckin' hippies," Rook said. "And hopefully without all the mud."

Cage lifted two fingers in a peace sign. "Peace, love and happiness, *maaaan*."

"Sex, drugs and rock-n-roll," his brother corrected him.

Cage nodded with a grin. "That, too."

"Trip's finally bitin' the bullet," Rev said on a sigh with a shake of his head.

"Think it's the other way around," Cage said. "It's Stella who needed the convincin'."

"Yeah," Rook answered, "he's been ridin' her ass about that, hopin' once it's official she'll agree to givin' him the babies he wants."

"Never thought I'd want one," Cage admitted, "but now I can't imagine not havin' Dyna."

"Yeah, well, you all have at it. I'll stick with bein' an uncle," Rook said, but his expression didn't match his tone as he stared down at his niece in his arms.

Holding Dyna was one time the man turned into a big softy.

"Should we take bets on who falls next?" Cage asked.

"Gettin' hitched or gettin' knocked up?" Rev asked.

"Fuck if I'm bettin' 'cause who the fuck woulda guessed Reese to be the first ol' lady knocked up?" Rook said.

"Speakin' of Reese," Cage started. "You can thank her for not gettin' a repeat performance of my blanket party."

"What d'you mean?"

"Not sure if I'm supposed to tell you, but can't hurt at this point." Cage shrugged. "Deacon had texted everyone in the committee to let them know Reese had already unclipped Reilly's leash. When you burst into the meetin' that night, we all already knew you were comin' and the reason why."

What the fuck? "You all knew before I even went in there?"

They hadn't acted like they knew. Even Deacon pretended like it was a complete surprise. Rev just figured it was so no one found out he already knew.

Cage grinned and nodded. "Yeah. How tight was your asshole puckered when you stood there in front of us?"

"So tight I couldn't shit for a week."

Cage and Rook both howled loudly, making Dyna chuckle in Rook's arms and Cujo start a hellish round of barking in the distance.

Cage whacked Rev on the back. "Makin' you suffer was part of the punishment. Good thing he gave us the heads up, 'cause I wouldn't wish that fuckin' blanket party on anyone."

"Yeah, but at least you had Jemma to nurse you back to health."

"Thank fuck for her," Cage muttered. "Now look at us, we all got a ball and chain around our fuckin' ankles. Dutch and Whip are the only single fuckers left at the garage."

"Dutch ain't ever gettin' nailed down again. He's havin' too much fun in his old age," Rook said, then glanced down at Dyna and asked, "Ain't your pop-pop the ultimate stud?"

Dyna jerked in his arms and broke into giggles.

Cage's daughter was a happy baby. She didn't know it yet, but she also had a whole club behind her. It went without saying that everyone in the Fury would bend over backwards to get her whatever she needed or to protect her. She didn't just belong to Cage and Jemma, she belonged to the Fury as a whole.

His babies, if and when he and Reilly decided to have any, would get the same treatment. Their kids would grow up a lot fucking differently than either of them had. Also, in a much better world. Most importantly, they'd be surrounded by people who loved and respected them.

Hopefully none of the Fury kids would ever feel lost, lonely or unloved.

All of that proved, once again, that family wasn't always blood and blood wasn't always family. But when those family bonds were strong, whether blood or not, they were practically indestructible.

Yeah, both he and Reilly had finally found their true family where they least expected it.

But they also found each other.

In the end, the sinner had become the winner.

And Reilly was his prize.

———

"Family isn't always blood. It's the people in your life who want you in theirs, the ones who accept you for who you are. The ones who would do anything to see you smile and who love you no matter what." ~
Anonymous

———

Turn the page to read the first chapter of Crash: A Dirty Angels MC/Blood Fury MC Crossover Even though it's a crossover book between the two clubs, it's also the next book in the Blood Fury MC series and is best read before book 9: Blood & Bones: Ozzy

———

Sign up for Jeanne's newsletter to learn about her upcoming releases, sales and more! http://www. jeannestjames.com/newslettersignup

Sneak peek of Crash: A Dirty Angels MC/Blood Fury MC Crossover

You are hereby invited to the wedding of Trip and Stella...

Turn the page for a sneak peek of Crash: A Dirty Angels MC/Blood Fury MC Crossover

Crash: A DAMC/BFMC Crossover (Unedited)

Chapter One

WITH BOOTS WIDE, legs spread and hands on his hips, Crash stood at the edge of the Blood Fury MC's courtyard and scanned the field beyond.

A sea of tents, campers, borrowed travel trailers and rented vans as far as he could see.

Sleds. Lines of them. The mid-June sun reflecting off all the chrome made them sparkle like diamonds. All badass bikes and not one of them a piece of shit. Mostly Harleys and a few Indians. All made in the good ol' U.S. of A. Not a crotch rocket to be found on the property.

As it should be.

Some of those sleds had even been designed and customized at his own body shop in Shadow Valley by Jag Jamison. And now Badger and Olly. The two newest patched members—with Olly being the youngest—who Jag took under his wing as apprentices.

Overwhelmed with all the custom jobs he was getting, Jag decided to pass his skills on and stick more to the designing part. Along with his artwork, regularly selling for a pretty fucking penny, the brother wasn't hurting for scratch.

Crash didn't have the patience for all the detail work needed to build a custom sled, so he stuck to the basics in the garage. Doing repairs and rebuilding the engines. It paid the bills, put some scratch in his pocket and fattened the club's coffers.

Business was good.

Life was great.

And this blow-out weekend was going to kick mother-fucking ass.

With the stops along the way, it took over five hours for the Angels to ride from Shadow Valley all the way north to Manning Grove. Luckily, it was a beautiful day to start off a hell of a weekend full of celebrating.

It was the first time all three clubs in the western Pennsylvania alliance were getting together in one spot.

His MC, the Dirty Angels, along with the Dark Knights, were invited to the Blood Fury MC's home base to celebrate their president's marriage to his ol' lady.

Right now Crash was ready to party and partake in some sex, drugs and rock-n-roll.

He grinned and brushed his palm over his short hair, cursing himself for shaving it all off in a drunken bet a couple of months ago. He'd shaved off his beard at the same time—unfortunately, also a part of the bet—and sported a bare face and a bald head for quite a while now.

Because of that loss—both the bet and his hair—his brothers had ridden his ass hard and without a drop of fucking lube.

It was finally growing back, but he had decided to ditch the beard for a while. In fact some of the women in the DAMC sisterhood threatened to kick his ass if he grew it back once they saw his chin dimple that had been buried under the bushy beard. That was what they called it, a fucking chin dimple.

Whatever. He really didn't give a fuck about any fucking chin dimple. The dip only made it harder to shave. This weekend he wasn't shaving once. The sisterhood could suck it if they didn't like it since he didn't answer to any of them.

Hell, he didn't answer to any woman at all.

He'd avoided it for over forty years and had no plan on changing that fact any time soon.

Most of the women he'd even remotely considered had been younger. Child-bearing age. Jonesing to start a family.

Crash was fine with the way things were now.

Ride free, die free.

Free of a ball and chain. Free of kids. The only responsibility for him being his garage, his MC and his brotherhood.

Simple.

And drinking to the point where he could lose a damn bet and it wouldn't matter to anyone but himself.

But, yeah, he missed his damn hair. Before losing the bet, it hadn't been cut since he was a teen and would get dragged to the barber by his mom when it got shaggy.

He turned around to face the courtyard and glanced to the right, where the Fury's pavilion was. It was double the size of the DAMC's but then, the Fury's farm had a lot more space than the property where his club's church and The Iron Horse Roadhouse were situated.

The DAMC's building and lot might be smaller, but because of that, their church was much easier to defend. He glanced around. Enemies could sneak up from all sides on this farm. Too much open space existed.

His gaze skimmed The Barn to his left. At least Trip had taken Zak's advice and omitted windows from the first floor of their church and bunkhouse. Smart thinking.

A hard lesson learned when the Warriors shot The Iron Horse up during a Christmas party, trying to kill them all.

At this point the Fury had no rivals, but he had heard mutterings about some local redneck militia wannabes. Trip assured both Z and Romeo, the Dark Knights' prez, that those hillbillies wouldn't be a threat this weekend.

Crash had no idea why this weekend would be different than any other, but it wasn't his problem, either way. It was up to the BFMC to protect the visiting clubs by making sure the event was safe, but, of course, the other two MCs would jump in if all hell broke loose.

Crash wouldn't mind a doing a little ass-kicking this weekend. Life had become a bit boring at home after the rival Shadow Warriors were obliterated and now with most of his club brothers living with their families in a gated community away from church.

Yawn.

Hell, Dawg had already become a grandparent. It would soon be time for them to break out their old fart motorized scooters instead of their sleds. Maybe Jag could customize those, too.

Crash snorted and glanced back at the pavilion when he heard some excited chatter.

Kids of all ages were beginning to gather in that vicinity to be entertained and babysat by a few of the house mouses both they and the Knights had dragged north with them. Not surprising how many kids there were since bikers tended to like to procreate. Or at least practice procreating.

Especially the Dirty Angels.

Once it got late, those kids would be taken elsewhere so any adults-only activities wouldn't be witnessed.

But not all of the kids were young any more.

The oldest being Zeke, Zak's son, now a very stubborn fourteen, followed by Ash, Hawk's son, and Violet, the oldest of Diesel's three daughters.

Crash wasn't counting Lily in the mix anymore since she

declared, loudly and often, she was now an adult at nine-teen. Dawg and Emma disagreed about the "adult" part. *Hell*, even their youngest, Emmalee, affectionately known as Lee-lee, was eleven already.

And now hated being called Lee-lee.

When the fuck did his generation of Angels get so goddamn old? He'd been a member of the DAMC for almost twenty-six years. Twenty-six fucking years! And he'd die a member, too. Even though he wasn't born into the club like some others in the brotherhood, it was still in his blood.

Family, that was what they all were. They all had each other's backs, protected the women and raised the children.

The saying "it takes a village" was about right. And the neighborhood Zak built behind electric gates and high walls —out of necessity—had certainly become a village between the DAMC families and Diesel's Shadows living in the compound, too.

It looked like Trip, the Blood Fury prez, was doing something similar here on the farm he inherited. Building an MC compound where everyone lived close. A true family and village of their own.

It was damn smart. No doubt.

A large, dark figure lumbered Crash's way, wearing a black leather cut that told everyone who he was and who he belonged to, but Crash didn't need to read any of his patches to know who he was.

Crash stepped into Magnum's path and, after chin-lifts, they clasped hands and bumped shoulders.

"Brother," he greeted.

"Brother," the Dark Knights' sergeant at arms greeted back.

"Where's your ol' lady?" It had been a minute since he'd seen Dawg's daughter, Cait. Ever since she hooked up with

Magnum and popped out Asia, their daughter, he hardly ever saw her around DAMC's church anymore.

"With her sisters and Asia," Magnum answered.

Cait probably spent more time now at the DAMC compound with Dawg's family than bothering to stop over at church to hang out. Magnum was super protective of his wife, and Dawg was still very protective of his oldest daughter.

Cait and Magnum did not live in the DAMC compound and didn't plan on moving there, either since he, and now Cait, wore Knights colors. Though, Dawg and Emma would prefer they lived close.

Crash didn't live over in the gated community of homes, either. He still lived above church with the rest of the single members and some of the prospects. Most of them a fuck of a lot younger than him. A total different type of generation than when he was that age.

He really needed to move the fuck out. At now forty-four, he was getting too old to live in a tiny room with an even smaller shitter. Living there rent-free for all these years let him save up enough scratch that he could buy a really nice place elsewhere and not go into hock to do so.

But if he did that, Zak would push him to build a house in the compound and Crash wasn't sure he was ready for that or to drop that kind of dough. A single guy didn't need a big house. He only needed something small and simple, just a place to rest his damn head or for privacy for when he needed it.

Yeah, all he required was a huge bed, huge shower and a huge flat-screen TV with surround sound for action movies and video games. A kitchen would be good, too, even though he'd be lost in it, but at least it would have a fridge to hold beer.

There were many bonuses to still living above church.

One, the commercial kitchen between the clubhouse and The Iron Horse, with line cooks and Mama Bear to keep him fed. Two, a help-yourself stocked bar on both the public and private sides of the building. Three, sweet butts at his fingertips whenever he was in the mood to get down and dirty. Four, sweet butts and prospects available to clean that tiny room and even smaller shitter.

Yeah, fuck moving out. He had it damn good where he was.

"Where are you stayin'?" Crash asked the man who had to be three inches taller and a good fifty pounds heavier than him.

"Some kind of emergency housin' setup on the other side of that tree line. Daddy Dawg and Emma decided to camp so they could have some 'alone time.' Lee-lee and Lily's stayin' with us."

"Surprised Lily wanted to come."

Magnum arched one dark brow. "She didn't. But Daddy Dawg said... Hold on, let me quote what my daddy-in-law said to her, 'Your ass ain't stayin' in this house alone when all of us are goin' north. Fuck that. We'll come home to the house in fuckin' shambles.'"

Crash barked out a laugh. "Yeah, that sounds about right. She just turned nineteen, of course she's gonna go wild when the 'rents are gone for a few days. We might be old but we remember bein' that age."

"Speak for yourself. I was bustin' ass at that time 'cause I already had two kids. Both of who made me a grandfather a while ago. Daddy Dawg also told Lily he's got enough grand-fuckin-kids already and that he ain't old enough yet to be a grandfather for a second time." Magnum grinned. "My answer to that was 'you're fuckin' welcome.'"

Crash laughed again. "Sure that put him in a good mood."

"Can't pass up a chance to remind him I knocked up his baby girl and plan on doin' it again soon."

"That probably spurred him to drag Lily along for the weekend."

"He would lose his goddamn mind if Lil got knocked up as young as she is."

"She ain't young," Crash reminded him.

"Right. She reminds us how old she fuckin' is several times a day. Thank fuck Cait ain't annoyin' like her younger sister."

"What the fuck happened to that sweet, innocent little girl?" Crash asked.

"Who? Cait?"

"Lily."

Magnum chuckled. "All of us. We're all a bad influence."

"Don't think Em is too worried about it."

"Fuck no. 'Cause even though we're bad influences, we'll kick someone's motherfuckin' ass if they fuck with her."

"Just like you with Cait?"

"Didn't fuck with her. Made her my ol' lady and then put a ring on her finger *before* plantin' my baby in her belly."

"That you did," Crash murmured. "Where you headed now?"

"Meetin' in their church. All the prezes, VPs, and sergeants at arms."

"Fuckin' badass church, ain't it?"

"Better than ours. Thinkin' we need to find a new place other than the shithole we have now."

Crash grinned. "Sully officiatin'?" Sully had married Diesel and Jewel a while back. And some of his other brothers when they finally decided to make their ol' ladies their wives, too. Being allies with another club who had their own ordained minister had its perks.

"Yep."

"Sounds good, brother. Go do your thing."

Magnum paused. "Where'd you end up? One of those fuckin' tents?"

Crash snorted and shook his head. "Fuck no. Hate campin' and too fuckin' old to sleep on rough ground. Rig and me are sharin' a room at the Fury's motel in town, think it's called The Grove Inn. He checked us in, haven't been over there yet."

"Club here's got a nice mix of businesses."

"Tell me about it. They're certainly buildin' a fuckin' empire."

"Nothin' wrong with that," Magnum answered. "All right. Gotta go, brother. Catch up with you and the others later."

Crash found himself standing alone again.

He watched Magnum walk through the wide-open double doors on the side of the Barn. As they'd all arrived today, they were told the bar inside was fully-stocked and to help themselves if someone wasn't manning the bar.

But what he needed first was fucking food. Then whiskey or a beer. Or a couple of shots of whiskey, *then* a beer or two. After that, maybe a woman, if he could find one who caught his interest.

With what he was seeing so far, he'd have no trouble finding one. All the ol' ladies were told to wear their "Property of" cuts today to identify them as off-limits, even if they normally didn't wear them. This weekend it wasn't an option.

Even as young as Diesel's girls were, they each wore a "Property of Diesel" cut in denim instead of leather. Of course, not for the reason the older women did, but because he liked to make it known who his girls belonged to.

Who his girls would always belong to.

Crash pitied any man trying to take his daughters away.

And not even in a kidnap type of way, but simply by trying to date them.

Vi was getting closer to the age where she'd want to start talking to boys outside of the DAMC family. God help them all. Her father was nicknamed "The Beast" by her mother for a damn good reason.

Crash strode across the courtyard giving chin-lifts to bikers he didn't know, hand-clasps and shoulder bumps to the ones he did. Someone had mentioned a spread had been set up inside to keep it out of the June heat.

He wandered through the same double barn doors Magnum had and was once again amazed at the Fury's church. It reminded him of a resort, but biker-style.

The pool tables were hopping, the music inside was rocking, a couple games of darts were in full swing, and a loud and rowdy poker game was happening in one corner. He spotted Slade and Moose sitting in on that game since they both were good at playing cards and could usually clean up and walk away with fat pockets.

Moose had brought along a stripper he'd been banging from Heaven's Angels. She sat in the big man's lap with her arms hooked around his neck and her huge tits smashed into his chest. Crash had no idea what her name was, but she had become his most recent regular. For this month, anyway. Next month it could be another stripper. And the month after that...?

Unlike when Dawg managed Heaven's Angels Gentlemen's Club, Moose didn't mind hooking up with his help. And he did so often.

Because of that, also unlike Dawg, he had to deal with a shitload of cat fights among the talent.

What Crash wasn't seeing right now was a bunch of skin. Of the female variety. That would change quickly once the sun went down and the kids were shuttled off somewhere else.

He swung his gaze around the large building with the center stone fireplace and the massive wood bar along the wall opposite of where he just walked in. Yeah, the sweet butts from all three clubs were still dressed, amazingly enough, though they were working some of the guys pretty damn hard so they might not end up clothed for long.

They'd just have to take it somewhere where little eyes and ears weren't around. Easy enough since there was a bunkhouse attached to the rear of The Barn and a field full of tents, RVs and campers to go hide in to take part in carnal pleasures.

Yeah, once the alcohol and beer began to flow and smoke—both of the tobacco and pot variety—created a huge cloud overhead, things would change real quickly. He was pretty sure even the older kids would have an early curfew this weekend, this way the adults could spend the next few days reliving their lives before they had those kids.

Another reason he didn't want any, they fucked-up your life. Nothing stayed the same after that. He'd seen the proof. It was almost enough for him to make an appointment to go get snipped.

This way there was no risk of becoming someone's "baby daddy."

He spotted the spread on two long tables along the front wall of The Barn and headed in that direction. Once again, forced to stop every few seconds to greet someone he recognized from the Knights or his own club. He didn't know any of the Fury except for Trip, so maybe once he filled his gut, he'd go shoot some pool and shoot the shit, too.

That sounded like a fucking great plan.

He was only a few feet from his destination when he heard it.

Female laughter that rose above the din.

He heard plenty of that before, but the husky sound of this woman's laugh had him turning his head. He paused his forward movement and his gaze skimmed the crowd around the long, custom-made bar.

He couldn't see her. Only hear her laughter again. She had to be behind the wall of bodies in denim and leather blocking his view.

Then he saw her. The one who belonged to that laugh.

At first, he could only see a flash of blonde hair as she moved behind the length of the bar. Then he got a glimpse of her face wearing a huge smile as she bumped shoulders with another woman working the bar with her. Both of them were pouring drafts and mixing drinks for whoever needed them.

She disappeared behind a mix of club members, then he caught another glimpse of her at the end of the bar closest to where he stood.

Fuck.

Too bad she was wearing a leather cut. She'd been claimed and belonged to someone already. That meant she was off-limits.

He shouldn't be disappointed because there should be plenty of other available women this weekend. Even so, he was. At his age, it took a lot to catch his attention. He didn't dip his dick in just any pussy anymore like he used to when he was younger.

Back then, it was only about getting laid and draining his nuts. Now, it was more about the experience. It was more about quality than quantity at this point.

He shook his head and turned his attention back to the food laid out before him and grabbed a disposable plate from the end of the table.

"Let me do that for you, baby. I'd be glad to serve you."

Crash turned toward the female voice and saw a girl, not a woman. She couldn't be much older than Lily. Maybe by a couple of years, if that. Possibly old enough to drink. He wasn't great at judging ages.

Being twenty-one, or close to it, might legally make her a woman, but Crash wasn't into twenty-somethings. The generation gap was too fucking big for him.

He was old school. He liked women who didn't whine. He liked women who weren't looking to put their claws in an unclaimed brother.

He liked women who knew what the fuck they were doing when naked and didn't need guidance on how to suck dick or do ass-play. Or whatever he was in the mood for.

Whatever it was, *for fuck's sake,* it definitely wasn't training some young thing in the sack.

Again, he was now more about quality versus quantity.

While this girl was cute and had *really* nice tits, that was where his interest ended.

She reached up and pushed the tip of her finger into his chin dimple. "That's so sexy!"

Christ, he was definitely growing his beard back, starting this weekend.

She snagged the plastic plate from his fingers and began to pile it high with a variety of shit. He stood back and let her do her thing and, as she mindlessly chattered away, he realized he would pass on anything else she offered him besides a plate of food.

After moving down the table and building a mountain on his plate, she came back to him. She kept a hold of it when she said, "There you go. I bet a man like you has to eat a lot."

"No more than anyone else," he answered, grabbing the full plate from her and finding a fork to go along with it. Before he could move away, she tucked a hand in his open cut and planted it on his gut.

"You have some hard muscles under there." The brunette smiled up at him and winked. "If you're still hungry after you eat all that, I have a tent set up and I'm not sharing it with anyone… unless its with you."

"Old enough to be your dad," he grumbled.

"I can call you Daddy, if you'd like." She winked again and, like the first time, it was kind of awkward and not sexy at all. She needed to practice that in a mirror.

But, *holy fuck*, her suggestion made him rethink blowing her off. If she had another ten years on her, he might have followed her out to that damn tent and had her call him Daddy and some other things, too.

He glanced down at his plate of food and back up to her. "You belong to someone?"

She smiled and shook her head. "Just you, if you want me."

"You ain't with anyone?"

"Nope. Just here to party this weekend. A good friend of mine hangs out with the Fury on a regular basis."

"Like a sweet butt?"

She nodded, with her bottom lip tucked between her straight, white teeth. She needed to practice that look, too.

"But you ain't?"

"No, right now they have too many of them and not enough brothers to share. If I become a sweet butt I limit myself on who I can hang out with."

Hang out with.

"Means right now you can fuck prospects but if you were a sweet butt you couldn't," he explained, knowing the deal.

"Exactly! I'm assuming it's the same in your MC."

"It is."

"Then you know the rules."

"I also got a rule," Crash said.

"What's that?"

"Don't do young girls."

"I'm not that young." She pouted.

Yeah, that pout settled it. "Too young for me. Appreciate

the offer, but right now I'm gonna go stuff my face. Then later I'm gonna find someone a little older to sit on it."

She removed her hand from his gut and slid it down to his junk, which was still soft and uninterested. "Well, if you can't find the right one, I'll be around all weekend." She did her awkward wink again and then, *thank fuck*, turned and set her sights on someone else.

He sighed and took himself and his plate over to the bar. And, more importantly, closer to the woman with the husky laugh so he could get a better look. He settled on a stool at the far end and dug into the mound of homemade potato salad. As he chewed his mouthful, he leaned forward a bit, glanced down the length of the bar and spotted her.

She was pouring a draft for someone hanging over the bar, who was not bothering to hide he was staring down at her tits. Her generous cleavage was stuffed into a snug white camisole with a bit of lace along the V-neck. The revealing top was tucked into her jeans and a wide black leather belt that matched her cut encircled her waist.

She was smiling at the man eyeballing her, not giving one shit he was checking out her tits.

Could he be her ol' man? If not, he couldn't imagine her ol' man would appreciate the obvious interest by someone else. Crash knew he wouldn't. Not if she was his. Nobody would be getting close enough to check out her goods. His goods. What belonged to him.

Yeah, too bad someone already claimed her. Maybe whoever her ol' man was wouldn't mind sharing.

He muffled a snort. If her ol' man was anything like any of the Angels, they weren't sharing shit. Once his brothers claimed their ol' lady, she was good and claimed. Nobody was touching or sharing their women. Except with their kids.

As he lifted another spicy as fuck Buffalo wing to his

mouth, she appeared in front of him like magic, waving a paper napkin in his face.

"I noticed that you need this."

He grabbed it from her fingers and swallowed the mouthful, trying not to hiss from the burn. "Yeah? Do I? Think I might need a beer to cool my mouth the fuck down after these wings." He wiped off the sauce from his messy fingers and his burning mouth. He was going to need more than one damn napkin.

"I made those wings."

He cocked one eyebrow. "You did?"

A slow smile crossed her face and she nodded. "Can't handle a little heat?"

"Baby, I can handle a shitload of heat. How 'bout you?"

"The hotter the better," she said with a wink that was certainly nothing like that other girl's. It came more naturally with her. And was a fuck of a lot more sexy.

"'Til the next mornin'," he murmured.

"Oh, are we still talking about chicken wings?"

His gaze dropped to her name patch on the front of her cut. "Lizzy," he murmured.

"That's me," she stated cheerfully. "I'll grab you a beer. Don't go anywhere."

He wasn't planning on it.

She was no twenty-one year old. More like early thirties. It wasn't her face that showed her age, but he could see it in her light-brown eyes. She had some experience behind her. She wasn't young, dumb and needing an education. She was at the point in her life where she could be the teacher.

He liked that.

He like that a lot.

What he didn't like was what he saw when she turned to head down the bar to grab his beer. The cut she wore looked just like the ones the ol' ladies wore, only her top rocker stated: "Property of," and the bottom said: "Blood Fury MC."

He frowned. *What the actual fuck?*

Continue Crash's story here:
mybook.to/DAMC-Crash

If You Enjoyed This Book

Thank you for reading Blood & Bones: Rev. If you enjoyed Rev and Reilly's story, please consider leaving a review at your favorite retailer and/or Goodreads to let other readers know. Reviews are always appreciated and just a few words can help an independent author like me tremendously!

Want to read a sample of my work? Download a sampler book here: BookHip.com/MTQQKK

———

Sign up for Jeanne's newsletter: http://www.
jeannestjames.com/newslettersignup
Join her FB readers' group for the inside scoop:
https://www.facebook.com/groups/JeannesReviewCrew/

Also by Jeanne St. James

* Available in Audiobook

Made Maleen: A Modern Twist on a Fairy Tale *

Damaged *

Rip Cord: The Complete Trilogy *

Brothers in Blue Series:

(Can be read as standalones)

Brothers in Blue: Max *

Brothers in Blue: Marc *

Brothers in Blue: Matt *

Teddy: A Brothers in Blue Novelette *

Brothers in Blue: A Bryson Family Christmas *

The Dare Ménage Series:

(Can be read as standalones)

Double Dare *

Daring Proposal *

Dare to Be Three *

A Daring Desire *

Dare to Surrender *

A Daring Journey *

The Obsessed Novellas:

(All the novellas in this series are standalones)

Forever Him *

Only Him *

Needing Him *

Loving Her *

Tempting Him *

Down & Dirty: Dirty Angels MC Series®:

Down & Dirty: Zak *

Down & Dirty: Jag *

Down & Dirty: Hawk *

Down & Dirty: Diesel *

Down & Dirty: Axel *

Down & Dirty: Slade *

Down & Dirty: Dawg *

Down & Dirty: Dex *

Down & Dirty: Linc *

Down & Dirty: Crow *

Crossing the Line (A DAMC/Blue Avengers Crossover) *

Magnum: A Dark Knights MC/Dirty Angels MC Crossover *

Crash: A Dirty Angels MC/Blood Fury MC Crossover

Guts & Glory Series:

(In the Shadows Security)

Guts & Glory: Mercy *

Guts & Glory: Ryder *

Guts & Glory: Hunter *

Guts & Glory: Walker *

Guts & Glory: Steel *

Guts & Glory: Brick *

Blood & Bones: Blood Fury MC®:

Blood & Bones: Trip *

Blood & Bones: Sig

Blood & Bones: Judge

Blood & Bones: Deacon

Blood & Bones: Cage

Blood & Bones: Shade

Blood & Bones: Rook

Blood & Bones: Rev

Blood & Bones: Ozzy

Blood & Bones: Dodge

Blood & Bones: Whip

Blood & Bones: Easy

COMING SOON!

Everything About You (A Second Chance Gay Romance)

Double D Ranch (An MMF Ménage Series)

Blue Avengers MC™

About the Author

JEANNE ST. JAMES is a USA Today bestselling romance author who loves an alpha male (or two). She was only thirteen when she started writing and her first paid published piece was an erotic story in Playgirl magazine. Her first erotic romance novel, Banged Up, was published in 2009. She is happily owned by farting French bulldogs. She writes M/F, M/M, and M/M/F ménages.

Want to read a sample of her work? Download a sampler book here: BookHip.com/MTQQKK

To keep up with her busy release schedule check her website at www.jeannestjames.com or sign up for her newsletter: http://www.jeannestjames.com/newslettersignup

www.jeannestjames.com
jeanne@jeannestjames.com

Blog: http://jeannestjames.blogspot.com
Newsletter: http://www.
jeannestjames.com/newslettersignup
Jeanne's Down & Dirty Book Crew: https://www.facebook.
com/groups/JeannesReviewCrew/

facebook.com/JeanneStJamesAuthor

twitter.com/JeanneStJames

amazon.com/author/jeannestjames

instagram.com/JeanneStJames

bookbub.com/authors/jeanne-st-james

goodreads.com/JeanneStJames

pinterest.com/JeanneStJames

Get a FREE Romance Sampler Book

This book contains the first chapter of a variety of my books. This will give you a taste of the type of books I write and if you enjoy the first chapter, I hope you'll be interested in reading the rest of the book.

Each book I list in the sampler will include the description of the book, the genre, and the first chapter, along with links to find out more. I hope you find a book you will enjoy curling up with!

Get it here: BookHip.com/MTQQKK